WHITE ROSE OF NIGHT

also by Mel Keegan:

Ice, Wind and Fire
Death's Head
Equinox
Fortunes of War
Storm Tide

MEL KEEGAN

WHITE ROSE OF NIGHT

THE GAY MEN'S PRESS

First published 1997 by GMP Publishers Ltd,
P O Box 247, Swaffham, Norfolk PE37 8PA, England

A CIP catalogue record for this book is available from the British Library

ISBN 0 85449 256 9

Distributed in Europe by Central Books,
99 Wallis Rd, London E9 5LN

Distributed in North America by LPC/InBook,
1436 West Randolph Street, Chicago, IL 60607

Distributed in Australia by Bulldog Books,
P O Box 300, Beaconsfield, NSW 2014

Printed and bound in the EU by The Cromwell Press,
Melksham, Wilts, England

Prologue

Rievaulx Abbey
1228 A.D.

I am old now, but my mind is as keen as it was in my youth. Much of what I am about to tell may be ascribed to the wayward memory of a man of my years, but I will only smile, for I know the truth. I am asked to write of great times and great wickedness, and I have been absolved by Abbot Michael to recount the entire truth without alteration, by change or omission. I will speak of places, men and deeds my reader may scarcely believe, yet every word is truthful. I will tell of kings and sorcerers, the Lionheart and Salah ad-Din Yusef ibn-Aiyub... Saladin Rex.

I am urged to write of what I saw, heard, and felt; and also of my beloved. I am Paulo, who as a youth was called the Fostered Boy. But Edward called me Paul. I am of a Spanish sire and Saxon mother, which accounts for my name and looks. My parents died before I was eight years old, and I was fostered by the old knight, Ranulf of Sleaford, who was as a father to me until I entered the house of Aethelstan. I remain what I have always been, one who dreamed of being a warrior yet never fought; one who loved, and was loved, who travelled far, and saw such things as I myself hardly believe.

The strangest of these tales, being of heaven and of hell, is what fetches me to the abbey when I have grown old, while my beloved is dead these five long years. Absolved, I will relate the sum of my memory and leave the reader to credit or scorn as he will. Mine is a tale of joy and sorrow, pain and pleasure past bearing; of evil, salvation and love... my one love. I have had no other.

Edward of Aethelstan was a Saxon knight of good family but poor fortunes. He was my life and destiny, and it is to him I shall turn in death. I feel the yearning tug of sleep, that last long sleep, from which I will surely wake in his arms.

They call me Brother Paul in this place, but I do not feel part of their order. I am confessed and have done an old man's penance. The scourge still burns, no matter the years, yet hurts less than the blaze of resentment. Who are they to judge me, or Edward? He is not to be judged, not by mere men.

In this state of grace, I write without fear of retribution. If I seem blasphemous, let it be understood I recount only what I saw and heard. These were the true words and deeds of men whose banners flew beside those of Richard, Lionhearted. I beg that the reader also absolve me, for I will speak of strange magic, of darkness and despair. If I sin again with my confession of the love that drew me into this turmoil of events, so be it.

Some of my tale is puzzled together from the testimony of others. Where I did not directly observe the scene, I place my faith in those who did, and here give their accounting. These are the sworn testimonies of men who loved Edward also, in their own ways. If I am a fool to trust, then I am a fool.

I gaze through the door of my cloister cell at the forest cloaking the hills above the monastery wall, and I remember the day our ship left England's shores. So long would pass before I would see again such sights as these abbey woods, yet seldom did I even think of home. My life whirled with forces beyond my control.

I smell the ramson and the forest, hear the chatter of finches, the bell calling my brothers to matins, and the high, sweet voices of the little boys singing, but my thoughts are summoned by the past.

In my heart I am a youth again, a little frightened and alone as I sit listening to muted voices in the hall at Aethelstan Manor...

PART ONE: KNIGHT AND SQUIRE

Chapter I

Their voices were muted by the thick stone walls of the old Aethelstan Manor. I sat in the hall outside their closed door, my hands about a cup of ale as I looked up at the great tapestry opposite me. Nuns had stitched into it the likeness of Elric, the grandfather of the young earl, and the likeness between the two was remarkable, save that where Elric was shorter, darker, thickset and hirsute, his young kinsman was tall, slender despite his skills with sword and lance, and as blond as sunlight.

I sat listening, and was apprehensive. I was sixteen years, and though I was well grown for my age and in no way unmanly, I was always pierced by the arrows of a terrible guilt that led me to a feeling of unworthiness. By the age of eleven I knew the truth about myself. I would look, enraptured, at the lissom young bodies of boys my own age, watch them playing in the river and be filled with urgency. I thought it a dreadful sin and would often seek a wandering friar to confess and take a beating as the price of my salvation.

Ranulf had grown old as I watched. When my parents died, almost nine years before I was sent to his house. People called me the fostered boy, but I was made part of the family of Ranulf's young sister, who was lately widowed. Her husband was buried somewhere in Palestine. Many young men had died in that war, as they have always died in others. There was grief but no surprise when another wife became a widow, and her children were orphaned.

Ranulf spoke with the thick accent of Norfolk, which had been his home before he came to Sleaford for the sake of his sister. I loved him as a father, and he treated me always like a son, as he had promised my own sire. Alberto Delgado had ridden to battle with Ranulf years before, but in the end it was not a heathen lance but fevers that killed him, and my mother too.

When I entered Ranulf's home I was seven years old and the young earl was even then mourning his own father, who was killed when the Saracens overran an encampment near Edessa.

Edward was named for the beloved old King in whose hands this Saxon land was free and happy before the Normans came. He was a man of learning as well as a warrior, and I respected him for this as well as his skills with sword and lance, and for his beauty. Oh, I may have been a lad from a poor house, but I knew him.

I had seen him just that morning, before Ranulf brought me to the Manor. Edward had ridden out along the hill above Sleaford on his great, steel-grey warhorse, with a hawk on his wrist and the morning wind tossing his hair about his shoulders. He wore it uncut and untied, and it was the colour of silver-gold, like moonlight on the water. I knew him well! But not as well as I had yearned to for more years than might be entirely decent.

It was Ranulf's paternal feelings that brought us to Aethelstan Manor that night. I studied the embroidered face of Elric and wondered apprehensively what would become of me. I sipped a little ale and frowned at the banner under which Elric had fought. The nuns had sewn its likeness into the tapestry but the banner itself, battered and wearing its honours proudly, stood by the door.

It was midnight blue, and onto it was embroidered the device of this house, a white rose, full open in bloom. The banner fluttered above Elric's needlework head as he trampled the Saracen underfoot. His great sword was on the wall over the fireplace – one saw it as he entered the house.

I took a sip of ale and listened to Ranulf's voice, thick with that Norfolk accent, so familiar. Then Edward spoke and my insides quivered. His voice was steely, taut as a bowstring yet filled with soft restraint and rich with humour.

"Come to the point, Ranulf," he was saying. "Tell me what you want of me!"

"What I want?" My foster father chuckled. "I want the best for the boy, what else would you expect?"

The best, from my point of view, would be to be swept off to Edward's bedchamber, undressed and put to some useful service! But this was not what Ranulf meant at all. He meant, what was to become of the rest of my life? I was no longer a child, and I must have a situation.

"He can read and write," Ranulf offered. "Have you need of a secretary? He has a strong back and good hands, if you need a groom. Edward, consider the lad. His father was a Spanish knight, yet what is Paulo? I can do little for him, you know that. I'm paupered after the war and I have my sister's little ones to look to. Paulo must make his own way, but what's he to do in a village like Sleaford? Would you have him herd pigs? That labour awaits him at dawn tomorrow if you send him away. I had no heart to tell him."

I cringed. It was the lowest of occupations, and I would refuse it. Sooner would I put on a cassock and enter holy orders than sink so low that I dishonoured Alberto Delgado's name. Ranulf was telling the earl the truth. He had spent every shilling on his campaign. Now, when his family needed him, nothing was left.

And what of me? The fostered one came last on the list of kin to be provided for. I chewed my lip, glared at the midnight blue banner with its white rose, and listened for the earl's steely voice. It was like

10

a drawn sword, ready to fight for honour. Would it ever fight for mine? I mocked myself for the absurd thought, but it might have been an intuition.

"I've no need of a groom or a secretary," Edward said almost regretfully. "You saw my servants packing as you came in. You know full well, Ranulf, I'll be gone within the month and shall not return for years." He paused and added softly, as if the word horrified him, "Crusade."

"I fought there in my day," Ranulf agreed. "Do you need a squire, then? Paulo is a well grown lad, and strong, like his father. Much like his sire in body, and half as hairy!" He laughed reminiscently. "He's tall already, and boys his age shoot up a hand's span while you watch. A wager, Edward. He'll end taller than you! He's as heavy already, I should say."

I gave my body a critical glance. I was quite muscular even then, and as he said, tall like my father. Would I be taller than Edward, stronger? I shivered as I imagined being a hand's span higher, and holding the much more slender Edward crushed against me, with my face buried in that gold hair. A terrible wave of lust caught me unawares and I admonished myself. I promised myself confession and penance the next time I saw a friar on the road.

"He's a responsible lad," Ranulf went on. "I have never seen him shirk since he was a little one, and have often seen him go to a priest, kneel to confess some wrong, then bear a hefty thrashing like a man. That is the guarantee of a good conscience and courage."

If only Ranulf had known what I had confessed! Which time had he seen me? When I admitted watching other boys and lingering over their long, sun-brown limbs? Or had I confessed to the sweet pangs of lust I felt as I watched the young earl of Aethelstan ride out falconing, with his lean, sinuous thighs widespread about the horse called Icarus. Icarus, I thought, who flew, and I pictured the great beast carrying Edward to battle in some heathen land, as if they rode the wind.

I would need a mighty penance, soon, I told myself as I imagined myself a hand's span taller, with the slender strength of Edward crushed to me. He was perfect in his nakedness, this I knew. The Manor lay close to my home, and I was familiar with every path through the woods. I knew the places where hare and foxes could be trapped, though shooting a deer would cost a man his hands. And I knew where the best swimming was.

I followed Edward almost every day through that last season before the banner of Aethelstan once again flew in the Holy Land. I never told him that I followed him, not in all the years we shared. It would likely bruise his pride, that he should have been betrayed by spying, and by me of all people. Yet I followed him, before he even knew I was alive. I would lie in the rushes, concealed by the willows along the riverbank, and watch him tether the warhorse. Icarus low-

11

ered his nose to graze and my lord put his foot on a rotten log as he disrobed. I would hold my breath as he folded the hose and for a moment stood in the sun to tie up his hair lest it tangle.

His uplifted arms hoisted the hem of his tunic and afforded a tantalising glimpse of bare buttock. I would beg the river gods to make him turn and show me his manhood before he dived into the water. His hair was pale in the sun, so he seemed not to have any across his breast and below his belly. I would feast my eyes on the long curve of his spine and pray for him to turn. His limbs seemed smooth as a girl's, but between his legs he dispelled that notion. He was big and fierce, reminding me of the haft of a spear. How I longed for that lance to sunder me!

I would find a friar, I thought grimly, kneel, take off my jerkin and tell him to lay my penance across my back with a heavy hand. What would Edward think of a squire who lusted shamefully while he polished the armour and groomed the nag? I finished my ale with a quivering feeling, sure I was destined for the swine tomorrow, or else a cassock and holy vows.

But Edward said softly, almost below my hearing, "I've no wish to take a young lad to war, Ranulf. You have seen yourself what becomes of them with the work, the heat and hardship, not to mention that they are preyed upon when the master's back is turned! You know what I mean."

Did he mean what *I* thought he did? I shivered again, realising of a sudden that my golden knight, my white rose, whom I had imagined almost a saint, so unblemished was he, was not so innocent after all. He knew the same things that I knew... he knew what boys had to offer, and what was sometimes taken from them, no matter if it was offered freely or not.

But Ranulf was laughing heartily. "Edward, have you seen him? He's like to break the arm of a beast who offended him!"

It might depend on the beast, and the manner of the offence! I knew of several who would not be rejected, and one in particular, who was even then speaking and whose affections would be paid for in blood if that was the only way to have them.

"I've not seen him since you brought him to Sleaford when he was a child. Where has he been?"

"At his lessons with the monks, and working in the fields with my sister's eldest. He's grown more than you might have imagined. Shall I fetch him in?"

"Oh, very well." Edward sighed. "I'd rather have him as a squire under me than see him levied for the army and chopped to tatters. Or take vows," he added soberly, as if guessing my own mind.

The door opened and Ranulf looked down the hall for me. I stood, straightened my jerkin and hurried toward him. A fire blazed in the chimney, at least twenty books were displayed on the shelves, and

12

silver cups were on the table in the middle of the room.

Edward stood by the hearth, hands clasped behind him, gilded by the firelight and the glow of a dozen fat yellow candles. I caught my breath at the look of him and went down on one knee. It was some time before I dared lift my head, and he did not invite me to rise, as if it were easier to look me over, judge what he saw, with me trapped in this position. It did not damage my knees, and as for my pride, there was no man I would sooner have knelt before, not even the King. Save that I might have wished Edward naked, and myself before him like this for another purpose entirely. Slowly, I raised my head, and found him smiling at me.

No matter how often I had followed him as he went out to hunt or swim, I had never seen him closely. It was the first time I had seen the colour of his eyes, the fine marble texture of his skin. Even his beard was so fair that he seemed to have none, where my own cheeks were shadowed with my youth's stubble and must grow even darker with time. Mesmerised I looked up at him, at his red robe and the fine, slender hand toying with his dirk, which he had drawn from a jewelled sheath at his girdle. His eyes were grey as a storm sky. I imagined them dark with anger, and swallowed; I imagined them dark with passion, with lust for me, and quivered.

At last he spoke. "Get up, boy."

I stood unsteadily and looked up a matter of inches into his face. Close to, his slenderness was even more obvious. Like my father, my frame was wide. Even then I had the impression that I was broader, though probably not stronger, since he was a soldier. He slid away the dirk and folded his hands into his sleeves. The Saxon-blond hair lay on his shoulders like a mane. I wanted to knot my fingers in it, and imagined holding him under me while we writhed and tossed ... being crushed under him while he rode me as he rode that warhorse. Insanely, I envied Icarus.

"You wish to be a squire?" he prompted quietly.

That was the last thought on my mind. *I wish to go with you. I would go anywhere to be with you, be anything!* He was waiting for a coherent answer, and I cleared my throat. "However I may serve my lord best, is what I wish." That at least was the truth.

"Then you'll leave England," he said, amused. His eyes were like quicksilver as he laughed. His fingers played with the ends of his hair. "There'll be danger. Perhaps you shall not return."

"Then I shall not return, my lord," I said softly. Nothing seemed important then. Nothing mattered, save that he took me into his house so that I could be near him.

He chuckled. "Bed with Master Jacob tonight. I'll see you tomorrow, and till then, a good night to you."

It was a dismissal. I wanted to stay but held my tongue, bowed low and left the room with a glance at Ranulf, who was mightily pleased. He shut the door behind me and I leaned on the wall to hear Edward's voice a while longer. Not that I wished to eavesdrop, but I loved to listen to him.

Footsteps along the hall alerted me and I saw the groom, Jacob. Older than I but younger than Edward, he smelt of horses and had big, callused hands. It was he who disciplined the boys, and if I fell into disfavour it would be Jacob who would put the birch across the cheeks of my arse. Wary of him, I ducked a little bow.

"My lord told me to retire. I was wondering where to go. He said to bed with you, Master Jacob, and I'll have my duties set out in the morning." I tried to speak diffidently but I was thrilled with an absurd sense of triumph. I would wear Aethelstan's colours in the morning. No more threadbare jerkins and patched hose. I would have the midnight blue, with the white rose over the left breast, and a blue cape. Edward's own colours.

Jacob cast a glance at the door as if he wondered if he should summon his master and make sure, but then he seemed to think better of it and led me out of the house through the back door, by the scullery where the kitchen maids were asleep. I heard light snoring as I stepped over the wolfhounds, and was soon in the warm air of the summer night. Jacob scattered the drowsy chickens as he led me to the stable, and prodded my behind until I climbed the ladder to the hayloft.

Hay makes a soft but itchy bed. I knew I had insects in my clothes by midnight, and wondered how Jacob managed to sleep here all the time, to tend the horses. I slept little and scratched a great deal, but when I did sleep it was to dream wilful, wanton things. Edward came to the loft, teased me awake, and when I rolled belly down in the hay that spear-haft pierced my loins, and he whispered that he had wanted me for as long as he had known me. Which would have been a matter of minutes, I reminded myself as I started awake.

The sun was not yet up and the cockerels boasted on the midden heap as I reeled out of my itchy bed to find Jacob standing below the loft with a tub of water, a scrubbing brush and a suit of livery for me. I hurried down the ladder and touched my forelock before him, but he curled his lip at me. He was an ugly, whoreson brute with hairy forearms and a big nose, beetling brows and gnarled fingers.

"Don't waste pretty manners upon the likes o' me, Master Spanish," he said tartly. He was never able to forget or forgive the fact I am not full Saxon blood. Being Saxon himself, and distrusting anything that was not, he had no love of me. "Take off yon rags and start out clean," he went on. "Thou'll start clean or I'll flay thy arse, by God, I will."

I needed to bathe after a night in the hay and would not have argued, but the water was cold and the brush he used on me was meant for horses. It almost flayed me anyway, fetched me up in great red weals, as if I had indeed been beaten. Jacob was cursed thorough too, as if he expected me to arrive here infested.

Perhaps other youths did, and he was right to suspect. I was clean, but out of respect for the skin of my buttocks I stood still with legs apart and let him scrub me anywhere the hair grew thickest yet shortest. I was wincing and fidgeting when I heard a slight sound behind me and looked over my shoulder, over Jacob's bowed head, to see the earl.

He was dressed for riding, leaning on the stable wall as he watched this performance with a mischievous expression. "Leave a *little* skin on him, Jacob," Edward said mockingly. Was he teasing me? His eyes roved from shoulders to feet, and as they settled on my rump I shivered. What he could not see was that my cock got up at that moment, and I seized a yard of sacking to cover myself. "Why, boy," Edward said, much amused, "are you skinned? I should have warned you, Jacob is not known for gentleness, but it's best to leave all traces of your last employment behind, eh?"

He meant, have the ticks and lice scrubbed out of me. I squirmed, flushed and nodded, swallowing my angry words. I had never had ticks and lice, any more than he had. Vengeful, Jacob thrust the brush between my begs and caught my balls a sharp rasp. I flinched and jumped clean out of his reach.

"Enough! I am cleaner than clean," I yelped, burning with help-less embarrassment, because under the sacking my cock was a poker. Edward would believe I covered myself chastely, out of modesty, but that was untrue. Had I not been aroused I would have shown him that I was more man than boy, with a good, strong prick for a lad my age, and heavy balls that made wickedness for me, sometimes four times in the night. He surveyed my breast which, like my father, was richly pelted. His eyes found my nipples, lingered first on one, then the other. When they stood erect I could do nothing to disguise it, and instead I lifted my chin and looked him levelly in the eyes.

I think he suspected then what manner of lad he had employed. My paps tingled with excitement just at his glance. Had he touched me I would have spilled my seed, and a slight crease of his brow warned me that he was wise to this. So my saint, my white rose, was not as innocent as I had dreamed.

Part of me was relieved, that after all there was the slightest chance he would look at me and see a companion for the night. Another part was disappointed. I had dreamed I would be the first, that I would take the blond head in my hands and be the first man to bruise his beautiful mouth with a kiss.

A moment later fear caught my gut in a vicious grip. He knew my heart, there was no doubt of that – but did he scorn me? If he was the kind of man who loved God before all women, and lopped the balls off men who bedded men, I may be in grave danger. Even before

15

I entered his house I belonged to him. I was nothing, a serf on his estate. If he wanted to use me as an archery butt, I could say nothing, supposing his games killed me.

I held my breath and searched his face. Perhaps my fear showed. I was very young, frightened, very much alone since Ranulf had left last night without even stopping at the stable to say farewell. But Edward merely lifted one brow at me and said to Jacob, "I'll take out Icarus. He'll benefit from the exercise after his idleness of late. Soon enough he'll be cramped in a ship, which neither he nor I will enjoy. I'll return in an hour or two."

"And the boy, m'lord?" Jacob asked as I fidgeted from foot to foot with the sacking clasped to my groin, my cock throbbing hard under it and my paps tingling, wet in the morning air, sore after Jacob's ministrations.

"Feed him and find him something to do." Edward turned away from me and paced into the stable. He had the walk of a hunting cat, I thought, lithe and supple. He was a warrior, it was evident in every stride he took. I lusted and envied in equal measure, and waited only until Jacob's back was turned before I rushed into the clothes, pulled down the midnight blue tunic to cover my hopeful erection.

Icarus clopped out of the yard minutes later and I watched him out of sight. I would never forget the way the sun shone on Edward's hair, and how he moved to the gait of the big animal. *I will have him. One day he will be mine, I must have him!* The thought fled through my head unbidden. I did not court it, nor did I deny it, though I laughed mockingly at myself as Icarus turned the corner and disappeared about the climbing roses and apple trees.

I put my palm over the little white rose on the left breast of the tunic. Beneath it my pap tingled sharply, and deeper yet my heart thudded as if I had been running.

Hearing my laughter, Jacob barked, "What's thee laughing at, knave? Off to the kitchen and feed thy face, then I'll find thee something to occupy thy idle hands!"

I had not eaten since early afternoon and was famished. The kitchen maids gave me bread, pickled pork and cheese, which was better fare than the cabbage and lentils we ate at home. There was never enough food or anything else in Ranulf's house. He was too proud to ask for charity and Edward was too preoccupied with the forthcoming campaign to notice the desperate want. With one less mouth to feed – mine, and a large one at that – the family must prosper. I ate until Jacob began to grumble, then left the kitchen with a muttered word of thanks, and went to work.

The Aethelstan livery gave me a sense of who I was. I felt I belonged to Edward, as much as I wished he belonged to me. My destiny was fixed even then. Where Edward went, I would go. If I had known where my passions would lead me, I might have turned back

16

that morning, but I like to think I would not. The hardships and pain in store for me were far outweighed by the joy. I have never been discontented, no matter what befell me, but only Edward ever gave me the gift I wanted most. The gift of love.

Chapter II

I might have wished he would want me at first sight, and that love would blossom out of lust at once, but Edward watched me almost as much as I watched him all that first day, and I was caught in a dreadful quandary, unable to guess if I was doing right or wrong.

I had my duties – to curry the horse, polish the saddle, oil his swords and feed the dogs. All this I did, conscientiously and without error. And every time I would look up, grey eyes were on me. Finding fault? I was fretted by evening, but still Edward had no word to say against me.

He entertained guests that night, men I had never seen before, but their names were great, and their manner grand. They ate venison and a swan stuffed with hazel nuts, and spoke idly of the King. They spoke also of money, and the price of armour and horses. These knights would be on the field of battle soon enough.

It fell to me to carry out the empty platters, sweep the table and keep their cups full. It was not elegant work but Ranulf had made sure I was no bumpkin. I knew my manners, which cup to put where, how to pour wine, and I was hardly likely to complain. It gave me the opportunity to be near Edward.

His teeth were very white. I saw the pink tip of his tongue flick out to catch a drop of wine, and he looked at me in the very moment I was imagining his kisses, as if he could read my mind. I flushed hotly as his eyes burned into me. Did he know what I thought? Heaven help me if he did. Those grey eyes brooded on me a while before he returned to his guest. Sir Lionel de Quilberon was big, burly, twice Edward's weight and much taller. He was a vile swine in his manners at table but, they said, a great warrior. And he was faultlessly kind with the dogs, who sat cadging at his feet. I knew instinctively, Sir Lionel was one of those men who cared nothing for life's refinements, could not read, nor remember a verse, but in battle he was worth ten men and in bed he would be so gentle with his lady, she would swear he was a saint though his face was almost ugly. Edward liked him greatly, and for this alone I would have pardoned his manners as he tossed scraps over both his oxen shoulders and wiped his hands on his coat. Edward was amused, and smiled as de Quilberon drank too much and began to snore at the end of the table.

17

I lingered as long as they might want a cup bearer, and fancied myself Ganymede, waiting upon a creature like Narcissus. Such is love, and aye, it is foolish. My lord seemed at one moment not to know I was there, and at another his gaze followed me until I blushed and was absurdly shy.

They bedded late, and so did I. My room was in the loft under the thatch. I heard starlings and pigeons squabbling above my head and mice scuttling along the wainscot. I seemed scarcely asleep, with a big full moon glaring in my face through the open shutter, before Master Jacob was shouting at me and yanking me out of bed by the ear. Smarting with indignation, I hurried down to a swift breakfast and my day's work.

There was so much to be done – preparations for war. The whole household was making ready for the master's absence, and Jacob was a swaggering, overbearing oaf. I hated him by midmorning, when he boxed the ears of boys much younger than myself and slapped the cheeks of girls older. By afternoon I was tired, filled with resentment, and I had not set eyes on Edward since first light, when he rode out on Icarus.

He had gone to swim, I knew, and I fumed. Had I been free, as I had been two days before, I could have followed him, lain in the reeds and watched as he stripped bare and bathed in the shallows. Yet I was clad in his livery, wearing the white rose of Aethelstan, and I had not even seen his face today. My hands were sore with polishing and my shoulders ached after the stack of firewood I had axed for the kitchen hearths.

At last, thoroughly out of sorts, I made an awful mistake.

I left by the postern gate for an hour's peace and quiet in the woods. I wanted to breathe free air, forget Master Jacob and look forward to better days ahead, when I would answer only to Edward, aboard a ship bound for the Holy Land. The great adventure – that was what I wanted. That, and Edward's fine, strong hands on me, and his tongue between my lips. Not Jacob devising every hard, dirty job he could think of, to mock me.

I enjoyed my hour's peace and could have returned then, no one the wiser, had I not fallen asleep in the glade. I had slept little the previous night and Jacob had kept me busy since dawn. I fell sound asleep and when I yawned awake I was shocked to find shadows marching across the water meadows like soldiers in ranks. I sprang up, guilty, a little frightened, and ran.

How could I run fast enough to escape Jacob's ire? I knew I was hastening to my punishment. It was dusk as I ran into the yard. Hearth smoke curled in the still, warm air. The girls were hard at work, the lads, the old women – everyone but myself seemed occupied. And Jacob had been waiting for me, likely for an hour. I swallowed at the grim look on his face, and ducked a bow before him.

What could I say? He growled dangerously, too angry even to speak for a long time. "Thou'rt a lazy, good for nothing cur," he told me fiercely. "Thou'rt a louse, a maggot, ye half-Saxon brat. Thou'lt learn a lesson this day that thou'll never forget!"

I opened my mouth to protest but closed it again. I had been foolish enough to fall asleep – no one drugged me or lulled me. It was my mistake, and who but I should pay for it? I studied the dirt at his feet as he passed judgement and sentenced me.

"Aye, a lesson for thee, and well remembered!" Jacob barked. "Robin! Harald!"

The two youths took me by the arms. They were keen to win Jacob's favour and would do his bidding no matter what he asked. I was caught in a snare of my own making. If I fought, the earl would likely send me away, and Ranulf would be so furious that I would have the same thrashing at home. If I did not fight, but let Jacob have his way, at least I would still be wearing the Aethelstan colours on the morrow, and Ranulf would never know I had shamed him so soon. I groaned and let them fetch me to the gatepost.

Jacob took off his belt and I breathed a little easier as I thought he meant to hit me with that, which is a boy's chastisement. But the belt looped tight about my wrists, stretched me taut with my hands over my head, and buckled. I had set aside my tunic and was bare to the hips. I felt Jacob maliciously tug down my hose to bare my arse also. The others were looking on, the soot-nosed kitchen wenches too. My face flamed with humiliation as much as dread. I looked over my shoulder and saw the birch rod, an evil, whippy cane, a full yard long.

It fell across my shoulders and rump, and I counted fifteen, the measure of Jacob's wrath – six or ten is a usual penance. I squirmed against the post and panted. It was not the first time I had been birched, but before this I had been struck only by an old monk whose best days were behind him, and whose arm was soft. Jacob's arm was muscular, and my poor back and arse were afire, the bones themselves throbbing, when he had had enough.

Robin and Harald let down my hands and I tugged up my hose. I winced as I covered my behind, and could not bear the tunic at all. Jacob cuffed my head for good measure, and I went to the stable without a bite to eat.

There I stayed until late, and fancied myself abandoned. I longed for the comfort of my bed in the loft and swore furiously as I thought of the scrubbing I would have in the morning if I slept in the hay. Jacob detested me, although I did not know why. I cursed and ached, stroked Icarus and whispered to him, secrets I could never tell to a human.

Much later one of the little boys came yawning to the stable and looked in. "Are you there, Paul? The master wants you."

19

Wants me? If only it were true. So Jacob had not only whipped me, he had tattled and now Edward would chastise me too. I pulled on my tunic, wincing as it scrubbed my raw back, and hurried to his door. It was on the upper floor, by the warm kitchen chimney. I could hear the servants down below and birds in the thatch above, and smell the cooking fire, the woods and him. I knocked and his voice called, "Come in."

I stepped inside, bowed my head and kept it down though I yearned to look at him. I had seen nothing of him since morning. He wore a robe as blue as my own livery, trimmed in white fox, and had combed out his hair. He was in the chair by the hearth. Parchment and ink lay to hand on the table, and I saw an unrolled map with its ends weighted with wine cups. I waited, hardly breathing.

At last he said, "Master Jacob told me you were punished this afternoon." I nodded and held my tongue. Edward looked me over from crown to toe. "What were you punished for, young Paul? What direst sin did he detect about you? Ranulf said you were a talented, trustworthy lad."

"I try to be, my lord," I muttered, flushing scarlet. "I went into the woods for a little time alone, and fell asleep. I slept hardly at all last night and could not keep awake. I was very late returning."

He leaned forward and I glanced up to see his frown. "And for that Jacob leathered you? It seems a hefty punishment for so slight a crime."

"The leather bound my wrists to the gate, my lord," I said ruefully, "and a birch rod did the business!"

His brows rose. "Take off your tunic and show me."

Lay myself bare before him? I looked nervously at his face, and a devil woke in me. Had I been thrashed for this devil, it might have been more fair. I turned my back, pulled off the tunic, and brazenly rolled down my hose to display my arse, which had suffered seven or eight of the most vengeful blows and was even then throbbing. My cock was bare, and I folded my tunic over it, hoping this show of modesty would absolve me. For some time he said nothing, nor did he move.

I almost looked back at him, and then froze as I heard the rustle of his robe, a soft footstep, and his hand fell on my back, stroking between the welts. It stroked down and down, and settled on the curve of my right buttock. I shivered, deep as the very soul of me.

"I'll speak strongly to Jacob," Edward said quietly but forcefully. "That he has his bones to pick with me is no reason to take his grievances out on you, though I can see why he did this."

"My lord?" I did look back then, and found him studying my abused behind while his right hand cupped the curve of my cheek. Beneath my folded tunic my cock leapt up. I was surely done for now.

There could be no escape, and I felt certain, when Edward was done beating me I would not own an inch of whole hide. I pressed my tunic against my wilful prick and closed my eyes. "My lord, I don't understand."

"No, you would not." Edward removed his hand and stepped away. "Undress and lie on the bed. You are in no fit condition to run Jacob's gauntlet, and he'll make sport of you. I should have known. You must forgive me, boy. My mind is filled with preoccupations – holy war is no small matter."

Somehow I managed to keep my back to him as I rolled down the hose and squirmed onto my belly on the bed, so he did not see the erection I sported. The thought that I was naked, lying on my throbbing cock on his bed almost finished me. If I came and stained the red quilt I would surely be separated from my balls! I thrust my hose under me without his noticing and studied the oak beamed ceiling as Edward paced the room. Shadows danced on the walls behind him, holding me captive.

"Jacob and I have had our differences," he told me. He took a deep breath and seemed to choose each word with care. "He... wanted very much to be where you are now." He glanced deliberately at the bed. "Do you understand?"

He thought me an innocent? I was certainly flushed enough, and he had not yet seen the front of me, to know I shared Jacob's yearning. "I understand, my lord," I said softly. "I've seen boys. Other boys," I added quickly, in case he reviled Jacob's desires. "It is quite common. Pleasure costs nothing."

His brows rose and he laughed. The sound thrilled me. "Then you are of Jacob's mind! Did he steal into your bed, and you spurned him? Is that why he took the birch to you?"

"No, he seems to hate me," I said, honestly bewildered. "He has only tried to make me suffer thus far, and I have neither said nor done anything to him to earn this."

Edward sat on the bedside. His fingertips traced the stinging lines of my welts, and they hurt. I winced and he looked at my face. "He hates you because you shall soon accompany me on Crusade. That is reason enough, since he remains here."

Of a sudden I understood. Jacob was jealous! I took a breath. "My lord, I did earn a thrashing. I fell asleep in the woods and was idle while others were at work."

"Which would have earned you six good strokes of his belt, a mere tickle by comparison to this," Edward mused. "By heaven, he flogged you. And the fault is mine, I suspect."

"Yours, my lord?" I frowned at him, thinking how beautiful he was in the firelight. He had a straight, perfect nose that could have been the work of a sculptor, and a mouth so lush and sensual, I could not see it without wanting kisses. I had to force myself to pay attention to his next words, and then was grateful I did.

He shrugged as if in resignation. "I like a comely youth. It is a sin and I confess it, but the Bishop of Lincoln will sell me absolution once a year for the price of a bull paid to the church. He swears absolution bought is as good as that suffered and laboured for, and I'll not argue with his grace's wisdom!" He stroked my behind again. "I've always liked a comely youth, but I have only ever looked and imagined. Jacob made it known to me, he would willingly warm my bed. I told him *no*, as gently as I could. He is..." He sighed.

"A brute without even manners or a lovely face to offset his bearish ways," I suggested.

Edward looked sharply at me and laughed quietly. "Yes. Oh, I've seen the pleasures of others, knights and squires. It is, as you say, common enough. But here at home... my family is close at hand, the girl who will be my bride lives on the hill above Sleaford, and the priests hereabouts are tattletales with no concept of the sanctity of the confessional!" He shrugged, and his hand gave my behind a luscious little pat. "I must have enraged Jacob more than I realised. It saddens me that it is you who suffered."

My nerves were singing, my head felt light. "My lord, Edward," I whispered, using his name for the first time, thrilled by it. "I'd be thrashed again, and have the birch gladly if it fetched me here." He was too taken aback to speak. "Onto your bed, naked, with your hand on my rump." I groaned. "It is worth the beating, and I dare say, if Jacob knew where I'd be tonight he would have hit me twice as hard!" I wriggled under the weight of his palm, which of a sudden began to stroke. Edward's eyes darkened, storm-grey and wide in the firelight as he looked down at me, and not at my face.

"Have you experience?" he asked, and I thought he was breathless.

I swallowed twice before I could get my voice. "Some little, my lord. Enough not to disappoint or deter you, no matter your need."

"My need? What of yours?" Edward shook his head over my welts. " 'Tis a salve and a cold compress you want, Paul, not an over-eager pizzle in you tonight."

The words ran through my belly like fire and I looked at his lap, where his robe was disturbed by what had lifted beneath. I had seen his golden cock many times, when he stripped to swim, but never blood-rich and hungry. My hand crept toward his legs, and he let it.

"Forget me. I am nothing." I slipped my hand into his robe and found the softness of linen. "Let me. Please."

He was not moving, nor even breathing. He closed his eyes as my hand sought the hem of his linen and slid under and up. I felt his thighs, lean and hard, and the softness of his hair, which I knew was as blond as his head. I found the firm bulk of his balls before I discovered the base of his lance. My head swam as I touched his testicles and felt them swell in my palm. Then I ringed his cock with my thumb and forefinger, and stroked him a little.

A little was all it took. He threw back his head, mouth open, and I realised, bemused, he was about to come. I saw nothing for the robe, but smelt the tangy odour of his sex as he surrendered, felt the thud-thud of the lance in my hand. My own body, neglected and aching, burst at the same moment, and it was fortunate I had slipped my hose between my belly and the quilt.

He cried out, sharp as a dirk, as he came, a wounded sound like an animal in pain. The shaft spent itself and softened in my hand. I cherished it – I might never get another chance. Edward's eyes opened at last and blinked at me.

"Where did you learn what you know, Paul?"

I took a shaky breath. "I know only a little. There was a boy called Grendel. He and I would fumble with one another, two summers ago. He was older, and was killed fighting in Wales. I knew a young monk called Benedict who liked pleasures of the mouth, and he showed me many gentle things." I saw Edward's gullet twitch as he swallowed. "My lord, I do not come to you sullied. I am virgin, I swear." *And shall be till you sunder me, or no man will have me!* I might have said that to him. I might have told him I loved him.

It would have been the truth. I loved him with every fibre in me, and I knew it with a flash of dizzying insight. But the face of innocence looked down at me as Edward regained his breath after I had released him so chastely. Innocence, not ignorance. Edward had seen boys, he knew what men did with men, and recognised those feelings. But he had been content to look and like before this. Perhaps he would have been content merely to look at me, stroke my welted skin because he felt in whole responsible for my suffering.

The scent of his pleasure lingered about his garments, he could not deny it. If the churchmen are right, and virginity is done for when two men touch at all, even just to kiss, then Edward was no longer an innocent. He had come in the hand of a young man. I was his first, I had my dream, or part of it.

But what would become of me now? I was no longer sure of myself, and began to fret as Edward stood and paced to the hearth. One hand leaned on the mantle and he looked into the flames. For a long time he said nothing, and then returned to the bed and smiled faintly. "Will you seek yet another penance? Ranulf told me you do this when a friar is in the district."

I blushed. "Perhaps. But between one penance and the next I am prey to temptation. Always. I am human."

"And do you expect me to confess myself and bare my back for the scourge?" Edward was teasing. His eyes glittered with humour.

"Pay the price of a bull to the church once a year," I purred. "Brother Michael told me once, it is as great a sin to *think* carnally of a man as to perform the deed itself, so one may as well have the pleasure as well as the penance."

"Evil boy," Edward said, but he chuckled also before sighing. "Meanwhile, this has done nothing for the skin of your back."

He crossed the room and threw open a leather bound trunk. I wanted to say, his kiss was all the balm my back needed, but I had not the gall. He returned with a pot of greasy brown stuff that smelt a little odd. I guessed it must be the comfrey plant, pounded into a salve with olibanum and perhaps mandrake. I knew something of these things, since I had spent some time with the old woman, Edith, whom it pleased the folk of Sleaford to call a witch. Certainly, she was wise in the uses of herbs and flowers. She might have made the salve he spread on my back and arse cheeks. I closed my eyes and purred as the coolness soothed me. I had not realised how sharp the smarting had been, and I lay there for lush minutes, savouring the feel of his hands. The last hands to touch me were Jacob's, cuffing me while the youths let me down from the gate. Edward's were so different. So gentle.

At last he finished and stopped up the pot. "That is the best I can do, Paul. Will you have a quack on the morrow?"

But I shook my head. "I'll have more of that, from your hands, and a smile." I wanted a kiss, but knew better than to ask for it. Was he the kind of man who would tumble another, use his body for pleasure, yet refuse him a kiss? A kiss is a token of loving, not the same as coupling for merriment.

I sighed and sat up carefully. I did not let him see the white stain of my coming on my hose, but I did let him see my crotch now, and his eyes lingered there. I am finely made, though it sounds like a brag, long and thick enough to comfortably fill a lad or lass, though not so bullish as to hurt. My cock was quiescent on my balls, which hang high and tight. I wondered if he would ever touch them, or if this chance encounter were the first and the last. The storm-grey eyes dwelt at the parting of my legs for a considerable time, until I began to feel the first twitches of life returning to my spent shaft. Had he eyed me one full minute longer he would have seen me resurrected.

But he turned away, and never saw my shoulders slump. "You had best go to bed. Here, I have a robe that will be softer than your clothes. Return in the morning, I'll salve you again. I would have asked you to ride with me, hawking for hares, but I doubt you could sit a saddle in that condition." He draped a soft red robe around my shoulders. It smelt of him and I held it about me though the night was warm. "Leave Jacob to me," he promised. "He'll give you no more commands, and no further discipline after this!"

I was too elated to feel disappointed as he dismissed me. Halfway through the door, I took his hand and pressed my cheek against it. "Thank you. I did earn some kind of lesson, and took it without

24

argument. If he told you I fought and cursed, he lied, for I never did."

He said nothing, but touched my cheek, and I felt his eyes on me the whole time as I walked down the passage and climbed the ladder to the loft. I sprawled belly down on my own bed, still covered by his robe, tingling and alive as I had never been before. My wilful cock was up, now that it had the privacy to be shameless. I took it in my hands and beat it into frenzied pleasure with my thoughts filled with him.

Chapter III

In the morning I was eager for the salve. Over the breakfast table, at which I stood, being too sore to sit, he studied me with a faint, perplexed smile, and when the maids had cleared away he withdrew to his bedchamber and called me to follow. Today I bent over the table and he salved me swiftly, unwilling to put me on his bed or linger over me. Did he regret what we had done last evening? I bit my lip as he stroked the comfrey into me, and tried to concentrate on what he was saying.

"This afternoon I ride to Sir Lionel de Quilberon's estate. Perhaps by then you shall be able to sit a horse. Your stripes are much improved." He patted my rump. "Jacob has had stern words from me already and is sulking." He restoppered the salve and stroked deeply with both hands. "Sir Lionel sails with us. His ship, on the Humber, will take us to war. Will you pine for England, Paul?"

Not if I go with you, I thought, but said, "My place is with you, nought else should concern you. I have shamed Ranulf already with last afternoon's performance. I shan't disappoint you further."

His hands stilled on my behind. "Disappoint me?" Edward laughed and patted me before his hands were gone and he reached for a rag. "Do you think I stand here, grease to the elbows, oiling the arse of any young lad?" Flushed to the ears, I pulled up my hose and ducked my head. "I like you," he told me. "Ranulf and I rode to battle together, and if he tells me I can trust you, I believe him. I thought to shock you with the confessions I made last night. Had you been God-fearing, you would have scorned and spurned me, and walked away in a fine fury, no matter the difference in our rank! Some things come before pride and privilege."

So he had been half afraid *I* would take umbrage when I learned the truth. I had blundered into a triangle of desire, come between the hopeful groom and his disapproving master. I smiled ruefully, noticing that in daylight his eyes were blue-grey, like ice, and his hair as near white as blond. "I'm no angel," I said quietly. "I have my passions, my lord. Perhaps God will burn me in hell for them, but I cannot change what I am. I have confessed and done penance so may times, yet... here I am, unchanged and unable to change." As I looked up at him I allowed my face to show some small part of the longing I felt for him.

He recoiled as if I had struck him. His brows first rose and then knitted in a frown, his mouth opened to speak, closed again, and he turned away to gaze through the tall, narrow window, over the estate as far as the river. It was a long time before he spoke. "Paul, this cannot be," he whispered. "What passed between us last night is more than should have."

My heart sank. I lowered my eyes from his slender body in the soft black leathers, and hid my disappointments as best I could. "Perhaps you are right, my lord." I stepped back to the door, telling myself it would be enough to be near him, serve him well, honour his house. I lifted my head again when I had my expression composed. "When do we sail?"

"Two weeks, if the weather holds, three if not. I ride to Lionel's this afternoon to make last moment arrangements for armour, horses and harness." He glanced over his shoulder at me. I met his eyes levelly, afraid of what I would see there, and was taken aback. They were filled with yearning and some deep pain. Bruised and troubled, they flayed me to the bone as Jacob's birch had not even begun to.

What had I done to him, what had I shown him, offered him, that he would never take from me? I had cursed him with desires that might never be fulfilled beneath his own roof. He stirred and raked back his hair. "I'll take out the falcons this morning. If you can sit a saddle, be ready at noon. We'll return tomorrow or the next day, and I'll instruct you myself in the duties of a squire.

He stalked out, and I heard his feet on the stairs as I tarried, breathing the subtle scents of him that lingered about his clothes and bed. I had hurt him, and the hurt would continue. Absurdly, I wished I could undo what I had done, but no sin is redeemed so easily. Perhaps coupling is called sin because of the pain it brings after a few moments of joy. Miserable, I stood at his window and watched him ride out with his favourite hawk on his wrist. He went into the woods and up toward the hill where the hares were most populous and must be culled unless they were to eat every blade of graze. I lost sight of him in the elms, and closed my eyes, castigating myself more brutally than a priest would have.

Jacob eyed me viciously all morning but stayed well back and was silent. I did not even look at him, when I could manage it. He snarled at the boys and maids, dealt cuffs and wallops all around, but I received only glares. Now, I did not care. I knew his secret and when I plucked up the courage I scornfully looked him up and down. He was a brute, hairy as a beast and coarse as a bonded serf. I imagined him naked and thought of a cock like a donkey and great, hairy haunches, and between, a hungry great hole, well fucked and ravenous for more. I shuddered, trying not to imagine him in Edward's bed, or in mine. I was lucky Jacob was jealous and hated me, for he could have done as Edward said, crept into my bedchamber and demanded my favours. Just as I had accepted his discipline, I would have had to serve him that way too. The newcomer had little choice.

I spent the morning idly, helping the maids, who were nice girls, fairy-slim and wide eyed. They liked me, and I enjoyed one or two invitations for bed, which I seriously considered. Edward's door was closed, and that side of me must be curbed. I told myself this over and over, and when a lass fluttered her eyelashes I whispered silly things in her ear.

Edward was back before noon with a brace of hares over the saddle. The hunting had been good. The maids took the meat to be cleaned, and he stood in the yard, looking long at me, searchingly, before he strode by without a word and went to his bedchamber. I feared I was in disfavour, but what could I do? I ate bread and cheese before I fetched out Icarus and a little black mare for myself, in case the invitation to ride to Sir Lionel's was still good.

It was. Early afternoon was hot. Sweat prickled my ribs and stung my half-healed welts as I mounted and sat gingerly on my striped behind. Edward lifted a brow at me. I flushed and nodded, and we turned east toward the de Quilberon estates. They lay much nearer the coast and I smelt the tang of the sea as we drew closer. I never saw the water, since the hills rose in a final serpent-back hummock between the house and the beach.

It seemed Edward was expected, for his stable boys scurried out to meet us. They took the horses and I stuck to my lord's heels as he paced into the house, where Sir Lionel himself appeared. He was big and loud, no better and no worse for being in his own home rather than a guest in someone else's. He embraced Edward, smacked his cheeks with kisses, and I sighed. Brotherly kisses were accepted, but the kind I longed for might hurt Edward more afterward than they pleasured him at the time. Such is the paradox of pleasures of the flesh. I held my tongue, stood behind Edward's chair as he sat and took wine, and I tried to listen and learn.

Sir Lionel had news of the King, and the Crusade. He spoke of Saracen knights, of places with names that suggested Babylon itself, strange and exotic. My half-closed eyes surveyed Edward's handsome profile and I imagined him beneath a star-spangled desert sky. I knew nothing, then, of the desert, but I could dream.

Some intuition told me, like a voice in my ear, *You will learn more than you will care to know. Beware!* I did not listen. I was too preoccupied with my scenes of voluptuousness, as Edward crept to me in the hours after midnight in a desert camp of war, placed his hand on my belly and said –

27

"Paul!" He had spoken to me several times already. I had not heard a word, and gave a guilty start. Edward frowned up at me. "What ails you? Are you in pain?" He looked at Lionel. "Just yesterday he had a cruel whipping, shoulders to arse, for nothing. Jacob's work, as you might guess."

The Norman spat a mouthful of gristle into the hearth and returned to the bone he was gnawing. "I saw Jacob beat a donkey half to death as it struggled under a load. I took a stick to him myself for that." Lionel's deep brown eyes frowned at me. "If you're in pain, go and rest. I'll think no worse of you."

"Thank you, my lord," I muttered, "but the truth is, I'll hurt as much if I stand or lie, and I'd rather attend Sir Edward, which is why I am here."

Lionel's brows arched and he leaned over the table to give Edward a nudge with one beefy elbow. Edward did not look at me. Did he not trust himself, or not trust me? "You've the makings of a fine squire there," Lionel said cheerfully. "Treat him rightly, not too many leatherings, good suppers and little treats, and he'll do you well enough through the whole campaign."

Little treats? I thought of Edward's body lying hot against my own, his cock between my thighs, or deep inside, or in my throat, and I swallowed hard. I was bound for hell, no doubt about it, and worse, just then I could find no will in me to care. Edward made a noncommittal sound, took a draught of wine and would not speak, even in jest. I could have borne gentle mockery. Did he worry for my feelings? He need not have, but I could not tell him that.

Instead, he returned to what he had said originally. "I was telling Sir Lionel, Paul, you can read. Can you read a map also?"

"Aye, my lord. Brother James taught me by showing me maps of Normandy and Aquitaine."

"Good. Then you can serve me too," Lionel mused. "I've three squires, but they're little lads and I'll take only the eldest and leave the whelps behind. I've no wish to see them come to harm. The only woe with this is that the eldest, Henri, can read neither letter nor map, though he's fine with nags and can hone a sword as well as I can myself. He'll study chivalry, not writing and manners." He cocked his head at me. "Have you no such ambitions?"

The question startled me. Study chivalry, be a knight? Though my father had been a soldier and had won his spurs in the old King's time, I had never considered the possibility that I should follow in his footsteps. I was the orphan, the Fostered Boy, for whom it was Aethelstan's livery or a herd of swine!

I was silent so long that Edward's fair head rose, and stormy eyes probed me deeply. He also was waiting, and I cleared my throat. "I have the same dreams as any lad," I said blunderingly, "but I hope I can tell the difference between what is dream and what is real. I am

28

a Saxon, and Saxon knights are few indeed."

"Edward is Saxon also," Lionel said pointedly. He sighed and leaned toward me. "'Tis more than a century since we Normans came here. Many of us consider ourselves English, not Norman, and sure to God, not French. Aye, my name is French and I speak that tongue as well as yours. But I can write neither. The lass I wed is Saxon, and my sons are as Saxon as not!" He turned to Edward, offered his hand, and Edward clasped it firmly. "We fight for God and the Lionheart, in that order. So forget your Saxon blood in this house, boy."

I wished he was right, but Edward knew the truth. His face was troubled as he listened to Lionel, as if behind his facade of calm he wished what Lionel said were true. But Lionel was one man – a great man, I realised, but just one. A hundred to his one were the Normans who would never call themselves English and who scorned to wed Saxon women, no matter how noble they were born. Edward was a knight by a mere fluke.

Before the Normans came, his family had owned much more land than they did that day we visited de Quilberon. The earldom was as old as time, so I believed. Even though his family capitulated to the invaders, Duke William stripped their estate to the bone. The Aethelstan house retained its nobility, but the Normans of that shire were reluctant to show Edward even common courtesy.

He hoped that if he fought in the Holy Land he might win favour with the King. Sudden insight blossomed, and my heart quickened. Edward fought not for the Lionheart, nor for the Church, but for Saxon pride, so that people of our blood might live better after the war. Instinctively, I shared that pride in being Saxon, and I lifted my chin and regarded Sir Lionel with a smile.

"I would study chivalry if it would benefit Saxon honour. If my lord taught me, I would be diligent. I would fight for the common blood all Saxons share." There, it was said. *Take that from me, Edward! Take from me that thread of kinship!* He could not, for it was born in all of us and I could revel in it without hesitation.

Lionel was amused. "You'd not fight for England, God, or a Plantagenet King?"

I shrugged. "It might seem so, but I am a Saxon in a Norman land. I must fight for what I believe in."

The big, burly Norman laughed and clapped his hands. "Well said! There, Edward. Will you instruct him?"

But Edward surprised both of us. "No." He drained his cup, put it down and fondled the head of the wolfhound which lay in his green-skirted lap. "No, I would not, for a lad who has been taught to read and write, and has grown to sixteen years without raising a sword is better employed in gentler pursuits. He is too old to begin. He would go out and be maimed or killed. I would fetch a body home for burial, or a cripple to be coddled the rest of his life, where at present I own a full-bodied young colt."

Was this how he saw me? I shivered, and my eyes were drawn to his, which smouldered like a fire banked down to last the night through. Lionel slopped another draught of ale into his cup.

"What say you of that, Paulo Delgado?"

'Paulo Delgado' might have felt his father's honour, heavy on his shoulders, and sworn he would win his spurs at any cost. *Paul* merely said quietly, "I am my master's horse." That devil got into me and I could not help but add, "to ride as he chooses."

"Or not, if he chooses," Edward said testily. He stood, smoothed his robe and walked over to throw open the shutters. It was very late in the afternoon, or early in the evening. "I am stifled, Lionel! I wish we could leave tomorrow. What of the armour? Has that smith finished yet?"

"That smith can no longer work," Lionel said broodingly as he studied me from beneath bushy brows. "The Sheriff of Durham's tax collectors visited him for the third time, over taxes from last year. He could not pay and they lopped his right hand. He'll work no more."

The story seemed to be flung challengingly at me, and I looked away. It was not my place to stand up for Saxon honour – I was lower than the smith who had been maimed. Edward was a knight, let him answer. His horse, this willing nag which he chose not to ride, would confine himself to carrying burdens.

Edward sighed heavily. "The man was the best armourer in this shire."

"And the best talent with an upthrust pizzle," Lionel said ruefully. "He has fourteen children and one on the way. The tribe of brats he has sired has paupered him, and now his eldest sons must do the work while he looks on and instructs. They are big, brawny lads and will do well, given the chance."

"Aye." Edward rubbed his eyes as if he was wearied. "Did no one speak on the man's behalf? He could have come to me."

"You spoke for a ploughman last winter and were warned not to meddle," Lionel reminded him. "The Sheriff of Durham holds the reins here, and you Saxons must mind your manners. Edward, you've more to lose than your armourer."

Edward looked at his hands, which clenched into white knuckled fists.

Lionel sighed. "You could lose your lands and title, and end with less than this – this full-bodied colt of yours! You ride a precarious path, and will be advised to remember it."

"I never forget it," Edward snapped. "Why else would I go with you to fight a Norman war against Turks and Saracens, for a God whose very name I doubt!"

The other man's dark face hardened. He stood, wiped his greasy hands on his breast and approached Edward with several long strides.

"Hold your tongue on these matters under this roof, my friend. I've some God-fearing, church-haunting stewards who'd be happy to see you tied to a stake amid a mound of faggots, and put a torch to you themselves!" Edward's eyes lowered and his lips sealed. Lionel spoke in the barest whisper, his eyes on me. "Know you, boy, what became of his family while his father, the old earl, was fighting out of the country for the King?"

I shook my head. Edward opened his mouth to protest but Lionel's fingers dug into his arm insistently, and he closed it again.

"Normans ransacked a house on the Tees, at Yarm where his mother and sisters were visiting. None was left alive save a little girl who told the tale. He was younger than you at the time, studying in a monastery, learning letters."

The word 'letters' was spat with contempt. I knew what Lionel – who could neither read nor write – was thinking. If Edward had not been in the monastery he might have been able to defend his women and the day might have ended differently. I was less sure. More likely, the ransacking Normans would only have sported with the young and beautiful boy too, and that night he would have been as dead as the Aethelstan ladies.

I swallowed hard. "You lost your faith that day," I whispered to him, hoping I was not overstepping the bounds of my liberty by speaking so intimately.

He took a breath, held it and seemed to summon his thoughts. "I lost what faith I ever had. The monastery had already weakened it, for I saw all manner of debauchery there, and absolution bought with money that had been earned by blood. I've no time for God, Paul. You should know this, if you're to serve me. You'll likely be shocked by much I say and do – or fail to do."

Then, if he was not afeard of God, why did he shut his door to me? I could not guess, but I knew I had begun to glimpse his secrets. I owed Lionel a great debt, also, for he had shown me the one chink in Edward's mailcoat through which one who loved him could glimpse.

And Lionel loved him – not as I loved Edward of course, but like a brother or even a son. A comrade in arms. I studied Edward in the evening light from the windows he had thrown open. He was almost the same height as I – he that little taller, as I would be slightly higher when I was done growing. He would not look at me, but said to Lionel,

"And we are to get our armour from the smith's sons?"

"By next week at latest." Lionel seemed relieved to have left the subject of Edward's family. "The price will be the same, but I've a mind to pay more, since this year's taxes will be no less hefty than last, and the man is maimed already."

"Rather lop his balls than his hands," Edward muttered. "Fourteen brats is more than enough! He's paupered by now, and his woman must be bow-legged!" Lionel laughed. "And you're right, we'll pay a little more for his sake, damn the Sheriff."

"And the armourer will keep his left hand," Lionel added. "He may learn to wield a hammer with that arm."

They spoke for hours of ships and fighting men, horses and weapons. I was shown sheets of numbers and told to add them, and I discovered an error or two in the accounting for the voyage. This pleased my lords, and Sir Lionel showed me his maps in the evening, when he was certain I could be trusted. They were priceless. I had never seen maps of the Holy Land, and I was hungry for their secrets.

A large, blunt forefinger stabbed at the word Jerusalem, and Lionel told me, this was where we were bound. We would camp, raid into the deserts, besiege the Saracen and raze his walls to the ground. It all sounded very grand, but I was not blind to Edward's dark look of unspoken qualm, and I reserved my judgement.

That night I slept with the three squires. The eldest, Henri, was a skinny twelve-year old with bright, shrewd eyes and a quick mind, like a monkey. He had a whippy strength and a native cunning that would take him far – if they did not get him into trouble first, I decided, and maybe hanged before he was twenty.

I shared his bed but he kept his hands to himself, turned his back on me and was quickly asleep.

* * *

The lady of the house woke not long after dawn. Sir Lionel's wife was a mother of five, broad in the hips and handsome. She must have been lovely as a girl, with her long, hay-coloured hair and blue eyes. She was past her best now but still would catch the eye when the light was just right, and Lionel thought she was the finest woman who ever lived. I believe he was right in that thinking.

I had known few women in all my life – where was the opportunity? Past her best or not, Lady Enid de Quilberon was the match of any I had ever seen. I liked her and I'll brag, she liked me also, and spoke to me with a smile when we breakfasted. Edward and Lionel were already dressing to leave and I was not invited.

They were riding to look at horses and harness at a manor down the coast. I would have enjoyed the journey, since my arse was mended and I always wanted to wander further afield than I could. But instead I walked over the hill, gazed at the sea and thought myself both blessed and cursed at once.

Had I still owned my liberty I could have followed Edward on a whim. Had I been just a common lad in the fields he might have tumbled me, laughing, and ridden me. At least I would have had that to remember. Had I been a precocious imp like Henri I might have stolen into his bed, begged him to fuck me and earned my memories that way. But I was none of those things. I had everything, and I had nothing.

I lay in the coarse sea grass above the beach, watching the breakers on the yellow sand and the wading birds that pecked for crabs and shellfish where the tide turned back upon itself. I called myself unfortunate, forgetting that if Edward had not taken me in I would have spurned Sleaford's pigs and taken vows of chastity and obedience with the monks.

Why did Edward shut me out? If his faith had been stripped from him as cruelly as a man could be flayed of his skin, he was unlikely to fear hell, or even believe in God's existence. So why did he send me away? I rolled over, cupped my chin in my fists and pretended that the heat of the sun on my back was his hands on me.

Before me the sea rushed in and out, lulling me to sleep. Soon that same sea would carry me away, but to what uncertain future, I could not even imagine.

Chapter IV

I saw nothing of Edward the whole day, and though I watched for him long into the twilight he did not return. Lady Enid was not concerned. Lionel, she said, would have decided to stay the night at another Saxon estate where fine warhorses grazed the riverside slopes.

In the evening a minstrel and fool entertained us. A whey-faced young priest said Benediction in the chapel, and I bedded with Henri once more. I was fretted and longing for sleep, but that night the boy was wicked, and whispered into my ear, carefully, since the younger boys were asleep.

"Are you coming to the Holy Land with us?"

"As Aethelstan's squire," I told him. "Go to sleep."

His hand crept onto my chest. "You're furry as a man. Why don't you stay here and get a woman instead?"

"I may find a woman there," I said drily as he explored my breast. I cannot say it distressed me. Many's the twelve year old who's more adept at seduction than his elders. Had this rascal been a man's catamite? Surely not Lionel's! He tweaked my paps, which made me squirm, and laughed. "You are a cheeky monkey," I scolded.

"And your tits are tender as a maid's," he chuckled. "If I pull on them, I wager your pole will rise up hard."

I caught his hands in a painful grip. "Have you any notion of what you are about, little knave?"

He yawned in my face. " 'Tis a sweet way to pass the night."

"And whose bed have you shared, to know about it?" I asked, releasing his right hand and letting him continue if he wanted to.

33

"I was bred in Baron de Rocher's castle. I often think I'm his son," Henri snickered. "If I am, I am double-damned and God will never forgive me! A bastard, to begin with, buggered by his own sire." He turned over and wriggled his narrow little hips against me. "Feel me there."

"I will not!" I may have sounded shocked, but in fact I was amused and endeared. Henri was Baron Michel de Roche's bastard, no doubting it. He wriggled and sighed until I brought my hand between his legs and slid it up between his cheeks in search of his opening. It was as oily as a well-kept sword and my thumb slipped straight in. I grunted in astonishment. "Why, you impudent – " I began, but he pushed back and snickered. "You like this?"

"How can I lie?" Henri panted as he worked on my hand. "I had no choice at first, but they showed me how to like, then crave it! I am evil, I know." He rolled over on his belly and his eyes glittered at me in the light of a single stuttering candle, half laughing, half inviting.

How long it was since I had done this to another boy! Grendel was years ago, and there was only one since, and a harlot of a girl who lifted her skirts one morning. Sleaford was not a place of plentiful opportunity! My hunger for Edward had brought me to dire straits and I was desperate for the release Henri offered. He would not scorn me tomorrow and I would do a favour for him if I could – anything but grant him my arse, he could not have that, it was for Edward or no man – and we both would sleep sounder for it.

I fumbled in my night linen, bared a swatch of myself and entered his oily little body with a deep groan. Henri twitched, muttered into the pillows and then settled. Beneath me he was so small and thin, I could not even pretend it was Edward. I bit my lip with a rueful smile that mocked myself, and fucked him as gently as I could, given my urgency.

He was pleased, came twice as boys can at that age, and curled up to sleep in my arms with his head under my chin. I had not invited him into my embrace, but he reminded me of the puppy I had cuddled to sleep when I was very young, and I took him gladly.

Oddly, I did not sleep much. My release in Henri's eager body was just enough to clear my mind and make me realise all I wanted from Edward. All I believed I would never have. I saw out the night with resignation and was even more fretted by dawn.

Edward and Lionel returned down the coast trail at midmorning, and I was on the dunes with a wave of greeting. Lionel cupped his hand to his mouth, shouting to me as I ran toward them, "The horses are arranged and he has a little chestnut gelding for you, the pick of the herd, discounting the warhorses."

I looked up at Edward as I slithered to a halt at his side, and smiled despite myself. He seemed flustered, as if he had not meant me to know the lengths he had gone to, to secure me a good nag. "I

34

am proud to wear your colours, my lord," I told him. "I'll take good care of the horse."

Bluffly, he reached down and tousled my hair. "I shall see that you do, mark my words! Do wrong by the horses and you'll find soon enough, Master Jacob is not the only one with a heavy hand."

I still smiled at him, if anything, wider. "My lord, were I to harm your horse by fault or neglect, I'd fetch the birch, bare my arse, confess and beg you to set me to rights, so richly do I cherish my duties."

For a moment his mouth thinned and his eyes sparkled with laughter. I had the better of him, but only he and I knew it. If I took down my hose and lifted my arse, it would not be for a beating, no matter what I had said or what Lionel assumed. I thought Edward would choke as he tried not to laugh out loud, yet I had also spoken the truth. I cherished his trust, and duty came first to me. His horses, his weapons, himself.

He shook his head over me and kicked Icarus's brawny sides. I jogged back to Lionel's house at the horse's shoulder and took his bridle as Edward kicked out of the stirrups. "Groom and feed him, clean his harness, turn him into the paddock, then you may sup, boy," he said in that mock-stern tone of teasing.

I bowed, back-cracking low, and heard Lionel say, "God's teeth, you work the boy too hard. He deserves a kind word. Know you not, by now, he loves you?"

"Oh, I know," Edward murmured as he and Lionel entered the house by the scullery door.

Behind them, I smiled and stroked Icarus's ears. He had a bony, sensitive face, brown eyes and big, feathery white hooves below four long white stockings. The muscles under his dappled, iron-grey coat rippled as I groomed him, first for duty's sake, then for pleasure. He liked to be groomed, and caressing him with a wisp of hay I could make believe I was caressing his master. No one else was in the stable and I told him many a secret. Who I loved and wanted; what I had done last evening with Henri. He snorted as if to chastise, and I laughed.

In the evening I served at table, and before bed I sat with Edward on the house's back doorsill and learned how to draw a sword and handle it safely. How to oil it, and pass its edges across the whetstones, different kinds of whetstones for different finishes. I only grasped half of what was said and knew I would have to ask Henri for the finer points later. Being near Edward seemed to chase the brains out of my skull.

The scent of him filled my head as we sat together, and I felt the heat of his shoulder against mine. The yard was deserted and the chickens pecked at our feet. Lionel's whole household had gone to benediction and we were alone but for the hens, the dogs and stable cats. As Edward finished showing me the grinding stones I put my hand on his knee.

He took a sharp breath and said, "Paul, please. Not here."

"Then, where?" I hissed. "My lord, I have told you in a thousand ways, I want you. Will I be driven insane? Kill me now, with this very sword! Do it quick and clean, not one day at a time, as you're punishing me." There, it was out. And now I was afraid.

He sighed heavily. "You don't understand."

"You hate priests and you don't believe God exists," I said flatly, "I know that. So it cannot be a fear of hell that keeps you from me."

"Not fear of hell," Edward said quietly. "But of my fellow man."

I shot a glance at him and frowned. The last of the twilight softened his face until he could have been a boy. He seemed no older than me, with his beard so blond that not a trace showed about his jaw. "Make me understand. Is it me? Do you find me distasteful?"

"Don't be ridiculous," he said tersely. "Why, just the other night you..." The faintest flush warmed his cheeks. He cleared his throat. "I do not believe that heaven would punish a man for loving, nor for doing what is natural to his heart, but there are men who repay love with pain. I want no part of that. I am on the wrong side of the Sheriff of Durham already."

"You spoke out for a ploughman," I prompted.

"Like a fool, I did. And the ploughman's eye was still put out, and now I am on a lengthy list of men the Sheriff calls his enemies. The Bishop is no friend of mine either, since it is Church tax rather than the Crown tax that makes the burden borne by my serfs so cruel. We can pay King or God, not both. I argued to his grace that he must lighten his tax, and he was in such a fury, I feared I would be excommunicated."

"But you would not fear that!"

"True," Edward admitted. "But if I am excommunicated I'll lose the hand of Edwina Montand. A marriage with her will double the size of my lands, secure a rich bride-price, buttress my house with Norman blood and..." He stopped and put his face into his hands. "I am a traitor, I don't deny it, but I see no other way. This is why I ride on this cursed Crusade. To woo Edwina's poxed old father. He is ancient and sodded, and cannot last long. His sons are all dead, killed in the Holy Land. He can will his estate to whomever he names as his heir, either me or Yves Guilbert. And if it is Guilbert..." he sighed. "Then a girl will suffer and Guilbert will become so powerful in this shire, he will swallow Aethelstan without a hiccup."

At the mention of Yves Guilbert I shuddered. I knew him only from tales and gossip, and I had always taken the stories lightly, but if Edward believed them, I believed. Stories of young girls tortured past believing, injured and violated. His fancy was not for boys. Boys he simply killed, willy-nilly, as he chose. Girls suffered much worse. And to this man, old Baron Montand would give his daughter in marriage? The man was mad!

Was that it, was he addled with the years? "His mind must be gone if he will sign his daughter away to Guilbert," I said darkly.

Edward's fair head nodded. "It is. In Guilbert he sees a great warrior. True, Guilbert is magnificent on the battlefield, but off it, he is toadspawn. Would that one of his girls would find a dirk to hand and put an end to him. But God sends the sweetest maidens to that castle, never a girl with nerve and strength, and a sharp knife." He shrugged resignedly. "I am caught, Paul, no means to escape. I must be without blemish, in a state of grace, as far as the stewards and priests hereabouts are aware."

I digested this and nodded. "We could be secret. I could come to you silently after midnight. Or we could go out. I know the forest well."

He was shaking his head as I spoke. "Many know the woods, and trappers and poachers are there every day, as well as King's men, foresters and outlaws. My servants sleep lightly and have keen ears. Remember that." He dared take my face in his palms, and I suffered a sudden rush of hunger to taste his mouth. "We cannot." He took his hands away and said, husky with regret, "Would you like to leave my service? I can tell Ranulf some tale that will credit rather than harm you."

But at once I made negative noises. "No, my lord... Edward. I would sooner be with you and bed alone than be without you. When Sir Lionel sails, we go together." I looked at the sky in the north. "The weather is holding fair."

"Yes." He stood, gathered his swords and handed them to me. "Be a squire, then. You know where everything belongs. And the horse?"

"Is fed and groomed, in the paddock, knee deep in gaze," I reported, "or I would be bare-arsed before you after all, and not for pleasure!"

He smiled sadly, and I hurried up to the room to put away his things.

That night I could not wait for Henri to offer me his body, but took it quickly. I was frustrated past reason, and pinned him down on the palliasse, humping into his oiled passage until he oofed and panted and swore. Afterward he punched my chest and said I had raped him.

"You lie, viper, you loved every instant," I argued. "Why else do you come to bed with that part of you washed out clean and oiled sweetly?" Then I stroked his soft brown hair and kissed his lips. "Did I hurt you?"

Henri giggled into my mouth and sucked my tongue. "No, not even at first. I've been buggered too often to be distressed even if you're quick. What is the matter with you, Paul? You rutted on me

37

tonight, where last eve I had to seduce you!"

We were whispering in the dark. The other squires were asleep at the far end of the loft. He stroked my mouth with his fingertips, and I saw a glimmer of moonlight in his eyes. Shrewd eyes, like those of the raven or the jackdaw. Yet, despite his shrewdness he was a likeable rascal, and I knew I could trust him. "Will you keep my secrets, Henri?"

"Secrets?" he asked eagerly. "Life and death secrets?"

"Life and death for me, if I am discovered," I sighed. He nodded vigorously, shuffled into my arms and pressed his ear to my mouth. I bit it sharply and thrust in my tongue. "Keep this secret, then. I am in love with my lord of Aethelstan, and he'll not have me." I told him what I had said to Icarus and felt Henri's jolt of surprise. When he drew back from me he took my face between his hard, callused little hands and sighed over me. "What, knave?" I prompted, but without sting.

"I am sorry, I did not know," he murmured. "Else I would have been less vile about seduction last night. I thought you might like to play, the way boys do, but you have become a man." Surprised, I waited and his slim shoulders twitched as he shrugged. "You speak of love. Only men speak of love and weep at night for it. Boys speak of fucking and sucking, and snigger at evils performed on the other side of a wall from the master's bed." He leaned over and kissed my mouth tenderly. "You can fuck me again if you like."

"Oh, Henri." I took him in my arms. "You are a man yourself, a little, if you understand these things. I'll couple you again if *you* like. There is the difference."

"Gently this time, then," Henri whispered, and turned on his belly for me to do it.

It was slower and better this time. I sheathed myself and thought of my blond Aethelstan rose who lay asleep below these very floorboards. Edward, curled on his side beneath the counterpane, sleep-warm, softened by slumber, with his gold hair fanned across the pillow and his long, dark lashes on his cheeks. I could have wept, and took my solace from Henri's tight young arse, which gripped my cock so sweetly.

I slept better that night with Henri wriggling in my arms, and in the morning when Edward decided we must ride home I managed to find a moment to kiss the boy behind the stable. In daylight he was a sharp-faced, sharp-boned little creature, pixyish, energetic. Very young. I tousled his hair and told him,

"We'll sail together and be away from home a long time. We'll both become men before we return. It's good to have friends before such a voyage, eh?"

He nodded, and then Sir Lionel called him and I returned to the hitching post where Icarus and my little gelding stood dozing. Edward wore his black velvet this morning. His steel-hard slenderness was emphasised by the costume and he commanded my eyes. Indulging myself, I celebrated his overwhelming masculinity and challenged heaven to fling a thunderbolt at me. My spine prickled the instant the challenge was made, but the sky remained clear and blue as Edward put boot to stirrup, mounted up and took the reins in his left hand.

Standing at the gate, with his wife on his arm, was Lionel. "I'll sup with you soon and fetch news of the ship," he promised, and slapped Edward's thigh with one gauntleted hand, brotherly hard. I almost yelped, 'don't bruise him!' A ridiculous thought, for Edward was a warrior.

"See that you do," he said, laughing, and leaned down to kiss the woman's cheek. "Your hospitality was most welcome, my lady. Stay safe."

She was Saxon, as was he, and I also, at least by half. It made us kindred, and for this I offered a grateful prayer as I followed Icarus through the posterngate and away from the sea. I was silent, just watching Edward's back for an hour or more, until it seemed he could tolerate my quiet no longer.

He turned in the saddle, found me gazing at him with some dreamy, loon's look on my face and gave me an exasperated sigh. "I was about to scold you for being sullen," he told me ruefully. "Paul, take that look from your face before someone sees it."

Flustered, I knew I was blushing. "What look, my lord?"

"You know very well!"

I did. My blush deepened and I glanced at the crows circling the carcass of a goat on the hillside. Edward reined back until Icarus was level with my little horse and said in a softer tone that thrilled me, "I promise you this. I can give you none of what you want, but you'll be safe with me. I'll keep you out of danger. You'll know only the hardship I suffer with you. This is the best I can do. You understand my position?"

The worst of it was – and it stung me like Jacob's birch – I did. I nodded miserably. "I understand all too well." Even there, miles from home, I had seen a woodsman on the trail. If we had stopped for a moment to steal a kiss, so innocent an expression of affection, we would have been seen. If I strained my ears I could hear a voice singing, an axe chopping in the forest. Nowhere could we be properly alone, and everywhere there was danger that could have me burned for a witch, and Edward with me.

It was well known, then and now, that when a man loves men he is a witch. I never fully understood the reasoning behind this. I suspect the churchmen who preach it reckon the devil gets into us, making us love others of our kind, and this make us witches. I would argue, it is God who gets into a man and makes him so beautiful he bewitches others. I was helpless before Edward, and he knew it. The turn of his cheek seduced me, the sun on his hair, the way he rode with his hand on his lean thigh. All this inspired wild thoughts and wilder passions.

He was gentle toward me, which was more than I could have asked for. He kept Jacob away, and for that I was grateful. That evening I served at table as he tore squabs with a monk I knew from the priory. Brother Hubert was begging money for a new roof. Edward could ill afford it, and promised the tonsured idiot some amount when the harvest was in and taxes paid. I stood by with the wine, half asleep with the wolfhounds in the draught of the fire as I listened to their desultory talk.

Then I was asleep, and the next I knew it was very late and the monk had gone. I stirred guiltily to find Edward looking at me with a perplexed expression. We did not speak, but his stormy eyes roved over me from crown to toe and back, and the mouth I longed for smiled. I struggled out of my doze but he shook his head minutely, putting me at my ease.

"I always seem to be falling asleep when I should be working," I said ruefully. "Will you switch me?"

"You've no fear of punishment, have you?" he asked thoughtfully. I shook my head. "You have been punished often." Not a question. I nodded. "Did Ranulf beat you?"

"No, my lord, but nor did he stop the brothers, when I arrived late for lessons or forget something. Often, I limped home, or did not go home at all, being too sore. Ranulf said it was not his business, and I survived."

"They know how to curb a boy's spirit," Edward said drily, and I remembered that he had been sent to a monastery for schooling. They could have treated him no more kindly than me. I tried not to think of him shuddering after righteous chastisement, as only churchmen know how to deal it. Still, Edward was half-trained as a knight by then, and would have borne it easier than the little boys who were being tutored as scribes and pages.

I sat, rubbed my eyes and watched him pour a last cup of wine, but this he gave to me. Astonished but delighted, I took it. He stood beside me, one hand on my shoulder, looking into the fire.

"I'll fetch you home whole," he promised. "If I can give you no more than that, I should give you no less. Trust me."

"I trust you," I said very softly as I savoured the wine and thought, *how I do love you!* To say it was impossible, and I clamped my teeth on the words. "All is ready?"

"We leave in a week. I must put my accounts in order, pack my belongings and farewell Lady Edwina." He bit his lip and his face darkened. "I made her addled old father promise not to give her away in my absence. He'll do as I ask."

"And if Baron Montand should die before we return?" I asked. It was something he must consider. If his chasteness was not merely to stay on the right side of the bishop and avoid a witch's horrible execution, but also to keep the girl out of the possession of a man like Guilbert, then Baron Montand's untimely death was something he could not overlook.

"If the old man dies too soon, she goes to the nunnery," he said very quietly. "I'd trust her to the holy sisters. She'll likely take vows and stay there." He shook his head slowly. "A waste of a young life."

"As a bride of Christ, her lands and fortune go to the Church," I added. He shrugged as if it meant nothing, but I knew at least one of his secrets. This was a troubled estate wearing a proud face. Beneath the pretence of elegance, Edward's fortunes were threadbare, and this foray to the Holy Land was a desperate attempt to repair them. If he won the King's favour and wedded Edwina Montand, he would keep his house intact.

And if he did not?

I studied him in the firelight. If he lost everything and became a lacklands soldier of fortune, he and I could be together. But the price he would pay for my pleasure was so high, I shuddered and drowned the selfish thought in my wine. He took the empty goblet and touched my nose with one fingertip as I looked up again.

"Go to bed," he said softly. "I shall sit up a while and think, but I want to be alone. Your presence... disturbs me." He forced a smile and nodded at the door. "A lad of your years needs his rest."

Obedient, I went to bed, but I did not sleep for fretting, and I thought often of what little Henri had said the night before.

Chapter V

I did as Edward wished and kept my distance, said nothing, did nothing that betrayed my feelings. But nothing can stop a man dreaming, and what dreams I had! Some were tender, and I went to him and was welcomed, or he came to me and we were gentle with one another. Others were violent dreams, and I was a captive of a creature such as Yves Guilbert. I would suffer torments before Edward fetched me to liberty, killed the brute and carried me off. Thereafter I was his, and he used his property in every way I could imagine.

Such was the realm of my thoughts in that last sunny week while we waited for Sir Lionel's ship to make ready. The real world was as ordinary as ever. Edward went about his business, I saw to his horse and weapons, and once or twice crept out to follow him, to watch from the rushes as he swam. Soon enough, I would have few opportunities.

One final duty fell to him in the days before we sailed, and he was grateful for my company. Early one afternoon we rode by Sleaford and up onto the hill, to the Montand estate. The old Baron was in his sickbed and I saw nothing of him, but Edward went to his room, spoke to him for almost two hours and emerged looking weary. I wondered if the man were dying, but Edward said not. His gout and his chest had sent him to bed, and it was his wandering mind and evil tongue that fatigued my lord.

One flower existed inside those walls, and how she flourished there I cannot explain. I was astonished when I met Lady Edwina, for she was only a child of twelve years. The same age as Henri, I thought... but what a gulf separated the squire who had been buggered since the age of nine, and the girl of the same years who was tiny, fragile and virgin.

She was white as porcelain with bones like a bird's. She reminded me of a dove, all white feathers and delicacy. Her huge cornflower-blue eyes would smile at me briefly and then return to Edward. She loved him. I knew at a glance, since I loved him myself. She and I shared that kindred spirit, but she would one day share his bed and ripen with his children, while I would count myself fortunate if I polished his saddles and won a smile from him. Resentment stung me like a swarm of wasps, and I idly wondered what God must think of me. Nothing good, I was sure.

In the evening we three sat on the terrace, on the hillside above Sleaford. I saw the red shingles of Ranulf's roof and fancied, if I shouted he would hear me. I saw the thatched hut too, where Grendel had lived until he was taken for the army. He fought for the Sheriff and was cut to tatters in a battle against outlaws. And there was the byre where I had first seen a man unclothed, first felt a man's hand, in lust rather than in love.

All my life had taken place in this fold in the hills. How often I had longed to leave, yet now I was on the point of it my heart pounded. I wanted to run home, slam the door – so long as I could drag Edward with me and shut him in too. I sat against the sun-warmed bricks and watched him with the lady. *Where you go, I follow,* I thought with a lazy, indolent sense of martyrdom. I would have gone to hell for him. In fact, I fully expected to, since in those days I still owned a thread or two of faith.

Often he looked at me, eyes brooding and stormy. It discomfited him gravely to be between the two of us – the lad he desired, the girl he must marry. He was fond of her, I saw that. He held both her hands in one of his and spoke kindly for a long time.

But Edwina was just a little girl. Her child's mind was full of nonsense about sewing and her sister's baby, and the scolding of the priest during her lute lessons. This folly amused Edward, perhaps as a respite from the business of war. He smiled as she chattered, and I imagined these two, years hence, when he had returned from Crusade with King Richard's favour and a heavy purse, and she had become a woman. I pictured them entwined beneath the red counterpane on Edward's bed, where he had rubbed me that night, and I envied Edwina so much, I was choked.

Yet I grieved for her also. She lived in a house where the sun never shone, with only a simple-minded old father for company, and she knew that if Edward failed to return she would belong to Yves Guilbert. I would wish that on no one, no matter my own passions.

So Edward must come back safe, for her sake. I turned my eyes to the evening sky, wondering if I were being punished, or if Ranulf was right. The gods of our forefathers, he said, are older than the Church, wiser, and a man might have better luck praying to the earth and forest spirits. Behind the pious face he showed Friar Aelfric in church lay a man whose faiths were in the things his fathers had taught him. From Ranulf I learned the names of Wotan and Tor, but never knew who they were. From Edith, the crook-backed maker of charms, I had discovered the ancient spirits, some of whom live in the forest, which is why people fear the deep woods, and no one ventures into them on Samhaine's eve. Ranulf rarely spoke of what he knew and believed, but he was never a foolish man.

And here was Edward, whose faith was shattered when Norman soldiers murdered the women of his house. Such raids were not uncommon in the shires, certainly not among Saxons. There are two codes of justice, one for the conquerors, one for the conquered. Edward held onto his rank by the last rim of his fingernails and struggled to keep even that hold. Otherwise, a holy war in a foreign land would have been the last concern in his heart.

"We leave soon, Edwina," he was saying to the girl, who was on the verge of tears. "But it will not be forever, and you will be a woman when next I see you."

Huge blue eyes looked up at him. "A year, Edward? More than that?"

"Yes." He paused, as if unwilling to tell her that it could be many years before we returned. "The King himself may call an end to the war, and if he withdraws, we follow. I have no longing to go to war, you know! I wish I could stay, aye, and wed you when you are a little older."

"I am old enough now," she protested. "My cousin Rachel was wed when she was no older than I!"

"And died in childbed in less than a year," he said sharply. "Let your bones grow first. I would only hurt you if you were my wife so soon."

She might have guessed the truth of that. She had never seen him naked, as I had many times, but Edward was so much a man, who doubted his virility? He was big enough to issue a fine challenge to the likes of me – a challenge I yearned to meet. But for a dove like

43

Edwina, it was best to wait. I at least could not get with child, but many women died that way. The young wife of the potter who was Ranulf's neighbour ended so. I spent a whole night listening to the poor woman's screams for God's mercy. He ignored every cry, and at morning she died dreadfully, and her child with her.

Edward leaned over and kissed the girl's cool forehead. "I shall return for you, never fear. And if Yves Guilbert should visit in the meantime, tell him you and I have sealed a pact and shall honour it come what may. That will hold him off."

She did not seem so sure, and flung herself at him. He stroked her hair, which was the colour of ripe wheat, and looked at me over her head with a sigh. I shared his expression of regret and exasperation, but nothing was to be done. Even Edwina was resigned.

She was the lady of the house despite her years, and sat in her father's place at the table that night. A poor troubadour and a lame fool entertained us, one unable to sing in tune, the other unable to turn a decent somersault, though both tried and we were too polite to notice their faults. Both had grown old in the service of this house and doubtless were doing their best.

It was still early when we bedded. The sky was not yet dark and I, as Edward's squire, was given a little cot at the foot of his great, wide bed in the guest chamber. It was very proper – this was the usual arrangement for knights and squires. Edward shut the door, threw the bolt and stood in the middle of the room, glaring at the floor for a long time. I could scarcely breathe. We were like statues and I would swear I could feel him without touching him.

"My lord," I whispered at last, "who would know?"

He looked up at me, frowning, and shook his head.

"But my lord... Edward." I breathed his name, full of longing.

"No one would know, it is true, but the memory would mock us, Paul. 'Tis far harder to break a cur of a habit once he has acquired it than to prevent him ever falling into the habit."

"You are cursed logical for a beauty," I said, mightily disgruntled.

His brows flew up toward his fringe. "A beauty? You think so?"

"A beauty that haunts my dreams."

"You dream of me?" Did his eyes darken? "What do you dream?"

Heat flushed my cheeks. "You can imagine. Oh, Edward, you are stubborn and disciplined. I have not your iron will. Of course I dream! What else do you leave me? Surely you don't deny me the right even to dream!"

He smiled sadly. "I also indulge my whims, but I know where to make an end of it." He took a step toward me, put his hand on my shoulder. Where he touched me I was fire and ice. "There's nothing in it for us but pain. You have seen my life. You have no place in it... I wish you had."

44

His voice was rough with sincerity but still he turned his back on me, dragged off his clothes and slid into bed before I had properly seen him. I bit my lip on useless curses, snuffed the candles and tugged off my own garments. I was half bare when I realised how bright was the moonlight. And that he was watching me.

The silver light shone in his eyes as he lay, bare chested in the enormous bed. I turned toward him, let him see me. *There, know what you are denying yourself!* I thought with a trace of malice. I rolled off my hose and stood naked in the rectangle of light from the window. He was silent, but his eyes travelled me from crown to toe, and under his gaze I felt my cock stir erect.

I heard the breath catch huskily in his throat. He murmured something, I could not hear what, nor would he repeat it. I was brazen before him, aroused and making no effort to conceal myself. But I was not lewd. I did not touch myself, but stood with my hands at my sides, not even posturing to fetch him on heat. He looked his fill – all he could bear, I think – then closed his eyes.

Tears of frustration scalded my own eyes and my balls throbbed painfully. I gazed at him long after he would no longer look at me. And then I slid quietly into my own bed and willed my stubborn erection to subside. For a while it did, but I had been half asleep for only minutes when I woke with a start to find myself humping the palliasse, which in my turbulent dream had been his back. I groaned, came, and was suddenly rigid with anxiety. Had he heard? But his breathing was shallow and steady. He was asleep. I relaxed bone by bone, turned over and grumbled into the pillow.

* * *

I slept only briefly and woke before him, when dawn was just a glimmer in the east. Our window caught the morning light and I stood beside the casement to watch him drowse on while the birds set up their din and then grew quiet once more. He slept on his back, his mouth lax and soft, his jaw not even shadowed because of his blondness. The quilt was low about his hips since the morning was warm, and I saw his chest, his little brown nipples, clearly and closely for the first time.

Then suddenly he was awake, and I gave a guilty start. Should I apologise? I was caught in my own snare. Instead, I only smiled sadly, and handed him his clothes. He swung his long legs off the bed – the opposite side to where I stood. As he stretched his limbs I reached out one hand and put the flat of my palm on his back. He did not flinch but froze, even his breathing stilled.

That was the sum of what we shared under Montand's roof, but in a way it brought us closer. Perhaps Edward knew after this, he could trust me even behind a bolted door. I would look, and dream my foolish notions, but I also knew when to 'make an end of it.' Resigned, I followed him down to breakfast. He was silent, but when we sat by the kitchen hearth to drink a cup of ale he smiled at me and my heart came alive. It was a little token of what he felt, fondness I would have done anything to earn.

The lady rose late and was still yawning when she farewelled us at the gate. Edward kissed her, on both cheeks and her pouting mouth that reminded me of strawberries. She was wet-eyed again and I gave the poor little dove my sympathies. It would be years before she saw Edward again. Though I was not at liberty to kiss him, at least I would be with him all that time. I felt privileged, and recognised the look of envy she gave me.

For Edward the parting was painful, and I knew what was in his mind. Would he ever return to claim what should have been his by right, and *would* have been if he been born a Norman? A Norman! I spat on the word, prideful of my Saxon blood, and his, as we drew rein on the hillside to see the town and the fortified manor above it, ivy-clad and hemmed about with gardens. Edward sighed heavily.

"Believe what you told Edwina," I said quietly. "It is not forever, and you will return with your fortunes mended."

He looked at me strangely, perhaps wondering if I read his mind. Truth was, the thoughts were plain on his face, which was as expressive as it was lovely. In later years he would learn to shutter his features, hiding what he thought and felt behind a mask, but I could always see through it.

"I believe," I told him, "just as she believes. She loves you, Edward." *As do I!*

To be allowed the liberty of using his given name thrilled me. I was not rebuked, and he nodded minutely as he gathered Icarus's reins to urge the big grey horse toward home. I rode a pace behind as I usually did, thoughtful and silent. Once or twice he glanced back at me, and I was attentive in case he needed some trifle. But he was merely looking, with an unfathomable frown, and when we stabled the horses he touched my shoulder in parting, another small token of his fondness.

I heard Sir Lionel's voice in the house, caught the words 'ship' and 'Humber', and I knew why Lionel was here. I groomed Icarus more hurriedly than usual and left one of the stable boys to look to my own little nag, so as to get quickly into my lord's company and hear properly what was being said. I hate to eavesdrop and get half a tale!

Plans were laid and time was short. The ship was waiting, Edward's bags were buckled down, and we tarried only for the final decision to depart. It was made while I poured a cup of wine. Lionel had already farewelled his family, and he came to Aethelstan on the way to Jerusalem.

Edward studied me as he drank the cup to the lees and held it out for a little more. "Leave a letter for Ranulf," he told me. "We depart in the morning, early. Write it tonight, for you'll get no second chance."

"I will," I said breathlessly. "My lord, is it long to the Holy Land by ship?"

Lionel laughed at my enthusiasm and ignorance. "That depends on the wind! Why, lad, do you fear the water?"

"No, my lord, not for looking at, bathing and swimming," I said dubiously, "but I have never been on a boat."

They laughed as if I had said something absurd. I shrugged off my inexperience and offered them more wine. As I filled Lionel's cup he swatted my behind and gave it a friendly rub. What would I have given for even that touch from Edward! My lord sat with his head cocked, one brow raised, watching me flush as Lionel made free with my arse. To Lionel it was nothing at all. He had no time for boys or men in that way. Edward was amused, and I found myself discomfited more by his amusement than Lionel's hand.

I sat over a letter to Ranulf at midnight. A tallow candle stuttered in the breeze at my elbow and the quill scratched over the coarse surface of the parchment. What could I say? I swore I would do him credit, come back safe and fetch him tales of glory – the glory of Christendom, Aethelstan, and Paul Delgado. I had begun to think of myself as Paul. I could not think of my name without hearing Edward's voice saying it, and I imagined it whispered in my ear, breathily, the way a lover would say it.

I set the parchment aside to dry and snuffed my candle, determined to get at least an hour's rest before the whole house became a chaos out of which we would hurry like thieves.

Too soon fists banged at my door. I was out of bed before I had my eyes open, and this morning Edward was about before me. Icarus was hitched in the yard, wearing his midnight blue trappings as befitted the steed of a knight on Crusade. He rubbed his bony face against me as I fed him an apple, and we watched the baggage wain loaded until it creaked on its axles.

Master Jacob stood at the gate to see us go. I touched my forelock to him, but it was mockery, and I dared this since I was on my way out, not to return until I was full grown. He glared, and I winked at him. I knew his secrets, and wanted him to know that I knew. I wanted him to spend years plagued with wondering if I was well bedded with Edward. My revenge would be slow but cruelly thorough.

The wagon turned. Edward rode before it, Lionel at his right hand, and I rode behind them with Henri. The boy babbled excitedly, eager for every new sight. He had been no further afield than Lionel's fences in the last year, and had before that been confined to the cloisters and bedchambers of his master's house – his master, who was like as not his sire, and his bedfellow. I shook my head over his plight, but Henri seemed to have taken no harm. He was wiry, strong, healthy and eager. He leaned close to me as we rode down to the river and said quietly, for my ears alone,

"We'll bed together often as not, Paul. I'll make you welcome."

I laughed and tousled his soft brown hair. "Evil child," I accused. "You know who I love."

"And who you cannot have," Henri said brashly. "Everyone knows Edward of Aethelstan is promised to Baron Montand's daughter." He stuck his nose in the air and pouted, a fair impression of a fine lady, untouchable and chaste. "Foolish to be moon-sick for a love that's lost before it's started," the rascal said, altogether too wisely for my liking.

"You would sooner I spoke of fucking than love," I chided him. "You are a boy. One day perhaps you will grow up."

My eyes were even then on Edward, who was deeply in conversation with Lionel, and I almost envied Henri his boyish carelessness. If I could have spoken of fucking and forgotten love, I would have been happier. But that would have needed a miracle, and the age of miracles is long gone. I sighed and began to watch out for the walls of the city of York.

We did not enter the city. Lionel's ship lay at anchor downstream, where the river is wide enough to allow a ship to turn about. I saw a cluster of gaudy pavilions, more banners than I could recognise, and we heard the jingle of harness before we rounded the last stand of oaks and came upon the encampment.

With Lionel's ship were many others. We were part of a great army that had gathered here and would sail, one or two ships at a time as the opportunity was right. I saw the standards of local knights and barons, and recognised the crest of a band of Knights Templars.

With Edward's specific instructions we stayed well away from the Templars, bowed and crossed ourselves as they passed us by. I had heard tales of them that iced the blood – how they would torture and kill in the name of Christ, and I wanted to know no more of them.

We followed Lionel to the great blue pavilion on the riverbank, and Henri pointed out a longship with furled sails, telling me that was de Quilberon's vessel. I shaded my eyes in the evening sun and admired it dutifully. Grander ships were anchored further out in the midwater channel, but to me a ship was a ship. This one would take us to the war as surely as any other.

At sunset we heard the Templars' singsong chant and stood in the smoky shadows to watch them kneel and pray, their swords thrust into the turf at their sides, their banner raised, their armour in absurd contrast to the benediction. Henri made faces after them and had his ear cuffed by Lionel. It was best not to aggravate such men. They had no sense of humour and no notion of forgiveness.

I was tired to the marrow and eager to rest, as was Henri. That night we lay under a blanket, back to back, ignored each other, and Henri snored softly the whole night through. I lay awake for a time, watching Edward toss and turn on a cot strewn with sheepskins. I could have lulled him to sleep; I could have eased him into rest, I told myself. I knew what his body yearned for. He had denied himself too long. At least I had Henri, and before him, a few others. Who had Edward had? He kept himself on a taut rein, allowing himself little save honour, which is a fine thing in a knight... but a knight is also a man.

And I know what you need, I thought hotly on the verge of sleep.

My dreams were wilful. He came to me on a riverbank, rising like the undine sprite out of the water with his hair streaming and his skin like pearl. He might have been a river spirit, but he was warm and strong, and when we coupled there was nothing spirit-like about the rod he thrust into my aching arse.

I woke with a start out of that maelstrom to find Henri dragging on his hose and pounding my shoulders. "We'll be late," he babbled. "They're taking the horses aboard. Come on!"

Eyes still half shut, I blundered out into the new daylight, and there was Edward, splendid in the Athelstan midnight blue, both hands leaning on the hilt of his sword while its tip dug into the turf, as he watched Icarus led up the ramp onto the ship. Suspecting that my hair was standing on end like a broom, I ducked a bow before him for the sake of those who were looking on.

"You let me sleep late."

"The sun is still hardly up," he argued. "You are looking care-worn, Paul," he added very quietly. He frowned, and so much was said without the need of words.

"It has not been easy, nor will it be," I confessed.

"Do you wish to stay behind?" he asked while his eyes seemed to brand me. "I'll release you even now. Go home if you will. What can I promise you but danger and – "

"Edward." I whispered his name. I did not want anyone to hear the little familiarity I was allowed. It might reflect badly on a Saxon knight who permitted a mere squire this liberty. "I would rather be with you than not, no matter where you go or what you promise me."

He smiled at me, exasperated. "You are a fool."

I shrugged. "Very likely, my lord. But I am sixteen years, and that is old enough to be my own fool, make my own mistakes, and pay their prices." I hopped onto the boarding ramp. "I must look after the horses. I have my duties, I've not forgotten! I promised Ranulf I would be an able squire. I have always been resourceful."

"Evidently," he said drily, with a shrewd expression.

I had excellent legs, and I knew it. When his gaze lingered on them I flexed them deliberately, showing them off. Not oblivious to my teasing show, he chuckled quietly before Lionel called and he left me to my work.

Before noon the ship shoved off. We stood in the bow, Edward, Lionel, Henri and I, watching the green English woodland slide by as the vessel nosed toward the sea. The sky in the north was clear and the wind quite warm. A priest had blessed us moments before we sailed, praying for calm seas, safe passage.

Thrills of excitement coursed through me and my mind whirled with half-formed fancies. How could I know what the desert looked like, or the tribesmen, camels, oases with date palms and the fluttering tents of the nomad. I had heard of these things but could scarcely picture them. I imagined many odd sights, all of them wrong – all of them strange, but not as strange as the reality toward which I was rushing without knowing it.

I turned to Edward and my face must have been filled with enthusiasm, for he was smiling, indulgent, amused, almost mocking until I blushed and he tousled my hair. I longed to kiss the warm palm of his hand, which lingered on my head moments longer than it need have. We looked at one another, each wishing impossible things. No one noticed that small transgression, and I treasured it.

The sail unfurled and filled with a westerly wind. It would not be long before we saw the sea, and I looked at England's green hills with a painful churning in my belly. How long would it be before I saw them again? What manner of man would I be when I returned? And what of Edward?

I could not know the answers to these questions, but had I guessed the truth it would have made no difference. Edward was my destiny. This I knew by some fey intuition, and it was enough.

PART TWO: PALESTINE

Chapter VI

Palestine. To me it was a word out of legend, since I had learned the tales of the First Crusade as a child, as everyone did. That great war was waged when Pope Urban II summoned a Christian army to the city of Constantinople, almost eighty years before I was born. For two years, the call to arms was carried throughout all of Europe, and in 1097 they gathered. Normans, Germans, Italians, barons and knights, priests, monks, and men who wished only to pillage and loot. It was the most massive host ever seen since the conquering army of William of Normandy. William's own son was with the force that rode to Constantinople, and from there to Jerusalem. For two years they fought the Seljuk, the Muslim Turk, the Saracen and the Kurd, until the Holy City was captured in the blistering high summer, after a punishing forty-day siege.

The massacre of Muslims and Jews that followed has indeed passed into legend, and where was the good of it? The captured lands were held by Christian knights – not handed to Pope Urban, as His Holiness might have hoped, but divided among the countries who had won them. The Kingdom of Jerusalem; the Principality of Antioch, which had been the first city to fall, in that Crusade; and the Earldoms of Edessa and Tripoli. This, they called *Outremer*. 'The Land Beyond The Seas.'

But Edessa was recaptured not fifty years later, and the result was yet another Crusade, more blood and horror. For a brief time the Christian knights maintained their grip on the Holy Land and pilgrims were safe on the road to Jerusalem. But a certain boy had already been born, and his name would one day also become legend. Salah ad-Din, the Kurdish General. *Saladin*.

His army captured Egypt three years before my birth. The same army of Islam, massively swollen, immeasurably stronger, had captured Jerusalem itself, just fourteen months before I first put on Aethelstan's midnight blue livery. Older, wiser hearts than mine were filled with dread, that the horrors that had taken place ninety years before would happen again.

My head was filled with a boy's foolish notions, but Edward knew the truth. I dreamed of valour and glory, and he would chill the very marrow of my bones with the true tales of the evil committed in the name of Christendom.

On the voyage from England we boys sat rapt in the evenings,

51

listening to such stories, related by Edward and Lionel. Henri was younger than I, and more foolish. He spoke of chivalry, which he studied with Sir Lionel, and in bed at night he would prattle about being a knight and slaughtering the heathen. For all my naivety, it was the talk of pain and suffering that touched me deepest, for I could not stop myself imagining Edward in those straits. Lionel told blood-curdling accounts of the Lion-hearted King, which gave me cruel dreams, a week's voyage from home.

Once, Henri woke me when I began to shout in my sleep. He shook my shoulder, and suddenly Edward was at the door to our tiny, stifled cabin. I was sweated and shaking, bedded on straw that had grown unfresh and pressed tight to Henri's squirming body. Edward thought me fevered.

"Come and take some air," he urged, and I was glad to go with him. He stood with me by the side of the ship and we watched the moon over the restless sea. "Are you sickened of the ship?" he asked. "There is no shame if you are. Many's the hardened seaman who sickens on his first voyage."

How could I tell him the truth? I had pictured him in the scenes Lionel had described, and that curdled my belly. King Richard searched the Saracen cities for treasure, and in his zeal to find it, when he over-ran the harem of some chieftain he ordered the women slit open in case they had hidden their valuables inside themselves. Bodies strewed the killing fields. Monks did the killing and cutting, and a bishop prayed for the glory of Christ while Richard looked on.

I could not tell Edward that I had begun to fear for him. The arts of war were his very life, and through them he would rebuild his fortunes. If he lived. I looked long at him in the moonlight, admiring his fairness. He knew I was watching him but was silent for a long time.

At last he glanced sidelong at me. "If you can sleep, you should. To bed with you. It is later than you know."

So I returned to the cabin and lay down, and at last I slept. I feared the dreams' return but my sleep was peaceful that night.

Other ships travelled alongside us. One belonged to the Templars, and this one accompanied us every league of the way to the ports of Palestine. Pilgrims and armies alike usually travelled overland, but that year France was war-ravaged, and Lionel had received word that we would be fighting within fifty miles of Calais. We would fight every step of the way, and our chances of making it through to Palestine at all were dismal. So for that year, and a few to come, the journey was made by sea, the whole way.

I had few complaints, for I grew accustomed to the rolling, pitching deck soon enough. I liked to stand in the sea wind, my half-closed eyes following the Templars' vessel, as it matched pace with us, sharing the same wind. Edward would watch their parchment-brown sail with a bitter expression, but when I begged to know what troubled him he said only, "Be wary of them. Stand aside when they approach and speak softly."

All this, I did. I crossed their path the morning we reached our destination, many months from home, and found myself in the way of a warrior monk who seemed to care nothing for my life or limbs. He might have run his horse over my broken bones, had I not cleared his path fast enough.

Of those first days, it is the heat and flies and dust I recall most vividly. We had been at sea for so long, my legs were used to the roll of the deck, and of a sudden we were ashore and I was reeling like a drunkard. Edward only laughed and explained, I must regain my 'land legs' just as I had won my 'sea legs' the hard way. He swore he also felt as if the dry land beneath his feet pitched and rolled, but he looked firm-footed to me... and more lovely than ever as he grew brown in the fierce Arabian sun.

The heat was stunning, like a blow to the skull. I had never before perspired till my body ran awash and my muscles trembled, yet the Arabs thronging the waterfront seemed hardly to notice it, and went about wrapped in robes and hoods.

Edward had visited Palestine only once, years before, as a squire apprenticed in chivalry. Squire he may have been, but he fought. He pointed out the black-robed nomad, and the blue-robed warrior tribesmen who had come to the harbour to barter for camels and slaves.

This was my first taste of the silk and sin of Palestine. 'Tis a heathen realm, no doubt of it! The market sold foods, meats and fruits I had never seen. I ate too much too soon, and my belly griped in pain. They sold animals that amazed and amused me – camels, lion cubs and monkeys. And they sold people. I watched the trade in lush young bodies, girls and boys stripped bare for display, and my heart jumped in my throat. Edward was silent as these unfortunates were sold or bartered away, but he was watching me.

"My lord," I whispered, "this is not right, it cannot be."

"You are not in a Christian land now," he said bitterly. "Much you will see and hear will be strange. This is their way, Paul. What would you have me do?"

At that moment the dealer was eyeing me with a rapacious gleam in his black eyes, and I took a step nearer to Edward. "I would have you keep me safe," I hissed.

He looked at me and laughed. "You fancy yourself a prize that would grace this marketplace? Perhaps you are. See that lad, there? He fetched the price of a mailshirt. The other, younger boy, the price of a whole suit of armour. Perhaps you would fetch such a fortune."

I was troubled, though I knew it was a jest. He cuffed my head and took me back along the glittering waterfront, past our ship, which had tied up beside a bleached stone jetty, and a small distance inland to Lionel's encampment. They had taken the horses ashore and my duties were to Icarus. Edward left me to work while he and Lionel went to haggle over the price of labourers. I watched him go and muttered darkly after him, "Aye, and keep safe yourself. You are too beautiful and too golden to be any safer than I, in this place!"

Such thoughts preoccupied me. That night I slept apart from Henri, for it was too hot to press together. We bedded on the sand with one rug beneath and another over us, and I thought I had never seen the stars blaze so fiercely. I watched them and imagined Edward, captive, property, in that marketplace or another, deeper in the desert...

He stood naked and was studied by chieftains buying purchases for their pleasure. Cool and remote, he ignored their exploring hands and carried himself with dignity as he was sold and borne away to some dire fate. I trapped myself between horror and desire: one instant I was the helpless observer who lost his lover to an enemy, the next I was that chieftain who had bought the fair-skinned beauty, and he was mine. I had brains enough to know the difference between the awful reality and the foolish dream. One affrighted strong men, the other titillated bored youths. Preferring amusement, I surrendered to the fantasy and rolled over on my belly as my cock betrayed me.

A giggle alerted me to Henri's proximity before the monkey landed on my back, all sharp bones and digging fingers. "You're wicked," I told him without real sting. I felt his little prick poking at my rump but did not worry. I knew he would not presume upon me. He knew how much I would allow and where I grew annoyed

"I am wicked – *I?*" Henri humped me under my rug. "It was you a moment ago, moaning and rubbing! Oh, be still!" His fingers dug into my shoulders and he humped harder.

I sighed and cupped my chin on my palms. I had more sense, more patience and more control than a little lad of twelve. Henri squealed sharply and wet my back. "Are you quite finished?" I asked indulgently.

Panting, he rolled off me. "For now. You have a soft, lovely bum, Paul. 'Twas made for bed sports. Your knight would take it if he had the sense he was born with."

I glanced at the pavilion where Edward and Lionel were still talking by the light of a brazier. The horses were tethered along the side and our labourers camped beyond. It was very dark away from the firelight. I watched Edward laugh at something Lionel said, and familiar hunger wormed through me. All at once I rolled over onto Henri and wrestled him where I wanted him. "My turn, knave!" He wrapped his legs about my hips and took me in. I puffed windedly, "Do you always come to bed in a state of readiness?" For he was slick with oil, I could smell its fragrance. He had probably thieved it from Lady Enid before we left, but it was to our benefit and I was not complaining.

54

He snorted scornfully. "What folly, to come into a man's bed and make invitations without being ready to fulfil them." This was uttered in breathless whispers, for he had me deep inside and I was energetic that night. Henri was enraptured, and before I came he had spurted again, as boys will.

After such bedtime antics and a long, busy day I overslept. The sun was high when I stirred and I found Edward standing over me. He was outlined against the cloudless, blue morning sky with a curious expression, half mocking, half exasperated.

"Well, young Paul," he teased. "Once you said to me, if you shirked you would fetch the cane and bare your arse for suitable chastisement."

I struggled up, dressed hastily and had the grace to duck my head. "I am asleep while the rest of the world is at work. Your horse is hungry and your swords unoiled. You set out your own garments, and I – I am at fault. Your leave, my lord."

Likely, he thought I needed to piss, which was true. He let me go and I flung myself into the work with a will. Icarus was fed, his swords oiled, his clothes set to rights, all within half an hour. As I was finishing I caught sight of the donkey driver's switch, a whippy stick that would pass for a cane if needs be.

My personal devil got into me again, and I can only plead youth, humour and love. I wanted to stir Edward, to tease him into a gesture of affection. I asked another young squire where he was to be found, and learned he was at the well, behind the encampment, in the lee of the pavilions. Private, perfect for my intentions.

I saw Edward at once. He was stripped to bathe, clad only in his hose, which clung tight to narrow hips and long shapely legs, and even that was wet and indecently revealing. His hair streamed down his back and a barber's knife scritch-scratched about his jaw. I hung back, revelling in the opportunity to watch him. On the voyage I had little chance. I could *feel* the smoothness of his skin, and my tingling fingers counted the knots of his spine.

Some sixth sense told him I was there, and he turned toward me as he finished shaving. I held the switch behind me and bowed my head as I approached. He pulled on a robe and waited. The morning was already hot and I wore only a linen shirt and my hose.

"Are you done?" He asked. "Icarus – "

"Is fed and watered," I assured him. "And I am ashamed of my idleness. You must think me a dreadful squire."

"Boys need their sleep and these last days have been a trial for us all. I fretted for you on the ship," Edward said easily. "I know you were unwell for much of the voyage. If you need to sleep an hour longer here or there, what of it?"

"What of it?" I protested. "Your fellows have seen you failed by one in your service! I have dishonoured you." With a flourish I produced the switch and handed it to him. "You would be as well to swiftly set matters to rights." Then I turned my back and put my hands on my knees. My whole body tingled. Not for a moment did I think he would hurt me – else I should have been sweated with dread, not prickling with the anticipation of his hands on me.

"Paul, what is this?" He demanded suspiciously. The switch rested on my buttocks, just lying there. "What maggot is in your brain this morning?"

I loved the sound of his voice when he spoke in these soft tones, half teasing and wholly amused. My devil made me tease him in return. Trying to arouse his humour, I rolled down my hose, as I had seen another boy do two days before. It was commonplace when chastisement was imminent. If pleasure were the intent, however, it would have been a mortal sin. I knew that, so did Edward, and this was the amusement!

"You," he said to my bare rump, "are a wicked imp." The switch ran once, lightly, about both my cheeks, caressing. "You have my measure and are complacent of me. So sure, were you, that I would not strike you?"

"So sure," I sighed. "It was a caress I wanted."

He also sighed. The switch bisected my cheeks and travelled the length of my cleft. It ran lightly over the tender heart of me, paused there and dealt me a press inward that made me shudder. "Your skin is like white velvet," Edward said absently. "Soft as... ah, damnation, you've fetched yourself to woe now!"

I had not time to look up or ask what he meant before the switch cut down across my arse, three times, and hard. I yelped, more with surprise than in pain, for with these kind of welts it takes some time for the smart to set in. As my head jerked up I saw Brother Gervaise coming toward us with a pail in his hand and a pious expression on his fat face. I groaned as my buttocks began to hurt, and pulled up my hose as Edward said gruffly, and for Gervaise's ears,

"Let that be your lesson. If I catch you again I'll strike twice as hard and thrice as long!" He thrust the switch back into my hand.

I limped to the other side of the well to draw a pail of water for my own use. Gervaise glanced at me curiously, then at Edward. My master told him quietly,

"Boys' pranks, best nipped in the bud."

"Oh." Gervaise did not seem surprised. "Will he have instruction? Or will you take him in hand yourself, Sir Edward?"

'Instruction' meant all night on my knees before an altar, and a birching that would take the back off me. I looked urgently at Edward, desperately worried that he would commit me to taxing discomforts, but he merely shook his head.

"No, he is well in hand and a promising boy – of full sixteen years," he said with such an appraising look at me that I blushed. "I'll give him what instruction he needs, but my thanks, Gervaise, all the same." When the old pilgrim had gone Edward came around the well, sat on the crumbling stonework and looked up at me with a faint smile. "What price you pay for amusement! You'll not sit in comfort for some time, and all for what? To show me your rump and win a caress... which you did not get anyway."

I sighed and very carefully placed my behind on the side of the well. It was not so bad and I smiled ruefully. "I hoped to make you laugh, Edward. And I did. You could have struck me harder."

"For Gervaise's benefit?" Edward cast a scornful glance after the man. "I never liked him. He accompanied the Lionheart on more than one foray into the Saracen camps. You heard from Lionel about that."

I shuddered visibly. "I'll never forget those tales."

"Aye. Well, we leave here before noon and march inland. You'll see King Richard soon enough."

"How long?" I asked eagerly as I washed my own face and hands.

"A week's march," he guessed, "if the weather is with us."

I thought he was talking about rain, and could not comprehend how it could possibly rain sufficiently to halt our progress. I had never seen skies as blue, nor so cloudless. It seemed this parched land had never known a drop of water.

But Edward was not talking about rain, as I learned two days after we marched east from the coast.

* * *

I knew these lands from the maps. We left the ship at Joppa, in the land of the Canaanites. Before us were the towns of Arimathea, Bethel, Ephrem and Jericho, in the land of Judaea. Here, Rome had fought the Hebrew. Judas Maccabeas led his forces to victory and drove out the Romans, before Christ walked the earth. Here, the Zealots fought for freedom on a mountain called Masada. To the north as we marched were Samaria and Galilee, and a town called Nazareth.

We were most fortunate that the Crusader armies had secured this part of the coast. Six months before we might have had to come ashore much further away and toil through the desert... In six months' time, if we desired to leave, or were compelled to, our escape route might be just as dubious. Each battle redrew the maps, and from one month to the next no one was sure what was enemy territory, and what was safe.

I pondered, as I rode behind Edward and Lionel, if these lands were the heart of a faith as great as Christendom, why God had let them fall into the hands of disbelievers. Why was the Holy City denied heaven's own protection? And I studied the Saracen, the Turk and the Jew at the roadside.

Little boys with eyes as dark and soft as those of deer; women wrapped in robes and carrying baskets and jugs; little girls who squealed and played like children anywhere; old men whose creased faces were the mirror of the desert as they smoked, laughed and gambled away the evening. And the tall, aloof, dangerous figures of the men from the desert. Nomads. Moors from the south of Spain. Turks and Saracens, tall and swarthy with crinkly black hair, earrings and the smooth brown limbs of warriors.

I saw no vile creatures, but other men. I was so troubled that when we camped, three nights inland, I was unaware of what went on about me, even of Edward's presence, until he had waited on me for some time. I returned to the present with a start. The stars were fierce, the braziers burned brightly and sounds of music and revelry issued from the tents around us.

"You are at odds with yourself," Edward observed.

"Have you watched me long?" I came halfway to my feet but he waved me back. I was sitting on a rug, away from the company, with only the donkeys for companions. To my surprise and pleasure Edward sat on the corner of my carpet, clearly waiting for a reply. "I am fretted with the whole world," I confessed, as if I spoke to a priest. "I ask myself, what right have we to come into another man's country and kill him."

"Ah." Edward's wide shoulders lifted in a shrug. "I've asked that question not merely of myself but of priests and the barons whose orders I obey... Their answers differ. Some admit we are here for loot, which is at least honest! Some are here to liberate Jerusalem from the demonspawn."

"Demonspawn." I stretched out and gazed up at him. In the dark, I dared set my hand on his leg and he did not brush it off. I felt the curve of his thigh, sinuous and beguiling. "Do you believe Saracens are in league with the devil?"

"Churchmen say so," Edward sighed. "But then, they say the same of men like us, because of what we feel for each other, and they are surely wrong. Were I the devil's puppet, I think I would know! I believe I am not... but do I dupe myself? Who is right? 'Tis a rare paradox. God knows but will not tell, and men fight and murder century upon century while their prayers are unanswered."

"The Mohammedan looks to me like a man," I said thoughtfully as I stroked his leg, "like any other, swarthier than a Norman, but often handsomer."

"You like their looks?" He closed his hand over mine to stop its wandering, but when I kept it still he left his own hand there, on mine, and his touch thrilled me.

"Some are beautiful," I admitted. "Especially the young men, my age or yours. But none are as beautiful as yourself, my lord," I added as an afterthought.

"You have become bold," Edward whispered. "A few months

ago you would not have dared speak so openly."

I sighed. "We were in England, observed at every turn by priests and barons' men. Here? The land is vast and the people blind to what foreigners do. We could slit each other's throats and no one would notice."

"Aye," he agreed. "There is much blindness. Much that is against every law, and yet is done daily! Christ, it distracts me."

I wondered what he meant, and realised belatedly that he was as restless and uneasy as myself. I sat up and deliberately left my hand on his leg. His eyes were closed, his face turned away from me. I wanted to touch his hair, his cheek. Instead I opened my ears and listened to what he had been hearing all along.

My rug by the sleeping donkeys was at the back of one of the pavilions and we could hear rustlings from within. I caught my breath at the faint sounds. A light burned inside and I saw the faintest shadows falling on the canvas. Two figures moved in unison, a steady, supple rhythm. Two male figures. I swallowed hard and looked at Edward.

His eyes were open now, and starlight glittered in them. "You have been in Palestine before," I whispered. "Was it like this? Did you hear these things, see these shadows, that time?"

"Knights and squires. Horse boys and servants picked up on the road. Slaves, eunuchs purchased for no other purpose than *that*." He sighed. "Last time I was here, I was your age, and was almost part of it. I stayed away from them, for my teacher would forgive me nothing if I was caught."

My heart leapt. "This was the sole reason why you... "

"Slept apart and remained virgin?" He took a deep breath. "Yes. I was not here for long. I came out with one ship and went back with another when messages must be carried back. Dispatches were my duty, you see. I was sorely tried and glad to leave."

Just as quickly as it had soared, my heart fell. My head drooped onto my breast and I said softly, "Forgive me."

"For what?" His fingers slipped under my chin and lifted it. "For being in love with me? Never apologise for love. There is too little of it in the world. But never confess this love to a priest, for it invites such pain as makes a mockery of tenderness."

My body was alight as he touched my face. "I've confessed a boy's sins before," I whispered. "Once, Ranulf saw me and assumed I had been with a girl and my conscience was pricking!"

"You had been with a boy?" Was he breathless?

My heart quickened. His fingers trembled a little as he touched my chin, and I inched closer. "A boy who was close to me all summer. In our own way we shared a kind of love, as lads that age understand it. I've grown up a deal since then."

"I imagine you have," he observed. He took his hand from my

face then, and I could have cried out with frustration.

"Edward!" I groaned his name and subsided on the rug. In the tent, the squires were pleasuring each other deftly and diligently. I heard a feral little sound as a boy came and my body pulsed with its own needs. It was painful to lie beside Edward, listening to the pleasures of others, yet be denied him.

"Shhh," he whispered. "I know." He got to his knees, as if he meant to stand, but hesitated. And then, before he left me he leaned over and his lips brushed my cheek in the lightest of kisses, hardly a kiss at all.

He was a dozen strides away before I could fully believe what he had done, and rapture lanced through my belly. Quick as a thief I tugged down my hose, and my seed was lost in the sand. The night wind picked up the musk and wafted it quickly away. Pleasure and pain often go hand in hand. One learns this with time and age. That night, as I looked after my lord's departed figure, despite the instant of delight it was only pain I felt.

* * *

With morning he looked tired, and I knew he had not rested. He was irritable, and the heat and flies annoyed him more than ever. He barked at the Arabs who sold oranges and dates by the road, for getting in our way, even barked at the squires, which was not his way when he was himself.

I stayed well back and made sure I did my duties promptly, giving him no reason to snap at my heels. He said nothing to me, yet he watched me with eyes that looked bruised. My presence pained him, and time was not healing his wounds. Those eyes followed me accusingly as we broke camp. Lionel was annoyed over a lamed horse but the farriers and grooms promised magic for the beast by nightfall. Edward ate corn and dried fish as the tents were folded, and shook his head over our tardiness. The sun was hours up and we were still not on the move.

The jingle of harness on the road heralded the arrival of another party. Henri and I shaded our eyes, and I saw their banner. It was the Templars, whose ship had sailed abreast of our own. They had set out days behind us and were sure to reach King Richard's camp before us.

In command of them was Friar Jean de Bicat, a man I had learned to dislike intensely in a moment, when he beat a dog for crossing his path. Edward despised him. When de Bicat drew rein to speak with my lord and Lionel, I watched Edward's features set into stone-hard lines. He spoke civilly, as he must to a man as powerful as de Bicat, but though I could follow little of their gabble – their French was much too rapid for me – I knew from their tone, the Templars were mocking and Edward's temper was short and sharp.

As they left, Lionel spat into the dust after them and threw down the remains of his meal. "By heaven, I'd show that man the chipped edge of a rusted old sword, if the chance came my way."

"Unless he tasted mine first," Edward said in a tone I had never heard from him before. "But he's right, we are late. Hurry your lads, Lionel. Paul had my wagon ready half an hour ago."

As he said this his sun-narrowed eyes lingered on me, as if they stripped the clothes from my body, then the flesh from my bones, and laid bare my soul. I swallowed hard. As Lionel strode off to hurry his lads I hovered close to Edward.

"My lord, am I at fault?" I whispered.

One brow arched at me. "What makes you ask?"

"The way you look at me," I mumbled.

"And how is that?" Edward snapped now, which he had never done before.

"What ails you? Are you sickened or hurt?" I knew much was amiss, and half believed he was unwell, though he looked merely tired after a restless night.

He sighed, rubbed his face and touched my shoulder. "Every mile along this cursed road takes us closer to a rendezvous I have no desire to make, and every hour we delay incurs Richard's wrath. He is waiting for us. He needs new men, fresh blood."

I had heard the talk among the travellers. There had been a lot of killing, when Saracen raiders came in the dawn, exacting a heavy toll on the Knights. The Crusaders, King and all, had been here too long. They were tired, stale, wearied by the heat, suffering local maladies and longing to leave. Beyond their encampments lay the wilderness, and where the raiders came from no one knew.

The glare of the sun blinded me. I had never seen so many miles of arid hills, stark cliffs, dust, sand and desolation. Once, I had considered a kerchief-sized beach to be a desert, but here was a whole land comprised of sand and boulder. It was so barren, what was there in the ground to hold a man in his grave? Yet this was the home of warrior princes whose names were whispered by squires who had learned them from loose-mouthed knights.

From Henri I first heard the name of Imrahan. The very sound of it shivered me, though I did not know why. They called him the Slayer, the Ravager, and even knights whispered his name in something very like dread. Imrahan was a legend in those years, and like most people, I was beguiled by legends.

Henri had heard that many Saracen chieftains kept Christian slaves. For what purpose they kept them, I did not know, but my imagination throbbed. I knew that Imrahan was a chieftain, at the head of a tribe whose standard was black and gold, with crescent moons. Lionel had showed me a depiction of the banner and I asked, what did the moons mean? They were the mark of Islam, he explained indifferently, the sign of the Infidel who prayed five times a day, toward Mecca; and he told me to listen for the wailing of the Imam and watch for the Muslim.

I did as he suggested, and saw them pray. When the caterwauling Imam summoned them, they turned to the far-off city and went down in a curious position, faces on the ground, haunches uplifted. It was a position I had always associated with another act entirely, and I was taken aback. Did even Imrahan, the Ravager, do this? I was fascinated, and made the mistake of asking Brother Gervaise a question.

"Why do we hate the Saracen?" I asked innocently. I got no good answer, only a slap across the face that left me angry for an hour, until Edward found me and demanded to know why I was furious. I told him, and he only laughed tersely.

"That will teach you never to address sensible questions to a pious old nanny-goat!"

"But why *do* we hate them?" I demanded. My hands were busy, cleaning and polishing harness leather.

"They reject our Saviour and follow a Prophet our Church disavows." Edward shrugged. "They have a holy book that is not our holy book, speak an odd tongue, wear different clothes and are brownskinned." He looked at me searchingly. "They veil their women and write stirring, passionate poetry to boys. Do we need further reason to hate?"

Poetry? I was inspired but it was days before I found a marketplace scribe who would quote me verses in a language I could understand. Stirring verses that spoke of the silk of a boy's skin, the black almonds of his eyes and the raven-fan of his hair across a pillow in the lamplight of lovemaking...

A shadow fell across my face, breaking the train of my thoughts. I thought it might be a cloud, but looking up I saw a vulture's wings. Edward sighed restlessly and tightened the baldric girdling his robe. "Fetch Icarus. If we don't move soon we shan't make shelter by nightfall, and I've no wish to camp in the open."

Not with the tribes on the rise in the desert, which was the reason King Richard had summoned every knight who would come to his aid. Even Saxons. I watched Edward mount, so fair in this land of swarthy men. I had seen Saracens and Jews alike looking at him, as if they had never seen a man with hair the colour of ripe wheat, and I thought of the battle toward which Edward hurled himself.

As I rode after Edward that morning, in the wake of the Templars, I could only imagine such verses or emotions. Love was like a freshly kindled hearth. I was no stranger to a boy's swift, unthinking passions, but what did I know of poets?

Edward frowned over me all morning yet never spoke to me. I

would raise half the courage to ask what I had said or done, then my heart would fail me and I would curse myself for cowardice.

In the mid-afternoon, when the parched brown hills shimmered with heat that dizzied my brains, a wind sprang up out of nowhere. It shot like a lance out of the east, toward the Dead Sea, and flung sand and grit into the air until even breathing was painful.

The horses took fright. Icarus tried to bolt and Edward shortened his reins. My own little nag tossed his head, dragged his harness out of my hands and wheeled away with the mules who had not yet been tethered. I chased them, but the wind was like a devil. Arabs and Jews alike were scurrying for cover, and for the first time I heard cries of the *djinn*.

Bad magic was all I understood of that word, and my heart squeezed. I shouted after my horse and the mules, but they were gone into the stinging curtain of the storm. My eyes were scoured, sore, and in moments after I blundered after the animals I lost all sense of direction. I coughed on the sand in my throat and fell to my knees, both arms over my head in a vain effort to protect my face.

I was suffocating already. My chest was afire, and belatedly it occurred to me that I could die. The wind screamed across the desolate landscape, and I believed the old stories of vile magic.

"Paul! Paul!" Edward's voice bellowed repeatedly from somewhere on my right. I lifted my head, but by now I was blind. "Paul, where are you? Can you hear me? Call out, boy!"

"This way, I am here!" I shouted, coughed, shouted again, and moments later caught sight of a cloaked, hooded figure on foot, coming toward me, physically leaning on the violent wind. I tried to stand but the storm of wild air was vicious and he shouted, "No, stay down! Stay where you are!"

Thank God, he had seen me. I knelt, arms over my head, and waited, and then darkness engulfed me, darkness that smelt of him, and I felt the heat of his body. His heavy cloak wrapped about me, shutting out the wind and sand, and his weight carried me to the ground. I was breathless in the womb-like cover of the cloak, and hardly heard as he chastised me.

"Have you no sense? You don't run into a sandstorm! It will strip the skin off your face and blind your eyes. Paul, are you hurt?"

His hands searched me for injuries. He found my face and hunted for blood, but I had kept my arms over my eyes and my skin was intact. Instead, I kissed his fingers and lay still. "I am not hurt," I croaked, though I delighted in his concern. "Edward, you should not have come after me. To endanger yourself – "

"Was cursed foolhardy," he finished. "So Lionel will tell me! But you've never seen a storm like this, and I have." He spoke against my hair and his arms were around me as the sand and wind screamed over us. "Lie still," he whispered. "We must wait for it to stop, and we'll be buried if it goes on long."

It could have continued for an hour, and it would have been over too soon for me. My arms crept about him, and he did not forbid me. I tucked my face into the curve of his neck and kissed him there. He took a breath and I prayed that he would not put me aside.

Instead, his arms gripped me tight. He sighed against my cheek and said ruefully, "You are a hussy, has anyone told you that?"

"Not lately," I whispered under the noise of the wind. "And I am not a hussy. I love you."

"I only tease, the better to bear it," Edward murmured. "Else I should be mad by now, as mad as I must be driving you."

So he was aware of my distress. I wriggled closer, yearning for the press of his body, which I had tried to imagine for so long. He was strong yet surprisingly slight. All over, I felt the sharpness of his bones, and what was not bone was steely muscle. I lay in the arms of a man, and almost laughed as I realised, it was my first time. I had been with *boys* before, beguilingly soft, giggling when they were aroused...

I was breathless with unfamiliar pleasures. It was not any man, but Edward of Aethelstan. I kissed his neck again, let him feel my tongue and heard him moan, deep and resonant. I found his ear and nuzzled before my teeth closed on his lobe. I thrust my tongue into his ear, as Grendel had liked, recalling how he would squirm and wriggle when I did that.

Edward shuddered, hands clenched on my arms. "Stop it, boy. Stop it!"

Thoroughly chastened, I drew back. "Forgive me. I thought to please you and have disgusted you instead."

"Disgusted me?" He spoke shakily. "I thought you had experience of men!"

"Only a little," I muttered. "Enough to know – to know cock from arse, and what goes where," I said coarsely.

"Enough to know that your tongue in my ear will fetch me up, quick as a wink?" Edward said drily.

I had not known for sure, though I had suspected. I mumbled another apology. "I shan't do it again."

His fingers clenched into my hair. "You frighten me, Paul."

This I could scarcely believe. I tried to lift my head but discovered a weight of sand on the cloak. The air inside was close and hot, growing stale. Often, Edward twitched aside the hood to let in a fresh waft from the lee of our bodies, but we were fast being buried.

As he let in a little air I took a deep breath and said, "Frighten you? I cannot believe a knight should be affrighted of a boy!"

"Fear wears many faces," he said acidly, "and not all are wicked."

"You have not believed in hellfire in years," I protested. "You know that lads far younger than I practise such 'sins,' and God would not burn them. Not children too young even to shave their faces. I

64

never had much faith, and if I am bound for hell, so be it. I've done too much already to take it back."

His hands clasped me to him and I smelt his musk as he made a wounded sound. "You'll be the death of me."

"The life," I pleaded. "Let me be the life."

I longed for his mouth. My right hand roamed across his back and my lips searched blindly for his in the hot, sultry darkness. I knew he was not breathing as he waited for me to be so unpardonably bold. He had never known the pleasures men have cherished since the beginning of time. He was a virgin man in the arms of a youth – though he was a knight, born to rank and lands, I boasted the experience, such as it was.

A few encounters with boys my own age, a quick, furtive grappling before we could be caught. Nights spent wriggling with Henri while we tried to be quiet and let the other squires sleep. None of it prepared me for Edward's mouth. His lips were soft and parted, his breath wine-sweet, his tongue quiescent, as if it wished to be hunted. I set my mouth over his as if I plundered him of something priceless.

Can virginity be sundered with a kiss? My lips were dry. I moistened them, and he moaned once more as his mouth opened a little. I slipped my tongue's searching tip inside.

For a second I was sure he would wrench away, then he crushed me with astonishing strength, and his tongue was in my mouth instead. Possessing me. I had never even imagined such a kiss. I drowned in him, sank in a limbo of wine and honey, never to rise again. Long, rapt moments passed and I was aware only of the circle of his arms and the press of his mouth as he fed on me.

At last we were suffocated, and as we parted to breathe he twitched the cloak for air and we realised the wind had begun to subside. As we listened it dwindled to a breeze and then to a breath. Edward struggled up, lifting a tremendous weight of sand that had drifted over us. The cloak peeled back and we blinked in the sun, blind for some moments.

I saw only his face. I wanted to see the mouth I had fed, and fed upon. His lips were a little swollen and red, his eyes stormy as he looked at me and seemed to struggle for words. I should have told him then, I loved him more than life, but I was as tongue-tied as he was, overcome by what we had done, and moments later Lionel's booming bass voice shouted across the sand-blasted slope.

"There! There they are, I see them! Edward, are you hurt? Edward!"

Mute, careful, moving with heavy-limbed slowness, Edward got to his feet and turned his back on me.

Chapter VII

"The mules have fled. Stupid beasts," Lionel said as he washed his throat with a cup of brackish water. "I'll fetch them back." Edward stood at Icarus's shoulder, washing the horse's eyes. The sandstorm from nowhere had cost every man, every animal.

"If they are alive to be brought back," Lionel said acidly. "I can send my lads after them."

Edward shot him a hard look. "In this place, where white-skinned, fair-haired boys fetch high prices?" He shook his head. "Send a man who won his spurs years ago, or purchase more mules in the next market."

"I'd buy fresh mules," Lionel grumbled, "save that our baggage has gone with those!"

"All the more reason to fetch them back." Edward wrung out the rag and threw it back into the pail of water.

He had not looked at me since Lionel and Henri stumbled upon us, as if he could not bear to set eyes on me now, for hate or lust or fury. I wondered which as I hovered, fetching things as I was asked, but Lionel and Gervaise had not granted me a single private moment in which to ask Edward his heart.

"They ran that way, Sir Edward," Henri piped, pointing south. "They'll head for water. The orange-seller said there's a pond in the desert."

"Then I'll ride there," Edward said tersely.

"Not alone," Lionel warned. "You also are a fair-haired, white-skinned creature. A little over-ripe for the taste of some, but your asking price would no doubt be bettered by the fact you are a knight, spurs and all." He spat out a date seed. "Take one of the soldiers, or at least young Paul."

I stepped forward at once, grasping Icarus's bridle. "I'll ride with you."

He looked haunted, with eyes that both invited and warned, and I physically recoiled at their mute accusation. Yet, a moment later he nodded. "Saddle yourself a nag, if you must."

I scrambled to fetch a horse. The afternoon shadows were lengthening already, and who knew how far we must go. If we did not catch the mules soon, they and our possessions would be forfeit to anyone who captured them. Edward put boot to stirrup and swung up.

Lionel gave him his hand then bellowed at his squires, "We camp here! Pitch your tents where you will. And you, Edward, take care. I'll wait for you. How long?"

"Till tomorrow eve," he said guardedly. "After that you'll only incur the King's wrath. Wait no longer, then make best speed. I'll catch you up on the road with the mules, if possible... and if not, bend my stiff Saxon neck and make my apologies to His Grace as best I can."

They spoke of the King without affection, and the thought of Richard, Lionhearted, filled me with trepidation. I wheeled my brown gelding about in Icarus's wake and hurried to catch up. The road and the haphazard encampment dropped behind and of a sudden Edward and I were more alone than we had ever been. I heard only the muffled beat of hooves on sand, the drone of flies and the stirring of a breeze that only an hour before had been a screaming *djinn*.

"No point looking for hoof tracks," I said, needing to break the unending silence. Edward did not answer. "The wind will have scoured them clean away." Still he was silent, and I sighed. "My lord, forgive me. I never meant hurt to you." Yet he had ravaged my mouth, fed on me, to assuage the need that had tormented him.

"There is nothing for you to apologise for," he said softly. "I myself am at fault."

"There was no fault," I argued.

He glared at me. "Had I the sense I was born with, I would send you home on the next ship."

My cheeks flushed and I averted my eyes. "Then, I am most grateful that you have too little sense," I whispered.

"Aye," he grumbled, "I told you, boy, you frighten me."

"I led you into temptation," I said sourly. I never imagined myself as Jezebel or Salome. What dance did I perform, how many veils had I dropped already? How many had I stripped from him? I made surly noises as we rode into the blistering south. The sun was westering and the heat shocked me. "Do you want me to go home?"

"Yes," he barked, and then in a gentler tone, "no. As a knight and the Earl of Aethelstan, I wish you had never accompanied me, for you'll lead me straight to ruin. As a man... oh, Paul."

Cheered, I brought my little horse alongside. "You punish yourself without need. Only you attempt to be immaculate while others could not care less. You are far from your old enemies, the Sheriff and Bishop. You are hardly at risk."

"With Brother Gervaise breathing down my neck?" he demanded. "He answers to both Sheriff and Bishop, and is a confessor from Durham, know you this?"

I shook my head. "Still, Gervaise spends hours in prayer. I hear him muttering past midnight, every night! You and I need fear little."

"You and I?" He drew rein and glared at me as if he wished to cuff my head. "You speak as if we are wedded."

Again I flushed scarlet, remembering my station. Yet I was the son of a knight, and Edward had fought alongside my foster father. "Forgive me," I mumbled. "I forget myself."

"I wish," he said fervently, "I could forget myself."

Lie down in my arms, I can make you forget! You would forget the whole world for an hour! I did not dare say it. Sense bade me hold my tongue, and I merely sat my nag, followed his example and pulled up my hood to keep the blistering sun off my tender English skin. My time would come, I told myself. I gave Edward a look, half longing, half bitter, and swore myself to silence.

The mules had run a good distance, frightened witless with the storm on their heels. Their tracks were obliterated but Edward believed animals could smell water for miles, and he knew the location of that pond, or 'watering hole.' I knew it from the maps, and he remembered it from the months he had spent in his land, years before.

It was late when we saw the date palms clustering about the pool in the midst of the rocky landscape. A goatherd and his flock were leaving, and a string of camels was passing, on the way to the town we had left that morning. They would be in the caravanserai by moonrise, while we would not make it back to Lionel's camp in the dark without risking the horses.

"The mules are not here," I observed as we approached the pool. The camels and goats were gone. I heard the tinkle of bells in the distance as they departed, and our horses hurried to drink.

"They will be here," Edward said shrewdly. "We need only wait. Likely they'll come to drink at dawn. We surely cannot hunt halfway across Palestine for them!" Deliberately, he swung out of the saddle and let Icarus drink. I was still mounted, and he studied me with that guarded accusation. "A night in the open discomfits you?"

A challenge – was I a sheep or a ram? Just as deliberately I swung down and let my own tired nag drink. "It does not," I said stiffly. "I'll set a fire and we'll eat."

He did nothing to assist me. The duties were mine in any event, but as a rule he never stood idly by. I collected windfallen wood, lit the fire, slung a kettle, unsaddled the horses, hobbled them and assembled what food Henri had hastily packed. All this time, a good half hour, he leaned on the coarse trunk of a tree by the water, watching with a hot, dark expression that burned me like a brand.

He was losing flesh. The heat did not suit him, and his robe hung more loosely, but the slenderness only fined his features and to me he grew more beautiful. The horses were dozing, the kettle simmering, and our parcel of bread, cheese, figs and onions was set on a cloth beside the cloaks that would serve for a bed. I had shaken them out on a pile of straw-like grass. Nights were as cold as the days were fierce.

"Will you drink?" I asked as I poured boiling water into cups and spooned a concoction of liquorice and herbs from an engraved brass box. He left the tree at last, and took a cup from me. I handed him the food, and he took it without a word. "It is a clear night. That cloudless sky will make for sharp cold, towards dawn."

He arched one brow at me. The moonlight was as bright as twilight. I thought he would chastise, but still he said nothing, and ate methodically, as if he did not even taste the food. I watched his mouth and remembered how he had fed on me. My body blazed until I almost groaned aloud, and the glimpse of his leg at the parting of his robe reminded me of the night when I had lain on his bed and touched him.

My eyes devoured his belly and breast, where he had pressed me in a furious embrace under the cloak, and I realised the truth. Before we left England I had thought I could be near him, do him good service and be satisfied. I was wrong. Soon I would be mad. The malady grew worse every day I was with him.

I could not eat, and he noticed. I heard him sigh but could not look at him. "My lord," I whispered, shamefaced and angry at once, "I'll go back on the next ship. I'll take messages, tell Lady Edwina you are safe."

"Fine service, this," he whispered, "from a lad Ranulf called trustworthy and responsible."

I took a calming breath. "I have failed you both. But there it is, my lord. It's holy orders for me when I return, for I'll not herd swine. My father's name deserves better than that. And I deserve better than this."

Of a sudden, grief, anguish and self-pity overtook me, and I turned away to hide my tears. Grief churned my belly as lust once had, and as love did, every moment, and I hated myself for the display.

I did not expect his hands on my shoulders, drawing me back to the warmth of his body. Sword-strong arms circled me, held me against him until I whimpered. "Am I hurting you too?" he said against my hair. "Every day I think of me and Aethelstan, never of you. I'm a selfish brute." I could not speak, but pressed against him, terrified that he would withdraw his embraces and leave me desolate. "I bruise you," he whispered, and rocked me for comfort. A sound of anguish tore out of me and my hands covered his, where he pressed me. "You've done no wrong, and offered so much," he said quietly. "Love is so rare in the world, no one can reject it. I am not angry with you, I swear it."

"You've glared at me for hours," I said brokenly, for I thought this must be the moment of farewell. In the morning I would ride back with a caravan and soon be gone, back to England and disgrace.

"I cannot bear to look at you," he whispered. I thought he meant, if he saw me he could cuff me, then the tip of his tongue outlined my ear and I shuddered. He felt this and sighed, his breath scudding over my cheek. "You make me long to be wanton. I might ravish you," he said self-mockingly.

I hardly believed my ears, but he was kissing my neck now, and bit me gently. All at once I could not be still, and twisted in his arms. My hands gripped his sides, likely hurting him. "You want me? You want me, Edward?"

His hands cradled my face. Gentle as he might be with a girl, he kissed my nose. "What have you to give me, Paulo Delgado?"

"Anything," I stammered. "I've been yours for so long, and not because I wear your livery. I love you, not your rank and estate!" I flung myself against him. "I've thought you hated me since this afternoon."

"No." His hands ran down my flanks. "I switched you."

"For Brother Gervaise," I gasped as he stroked me there.

"Did I hurt you?" He rubbed his cheek over my hair.

"Yes. It didn't matter." I lifted my head and offered my open mouth for his delight. My delight. Who would see us here? Who would ever know? We might have been the last two men alive, with only the blaze of the stars for company, the wind and the quiet lap of the water.

His tongue plundered me and I invited more. He drew me onto the bed I had made and explored my breast. "I have no knowledge. I am older than you but in this, not wiser. I know what I have heard and seen... what I want. But I'll not pretend to learning or finesse."

"I know a little," I admitted huskily. "Let me show you."

He seemed to resist for a moment, then every sinew relaxed. Supple and yielding, he subsided onto the cloaks, the moonlight full in his face and his hair like silver. I knotted my hands in it, put my mouth on his, and soon we were breathless and I was alight.

Once before I had stripped for him in the moonlight. I recalled that night as I stood and undressed once more. But that night he had only looked, then closed his eyes to shut me out. Tonight he was waiting, chest heaving, eyes wide with longing.

Naked, I knelt beside him. He was about to help me disrobe him but I stopped him, did for him what many a squire has done a thousand times for his knight. His thighs were roped with slender muscle, not full like mine but long and lean. Between them his cock jutted proudly, and as I bared him I gave it my attention, and my breath caught in delight. Despite the many times I had seen him bare, I had never seen him aroused. I measured him with my fingers for length and girth, and found him nothing like the boys I had known before.

His musk was strong, seductive. I bent to his groin, set my lips on him and felt him shiver. His eyes closed and his head rolled to and fro. His mouth opened, but no sound issued from it. Had he ever felt a hot, suckling mouth on him? I put down my head to offer that while my fingers explored the mystery of the sac between his thighs and felt his balls stir, heavy in my palm. I cradled them while I took his lance between my lips, and now he moaned aloud. I lowered my head slowly and he arched his back, helpless, caught in the magic. And I was the enchanter with this dominion over him.

A sense of power possessed me. Edward owned me because I loved him, but I had this. I could keep him for my own with this magic, I told myself as I bobbed my head and the shaft of him went into my throat. It stole my breath, and I stroked his balls, gave them a light squeeze. His musk prickled my nose as my fingers charted his belly. My own body was like a furnace, and my cock thrust like a dirk.

"Paul, no!" He whispered at last, and his fingers clenched into my hair to urge me away. I knew why, and I would not let him. I wanted his seed. He could never take it back. His musk filled my head, dizzied me. With a cry he came in my mouth and I swallowed, and swallowed again. Whimpering like a boy, he fell back, spent while I throbbed with urgency. I clambered shakily onto his belly. My cock was slick with anguish, and I was almost hurting.

I stretched out on him, hip to hip, and he purred like a cat as I began to hump. Getting his breath back in great whoops, he held me, encouraging as I pushed and shoved, my cock jabbing his hard muscles. His hands cupped my arse, pulled me down hard, and I was wild. I shouted his name, felt almost complete yet a thousand miles from completion when, by some blessed instinct, he pressed the blunt tips of his fingers against my tender anus. I was too tight and dry to swallow his fingers up, but the pressure found the heart of me, and I erupted as he pressed where I had long desired him to pierce me.

Climax ripped me and I collapsed on him. He held me, kissed me, though I was in less need of comfort than he should have been. He had been virgin, and I struggled to remember this, as I lifted my head. I know not what I expected to see in his face. Fear, or revulsion, now that the deed was done – or anguish for his lost immortal soul? Instead I saw heady repletion, glittering eyes and swollen lips that smiled.

"You said once," he said thickly, "you had some small experience. You did not lie."

"I would not lie to you, my lord," I panted.

"You call me 'my lord' after that?" He chuckled and stroked my back. "You were my master a moment ago. You don't scorn me, now I have demeaned myself."

"You count love a dishonour?" I recoiled. "Then I also am debased, and worse than you, since it was your eager pizzle in my gullet, your seed hot in my mouth!" He groaned and I tongued his lips. "I have never counted love a dishonour. And I shall woo you back to passion when we have rested."

"Fine chance," he said drily.

"You're young, strong," I purred. Rest, and let me show you what else men like." I kissed his eyelids. "Are you cold?" I reached for our cloaks.

His hand stopped me. "Lie against me. I love the heat of you. I've never felt anything quite like it. You are almost like Eleanor, to touch!"

Eleanor was a lapdog – he was likening me to the silky feel of a cuddlesome pet, not to a woman. I threw back my head and laughed as he stroked my breast. "I have always loved you." I nuzzled his chest, suckled the sensitive little nubs of his paps, and he stroked my hair.

"What is to become of us, Paul? What have I to give you?"

"I ask nothing," I whispered. "Nothing you cannot give freely. A smile, a soft word, your bed on a night when none but us shall know. I learned discretion long ago, or I would have been burned for a witch before this! Men who love men are witches, did you know? 'Tis the devil in us." We kissed, and his tongue greeted mine readily. His hands clenched my buttocks and squeezed till I was suddenly erect.

"I'll hurt you to couple to you," he murmured. "I've heard squires weeping with pain."

"But it hurts only the first time," I added, "and even that is not past bearing, nor does it last the whole deed. If you are gentle, and I am patient, you'll pleasure me before you are done. I am ready! And if you will allow me... "

He could not have prevented me. I nuzzled his half-hard cock and sucked diligently until he was eager. Still, I was afraid when the time came. He had a phial of olive oil, which he rubbed into his face daily in the dry desert winds that chapped his skin. I knew it was in his bag, and while he was wondering how the tight, dry clench of me would permit him even an inch's welcome, I oiled myself.

His eyes widened and in the moonlight I saw his throat bob as he swallowed. His cock twitched eagerly. He was ready for me. I crawled onto the bed and knelt with my cheek on my hands and my arse uplifted, hiding my face lest he should see my fear. I would not turn back, when I had come so far and fought so hard to win this prize. Shivering, I felt his hands on my hips. One finger entered, deep and quick, but I had used a lot of the oil. I whimpered and bit my lip, and then his finger was gone and I felt the fine, proud shaft of him.

He hesitated. "Are you certain?"

I took a breath to steady my voice. "Aye, my lord, I am."

"Then, forgive me," he begged. "Absolve me before I begin."

"I love you," I whispered. "That is absolution enough for us both."

He stroked my flanks, and I felt his cockhead graze me and push. Like a lance that would not be turned aside by a mailcoat, he sundered me, and it hurt. I knew it was not pain past bearing, but still it tore a cry from me. I bit my arm to silence myself as he sheathed himself like the great broadsword with which he would slaughter the Saracen.

72

I was sure I would be ripped hip from hip before he was in, and could scarcely breathe. He seemed to fill me to the heart before he stopped, and my erection dwindled. All I knew was the anguish of my poor arse until, little by little, the torment stopped. Pleasure did not begin at once – it was more like tolerance of an ache, till he began to thrust, and the pain returned... faded... faded...

Then I was as breathless with delight as I had been with pain. I pressed back, and every thrust found a place inside that wreaked agonising pleasure. Did he think he was hurting? He stopped and it took all my encouragement to make him begin again. In the end, to convince him, I caught his right hand and set it on my cock. "Edward, were I in pain would I be like – "

"A poker," he gasped, and began again without hesitation.

I thought I would die before he was done. It was over for me before he was ready, and he kept me captive while he battered me to the heart. It was the sweetest kind of punishment, like the bite of a lash that brings wafts of pleasure, echoing the bittersweet storm of release. He gave a cry, his cock jerked in me and I tensed, intent on that part of him, and of me. I had him now. I had his seed, and he was mine.

Exhausted, he withdrew and collapsed at my side. I went down on my belly and panted for air, unable even to move until I began to worry for my sore arse. I struggled up, fingered myself and found the slickness of oil and Aethelstan seed. Blood? I prayed not. Edward watched with drugged eyes, and I leaned over to kiss, if only to reassure him before I bathed him clean and doctored myself.

I squatted at the water's edge to wash. The water was warm, and I was woeful sore, but I counted the deed worth thrice the cost. Satisfied, I patted dry on my discarded tunic and crawled toward him, hoping he would offer me his arms.

He did. I was still quivering, and he whispered, "I hurt you."

"Also pleasured me," I insisted. "I am well pleased. I've had the gift I've wanted for so long. And you?"

"I am still drunk," he confessed. "I have never done any such thing before. Not to a boy or a man. Your body is... "

"Yours," I finished, and stroked his chest. He was beautiful in the moonlight. I told him so as I buried my face in his hair. "I love you," I added wearily. "Sleep now. The mules must come to water at dawn and we must be awake to catch them."

He tried to speak again but I silenced him with my mouth and he surrendered. Somehow he was asleep before me and I lay propped on my elbow to study his face. In repose he seemed so young, and not as stern as he appeared when awake. I felt a thrill of pride. I was the lover of an earl, a knight. Yet I could never speak of my love, or else be branded a harlot, even a witch. This thought possessed me as I drifted down into sleep, and my last waking thought was sad.

Chapter VIII

His hand on my shoulder woke me to the brilliance of full daylight, yet I was cold. Desert nights are as bitter as the days are like a furnace. I was rolled in the cloaks, and as I pried open my eyes I saw that he was already dressed heavily for the chill of early morning.

He had interrupted a confused dream and I was fuddled as he leaned toward me and said, "Dress quickly. I hear camel bells approaching – we'll soon have company." He spoke tersely and I realised he meant me to be alert and wary.

As soon as he mentioned it, I heard the bells too. You cannot hear a camel's feet, for the beasts have enormous, soft hooves that make no sound. They are evil creatures that bite and spit, but in the desert a man is better mounted on one of these demons than on a horse, for the camel can live days without water while a horse quickly expires.

I struggled into my clothes and dragged my fingers through my hair, all the while watching Edward lay his weapons close to hand. He slid a jewel-hilted dagger into one sleeve, concealed there, and I guessed we would soon be at risk. I gazed into the east, blinded by the early sun, which sat on the shoulders of the parched hills. Where were our mules? How far had they run, that they had not come to drink with daylight? And then I saw the caravan coming on, and before it, a black banner with four gold crescent moons. Even I knew it. Who would not? I touched Edward's arm.

"I see it." He shaded his eyes, watched the flag approach at the head of a dozen camels and three score figures on foot.

They must have broken camp along the road and were likely headed for Joppa to trade. But that banner belonged to Imrahan, the chieftain whose men had harried the Lionheart's knights, killed scores and captured many more. I had heard tales of battle that made my blood congeal, and as the camels picked up their pace when their twitching noses scented water, I took a step closer to Edward.

Icarus was tethered by one of the trees, in the shade with my gelding, but neither was saddled. I wondered if I should surreptitiously harness them, and Edward guessed what was in my mind. "Be still," he warned. "If they see us trying to run they could make sport of us. Stay silent and beware, but look – half of them are women, and the ones in the rear are hobbled. Slaves. And see, behind them! Are those our mules? I think we must buy back our belongings."

He was right, I knew those mules well. I stood in the shade, stroking Icarus's face, and we watched the whole party come closer. The standard bearer was a big man, his face and body swathed in robes. He thrust the flagstaff into the sand and the breeze caught it, flared it out to display its four crescent moons, the signature of an Islamic clan.

The slaves were not hobbled tightly enough to hurt, just sufficient to make running impossible. Even these restraints were loosened when the camels had knelt to allow their riders to dismount. Men and women alike, slaves, freemen, wives and children, all wore the swathing robes, even their faces obscured. Yet there was no doubt as to who was their leader.

He stood straight as a young oak, feet splayed, head high, one hand rested on the hilt of the long, curved sword at his left hip. His face was covered but regal bearing is unmistakable. He surveyed the pool, the warhorse, Edward and myself in that order, the order of value. Water first. Then as fine a horse as ever walked these lands – Arabs have always cherished horses. Then, the tall, slender young man whose blondness must catch the eye in this place. Lastly, the boy, broad framed and dark, whose value was reckoned in his youth and, perhaps, his handsomeness. Had I not been sweet to the eye, I would never have seduced Edward.

Slaves, servants and women set to with the efficiency of a military company, but the camp they pitched was more sumptuous than Lionel's. They drove tentpoles into the sand, hoisted canvas, and rich rugs were unrolled on the sand before cushions were piled deeply for comfort. A fire was lit, and before the tents were pegged down against the lively wind I smelt the aromas of coffee and mutton.

All this time, Edward and the Saracen chieftain stood looking at one another, eye to eye, eight or ten paces apart, and neither broke that eye contact nor spoke. My chest began to burn and I realised I was holding my breath. No one paid the slightest attention to me. I was a mere observer and might not have been there at all.

At last, a boy approached the chieftain with a tiny gold cup of rich, sweet coffee, and knelt at his feet. He looked down at the lad, the first time had moved in minutes. He said something in that strange language of the tribes, and the little boy lifted the cup to his master with a smile.

The chieftain took it with his right hand, and with his left removed the silk from his face. I caught my breath, for he was quite pale skinned, as if he always kept himself covered, protected from the ravages of sun and wind, and his handsomeness would have turned heads at any court in England.

He was surely a kinsman of Imrahan, but he smiled, and his voice was soft, schooled, his English thickly accented. "Well met, sir knight," he said. "You are welcome at my camp."

Edward accorded him a bow. "I am Edward, Earl of Aethelstan." The Saracen did not offer his name or rank. Edward took a breath. "I see you caught our mules. They fled in the storm yesterday. We were searching for them."

Dark brown eyes glanced at the animals and then back at Edward. "We caught them last evening. You wish their return?"

They belong to a company of knights, Edward could have said, a company on its way to Jerusalem to make war, but he had more presence of mind than to elaborate.

Our host examined him from his midnight blue tunic to his boots, his sword, and then looked back into his face. "Drink coffee with me and we shall discuss the animals."

"Paul." Edward beckoned me.

He did not want us to be separated. If I were out of his sight and found myself a captive with a knife at my throat, what a hostage I would be. I hurried to his side and dropped a bow before the chieftain. The closer one approached, the more handsome he became, the more piercing his eyes. His skin was the colour of the fallow deer, while many of his countrymen were swarthy. His eyes sparkled with humour, for he knew we were on our guard, and was amused. Had we been assaulted, we would have stood no chance, so vastly outnumbered were we. Yet this chieftain knew also, if Edward were challenged, he would spill a considerable amount of Saracen blood before he succumbed.

Our host invited us into the most sumptuous of the four tents. The banner fluttered beside it. The carpets were rich and the cushions were piled deep. Two girls and three boys reclined there, all slaves, and all naked. Their whole purpose was pleasure. They were plump, soft skinned and idle, without a mark on their lovesome bodies to speak of ill treatment.

The boys smiled coyly as their master stepped into the tent and seated himself. A pace behind, Edward flicked a quick glance around, but the warriors were nowhere near, and only a single burly guard shadowed us as we were urged us to sit and take coffee.

It was served by one of the slaves, a girl with ripe breasts and rouged nipples. She wore a jewel in her navel, and silver bangles on her wrists. She brushed my arm as she gave me a tiny cup, and I felt a rush of heat, though my eyes were on Edward. What instinct told me, our host was a prince? He carried himself proudly, his people trod lightly about him, and even Edward spoke respectfully as the two exchanged pleasantries and debated the fate of the mules, for all the world as if they were old acquaintances at market.

Yet Edward's hand lingered close to his sword even while our host reclined carelessly, stroking his favourite boy, who sat between his feet. He appraised me overtly and for a moment, as he deliberated over the price of the mules, I had the suspicion I might be the price myself.

"I shall not rob you," the Saracen assured Edward as they finished the coffee. "Allah would see to it that I were myself robbed within the day! But the mules have eaten our feed, drunk our water, and been safe with us through the night. I desire a fair price."

"For the mules and the burden they carried," Edward added. "Their load was just personal oddments. You can have no need of them."

The chieftain leaned forward, both hands on the shoulders of the plump little boy. "A thief would charge you for your chattels also."

Edward's brows rose. Putting down his cup, he twisted stray ends of his hair between his fingers. "And will you?"

A smile creased the Saracen's honey coloured face into pleasant lines. "I am no thief, Sir Edward. Nor," he added as the smile widened, "do I murder. You are bound for the Crusader camp, on the Jerusalem road."

"I am as yet innocent," Edward said carefully. "I have not spilled a drop of your countrymen's blood. If you wish to execute a murderer, capture me on my return to the coast and kill me then."

Wide shoulders in rich, dust-gold robes shrugged. "You are a soldier at war. Shall I execute you for killing other soldiers fighting the same war? Who decides who shall be executed? I am not qualified. God alone makes such judgements." He lifted a brow at Edward. "You consider yourself fortunate?"

"That I find myself in the company of a gentleman? I do," Edward admitted. "My squire and I could have been jackal-feed by now. Or shackled with your slaves, for market in Damascus."

"True." Our host stroked his smooth chin. "You would fetch a handsome price. A better purse than you will pay for the mules!" He looked at me then, eyes sparkling with mischievous amusement. "But were I to sport with freemen and warriors, shall not men of your race sport with me, if a day comes when I chance to fall into the hands of your fellows?"

His reasoning was sound, and I knew this lore. The old folk of Sleaford recall the wisdom of the Britons who inhabited those hills before even the Saxons came to England. They speak of a law of rebound. Even the Bible says, 'As ye sow, so shall ye reap,' but the Britons swore a man is answered in the same tongue as he speaks. If he injures others, he shall suffer himself. This I learned from an old woman who lived in Sleaford's woods when I was a child. I would see her gathering herbs, but she never came near the village. She patted my head and told me things learned from her fore-mothers. Was she a witch? I never knew, but her eyes were kind and her hands gentle.

The chieftain laughed, a seductive sound that shivered me. I wondered what delights his little slave could tell of. Caresses that stole away the mind, pleasure that enraptured him, made him a slave more surely than a collar or shackles would have. He was twelve or so years old, I judged, like Henri, but made of different stuff than the bumptious little squire into whom Lionel hoped to instil the rudiments of chivalry.

"Go free and take your mules," the Saracen said in an amused tone. "Are you an honest man, Sir Edward?"

"When I can be," Edward said warily.

"Then tell me," our host invited, "why you neither look nor sound like your countrymen."

Edward lifted his head. "I am Saxon. Perhaps you have never seen one of us before. My hair is yellow, my eyes are blue. Most Englishmen of your acquaintance are Normans."

The chieftain frowned. "What I know of your country is little. Are you at odds with the Normans? I know England makes war upon Normandy, since Count John made gifts and grants of English lands to Norman barons, in the hopes of buying their favour. But where stand the Saxons?"

"The Saxon is an outcast in his own country," Edward said quietly. "Few are like me, blessed with rank. Most are like my squire, reduced to servitude beneath foreign masters."

"Ah." The Saracen studied me thoughtfully. I bowed and felt the weight of his scrutiny. "Then you know how my people suffer. Our women are raped and mutilated, our young men are killed." He fondled his boy and sighed. "If you are an honest man, take the truth with you when you leave this camp."

"What truth?" Edward asked quietly.

"That you were entertained not by a barbarian but by a man who returned your property, gave you your liberty, when both might have been forfeit, and your life too. Tell this to your fellows when you journey to Jerusalem, to murder my kind."

"I do not go to Jerusalem for murder," Edward protested. "Nor even for war! I shall do as little as I may and stay in my King's good graces and, if God wills, I'll endure the years of my exile and kill no one at all."

The chieftain stood. The boy rose with him, cuddled to him for a moment before he scampered away with the empty cups. I cast a glance after his waggling bare bottom, thought of what Edward had done to mine, and shivered. "Then why do you ride on Crusade?" The Saracen challenged as he clapped his hands to summon his guards.

"To win favour for my name, before I lose my lands and end as impoverished as my countrymen, herding swine for my keep," Edward said with brutal honesty. "Little else is left to Saxons. I did not come here for hatred of your kind, nor for love of any God, but for survival."

The two frowned intently at one another. Both were tall, lean and beautiful, each in his own way. Both were warriors and survivors, and I counted myself honoured to have sat with them. A big, brawny guard stepped in out of the sun, crossed his hands over his breast and bowed low in salute. For the hundredth time I wondered, who was this man whose slaves loved him, whose women smiled, whose warriors offered obeisance.

"Attend to the Saxon knight, Shoab," he said levelly. "He is to receive his mules and the baggage they carried." He spoke slowly, deliberately, to demonstrate that his people knew our tongue. This shamed us, since neither Edward nor I spoke a word of theirs.

"It will not be simple, Imrahan, my lord," Shoab said in strangely accented English. "The goods and chattels borne by the mules were distributed for the usage of our people."

"Then find and return them, and allow Sir Edward to ascertain that nothing is missing before he pays in coin," our host advised.

The name had not penetrated my bewildered mind. Shoab used it again before I heard it properly: "It shall be done, Imrahan."

With that Shoab left, and my chin fell. *Imrahan.* I had recognised the banner of the chieftain whose warriors had made such woe for King Richard, but I had assumed that Imrahan himself must be far away, enthroned on marble and gold, merely pulling the strings like a puppet master while his young lions did the bloody work.

Brown eyes glittered with amusement as he saw our recognition at last. "You did not know me," he observed, and chuckled.

"No, my lord." Edward dropped his eyes and bowed, deeper than before. Imrahan outranked him by many a league. As an earl bows to a duke, and a duke to a prince, Edward of Aethelstan showed Imrahan the respect he was due. "I knew only your name and banner and imagined you were Imrahan's colonel, perhaps his kinsman."

"Will you tell this tale to your fellows?" Imrahan asked mockingly. "That you were the guest of the plunderer, the slayer, yet were neither slain nor ravished?"

"I shall," Edward said levelly. "Know you, I am a Saxon, and my fight is not with you. This is a Norman war to which I pay lip-service, for as long as I must."

Imrahan's brow creased. "Yet you are a Christian, fighting for the glory of Christendom."

"I own no faith," Edward said, quietly and honestly. "I am a sinner in the eyes of the Church. I have renounced God, drunk wine on the eve of the pagan feast of Beltane, and bedded in love with a young man." He glanced sidelong at me.

Imrahan saw. "This young man?"

"Aye." Edward squared his shoulders. "Were I a Christian, I should burn in hell forever. And this," he added, with a vague gesture into the east, where lay besieged Jerusalem, "is not my war."

For a moment Imrahan seemed to consider, then nodded. "So be it." He offered his hand, his sleeve drawn back to bare his sinewy wrist. "Clasp as warriors, part in peace... but if we meet in battle, I promise you no favours."

"Nor would I ask them," Edward said blandly. He took the man's wrist firmly. "With luck, we'll not meet. Pray for me, since you've the faith for it. Ask your God to keep me from battle, not because I am a coward and too affrighted to face Saracen wrath, but because I've no wish to kill anyone, least of all men who find themselves in a hell we Saxons share."

Thoughtfully, Imrahan agreed. "I shall ask for your boon, Englishman. If you are favoured, would you not, therefore, become a believer?"

Edward recoiled in surprise, but quickly saw Imrahan's teasing and answered with a smile. "If I am granted the boon I shall certainly reconsider the matter of faith."

"The knights of Islam never wantonly murdered our enemies for their infidelity," Imrahan said earnestly. "When we overran a city we gave every man the choice. If they only embraced the faith and became like us, they were free. It is the secret by which we blossomed so swiftly across the world."

"I've not heard this," Edward confessed. "We are not taught these things. 'Tis a bad day, my lord, when our houses are at war."

"My clan is the Black Wolf." Imrahan drew back his sleeve to expose his arm, on which was a tattoo of a wolf's face. "We fight to survive in a land gone mad, filled with Normans, Germans, Templars, barons, land-pirates, and priests of a foreign faith."

Footsteps from the tent's open entrance announced Shoab. Again he crossed his hands over his breast and bowed. On his heels was Imrahan's favourite boy, this time with a pitcher of water. He knelt at his master's feet, and Imrahan tousled his rich black hair gently.

"The mules are loaded, every item recovered," Shoab swore.

"Then, be on your way, Saxon," Imrahan invited.

Edward slipped his hand into the folds at his waist and produced his purse. This, he handed to me, to count out a fair weight of silver coin. Shoab watched, but Imrahan seemed uninterested. Shoab took the money and I returned the pouch to Edward.

"Fetch the mules, Paul," he said. "Then saddle the horses. I'll join you in a moment."

It was a show of good faith. Edward no longer kept his hand close to his sword, and he turned his back to Shoab, inviting treachery. None took place. I followed Shoab out and saw that the panniers were all repacked. Women opened them for me to examine the oddments, but I waved dismissively. It would have been ill mannered to actually search.

I took the mules by their halters and led them to the tree where Icarus and my gelding were tethered. The Saracens rhapsodised over the warhorse, pointing out his glorious form as I got the saddle onto him. I ran up his girth and checked his harness as I watched for Edward.

He was still in the tent, talking with Imrahan. Even now it was not too late for treachery, and my heart did not begin to slow until he walked out into the brilliant morning sun, while Imrahan reclined on the cushions and lifted his boy into his lap to be fondled for pleasure.

I held Icarus's bridle, and Edward mounted. The mules were tethered to our saddles, three to each. We wheeled the horses about and left the encampment, and we put half a mile behind before I dared look back. The sun glittered invitingly on the water. "My lord," I said hoarsely, "I cannot believe who that was! Or that we did not meet a horrible end."

"Believe," Edward said darkly. "Imrahan is an honourable man." He glanced sidelong at me. "And we were lucky." He reached over and gave me his hand, which I kissed. "What thought you of him?"

"He is handsome," I said rashly.

"And you are a fickle imp," Edward said bitingly.

"I am not blind," I protested. "Are you jealous? I love you, Edward. I proved that last night."

In answer he drew rein, nudged Icarus closer to my horse and leaned over to catch my unresisting head between his hard, callused hands and have my mouth.

* * *

Lionel's lads were breaking camp when we rode in, late in the afternoon. Henri flung himself at me, babbling that he had never imagined he would see us again. I almost explained to him how very nearly right he was, then thought better of it and sealed my lips. He would never believe a word.

While the squires and servants broke camp for the evening's march to the next town, where we would eat and sleep before pressing on, Edward and Lionel sat over a cup of wine and spoke in whispers. I was busy with the nags until Edward sent for me.

"Come here, Paul," he commanded, "and assure Sir Lionel that every word I have said is the truth. He believes I am jesting!"

"All is true," I swore, wiping grease and harness polish from my hands. "Every word, my lord, I swear."

"Loyal squire," Lionel accused. "You've heard not a thing Edward said to me, yet you'd swear to his truths even if it sent you to the stake with an apple in your mouth! Come here." He collared me and pressed me to his barrel chest, which was an agreeable feeling. "Now, tell me the tale in your own words. And mind, if your story argues Edward's, I'll laugh in both your faces!"

So I described Imrahan and his beautiful little slave, the caravan, the capture and sale of our mules. I did not mention the direction in which Imrahan's party was travelling, for I did not wish to betray them. How easy it would have been for Lionel to send a troop of knights after them.

When I was done he was speechless. He walloped my behind and gave me a push, which brought me up against Edward. "So it's true," he mused. "The plunderer, Imrahan of the Black Wolves, is in these hills. I shall tell the King, of course."

"It would be your duty," Edward allowed. "But Paul and I have come back unscathed. Imrahan is not my enemy. He fights for his freedom in a land overrun by foreigners, and I know his heart."

"Saxon," Lionel accused. "I imagine you do! Ah, what of it? Not all devils have black horns and spiked tails!"

The image of Imrahan in such costume made me chuckle as I went to help Henri. After the long ride I was tired and a little sore of the saddle, but Lionel promised us an inn, with decent accommodations, and we would travel only slowly.

We reached it just as the first stars began to burn in the east, and the moon was up in a sky still peacock blue. I smelt spices, strange herbs and unguents, heard the tambourine, the hurdy-gurdy, and the little bells the women wear on their fingers and toes when they dance, veiled and aquiver, before gaggles of admirers. Tonight I was too weary to watch.

Edward led us into the inn belonging to a caravanserai, and I dozed while the younger boys fetched food and drink. Fermented date wine had a better flavour than brackish water. I was parched, and drank a lot to wash down mutton and apricots, while Edward and Lionel made plans.

Yawning noisily, belching after his large meal and rubbing his capacious belly, Lionel said he was for bed. Henri was asleep already, and across the table Edward studied me guardedly.

"It is late," he said quietly. "We must start early if we are to make the King's acquaintance by vespers. Saints preserve us from his wrath if we do not! Sleep well, Lionel."

He shepherded me up the sagged, creaking stairs to a tiny room over the stable. A single room, shared by knight and squire, so that the boy could serve his master, if he was needed. I shivered as I went ahead and closed the door. The mattress leaked straw and the smell of donkeys and goats wafted up from below. I hardly noticed these things.

Before the door was properly closed Edward had me against him and his hands raced over me. He was hungry for me and tonight needed no encouragement. I whispered for him to slow down but he ignored me, tore off my clothes and pressed me onto the bed before he had even undressed. He merely hoisted his tunic and squirmed down his hose to bare his groin to mine. Cocks crossed like swords and we both panted.

"Edward, stop," I whispered. "Edward!"

"I have wanted you for hours," he growled in my ear, "I am mad for you, I must have you or be insane. Christ, I knew how it would be

82

if once I let you... "

So it was my fault! I seduced him, forced him to embrace me. Resigned to guilt, I tugged his tunic over his head. His hose were almost off, I heard them tear as I did away with them, but he was past noticing, or caring.

We writhed and twisted on the drooping mattress, and he ate me alive. I knew what he needed, but not until he moaned his frustration and grew wild could I get a grip on him and roll him onto his side to bury my face in the moist, warm place below his belly. The blond curls there tickled my nose.

The swift eruption into my mouth was his salvation. Sanity returned in moments, and with it an anguished content. I sat beside him and feasted my eyes on him in the light of a smoking tallow candle. His chest heaved, the fine muscles there inspiring my fingers to caresses, the little plum-brown nipples inviting kisses. Against his thigh my cock throbbed pitifully.

I jumped as I felt his hand close over me. He held me in his palm and tugged me closer, the better to see me. I held his head between my hands, smoothed his tangled hair and remembered the warm afternoons when I had seen him in this state of glorious nakedness. How I had wished in those days that he would fuck me, just a quick tumble in the woods for pleasure.

Now love scorched me and it was no quick, eager passions I wanted. I never expected him to lay his lips on my cock, and when he did I was finished. He did not suck, for it was all too new, but kissed me tenderly while he stroked my length, and it was enough. I filled his palm with my seed and collapsed, winded and exhausted. He frowned over my cream in the grudging light of the candle.

"You did not need do that," I whispered. "Your touch was enough."

"You had no desire for my kiss?" He teased as he wiped his hand on a corner of the sheet and settled beside me.

"I would die for it," I murmured, "but you are a knight. To kiss your squire that way is not asked or expected. Rather, let me kiss you." I leaned down and did as I promised, with one lick for the blunt crown of him and another for each of his balls.

He sighed and pulled me into his arms. "I behaved shamelessly just now. If I should apologise, I do."

"No." I caressed his shoulders. "You wanted me, and it was like a gift. Everything I have is yours."

"And this?" He slipped his hand between my legs, sought the centre of me and rubbed his knuckles over it.

I arched against him. "Whenever you desire it."

He kissed my ear. "You are a fool to love me, as much as it pleases and endears me. I'll only fetch you grief. I'll be married when we return to England, and you have always known it." Yet he kissed my brow and then my mouth.

"I know," I agreed. "But that is years away. If I'm to leave your house for propriety's sake when you wed, and if I'm to be a monk, with only memories to warm me – then let me have some memories to savour!" And I pressed tight to him, and gave him my mouth, and he took it hard and deep.

Chapter IX

He was called Richard, Lion-hearted, and he was the lord and master of Norman, Saxon and savage Welshman. Yet I disliked him from the first, even before I was near enough to see his eyes, hear his voice, smell his perfumed body. I stood dizzily at the back of the pavilion with a knot of squires and servants, watched my own lord kneel at the feet of a Norman, and what I felt was resentment.

Edward waited with the newly arrived knights, tall and fair beside the banner of his house. One by one they were presented to the King, and one by one they knelt, a kind of abasement, and waited for his command to rise. I watched the others perform the rite, and felt nothing much, but when Edward knelt anger seethed in me, righteous, foolish and stubbornly refusing to be quelled. *Get up!* I thought absurdly, *you kneel to no man!* To see Edward abased was painful, and I wondered if he felt the stinging discomfort of dishonour, like the swift cut of the birch.

Yet part of me knew we should consider ourselves honoured to be there. I was tired, hungry, thirsty and aching after a day of effort, travel and work. We had broken camp at dawn; I tended the nags, bathed Edward and saw to his needs in bed, where he was becoming more demanding as he grew accustomed to temptation and quick, sweet fulfilment. I fetched food for Edward and the horses alike, carried water, and in the late afternoon cleaned harness, mail, swords, before I laid out Edward's clothes and lastly, my own. By evening I was worn to a nub in the heat, and had not eaten since noon.

My sinews were tight-strung as I imagined being in the presence of the King. I put the buzz of my head down to effort and weariness, for I needed a night's sleep, a meal and the kisses I longed for, but all that would have to wait. First came the honour of a formal presentation to His Grace.

Rich honour! My gold-maned lord of Aethelstan was a Saxon, and many's the Saxon who has been cast out of his home, even maimed, for no more than the accident of his birth. I bit my tongue to quell my anger as he knelt humbly, and I looked, instead, at the King.

So this was Richard, Lion-hearted. He was shorter than I had imagined, and not as handsome as he was called. Perhaps Kings are called handsome by men desperate for his favour – or by minstrels too tactful to tell the truth! Richard was a red-haired, blue-eyed, Norman; his skin was pale, despite the desert sun. His frame was wide, his belly large, his shoulders vast, but he was not a tall man. His hands, resting on the arms of his great, carved wooden chair, seemed so incongruously fine, I wondered if he he had the calluses to handle a broadsword. But the name of 'Lion-hearted' had been earned, no doubt of that.

I knew swords well by then, so often had I cleaned, honed and oiled Edward's. It was a service I enjoyed, though not as keenly as I cherished the good-keeping of his other sword, the warm, hard blade he was furnished with by Nature. I knew the hands of a warrior too, and as I studied King Richard, I deliberately compared him with Edward.

Edward was then in the best of his young manhood, not a line on his face, his back straight, his body slender and iron with youth. He had the resilient strength of the fine, thoroughbred horse, bred to hunt and run. King Richard was shorter, thicker, probably stronger but not as graceful or agile. His mouth was petulant and his eyes were cold as they looked down on the bowed gold head.

My spine prickled. Did he so despise Saxons that he would refuse Edward the right to win honour, even on Crusade? Already he had kept him on his knees far longer than the other knights, who were dark-haired, whey-faced Normans. And then,

"Well met, Aethelstan. Rise."

His voice was thin and mild, not at all the bark I had anticipated. He snapped his fingers and a steward brought wine. My own throat was parched by the heat of a long day's ride, and the dust of the road, but the squires would not be served until our masters had dined. I knew better than to ask.

The King invited Edward to take a cup. "The honour of Aethelstan is in your own two hands, here," he said shrewdly. "I shall place a weight of responsibility on your shoulders."

"Willingly accepted, Sire," Edward said graciously. "For this purpose, I made the journey here." He lifted his cup.

It was the right thing to say. Normans, barons and monks in dark habits and cowls nodded and murmured approvingly. But Edward's moment with the King was already spent and the next knight was beckoned forward. My lord looked over the heads of the assembly, searched me out, and I was full of pride, tickled by that unholy, unrepentant lust. He was beautiful in the lamplight. My loins were whipped by my imagination, and I scorned the rest of the company that thronged the enormous pavilion.

He wore his chainmail, glittering like starlight about his chest and arms. Over this was the coat of Aethelstan blue, which made him seem even blonder, and on his breast, the white rose. At his side was his great sword, and in his right hand, a goblet of rich wine.

The night was hot and the crush of bodies oppressive. Sensations rushed through me, some familiar, some new and disconcerting. My eyes devoured Edward as my mind thickened, and I ignored the inane chatter of the servants. I had drunk no wine, yet I was quite drunk. Smoke seemed to fog my head and I was jostled by the stewards who had begun to carry in the great tables that would be set for the evening feasting. There was a feasting every night, no luxury spared, while I had heard that in many Saracen camps food was scarce and men injured in battle died of want.

In the back of the tent, I found myself pushed again the thick canvas wall. Edward was unaware of me, or he would not have stood listening courteously to the King, looking cool and pure, while I sweated and panted in the grip of this peculiar drunkenness. The lamplight dimmed then, everything I knew seemed to jolt, and in the sudden semi-dark I saw the glitter of stars.

He stood above me, and I realised the glitter was a reflection off his mail. His cloak was flung over his shoulders, a white cloak that seemed like the wings of an avenging angel. The wind floated his hair about his face like a halo, and in his hands was his sword. I feared terrible retribution for something I had done, though what it was, I did not know. The sword lifted. I never saw his eyes, and the breath tore out of me. He was waiting for me to accept punishment, but what had I done that was so vile? Yet, if he was so certain I was evil, how could he be wrong? If he made it quick, I must be grateful. I bared myself, waiting to feel the tip of his sword. He turned me, thrust me to my knees, lifted my hips. Dear heaven, would I be impaled, as male witches accused of sodomy were sometimes killed? The touch came, but it was not cold and sharp, but hot and blunt, and another kind of sword sundered me. I was knocked off my knees by the force of his possession, the air stripped from my lungs and the thoughts from my mind...

* * *

Darkness. Had the lamps burned out? I struggled to see while sickness churned my belly and my loins were afire. Was I blind? Fear clenched my heart like a fist in a mailglove, and I threshed, on my back on some soft surface. The last I knew, I had been in the King's pavilion.

"Hush, boy."

Edward spoke softly close by my ear, a hand fell on my shoulder, and I felt a slight weight on my face. It lifted, I heard a splash of water as the light returned to my eyes, and I realised that my blindness was due to the wet cloth that covered and cooled my face. I heard the sounds of the pavilions then, where the knights and squires camped, and the bark of the dogs. We were in our own tent. I tried to croak a question, and though I made no proper sound he said,

"They carried you here and I stayed to tend you." He bathed my chest with another cloth. "You fell, burning with fever. The servants thought it might be plague. Sickness hovers like a buzzard around battlefields, and this land is strewn with dead. The King's physician said it could be an ill of the bowels, and I near fainted. I thought I had killed you."

I recalled my dream – he had been an angel of vengeance, a sword poised to cleave me, and then he had indeed sundered me, but not like that. He lifted the cloth from my face, I prised open my eyes, and a worried face frowned at me in the light of a single lamp. The tent was closed, no one the wiser, and I reached for his hand.

"Are you griped?" He felt my belly. "Just last night I... "

"I have not forgotten," I chided softly. "Last night you threw me on my belly and rode me like Icarus. It was glorious, I exploded like thunder! Have no fear, my lord. There was no blood, nothing save vast pleasure. You have not hurt me."

He slumped onto the bed beside me, and when I touched his face I found his cheek wet. He was weeping. I opened arms that were weak and trembling, and urged him closer. "My lord, what is this?"

"Guilt," Edward murmured hoarsely. "A thousand times tonight I almost called for the physicians, intending to tell them what I believed your ailment to be. I would have summoned a priest and confessed."

Horror eclipsed my weakness and I struggled up. My head spun and I grasped his shoulder for support. "Edward, never do that! If you made that confession, they would flog the hide off you at least, and at worst they could burn you. No matter what, you must never make the confession!"

"Not even though I killed you?"

"You have not killed me," I protested.

"I might have."

But I shook my head. "You think I'd allow myself to come to harm? Do you think you would allow yourself to hurt me?"

He closed his eyes, and I kissed the lids. "Last night I did not ask, but threw you down and took by force everything you had."

"By force?" I actually laughed. "You took nothing I was not prepared to give. If you had asked, I would have been wanton. That you did not ask... well, I am a vassal in your service. There is no necessity to ask, no matter what you desire."

He sat against my pillows. "You are stronger, by the sound of you. Not griped? You are certain?"

"I was overcome by heat, weariness, lack of food and drink. And anxiousness," I added sheepishly. "It was overpowering hot earlier, and I worked without regard for myself."

"And Lionel and I let you do it," he said wryly. He wet the cloth again and wiped my face. "I sent for the King's physician but he told me, till you woke and told if your bowels protested, we could not know what ailed you. You were not sick, merely limp as a rag, and your heart was fast. Do you thirst?"

My mouth was parched and I nodded. A pitcher of water was nearby, and he held it to my lips. I drank it all, and as the water eased my belly I felt better. My head throbbed but he seemed to know, and rubbed my neck.

"And still, I'm guilty," he told me. "I shan't do that again, Paul."

I struggled to understand, grasped what I thought he had said, and panicked. "You won't bed me again, won't fuck me? But, Edward – "

"I did not say that!" he chided. "I will be slower in future, and will ask, let you prepare for the punishment of penetration."

Punishment? My head reeled again. I turned into his arms and rested my cheek on his. "You have never punished me, Edward... save once, when Brother Gervaise caught me trying to play a game, and my hose were already down, and the switch in your hand. You had no choice but to lay it on me! The game was my own, I took my stripes in good part. As for the other... being fucked is no punishment."

He sighed over me. "I don't understand."

"I know you don't," I agreed, more clear headed by the moment. "I shall try to show you what I know, when we have some opportunity."

"When you are better. Here, drink again, and eat a little. There is some fruit. And your belly... ?"

"Growls with hunger, not with maladies caused by the water, the flies, or... " My fingers slid into his lap, touched the soft curve of his cock. It twitched and he closed his eyes. "Did the physician examine me?"

His cheeks flushed visibly. "Not between the legs."

"Then you must." I squirmed over. I was in his own bed, covered by a thin sheet; it was still warm in the tent, while outside the wind would be strikingly cold by now. I had lost most of my sense of time, but it could not be past midnight.

He faltered. One hand rested on my buttock, through the linen. He leaned over and I felt the brush of his hair on my back. "What is it you require?"

"'Tis you who requires it," I said into the pillow. "Assure yourself, I am whole, healthy, and take no harm from your loving."

"Is it proper? I am not a physician."

"No, but you are my... " I took a breath and hoped that he would forgive the liberty. "You are my lover as well as my lord. If you chose, you could lop my hands for the mere accusation of stealing, my balls for the suspicion of sodomy, and my head for trying to run away. All I have belongs to you! If you cannot put your fingers where your cock has been, no man has the right." I spread my legs.

"You are being wanton," he whispered.

"I love you," I said, hushed. "And I wish you would examine me. Thereafter, you can throw out this guilt. You fret without need, out of the goodness of your heart. Many lads have been hurt by men, but not by being ploughed the way you possess me. Your lance was big and wondrous hard, but I was oiled and as excited as yourself."

He hesitated, then reached under the bed for his chest of personal things. His shaving knives, a silver comb; a crucifix, the gift of his mother, on her deathbed. And a phial of thick oil with which he had anointed me several times. He was inexperienced but never cruel, and sense told him, a lad's tightness must be eased before the plunder.

But he had never put his fingers deep inside. He would stroke the oil onto himself, and dab just a drop on me. All that had been in me was the sword God gave him, and the slender finger of my boyhood friend, and on rare occasion, a heathen toy, the likeness of a pizzle, made of wood, thin and not very satisfying.

Counterpart to my ignorance, was his own. If I had never felt any such caress, he had never felt the butter-soft insides of a man. I watched over my shoulder as he bit his lip, working up his courage. Nothing distasteful was in his face. More likely, he feared he would deal me the very hurt he sought to protect me from! I smiled in encouragement. He sighed and slipped his first finger into me.

He swallowed and looked into my face. I was dizzy, and my head gave an ominous throb as blood pounded in my ears, but I spread wider and invited him to explore. The fascination of discovery consumed him, his brow creased and he felt me slowly, thoroughly. I squirmed in delicious agony as he examined the shape and form of the muscle that guarded my entrance, how round and tight it was, which is what the Latin word *anus* means: ring. I relaxed, and he slid a second finger in to help the first. I pillowed my cheek on my hand, and he murmured, as if he had never imagined the wonder of a man's insides. Even I knew little, though Grendel and I had explored, as he was doing to me.

His hand turned, he found the nub, that untold secret inside every man that makes the pleasure flood. He grunted, and I was too breathless to speak. "Paul, what is this? A lump inside. Is it natural, or must the physician see to it? Does it hurt?"

"No," I moaned. "It is natural, it does not hurt. It feels... " I was boneless. Grendel had first found this nub inside himself, and took fright at having a definite lump. Then he found I had the identical nub, and identical pleasures when it was stroked. I pushed back onto his fingers. "It is the root of pleasure. When you fuck me, this is where you stroke, and why I am filled with delight."

"True?" He whispered. "Can I make you come like this?"

I was lightheaded with rapture, and wriggled helplessly. "I believe you could."

"You're whole and healthy," he said drily.

"I told you." My hips did shameless things. I know not what he thought of me just then, for a harlot from a Joppa brothel could have been no more lewdly inviting. I was waiting for chastisement, a stinging slap, or the withdrawal of his hand and a verbal rebuke, but instead he scooped his left arm under me and sat me on his knee with his fingers still embedded. Delight ripped a moan from me, and I came with an unholy force. I weakened at once, slumped across his lap, where his musk was sharp, and fumbled with his robe, but barely had I opened it when footsteps outside interrupted.

Sir Lionel's voice called through, "Edward, has he woken?"

Edward's face shone with sweat. He closed his robe and held it bunched over his belly to disguise his erection. He plunged his right hand into a washing basin and threw a handful of sandalwood into the brazier, which would almost erase the acrid scent of my coming.

"He is awake," he called, and wiped his face before admitting Sir Lionel de Quilberon.

Sir Lionel was like a bear, big, bluff, hairy, strong, yet faultlessly gentle with his women and squires. Henri had nothing bad to say of Lionel, and I had liked him from the first, as surely as I had taken a terrible dislike to the King. Edward was rigid with frustation, but Lionel's concern was for me. He bent over me, put his hand on my head and swore.

"The lad is sweated. Convulsed?"

"Sweated by the warmth of the tent, my lord," I murmured. "I was overcome by the heat and long hours of work, and I regret my disturbance."

Lionel grunted, as if he did not believe a word. To my dismay the sheet was snatched away and he began to prod my belly, thorough and firm to the point of pain. My muscles protested, and fresh sweat sprang out. Edward's efforts had left my abdomen tender, and I yelped as Lionel prodded.

"Do you hurt?" he asked.

"Only if you keep jabbing me," I said as tears began, but at last he stepped back and I sighed my relief. "I need only rest."

He regarded Edward with an arched brow. "You work him too hard. Is he afraid of a whipping?"

"Good Christ, no," Edward said tersely. "I have never raised my hand to him."

Lionel snorted. "That is not what Brother Gervaise told me. He said he watched you deal three stripes to his bare arse."

"Oh, that." Edward turned away. "Tell him what you will, Paul."

My mouth flapped like a fish out of water. "It was just chastisement, Sir Lionel," I said with a stammering that could have been sheepishness or shame. "My lord struck me lightly, and deservedly. I had been gambling, which is not merely a sin but a stupidity."

"Gambling?" Lionel's bushy brows rose. "What did you lose?"

I warmed to the role, since I saw he believed me, and both Edward and I were off the hook. My cheeks warmed and I feigned a squirm. "My lord's dagger, one of his favourites. Had I been Sir Edward, I would have beaten my squire bloody for such stupidity. He only smarted me, enough to make me recall for an hour the fool I'd been."

Lionel laughed. "Do you gamble now?"

"Never! I suffered a thousand times more over the loss of my lord's property. Had he beaten me blue, I would have accepted his wrath, but he was surpassing gentle, even in the midst of punishment."

Lionel laughed, and threw the sheet over me. "So, now you work when you should be resting, in attempts to please him?"

"No," I corrected with mock-humbleness, "I work for him because it is my pleasure. So many duties fell to my hands today, I thought I'd never be done. I had no moment for myself." I glanced at Edward's broad shoulders, slender back and narrow hips. He had not yet looked at me, despite my story and Lionel's complete belief. "My lord, did I shame you? Does the King wish some reparation from me?"

But Lionel shook his head and helped himself to wine. "No. Indeed, he asked after you when the company retired. Not out of care for you, lad, before you flatter yourself! If your belly was clutched with colic, by morning half the camp could be down with it. 'Tis common in these parts, when the streams run low. Inside the city walls, disease is often rife. It is the means by which a siege is soonest ended."

He paced to Edward's side and slung an arm about his shoulders. Edward stirred and accepted a sip from his friend's cup. "Paul will recover by morning," he said quietly. "I did the best for him I could."

"So I see," Lionel said musingly. "He is in your bed."

"His own is too hard and small for a sick lad," Edward said testily. "He was threshing and would have fallen to the floor."

"Aye." Lionel finished the wine in one swig and tossed the cup down. "Still, get him out of there, soon as you can. There's a fiend by the name of Friar Angelo in this camp. Let him see a naked boy in your bed, and you'll both be answering to higher authorities. The King disapproves of such things."

"Such things as a sick boy taking his ease?" Edward hissed.

"As sodomy!" Lionel said brutally. "Oh, come, Edward, even you are not so blind that you cannot see what others would make of

91

it. He's a handsome lad, and we all know what goes on at night."

"Do we?" Edward looked away.

Lionel grunted. "If you're buggering him, 'tis your business, not mine. All I say is, keep this small truth away from prying eyes and eavesdropping lugs. If Angelo sees or hears any morsel he can chew, he'll not rest till there's a repetition of what transpired here a week before we arrived."

I sat, swung my legs off the bed and stood, wrapped in the sheet. "What happened?"

"Cheeky monkey," Lionel teased. "First rule of squires: Speak when spoken to, be seen and not heard, and contrive not to be seen until sent for! Still, you're somewhat older than the brats the rules were written for. You're out of your lord's bed, I see. Stay out, at least until you have looked out for the monks in this camp."

"But, what happened before we arrived?" I took a bunch of black grapes from the fruit dish and at last began to put some food in my empty insides. I felt bruised after Lionel's probing, tender, a feeling that reminded me of Edward, and made me tremble.

"Are you sure you're not feverish? You're pimpled as a plucked goose," Lionel mused, but I shook my head and spat pips into my hand. "Angelo had the spurs off a knight and the balls off his squire, for the sin of buggery, like that." Lionel snapped his fingers. "They were discovered. Now, Sir Geoffrey is plain Geoffrey of Ainsworth, a soldier with the infantry. The boy, Gregory, has gone."

"Gone? What do you mean?" Edward shivered visibly.

"A trader passed, with goods for market in Damascus. The boy was under considerable pressure to join a monastery choir, where he would spend the rest of his life in holy service, whipped for every unchaste thought. The morning the merchant left, it was discovered that Gregory was gone. Now, perhaps he was stolen away, and perhaps he was seduced. I have heard Saracens are often gentle with eunuchs. Know you this?"

Edward looked at me, and I saw his eyes darken. "We saw boys in Imrahan's camp. If Gregory was beautiful, a Saracen warlord might cherish him, teach him a new faith, make him welcome with the very pleasures he can never have in England."

I remembered the boy who had gazed at Imrahan with shining eyes. I thought of Gregory, and as my balls twinged painfully I sat on my own small bed, at the foot of Edward's, and pulled my knees into my chest.

"Well, take more care," Lionel said awkwardly. He fixed Edward with a baleful glare. "If you're buggering that lad – "

"I wish to Christ you would stop saying that," Edward snapped.

"Then, 'tis true?" Lionel exhaled through his teeth, like a dragon's breath.

"It is nothing to do with you," Edward muttered.

"I dare say not," Lionel agreed. "But I smelt a man's seed under the sweet reek of sandalwood, when I entered this tent. Take better care, both of you. Wait till the camp has bedded before you make merry."

He was trying to jest, and we were both grateful, but I was scarlet and afraid. I had no idea who Bother Angelo might be, but I had seen so many priests, monks and Templars in the few hours we had been here, I was already aware of the dangers Edward and I faced.

My heart sank. Months and years we would be here, and when we returned to England he must wed, and where would I be? It would be holy orders for me. I wondered if Gregory would find himself a Saracen protector whose house would be his home, whose bed would be his refuge. I hoped he found what he needed, but for Edward and me I fretted all the more.

Lionel poured another cup of wine. From the barracks I heard a horn as they changed the night guard for the watch till dawn, standard duties in a camp of war caught between the walls of Jerusalem and the desert.

"We've a duty to perform in a few days," Lionel told Edward as he drank. I was eating, but listened intently. "We're to probe into the east, in search of the cause of all the disturbance."

"What disturbance?" Edward perched on the edge of a chair. I looked at his lap and saw that his erection had gone. For that, I mourned, but I would see to his needs after Lionel had left.

"Some say angels, some say devils. Wrath of God or Satan, depending on whose livery you happen to be sporting!" Lionel sounded scornful. "There have been strange tribesmen in the hills, and voices in the wind. They call it sorcery, but I tell you, it has more to do with wine!"

My belly lurched and I looked up at Edward. The mention of bad magic disturbed us both. "I'll have nought to do with sorcery," he said quietly.

"You'll go where the King sends you," Lionel scoffed. "What, hocus-pocus frightens you? You and Paul likely dream of angels and demons," he said tartly. "You are ridden by guilt, are you not?"

"No," Edward glared at him. "Should we be?"

"The city of Sodom was struck off the face of the earth, for your self-same pleasures," Lionel observed.

"If one believes Hebrew legends," Edward hissed.

"Hebrew legends?" Lionel laughed. "You've gall, Edward, I'll give you that. But hold your tongue outside this tent. You may be faithless, but bow to the priests, or Aethelstan is damned, and so are you."

"I'm not a fool," Edward said with that steely tone I knew of old. "Neither am I guilt-stricken, and nor do I imagine angels and demons coming out of the air! This is what we are to investigate?"

"King's orders." Lionel stretched and rubbed his large belly. "I am weary and the sun is up in four hours. With your leave, I'll return to the surgeon who sent me to ask of the boy, then lay down my head."

"Good dreams," Edward said softly as he escorted Lionel out and laced the tent shut behind him.

No one could simply walk in, now. So long as we doused the lamp, which would throw betraying shadows, and kept quiet, we could do as we pleased. I listened to Lionel's retreating footfalls and watched Edward blow out the lamp. In the sudden gloom I heard the rustles as he disrobed, and mourned that I was blind. I heard the movement of his bedlinen, the soft sound of a pillow. I slid out of my own bed, which was narrow and absurdly hard, and back into his.

His arms opened for me but he said, "You shouldn't be here."

"Does your heart say that?" I nuzzled his throat. In the dark I was more aware of the roughness of his beard than I ever was in full light, when his blondness made it so impossible to see the stubble that I forgot it.

"Good sense says that!" he said, and for a moment I was sure he would fend me off.

I stopped and held my breath as he seemed to battle with himself. It was a battle he lost... or, a struggle his cock won, for it stiffened like a spear against me, and it would not be wrong to say that it was the blade that cut out his heart. He clasped me and I turned over in his arms. He was on his side and all I had to do was shuffle back, and he was in me.

I had had his fingers only twenty minutes before, and it was easy to take him like this. I had not realised how he had opened me. Most men never know what even their own bodies are like, an inch under the skin. Only surgeons have that knowledge... and lovers.

He was eager yet anxious, and when his arms closed about me I held them to my chest. He squeezed my paps and I sighed and rose again, boyish, wanton as a hussy. He was sobbing into my neck, desperate for the relief denied him when Lionel arrived at that awkward moment, but the gift was mine to make, and I made it with pleasure. Aethelstan seed filled me, and for a long time we were one body with four arms and four legs. He left me at last, turned me and hunted for my mouth.

His kiss was savage, as if he must punish me for leading him astray; and then he gentled as he realised what he was doing. "Sorcery in the desert," he whispered. "I meant what I said. I'll have no part of that."

"The King's orders," I added. "If choices were granted to Saxons, I'd choose to go home!"

"Choices?" He laughed, a harsh, bitter sound. "To a Saxon knight with an empty purse and doubtful honour, and a squire whose race and station are beneath the King's attention?"

"And whose sore arse is well bedded," I added wryly.

He cuddled me closer. "I hurt you?"

"Only a little." I revelled in his embraces. "Ask any woman after lovemaking, she'll tell you the same. Her body is a delicate instrument of pleasure. A man's is just the same. Don't be concerned."

"Then, I'll not be concerned," he said affably, content with that. "Go to sleep. As Lionel said, it will soon be sunrise, and you should have been resting, not rutting, this night."

His choice of words amused me greatly, and I slid down into grateful sleep, still chuckling.

Dreams possessed me at once, and pursued me till I woke, and Edward was the heart of them all while Lionel's words haunted them... I was stretched on the rack, while a faceless monk demanded my confession to sodomy. The admission would burn Edward as a witch, and I was silent. To have the truth, the good friar instructed his acolyte to suck my cock while I was stretched naked on the rack, and its rising was taken as proof of my sins. Edward would be burned with me...

I woke, shouting, but he caught me and I plunged back into dream, though not the same one. Now I was naked beneath a midnight blue desert sky, and a warm wind caressed me. Edward rose like a water- sprite out of a reed-hemmed oasis, and beckoned me. I went to him, he pressed me into the rushes, and the cool, welcoming water swirled over my head. Rapture filled me, even when I knew I was drowning, and I did not care that I was drowning, since he held me tight.

In later years, I have often recalled that dream, and thought many times, how odd it is that dreams sometimes give us a clearer picture of the truth than we like to believe.

Chapter X

The King came to our pavilion in the morning, and I could scarcely believe my fortune. He came to see me, though not out of concern for my health. He was fretted for his troops, and with him came a bevy of physicians, not ten minutes after I had shaved Edward, bathed myself, bundled up our bedlinen and dressed us both. My body was merely begging for rest after the rigours of the previous day, but I was to get little.

Eating dates and wine, Edward sat at his table, a book open before him, a quill in his hand, an inkpot beside him. I was about to throw out the pail of bathing water when I looked up and saw three golden lions, rampant on scarlet. In the next instant I saw the King's forbidding face and, to my shame, I flung myself to my knees. Edward also knelt, but this time the King bade him rise at once.

"Get up, Aethelstan, and tell me of the boy," he said. "Was he sickened in the night?"

"Merely tired and anxious, Sire," Edward said. "I believe I asked too much of him yesterday. The heat punished us all."

"My own physicians will dose him." Richard strode into our pavilion as if he owned it – which he likely did. He folded his arms on the glorious red surcoat and stood back to watch as the physicians loomed over me like any two horsemen of the apocalypse.

They were old, grey-bearded, and they were already impatient. I was disrobed with forced, jerky movements, and told tersely to prostrate myself. I looked swiftly at Edward and did as I was told. My fear was that they would prod between my legs, where I was no virgin lately. Any good physician would recognise the tell-tale signs, and then I must lie about my lover's identity, to safeguard Edward. My dreams of the night before haunted me as I endured their insensitive hands.

My belly was certainly prodded, but they paid no attention to my buttocks. One of them examined my balls, commented on their tension, and his colleague scoffed. "Of course they are tense, Robert! See his age and stature, recall the chastity of knights on Crusade, and their squires. He looked into my flushed face. "How long since you bedded a wench, boy?"

"Two years, my lord," I mumbled, speaking truthfully of the hussy who had hoisted her skirts to me in the woods outside Sleaford. Could that be called bedding a wench? I had her in the grass for under half a minute, when I was just fourteen years. She was he only girl I had ever touched, or ever would, and it was done for curiosity.

"His balls are likely swollen with seed," the old phsyician decided, "and there is no cure but prayer and chaste thoughts. Do you pray, boy?"

"Often, my lord," I said, also true – a second before I had been saying a prayer of sorts: *Gods, make them go away and leave me in peace!*

The quacks sat me up and listened to my heart with their ears pressed to my back. King Richard looked on. What a face he had! I remember it best as a visage without any suggestion of mercy, and I remembered Lionel's stories, tales he had heard from men returning from this Third Crusade in the last year. At last the doctors stood back, and the King waited for their judgement. Grey bearded, rheum-eyed Robert bobbed a bow and said, "He seems well, Sire, but I'll purge him, to be safe."

I clutched a sheet about myself and watched while a cup was mixed and thrust into my hand. I did not want it, for nothing ailed me, but when I attempted to protest Edward made a tiny gesture, silencing me. I swallowed the whole cup, which seemed to please

King and doctors alike.

Richard, Coeur de Lion, glared at me for a full minute as if I were the direst criminal, before he beckoned Edward and left the tent. Alone, I sat on my bed and felt the herbs begin to work. I cursed and swore, and as the day grew hot, sure enough I began to run back and forth to the privy. That cup turned my innards outside, and by nightfall I was almost ill, sick with shivers in the belly and so sore I could hardly bear to sit.

I had not seen Edward the whole day, nor Lionel. Little Henri popped his head into the tent as dusk began to thicken, and asked if there was anything I needed – unless the malady was catching, in which case, I could take care of myself! I sent him for a flask of olive oil, and squatted to bathe for the tenth time. He returned with the balm and I used it with curses for the damnation of all physicians. Henri watched, and whistled through his teeth.

"You look raw as blood! What did they do to you?"

"Dosed me with herbs," I muttered. "Fetch me something to eat, Henri. I can't wait on my lord tonight. I was not ill before this, by I am now."

He ran for bread and a squab, fruit and pickles, and still Edward did not return, so I bedded alone, and drowned my woes in several cups of wine. My belly was easier, with only the soreness to show for the 'care' of the physicians. Perhaps they purged me to please the King. With a lot of wine in me I went to sleep, and did not even hear the horns braying across the camp to call the guard to duty.

When I woke again it was very late, and a hand fell on my shoulder in the darkness. Had the lamp gone out, or had it been doused?

"Paul?" he murmured. The lamp had been doused, then. "How are you?" Edward was anxious, and his hands sought my face. "You were ill, Lionel's squire told me."

"That cup they gave me," I groaned as I went gratefully into his arms. "I'll mend."

"Bed with me," Edward murmured. "I shan't sleep if you don't lie with me."

Those words healed me more than a dozen salves. My heart lightened and the throb in my head vanished in a moment. I fumbled with his laces, disrobed him clumsily, which he forgave without question. Then we were in his bed. A horn shouted across the camp once more, and I had learned to tell the hour by these calls. It was the small hours of the morning and, but for the guardsmen, we might have been the only ones awake. We were safe.

I curled in his arms and he ate me with kisses, but when he tried to turn me and felt for my buttocks, I had to stop him. "Another time. Blame the King's physicians! I'm salved for my comfort, not your convenience."

"I should have known. I felt the oil, and... " He kissed the tip of my nose. "Go to sleep."

But he was a lance of tension against my back, and I turned over with a snort of derision. "And fail you in every way possible?" I threw back the sheet and put my lips on him. He fucked my mouth almost ruthlessly, which was the measure of his need. For me, it was wildly exciting, though it left my lips chapped. When he was done I crawled back into his arms and said,

"What devil has got into you, my lord? You were wild!"

He toyed with me as if I were a plaything. "I spent the whole day listening to a lot of old fools, priests, knights, barons, recounting the atrocities they have committed, and are about to commit. We are within sight of the walls of Jerusalem, and if you can bear a saddle tomorrow, we'll ride out and see the city. The Saracen King-General is more powerful in this land than Richard Lion-hearted will ever be. And not so brutal. We are holding, just outside this very camp, more than four hundred Saracens, Turks and Kurds, all of whom are to be put to death by the sword in a few days. You'll hear the carpenters tomorrow, building the scaffold." I felt him shudder. "With luck, we'll be gone before the bloodshed begins. I have no wish to look on as soldiers are slaughtered for the colour of their banner and the name by which they call God."

"Edward." I touched his face. "You should not be here. There must be another way to secure the Aethelstan fortunes."

"I wish there were." He kissed my lips and his grip tightened on me. "The King will watch as the Saracens are led to the scaffold, blindfolded and one by one beheaded. I don't want either of us to be here when it begins, so I offered to lead the first party into the east. Lionel was to take it, but I begged the honour. I should leave you behind, since you are so young, but I thought you'd not like to be here when the latest of Richard's atrocities begins."

"I would not let you go alone," I corrected. "'Tis not Richard and bloodshed I cannot bear, but being parted from you."

"It may be dangerous."

"Then it will be dangerous. At home, I could have been accused of stealing or poaching, and had my hands cut off, or of neglecting my taxes, and had my eyes put out. Is that not dangerous?"

"We could be killed," he elaborated with brutal honesty.

"Then we will be dead," I said, with the youth's calm disregard for death, which springs from his belief that he is immortal... someone else always dies, not oneself. Accumulating years cure this impression. "I shall die with your name on my lips and be buried at your feet," I said recklessly, "like the hound who loved you best."

"Young fool." Was he exasperated? He pulled the sheet over us and gave me a hug. "You're growing."

"Growing?" I considered my cock, which was useless tonight, and did not know what to make of that remark.

"Taller," he said succinctly. "You are putting on the last spurt, and will grow swiftly in the next year." He laughed softly. "I think you will be taller than me."

I shivered as I recalled my old fancy. How often had I pictured myself, broad and strong, holding him against me, protective, since Edward was slender and under my height! It was nonsense, but sweet nonsense. Edward would always be a warrior, and I would never be a fighter. Sooner would I run, and take back home a tale of survival rather than a story of glorious death. For now, it was Edward who held me while my insides quivered in the last throes of the brief indisposition imposed by those damned physicians.

* * *

With morning I was recovered. I drank goats' milk, ate a little bread, and bathed while it was still not even light. Edward lay in bed, watching as I laid out his clothes and poured him a cup of ale to slake the morning's thirst. He caught my wrist as I handed it to him. "Better?" he asked as I sat on the side of the bed.

"Much." I kissed his face and stretched. "I think I could sit on a saddle. Will we go out this morning?"

The city of Jerusalem lay only a short ride west of the camp. By that year, Saladin – Salah ad-Din Yusef ibn-Aiyub, Sultan of Egypt – had recaptured every city in *Outremer*, the very cities that had been 'liberated' in the Second Crusade. This audacity made it imperative that the forces of Richard, and Philip II of France, and the German Emperor, Frederic Barbarossa, joined to expel the invaders. But as I recall the story, Frederick died before he even reached the Holy Land, of heart failure, when he fell into an icy mountain stream, which left left Philip and Richard to share the glory; and the two monarchs had never seen eye to eye. No one was surprised when they quarrelled, and Philip abandoned the Crusade – and the Saracens – to Richard's tender mercies.

Tenderness was the last quality one would have ascribed to Richard. I think he had some of the madness of his brother, Count John, and all the terrible ambition and ice-heartedness of their mother, whose shrewdness and merciless vengeances are legend, even in the shires.

As the sun arced into a burnished blue sky, Edward called for the horses, and with a party of falconers, boys, knights, squires and pages, we rode west toward the Holy City itself. Even the name of Jerusalem was magic. Banners hung along the walls and the sun shone on the bleached stone. It was still in the hands of the Muslim Turk, and I was sure I smelt the rankness of death. So many battles had been fought, so many warriors had been taken back there to die. Surely, I thought, the conflict must soon end. Saladin's power was overwhelming, and every man in England knew how ill Richard could afford this Crusade.

Yet it was the kind of war that can limp on for ever, as first one army commits an atrocity, then the other, and vengeance comes in endless waves, like the ocean. Hundreds of Saracen men were shut in the pens, in irons like slaves, awaiting execution; Saracen women had been butchered by the score by the Templars, because someone had whispered that the riches of a town were often hidden within its women's bodies, and if they were cut open diamonds would spill out. The story sickened me, but I believe it was true. What vengeance would the Saracens reap for that? And so a war limps on.

I listened mutely to the others, following Lionel's instructions on the duties of the squire. I rarely spoke, but kept to Edward's side, waiting to be summoned to work, and I learned more of the state of affairs in the Holy Land from the squires and falconers than I could have learned from any tutor in England.

The Saracens were snapping at the flanks of the Crusaders; no one was without sin, without pain. This Crusade was lengthy and expensive, in money and in blood, and Richard was near the end of his patience. Saladin was said to be fretted, and in Normandy, men swore, Philip was attacking the lands Richard considered his own. Since the fall of the city of Acre, where the King had won his title of 'Lion-hearted,' much had gone wrong for him. He had hurt the Saracens, but his fortunes in Normandy were worsening. Every moment he kicked his heels within sight of the very walls of the Holy City, he yearned to be making war on Philip's troops, who ravaged, burned and raped their way through Normandy with the impunity of Knights Templars.

In the morning sun Edward's hair shone like that kind of silver-gold, argentiferous gold that falls from the sky, fire from heaven. I sat on my pony, gazing at him as he studied the distant walls, and perhaps he felt my eyes on him, for he turned to me.

The difficulties of our life here were manifest to me then, for no flicker betrayed him, nothing of our affection showed in his face. I felt chastened, as if he was telling me, mutely, *Do not look at me so, you will betray us both!* I looked away, blushed, and hid my flushed cheeks behind a cough.

The camp was gaudy, colourful and filled with activity. Pavilions spread out north and south, and the banners of a hundred baronies, houses and shires fluttered, while the three gold lions of the King flew above them all. When we returned just after noon, however, it was to see the carpenters already at work on the great scaffold where the captives would be executed.

We had seen few Saracen warriors at close quarters, to that point – only Imrahan and his men – and I admitted my fascination as Edward and I ate with a party of knights and scribes. He indulged my curiosity with a sigh, and we walked a distance from the pavilions, to the pens where the unfortunates were housed.

I do not know what I expected to see. Brawny, hairy, fierce men, perhaps, who were ugly or physically repellent, so that I should feel nothing when I remembered, they were all condemned. But chained in the pens were young men and youths very like myself. Some might have been Edward's age; some, I fear, were younger than I. They were smooth shaven, with long, dark hair, black as the raven's wing, or else curly-haired. Some were very beautiful, and many wore rings in their ears. Dark eyes looked at me without accusation, though they were sad.

I thought of the families, friends and lovers they left behind, and I grieved, but they were knights of their people, just as Edward was a soldier. He guessed what bedevilled me and shepherded me to the tree-shaded well not far from the pens. I drew a pail of water and offered him the first drink. Across the great camp of war came the hammer strokes, each one beating another nail into the scaffold where those young men would die. Every beat assaulted my ears. What was on my face, I do not know.

At last, he touched my arm. "We'll be gone before the bloodshed, and shan't return till it is over. They'll burn the bodies before we are back."

I nodded, needing his embrace, but there was no chance.

Edward sighed. "We leave soon. Tomorrow eve a priest will confess us, placing us in a state of grace, in case we are killed on this skirmish."

Again I nodded. He threw the last of his water into the pail and strode away, as far as the hitching-post where a string of mules was tied. He busied his hands with a bolt of silk, as if he was at a loss to know how to ease me. Perhaps I looked very young in that moment, or very vulnerable. This is how I felt. I wished I had remained in England... wished I was older, and a fighting man... wished Edward had been born Norman, and had never had to come here. Useless wishes, of which I said nothing.

That afternoon we began the preparations for our journey. Edward and Lionel were called to the King, where he lectured them as to their duties and objectives. I eavesdropped on the pages who served the company, and learned at second hand what was said in the pavilion where I was not allowed to set foot.

Voices had been heard in the wind, crackles of dry lightning licked out of a clear sky, dust-devils twisted like the dervish, strange horsemen haunted the horizon, flying banners no one knew. All this was ascribed to sorcery. It was well known – how, I never understood – that Saladin was a wizard who could summon every demon of the Sephiroth.

I had no idea what the Sephiroth was, and when I asked a priest that evening I earned a cuff for my head and a penance! I could only assume they were demons out of hell. I knelt before the image of the crucified Christ and droned the prayers, knees aching, heart rebelling, mind spinning with all I had heard from the loose-lipped pages.

Satan was out in that desert, and the soldiers of Christ must root out the evil, else the Crusade was done for. I groaned. I was not superstitious, but what I knew of magic was enough to make me cautious, and my reasoning was the innocent sense of a child.

If witches had to be burned, they must be so powerful that the Church sweated in fear of them. If they were powerful enough to arouse terrible fear in the bosom of so mighty a body as the Church, what hope had a paltry company of knights? What protection was a mailcoat and a sword against the powers of darkness?

Misgivings possessed me as we bedded, but Edward would not comment. He rolled me over, pinned me to the bed, and that night I gave him my arse. I felt well, and it would be our last opportunity for proper lovemaking until we returned. I hooked my legs over his shoulders and he thrust at me for a long time, came in me, rested, and began again. But just as I feared he would be insatiable and rough, he gentled, and the second coupling was much more pleasant. He was tender and saw to my pleasure too, with his hand. A little before I came he kissed the head of me, and in the darkness I half saw the tip of his tongue touch the eye of me. The sight was too much and I spent at once.

This was love, and I was complete. If I never had any more, I was fulfilled, and I said so as he held me against him in preparations to sleep.

"Love," he murmured against my hair, while his own hair was a cool cascade across my shoulder, veiling our faces.

Was it an admission of what he felt, or at last an acceptance of what I had so often told him I felt for him? I had been content to love him, and know he did not fear my emotion. His lust had grown feverish and his boldness was also growing. Now, he never hesitated, and while he showed me immense tenderness he had no qualm about placing me where he wanted me. I revelled, content to know I was desired, and that without me in his bed he could neither rest nor sleep. But I never dreamed I would hear him say he loved me.

Chapter XI

Work occupied my hands the whole day and I was exhausted by evening. Henri and I worked side by side while Edward and the other knights studied maps and listened to every tale that could be told of the east, the desert, its people, and the heathen sorcery that tormented the night.

When I was done Icarus shone, and I had checked his shoes. My lord's harness and weapons were sharp and polished, and every personal item I thought he might want or need was packed. I was red as a beet, heavily sweated and my head throbbed, when at last Edward returned to the pavilion. The day had been stifling, every moment of it endured in the constant ring of the hammers, as they built that terrible scaffold.

In a rare moment's privacy, Edward touched my face and bade me go and bathe before the priest came to confess us, and I was eager to obey.

Bathing took place in a shallow, brackish pool of tepid ground water where pages, squires and foot soldiers crowded beneath the trees. I lounged for an hour, drowsed and watched the sky grow bloody with sunset, and with great reluctance dragged myself out and returned to face the priest. Confession was always something I hated. Lying is also a sin, yet even in confession I must lie, or forfeit my very life.

I knew Friar Angelo by now: a man of middle years, middle height and sour manner. Edward's confession had been heard already, and he knelt a small distance away before the cross of his sword, driven into the sand. His hands were clasped, his eyes closed as he said whatever prayers were required to cleanse his soul, get him back into the Almighty's good graces.

Sighing, I knelt before the monk and crossed myself. "Bless me, absolve me, for I have sinned, good Friar," I began. He waited. "I am beset by doubts," I said, fairly honestly. "All about me I see savagery and pain. I find my faith shaken. I neglect my prayers and am given to... " I hesitated. "Fancies."

"Fancies?" Brother Angelo's hand rested on my shoulder.

"I am a young man, and my fancies are likely common. Still, they bedevil me."

That much was the truth. I stole a glance into the monk's face. He was satisfied. He made the sign of the cross before my forehead and gave me a round of prayers I must say without delay. I kissed his hand, smelt jasmine and lilac on his palm, and got to my feet.

By then Edward was finished, and I wondered what his confession could have been, since Angelo had given him a very scant penance. My own prayers consumed a good quarter hour, while Edward checked his bags and spoke briefly to a page. He was to dine with the King tonight, as we expected. Knights were feasted before they set out, to honour them a final time. Many did not return.

This at least was not ascribed to sorcery. The loss of so many knights was more the doing of a man they called the Jackal, a chieftain from the mountains. He was a Saracen or a Turk, neither of Imrahan's tribe nor of Saladin's; and he was, so men swore, a devil in mortal's flesh. I had heard stories that curdled my marrow. The Jackal spared no mercy for soldiers of Christendom.

Edward sat waiting for me to complete my lengthy penance, and when I was done he smiled. "You are in a state of grace!" he observed. "Do you feel very pure this evening?"

"Pure?" I scoffed. "My knees ache! I set nothing by it, as well you know. If God loves us all, we'll not be condemned for loving each other."

His face softened. "You confessed some strange, boyish fancies? You would have spent less time on your knees if you had kept that secret."

"Angelo would have suspected me of holding back the better part of my confession. A boy my age, and supposedly chaste, *must* have fancies. It stands to reason."

He laughed quietly. "I suppose so! I confessed as much when I was younger than you."

"To your family priest?" I was taken aback.

"No! I was at lessons in that damned monastery. I admitted to dreams that kept me awake, and they birched me. And before you ask, it stung like a whole nest of hornets let loose on my backside."

I shuddered sympathetically. "At least I had only to say a lot of prayers, yet I've done more to deserve the birch than ever you did."

He tilted his fair head at me. "What fancies?"

My face flushed. "Surely, you've no need to know the very details!"

"No need, but something of a desire," he said lazily. He was in a sublime mood, drowsy in the heat, a cup of wine in his hand, his eyes heavy, his gaze hot on me. We were alone in the pavilion and the noise of the camp would mask any and every word I said.

"But, my lord!" I protested, while my heart quickened. He arched a brow at me. I came closer, and dropped my voice. "In one, you suspect me of infidelity."

"Were you unfaithful?" His breath was moist on my cheek.

"Never, but you believed it, and were enraged." I met his eyes with commendable courage. "Would it anger you, in fact?"

"It would," he admitted, in that moment not teasing.

I smiled. "So it did in this fancy! I came home late – to Aethelstan Manor, not to this cursed tent. You were waiting, you threw the bolt on the door of your bedchamber, locking me in, and you... " I swallowed. I had woken in a sweat after dreaming this, before we became intimate. In those days, which I had begun to forget, I was painfully frustrated and dreams of every sort plagued me. Edward was waiting. "You did as Master Jacob once did. Laid your baldric across my poor arse until I was afire."

"A strange thing to imagine," Edward mused. "You've no taste for pain."

"It was an anxious dream," I said, unable to explain it otherwise. "I believe I turned to it as a means to have you claim me as your own."

"By beating you?" He sounded scandalised.

"For my infidelity," I corrected, half laughing. "The harder you hit me, the more you insisted on my devotion, and the angrier you were that I strayed into the beds of others. Which," I swiftly amended, "I never did."

"I see!" His eyes sparkled. "Did I strike hard?"

"The force of your arm bowled me off my feet and smote the air from my lungs," I said with a peculiar kind of contentment. "I howled fit to raise the dead. I knew you wanted me more than any other, after that, and though there was more in store, I bore it with a smile."

"More?" He recoiled. "Surely, not even in your dream did I set about you with a birch, as Jacob did!"

I looked about, saw we were alone, and kissed his hand. "You had a basin of hot water, and made me kneel over it while you washed my insides, to 'wash him out of me,' so you said. That also stung, but afterward I felt righteously clean and was ready for the most vigorous of rides... which you gave me."

He shook his head over me. "Never in a year would I dream of treating you so cruelly."

It was my turn to recoil. "Then, I could stray, and you would do nothing?"

He had clearly never considered this. A shadow appeared in his eyes, and I regretted my words. He cleared his throat. "Would you stray?"

"No," I said, adopting a wounded aspect. "But if I did, you would not care that I did? Not even enough to take back what was yours?"

His brows arched. "This thought has never troubled me. I would be angry. I suppose I might rail at you. I would certainly bolt the door for privacy's sake! I may even bathe you vigorously to wash out the taint of another's seed. How could I enter you, otherwise, knowing another had been there before me?"

I shivered. "You would rail until I begged forgiveness?" He bit his lip and nodded. Time to set his doubts to rest. "You would fetch water and wash away my infidelity? Then, I would be yours again," I said coaxingly.

105

"Would you?" He touched my face. "I could wash the smell of another from your skin, but not expunge the desire from your heart. Beating never purged a man's soul."

"It was but a dream," I said, exasperated. "And not the only one! There was another." He cocked his head at me. "It is Yuletide, and snowing," I purred as close by his ear as I dared. "You send me out to find kindling, and I lose my way in the snow. I stumble into a sheep pen and am sure I will perish before morning. Only one thought comforts me, that I will die in your service, and you will mourn me. How did I misjudge you."

"I would not grieve?" Edward was bemused.

"No, my lord, since you cloak yourself and turn the woodland inside out, searching for me! Next I know, I am in your bed, a fire roaring in the hearth, and you are drinking wine from my navel, licking honey from my paps. You make me sit astride your shaft and sunder myself, the instant I am well enough to stir." He closed his eyes. I touched his cheek, and he caught my fingers. Foolish, since the pavilion was surrounded by men, anyone could have come in.

"I'll have you like that, if you wish," I whispered. "Ride you, with a lance for a saddle under me."

Footsteps at the entrance spun us about, but it was only Henri, come to fetch Edward to the King. I was astonished to discover I also was summoned. I would not sit with Edward, of course, but would dine with the squires who were to accompany the knights at first light. The boys were respected for our courage. I left Edward with a smile, and noted with pleasure the blush on his fair Saxon cheeks.

We filed into the King's pavilion and separated at the entrance. The knights sat with the red-haired monarch at the far end, while squires and pages sat together, dining on simpler but still sumptuous fare. I knew a few of the other youths quite well. Seward, tall as me and tow-haired, scrawny and shifty-eyed. Gerald, brown-haired and lush-lipped, with one of those mouths that pout endlessly either in petulance or invitation; chubby little Aldred, with blue eyes and curly black hair, and thighs like a woman. I wondered what his knight did with him when the lamps were doused! Much the same as mine did with me, I suspected, and when Aldred caught my eye we shared a chuckle. He was a pretty boy of fourteen, far too young to be with Sir Ivor in this land, this camp, much less ride with him tomorrow.

We listened to the King and knights, and learned what we could. The Jackal had been seen not far to the east, and we were admonished to take care. One of his captains had been a prisoner of Richard's, but escaped during a raid in which it was said, fancifully, Saladin himself took part. This captain had one eye, and a scar on his face; he fought with a great sword the size of a man's arm, so heavy, a lad like Aldred or Gerald could not even lift it. He was the Jackal's kinsman and the two had fought together since they were boys... It was nearer myth than truth, but we were breathless with excitement.

These were the raiders of whom we must beware. They were the *djinn*, spirits of death who could walk out of any sandstorm and pluck the soul from a man's body. My flesh crawled as I listened to the tales Friar Rupert told. He had once ridden with the Templars, and seen such things as nightmares are made of.

Few men regard the Templars fondly, but imagine the malice Saracens nurse, if Englishmen bear the Templars no affection. A column of knights was waylaid and fought bravely, a whole day long. At sunset hardly a dozen were alive, and these were captured when a weighted net was thrown over them. It was said the Jackal himself drove them to the slave market in Damascus. There, reportedly to the vast amusement of Saladin himself, they were displayed naked, gelded, and from the market were whisked away to brothels where they would end their days. This fate, we were told, awaited the fairest of Christian knights. A fitting vengeance for the bloody acts committed upon the Saracens? I recalled the old, sacred rule, eye for eye, tooth for tooth. Even the scriptures acknowledge cruel justice.

But the darker threat of sorcery left King Richard perplexed. The knights scoffed and said these fears were the result of drunken revels, yet several men reported what they had seen. Gleaming phantom shapes that seemed to ride out of a dust cloud, battle cries adrift on the night wind, bolts of lightning out of the clear sky. Richard leaned toward his knights, fixing them with a glare that would have withered lesser men.

Red-haired young Cedric Duval lifted his head. "Sire, I saw these things with my own eyes, and I was not debauched. No wine had passed my lips, I swear. I cannot name what I saw, but I saw it. A column of ghost riders came out of the veil of dust which filled the sky, flying banners of green and black."

"Demons?" Richard pressed.

"I know not," Duval mused. "I saw nothing about them to suggest angels, no wings, nothing to fetch them out of the sky. Save sorcery."

"Black magic, then," Richard breathed, and sat back.

"Sorcery," Edward whispered. Eyes turned toward him. He had not spoken before. "I know little of magic, Sire. Perhaps, if you were to consult a priest or an astrologer?"

Wine slopped into Richard's cup. "They swear they have worn out their knees in prayer, and there is no more they can do to exorcise the evil."

"Time," Friar Angelo said quietly, but well within my hearing, "to send Christ's soldiers to cut out the rot, since no prayer will dispel it.

I wanted to cry out, if heaven's own angels did not set the evil to flight, what faint chance did soldiers stand? We were being sent to our death, either by sorcery whistled up by the Saracen, or on the swords of the Jackal. But I kept silent and watched the King with brooding eyes.

Once or twice Edward looked my way, and I saw no cheer in his face. This talk was driving him to distraction. He hated the casual cruelty of churchmen, which in its own way is as evil as any ill done by a sinner, and he was near the end of his patience.

Just days before, Saracen knights had been seen in the parched brown hills not far from Jerusalem itself, and the banners of the Jackal had also been sighted, closer to the coast. No company of knights could go looking for a fight now, and not find one. Edward and I shared the same misgivings. We were sacrificial goats, thrown to the slaughter since the priests could do nothing to exorcise these apparitions.

The fear of dark, Saracen magic was rife. I wondered if Richard half believed that the spilling of the blood of hundreds upon that cursed scaffold would arouse heaven's interest, win answers to the prayers of his corps of priests.

Sir Lionel de Quilberon sat back, listening mutely. He was to have taken the first column under his own command, and perhaps he guessed that Edward had volunteered, so as to be absent during the massacre. Or did he suspect my lord of trying to get quickly into Richard's affections? If he believed Edward eager for reward, so be it, for my lord had the fortunes of Aethelstan to consider. If serving this duty now, rather than in a month's time, would endear the King, let it be done! And if Lionel believed him squeamish, well, de Quilberon had known Edward's heart for years.

It was late when we were dismissed, and I had drunk too much. My head buzzed, and I knew I would regret my indulgence in the morning. The night air was cool, refreshing, and I stood for a time outside our pavilion, watching the stars. In England the night sky is black, but in the Holy Land it is never dark, but as blue as the Aethelstan livery. The stars burn more fiercely than I can describe, and one can believe that we are watched. Little wonder that this land gave birth to men whose faith at times seems to outstrip their sanity.

"Come inside," Edward called softly, as my head began to clear.

I did swiftly as I was told, and shut the canvas behind me. The lamp was already doused and he was abed. It was past midnight and we would be roused at dawn. Our column must be gone before the sun was an hour up, and we had many miles to cover.

I shrugged clumsily out of my clothes and noticed, for the first time, how short my sleeves were. He was right, I had begun to grow rapidly, the last quick spurt I would put on, while I surpassed his height. As I turned to the bed I saw him, outlined against some light from behind the canvas. He was on his back, one arm under his head, and the linen was kicked down about his feet. My nostrils flared as I smelt his musk, and the light, sweet scent of the body oil we used.

Always, when he was anxious, he was eager for me. I wondered what he had done before we were together. Did he snarl at his servants and dogs, or did he retire to the privacy of his chambers and set his right hand to good use? He was young, healthy, virile and, as de Quilberon frequently observed, my Edward was godless.

His voice was a steely purr, like the sound a sword makes as it is drawn. That tone made me shiver and get up hard. "Come to me." I wondered what he would say or do were I to resist, even refuse. But that was never in my heart. I went to him blindly, without question. Hands took my arms, dealt caresses, tweaked my paps. One palm explored my belly and found my eager cock, for he always ensured that I was eager before he required more. I blessed him for it on that night, and a thousand after.

I held my breath and let him do with me as he would. His scent dizzied me; love thrummed in my chest as he turned me, my back to his chest, and sat me on his belly. I smelt the oil, felt its slickness. He had anointed himself rather than me, growing bolder, surer. I knew in a blaze of intuition what he wanted, and trembled as I let him do it. Helped him do it. He sat me on his cock, and my weight plunged it into me like a dagger. His hands splayed over my back as I rode it down all the way, like a broadsword impaling me to the heart. I cried out, but he sighed, a soft, voluptuous sound. My buttocks were on his belly, and I took his bony shins in my hands.

"Ride me," he murmured. "As you promised."

"Like Icarus," I gasped, tensing for effort. He bucked, and it was quickly over for him. I was winded and frustrated, but his hands joined my own as I sat in that wondrous peculiar saddle and finished myself. I sagged down onto him, kept him safe inside me, and my head was on the pillow with his as he kissed my cheek and rubbed my seed into my belly.

"It was not a punishment," he whispered.

"To be filled with you? No punishment, my lord! I am the scabbard for you. I was made so, for you alone."

"My scabbard!" He teased fondly, breathless at my choice of words. "A devilish hot scabbard! I fear you must release me."

That old demon possessed me – the devil that made me show him my rump, after Master Jacob had thrashed it. "I've no wish to," I cajoled. "What use is an empty scabbard? You feel comfortable. Stay there a while."

"And you're baking me like an oven," he protested, which was only the truth. I could feel the sweat running freely off him.

Instead, I wriggled down, and he tolerated this for several moments before he simply took me in his hands and demonstrated the strength I envied. He lifted me off, and it was my turn to groan as he left me empty and aggrieved.

It was too hot to lie close together. That night the tent was stifling. Sleep did not come easily, since we were plagued with misgivings, and when the horns roused the knights who would ride with us, I was more weary than when I had set down my head.

Chapter XII

Fourteen of our company were Templars, from a monastery somewhere near Lincoln. I had been warned to avoid them, and that command I was pleased to obey. They seemed hardly to notice my existence when the company mounted, with the sun still low on the horizon and the land of Palestine like a great, sleepy dragon waiting to stir.

Their commander was Brother Jean de Bicat: tall, angular, Norman to his marrow. I hated him in an instant and found his looks disturbing. I saw a cruelty in his features that repelled me utterly. No matter my wilder fancies, Edward was right, I had no taste for pain. In the days before he put his hands on me, the imagined sting of his belt made my dream-self feel owned, his rightful property, which is all I had ever wanted. To belong.

Brother Jean's eyes were cold, his mouth thin, his nose aquiline as a rapacious eagle, yet something about him whiffed of the erotic. The saying is true, 'like knows like.' Not till months later did I realise what I had unconsciously known about de Bicat at a glance. I saw him half bare, doing penance, as all his kind do with grim regularity. New welts overlaid the old as he was scourged to blood, all the while gazing at the body of Christ Crucified, and in his eyes was an unholy gleam. I realised later, it was lust, not for God embodied in Man, but for that sculpted body, naked and taut with agony. This was Jean de Bicat.

That morning as we left the Lionheart's camp, I rode a little dun horse and kept well away from the Templars. They wore white, carried shield and lance, as did Edward, and before them was a great golden standard, and King Richard's banner, the three gold lions rampant on a field of blood-scarlet. Edward rode at the head of the column with de Bicat, and I rode far behind, chewing on dust with the squires and servants.

The lads had been eavesdropping on their lords, and knew a little of where we were going. I had no need to eavesdrop, for Edward had shown me a map, made by the King's own scribe. I had seen the position of the watering holes, the ruined towns, where the likes of de Bicat had put so many Saracens to the sword. De Bicat hated Saracens with senseless fury, for their 'crimes,' and at once I understood

Edward's deep scorn for hypocrisy. When Christian knights slew the folk of a Saracen town – women, children, old men and all – this was a great deed. But let a Saracen take vengeance, and he was the devil incarnate.

I had sense enough to keep my own counsel, and merely watched de Bicat, and hated. In every way he was Edward's opposite, cruel, vain and arrogant, and he was a monk! He had no notion of compassion, and was deranged when his temper was up. The first afternoon after we departed, we witnessed his wrath, and it was terrible.

In the blaze of the sun he punished one of his own knights and a page, for different crimes, but with the same heavy hand. I shuddered, knowing he had the right to discipline any one of us. Edward would not be able to safeguard me. De Bicat was responsible for our spiritual well-being, and it seemed that to be wholesome we must be constantly on our knees, thinking chaste thoughts in the midst of fervent prayer.

If de Bicat had known the thoughts uncoiling in my brain that day, he would have flayed me. I dwelt on my Edward and lusted fiercely. If I squirmed in the saddle I could still feel the slight rawness of his possession, and cherished it. Silence, lowered eyes and diligence were the best policy, and though de Bicat glared at me when I came near, he never had cause even to ask my name. He knew I was with Edward's party, for I wore the Aethelstan livery, which sweltered me in the heat, but I gave him no reason to notice me.

At sunset, after a day's ride that was merciless on men and horses, we made camp. My eyes were gritty, my face burned by the ferocious Palestine sun. I slid from the saddle and imagined my backside saddle-bruised while my legs were stiff and numb. First, food and water for Edward; second, water and grain for Icarus and my own little horse. Third, pitch our tent, unroll the beds and lay the table for the evening repast. Then, hurriedly scrub myself of dust and dirt, just in time to fling myself to my knees as Brother Jean rang a bell.

Vespers was sung in Latin. I knew enough to mumble along, move my lips intelligently whenever I felt de Bicat's eyes. I screwed shut my own eyes and begged silently, *Look elsewhere and leave me alone!* That night my prayers were answered. Another squire was given a hefty penance in prayer for arriving late to Vespers, but at least the skin of his back remained intact.

I was so tired I had not even the energy to eat. I flopped face down on my bed, on the cooling sand, while Edward and de Bicat were still reviewing the day's march. I could not even lift my head, and did not realise Edward was with me until his hand fell on my back and he said, close by my ear, "You didn't eat. You must, or you shan't have strength enough to make this march. You could have set out my bed and garments after Vespers, or left some work for me. Here, eat this."

He had brought me dates, salt meat and bread. I sat up, knuckled my eyes and gobbled the food. As soon as I took the first bite, I realised I was ravenous.

The camp had settled; the Templars were ensconced in their great pavilion, and Edward and I were in a much smaller tent, alone. I did not dare approach him, but he lit a candle, and in its light I feasted my eyes on him. Insects danced about the flame; he watched them, preoccupied, oblivious of me. Something was awry, and my belly churned.

"What is amiss? Am I at fault?"

"No, not at all," he said quickly. "But Jean de Bicat infuriates me. Tomorrow, he says, we will make better time and put more distance behind us. Today's ride was hard enough! Does he wish the horses lame? Does he wish to exhaust us so that by the time we race into the Jackal's heartlands we'll be in no fit condition to fight?" He shook his head, and with his fingers teased at his tangled hair.

It was permitted for a squire to comb his master's hair, and I did this when I finished eating. It gave me a small opportunity to touch him, and I revelled in the intimacy. "I think," I said softly, "Brother Jean is trying to impress you."

"Impress me?" He leaned his head into my hands and I longed for kisses. His lips were sun-chapped, but if I licked them to moisten them, they would become soft and cool. I lectured myself sternly for dangerous wantonness.

"He has a score to settle," I guessed. "Less than a century ago, a monk's place was in a monastery and fighting was left to professional soldiers. He'll likely drive us hard, so that when he is the last on his feet we will see he is the strongest knight beneath Richard's banner."

Edward sighed. "I hope I can curb him. Lionel and I spoke about the Jackal last night. The rumours are rife everywhere that he is at the heart of this Saracen magic, not Imrahan, not even the great Saladin."

"Where did Lionel come by these tales?" I teased the final tangles in his hair, then combed it for the pleasure of being near him. I could smell his body, pungent after the day's exertions, as no doubt he could smell mine.

"Market square tattle," he admitted. "But I have observed, merchants who deal in rugs, ivory and slaves are returning from the places we are still struggling to reach. Who better to ask of the unknown?"

"What do they say of the Jackal?" I put away the comb, sat at his feet and dragged his swords toward me. I uncorked the oil with the intention of using it on the blades; this guards the steel against rust, but the feel of it on my fingers made me shiver as I recalled its other use.

Preoccupied, Edward did not notice. "Carpet merchants dealt with him, twenty leagues from here. They told of a sorcerer in his camp." His teeth worried at his lip. "I do not understand much of what they said... Perhaps the language is against us, and the storyteller misinterpreted what he heard."

"So strange?" I looked up at him, intrigued.

"Strange enough," he said drily. "What say you, boy, of horse-men who ride out of the midst of a dust-storm... and a man with skin as green as a grass snake."

I had to laugh. "I could not believe it, unless he was before my very eyes, and then I'd blame my cups, last night's supper, anything but my reason!"

"So I thought," he agreed. "Finish the swords and put your head down. You must sleep. I swear, I'll see that you do."

"But not oversleep," I warned. "Brother Jean has a heavy hand and the thickest birch rods I have seen."

He made bitter sounds, for his dislike of de Bicat was boundless. We both slept lightly, and when the Templars' taskmaster called their company to order I was out of bed with my eyes still closed.

Edward had slept a few feet from me, and though we never touched I felt we were together. He lay still, heavy eyes watching me as I set out his garments and fumbled with his breakfast and shaving knives. I was yawning, hair on end, belly growling, and at last he chuckled over me. I blushed and looked down at his chest, bare above the sheet. My eyes were drawn to his nipples, brown-pink and erect as the morning air touched them with caresses that should have been my own.

Matins was a repetition of Vespers, sung as the sun sat on the east horizon. Brother Jean had a passing pleasant voice and a good grasp of Latin, but no sooner did I admire him for this than I deplored him again. A petty offender was punished for some vice, and I clapped my hands over my ears, not wanting to hear it. I wished de Bicat in hell.

We rode on with the sun at our backs. I watched de Bicat's bucket-shaped, white-plumed helmet, and what I imagined! He was a slave in a Saracen camp and must suck the eager cock of every man come sunrise and sundown, or be buggered by the blunt haft of a jousting spear, that split him asunder. He was the slave of a chieftain from the desert, and must bathe his master's body nightly, inflaming his owner so that a possession followed which aroused de Bicat to screams. He was the property of a brothel keeper, his arse was sold to any man who wanted it, and at a gasp of protest he was flayed by the birch and sold to a band of vengeful tribesmen.

Such was my hate for de Bicat – and it was fanned by his overt scorn of Edward. My lord did nothing to invite scorn, save to argue in favour of resting the horses and young squires now and then. De Bicat's lip curled, and instead of granting us the rest we needed, we quickened our pace.

Young Aldred, Sir Ivor's squire, was the first to faint from heat and fatigue, and Edward's lips compressed in anger. He knelt by Icarus, feeling the horse's legs, and meanwhile I held Aldred's plump little body in my arms. He was a child, no matter that he was but two years my junior. At that age, two years make a vast difference to a lad. He was feverish, prickled with heat rashes, and I feared for his life.

I took him on my horse, across my lap, with a cool rag on his brow, and somehow I felt my own fatigue less, since I was responsible for the boy.

By nightfall Icarus looked lame, and my own poor nag, which had borne a double weight, was sore. We camped by a palm-fringed pool, and I missed Vespers. I took Aldred, plunged him into the water, sat bathing him from brow to feet, and damn to Friar Jean de Bicat. The boy enlivened, but was still sick. His fevers made him a little delirious, but his head cleared as he grew cooler, and he sighed and moaned in my hands.

I rubbed his belly. "Better?"

"Aye," he croaked, and produced a shaky laugh. "If I were well, what you are doing would make me rise up like a little bludgeon."

"Shh, for the love of Christ!" I hissed. "If you are heard, you'll have us both flogged!"

"I know." His head lolled against my arm. "Your knight is beautiful."

"He is," I agreed as I slopped water over his head and watched the green parrots, which came to drink at the last of twilight, each night.

"Do you not love his touch?" Aldred whispered.

I gave a guilty start. "How did you know?"

"How could I not?" He sighed. "Aethelstan is made of different stuff to my knight."

"You've no taste for Sir Ivor?" I wondered.

"Not much," he admitted. "He is tender, but he humps with a clumsiness that makes me despair."

"Oh?" I washed his plump, sun-scorched face. "And what wideness of experience have you, which leads you to these conclusions?"

He giggled. The cool water was fetching him rapidly to life. "I was first fucked by a priest! He had the best hands, and the best pizzle I have ever known." He looked up at me from beneath a tangle of wet ringlets. "It was quite ten inches long."

My jaw slackened. "Vile nonsense, that. Your undersized little body would not accommodate it." I wondered if my own would take that much, and suspected it would not.

Aldred merely shrugged. "He shoved in what part would fit, and rammed me deliciously after my pains stopped. Thereafter, I could not wait for Latin class, and confession."

Now, I was scandalised. "You committed sodomy at confession?"

He stretched and yawned. "Before I made confession! Then, I would confess it in lewd detail, and he would absolve me."

"Indeed?" I said tartly. "And pray tell me, who heard the priest's own confession?"

"That, I known not, nor," he admitted, "did I care to ask."

I stood and washed my face with both wet hands. "Since you are feeling better, I ought to tackle my work before my lord is shamed."

I left him sitting in the water, watching the parrots and the last, fading sunset, and was busy with Icarus, forgetful of Brother Jean, when I heard footsteps behind me. I froze. They were not Edward's steps. I swallowed my heart and turned about. It was not de Bicat but another of his company, Brother Francis, a tall, dark-haired boar of a man, whose yellow teeth did indeed give him the aspect of a wild pig.

He loomed over me. "You were not at Vespers."

"My lord," I pleaded, "the boy, Aldred, was sick. I was tending him. I'll pray later."

"So you shall," he hissed, "and in my sight, so that I can see it well done! Come to me after you have eaten."

I bobbed him a bow. His spurred heels had retreated across the sand before I dared return to the grooming of Icarus. My face burned, not with remorse but with anger, and when Edward appeared some little time later, I could not wait to tell him. I was hopping with rage.

His mouth was tight with displeasure, but he merely shook his head and said softly, "If this will sweeten Brother Francis, so be it."

"You want me to – ? I began.

"To go and say your prayers in his hearing, as the rest of us said our own." He smiled crookedly in exasperation. "I do not ask you to believe what you say, but to say what *they* believe!"

The subtle difference impressed me, and I worked on, eating while I worked, and asking myself for the first time the question which has doubtless plagued all thinking men since time began. What *did* I believe? I struggled with this, and almost forgot about Brother Francis.

I believed in love. There, my faith began and ended. Not in love of God – I had seen priests in Richard's service do too much evil for me to own that kind of blind faith. I believed in the love of Man. The caring of a man for his kin, even his dogs. His impersonal caring for the great ocean of Mankind. The love of a man for his wife and children. And the special love of one man for the body, heart, mind and soul of another man. Love is our only claim to heaven.

"Paul?" Edward's voice surprised me, and I looked up to see him outlined against the starlight of early night. "Time you satisfied Brother Francis. Don't keep him waiting, and have an earnest look about you when you say what he wishes to hear!"

I was reconciled, circumfused with the pleasure of the thoughts I had entertained minutes before. I went to the Templar with a smile, ducked my head before him, and said,

"The little boy is well, I have seen to my lord's needs, and I should like to say my prayers for you now."

His brows rose in surprise. Had he expected my resentment? He drove the tip of his sword into the ground to make a cross, and I knelt before it, crossed myself and said what pleased him, while I dwelt on the love of Man. He was satisfied, and when I was done, to my astonishment he looped about my neck a silver chain on which hung a heavy crucifix.

"I did you wrong, boy," he growled. "I thought to chastise you for a damning lack of piety. I see now, you cared for a boy's welfare before all else, but would have given God his due an hour later."

I fingered the gift, and my impression of Brother Francis changed in an instant. "I thought my prayers would wait just a little, while Aldred had fainted. I feared for his life."

His lips pursed. "The pace Brother Jean has set is punishing, I own." He shook his head solemnly.

"It'll see off the nags," I murmured. "My lord's great animal is half lame, and will be fully lame tomorrow."

"So is my own beast," Francis muttered sourly. "I shall have words with my brother when we are settled." He angled his head at me. "What is your name?"

"Delgado, my lord." I palmed the crucifix, pressed it to my chest, over the white Aethelstan rose. "If I may serve you, tell me how."

He fended me off. "Your hands are full, serving your own knight. Be off with you!"

I was pleased to go, and returned to our small tent to find Edward absent. I wondered where he could be, but if I cocked my ear to the wind I heard his voice, and Sir Ivor's, and they were arguing. Then I heard de Bicat's brittle voice, and he was furious.

My mouth dried as Edward took him to task, for it could go so badly. I could not pick out their words, but the dispute went on and on in sporadic gusts, like an autumn wind that sometimes dies away and then springs up squallishly. De Bicat grew agitated and I hoped desperately that Edward would watch his words, put his safety before his temper.

Then Brother Francis came between them, shouting out across the camp: "Look! For pity's sake, look!"

There was a great commotion as we ran out into the cool darkness, and the whole company saw at once what he had seen moments before. There, over the dunes in the distance, toward the ruins of a nameless Saracen town that had been burned and plundered a decade before by the righteous, rampaging Crusader armies, lightning crackled out of the clear sky, evil and wicked, like the gleam in the eye of the devil himself.

A wind stirred, howled, flung up a twisting storm of dust and sand... and I heard voices in it. With my own disbelieving ears I heard battle cries I could not understand, the drum of hooves and the terrible clash of swords.

Chapter XIII

A great restless silence settled over us all. Some said it was Saracen magic, others swore it was the Apocalypse. The day of Armageddon was at hand. Cold sweat bathed me as I heard this, spoken in all sincerity by Templars, for Armageddon will end the whole world. Yet, who would be judged the more harshly, men like de Bicat and Richard Lionheart, whose wanton cruelties will surely pass into legend? Or men like myself and Edward, whose hearts were gentle with love?

I kept silent, kept my eyes on my work. Aldred rested the night through and in the morning was weak but able to go on. The black-smith examined the horses, and after all was said and done it was he who persuaded de Bicat to slow our pace. He warned that half the nags would be lame before we reached the hills where the Jackal was known to camp. What use was a force of lame cavalry?

De Bicat strode about with a dark look on his lean, hard face, and the birch was busy. We broke camp in the coolness of morning and put Jerusalem and the safety of the great army even further behind us. The bloodshed would have begun there by now. Three hundred prisoners for the scaffold. I thought of the young men I had seen in the pens, and grieved. The same was likely on Edward's mind, for his eyes were stormy, his manner distant. I would speak to him and he would not hear; later, I would look up to find him brooding as if he longed for me.

Scouts went ahead on the swiftest ponies, not weighed down by armour, and every few hours these vanguard riders would scurry back with news of the trail before us. It was they who first saw the banners, the pall of risen dust, spiralling sand, and they hurried back in the afternoon of our fourth day out from Jerusalem with a great shouting and waving of arms.

"Black banners! Black banners, Brother Jean!" They rode to the Templar, when they should by all accounts have made their report to Edward, but de Bicat was dangerous, domineering, and I do not believe Edward cared to press the point.

My mouth dried like a husk. Black banners? Black, with a single white crescent moon, was the pennant of the Jackal. Then this was the fight we had come looking for, but now that it was about to begin my heart betrayed me. It beat at my ribs like a hammer on an anvil, and if I could have summoned an angel, demon or sorcerer I would have spirited myself and Edward away in an instant. No enchanters rode with us that day. Instead, the *djinn* raised up its fearful head.

Edward lifted on his helmet. It was one of those terrible helmets like an upturned pail, with a cross cut out of the front for a vision-slit.

He told me he hated it. It was hot as hell, his own breathing sounded like a rasp-file, deafening him, and his breath was humid-hot, chokingly oppressive. I loathed it. With the thing on his head he was an anonymous shape, so like the Templars, from a distance, cloaked, I was unable to tell him apart from them.

Shouts and commands, orders and horn calls fetched the whole company to its toes. We squires and the boys kept back and I groaned, knowing what was to come. I had never seen a battle, never heard the bell-like chime of steel on steel, nor smelt the sweet-rotten reek of death, but I had heard the tales of a hundred veteran knights in the camps and on the ship, and I had dreamed too much.

In my foolish dreams I had stood on the edge of the fray and watched Edward fight. He swept through the enemy like a divine wind, with lance and sword putting the Saracen to flight, and they fled before him. The tales of glory mocked us all now. The reality was before me, and heaven was deaf.

I was with the squires and all we could do was watch our knights ride away toward a far-off encampment where the scouts had seen those black banners. Where they would fight, I did not know. I would see nothing of the conflict, and must wait like a helpless maid. For the first time I felt something of the pain women feel when they farewell a man, watch him take a road that leads inevitably to battle, and to the death of one foe or another. Many knights never return from the Holy Land. Many died terrible deaths.

My heart was squeezed, and while other lads knelt and beat the deaf ears of the Almighty I stroked the nose of my tired horse and waited. My belly churned in sickness, my eyes stung with sand and sun. A boy handed me a cup of water, but even that much sickened me, and I could have retched. I saw it all in my mind's eye – Edward, glorious, rampant and victorious... Edward, bloody, twisted and fallen. I saw a thousand images, each more dire than the last. And each of them, by whatever mercy, was wrong.

The sun was punishing and we took the horses into the shade of a hillock, watered and fed them. Aldred and the younger boys sat and shivered. The older lads like myself climbed the hill and looked out toward the field where battle had been joined. We heard the distant ring of swords, and voices, carried on the rising wind.

That wind was rising fast. All at once the breeze in my face was a scream, and sand scoured my eyes. Once before I had felt this. I had chased the mules into a storm, and Edward had found me, or I would have died. I slitted my eyes against the flying dust and put up a hand to shield my face.

The others scattered, some running the right way, some the wrong, but I had sense enough to fling myself to the ground and cover my head with my arms. Breathing was difficult, and soon I was choking. I had no cloak, and the sand began to drift over me. I would soon be buried, and suffocate – now, I knew only that I must find shelter.

I reeled up and staggered drunkenly, not knowing where I was going. I could only keep the wind at my back and hold my shirt over my face. The sand invaded everywhere, my eyes were soon raw, and the wind deafened my ears while my own blood roared in my head like a lion.

Which way was the camp? Surely, not even the Templars could make war in these conditions! I stumbled blindly, stopping my tongue before I could absurdly shout Edward's name. The sky was dark and all about the parched hills were veiled by a shroud of yellow-grey that stripped my lungs.

I was lost, I knew this in moments. It was scant consolation that the dust-devil would have stopped the battle. I saw no sense in shouting, for there was no one to hear, and the fierce wind ripped away every word. My breathing laboured like an old man's and I dizzied. My chest seemed full of sand and I was blind. I fell to my knees, gasping through the mesh of my fingers, and darkness lapped over my head.

As I starved for air, in the end I did call his name, though sense told me it was useless. I pitched onto my face, crawling along, fingers digging into the dry earth as the wind skinned my back and arms.

Then the darkness was total, and I welcomed it.

Voices spoke to me out of the void. I heard my father and old Ranulf. I heard the monks who had taught and tormented me... my boyhood lover, Grendel. And I heard Edward, who whispered into my ear what he had never said in reality. "I love you, have always and will always love you. You are mine. Come to me. Come to me."

I rolled over, in that delirious state thinking it was his voice, that he had found me, but I saw only blinding dust in the instant before I surrendered to merciful oblivion.

How long I lay there I can not say, but at last I stirred, coughed and retched. I came to my knees, sore and aching, and knuckled my eyes in vain attempts to scratch out the sand and restore proper vision. When I blinked about me, I saw clear air. The *djinn* was gone.

In its wake it left destruction, and such a storm could easily reshape the whole landscape. I had not expected to recognise my surroundings, and was not surprised to find strange slopes about me. Weak and ill, I struggled to my feet but the world spun like a top. I crumpled to my knees again, clutching at my aching head. Even my belly felt full of sand. My mouth was so raw, I might have been sucking a whetstone. I heard no wind now, only the cries of the kites and hawks that hunt over the dry hills, searching for vermin.

And then... what was that sound? Jingling? Bits of metal, cast together and rattling? A rhythmic thud-thud? Hooves? Horses?

My heart leaped and I fought for my senses. I shuffled about on my knees, still unable to rise, and peered into the east, where I saw only dim shapes at first, as my eyes were weak. Then I saw the great, blurred shapes of horses.

"Edward?" I blinked repeatedly, and tears washed my eyes, clearing them a little. "Sir Ivor?" I would even have called the name of Jean de Bicat!

Little by little my sight cleared, and I saw a lance, pointed at the very heart of me as I knelt there. Behind it, I saw the billowing white robes of a knight of Islam. And behind him, in the hands of his turban-headed standard bearer, was the black banner adorned with the single white crescent moon. The banner of the Jackal.

My heart turned to bricks in my chest, and my belly sank. I looked up into the swarthy face of the Saracen who brought his horse to a prancing halt not a yard from me, and the tip of the lance touched my breast through my tattered shirt.

PART THREE: A PRISONER

Chapter XIV

I have two stories to tell now, and I beg the reader's forbearance. One part of what follows is of necessity puzzled together from the testimony of others. While I was a captive Edward was free, and many miles separated us; but from his friends and other witnesses, I learned what he did, where he rode, and some little of what he felt.

First, I must tell my own story.

I knelt in the sand as the windstorm passed, and looked into the white-swathed face of the Saracen. I knew the banner in the hand of his standard-bearer, for how often had I heard Edward and Lionel speak of that device? These knights of Islam were from the tribe and clan of the Jackal.

The tip of the lance broke the skin of my breast with a stinging scratch that reminded me of my mortality. The magnificent Turkish warhorse halted, and my heart beat painfully as the man uncovered his face and peered curiously at me. I wondered if he spoke English, for I surely spoke none of his tongue, but he addressed his companion rather than me.

They spoke briefly while I studied the warrior's dark, bearded face, and while the lance held me docile on my knees, the standard bearer stabbed the blade of the great, black flag into the sand by his horse and swung down from the saddle.

I did not struggle. Even then, I knew that my choice was between being beaten into submission, or bowing to their wishes and keeping a whole skin and sound bones, the better to make a break for freedom. My hands were simply tied behind me and I was hoisted over the withers of the standard-bearer's horse.

Edward would believe me dead, and he would grieve. More than anything, I suffered for his pain of loss. The horse danced under me and my breath was pressed from my chest as the Saracen mounted, retrieved his flag and turned the animal back toward the column of their soldiers. Twice, I tried to lift my head to see where we were going; twice, I was cuffed hard enough to rattle my brains, and thereafter I kept my head down.

At last, when my belly was bruised and my head throbbing with this peculiar attitude, we entered a camp and I was dumped to the ground. I fell heavily but was not about to complain, for it was the first chance I had enjoyed to breathe freely in minutes.

Winded, I knelt and gasped while all about me milled restless, angry white-robed men. I heard the cries of the injured and dying, men who had fallen in the skirmish. Had Edward won? Had these Saracens been beaten off – was the Jackal himself dead, and if he was, had he fallen to Edward's sword?

These absurdities rushed through my head as I got back my breath, notions born out of fear. Stories were often told in England of Christian suffering at the hands of Muslims. Any captive could only live in dread. In the time of the First Crusade, just thirty years after William of Normandy seized England, such tales were recounted that Europe raised a rabble army that was vanquished entirely. They blundered into Turkey and were slaughtered by the thousand by the Seljuk Turk, Saracens and Kurdishmen who were harassing Constantinople.

My belly churned as I was caught by the shoulders and bundled out of the sun into a tent. At first it seemed very dim, and smelt of sandalwood and coffee. I was pushed to my knees once more, but when I lifted my head no one stopped me.

A man sat on the cushions before me, and at a glance I knew he was a warrior. There is something very definite about a fighting man. He has none of the softness, the paunch and pink hands of a languisher. I had bedded with a warrior for some time, and knew these things. I saw the steel in this man's face, the lean hardness of his body, the leather of his hands. He was handsome, early in his middle years, and I saw no cruelty in his face. He wore a soft, silken beard, and his eyes were deep, dark, beneath heavy brows. His head was wound in a blue and white turban about which was a gold chain, which I took for a badge of rank.

Behind him was that black banner. I looked at it, and at the man before me, and swallowed my heart. Was this the Jackal, or a colonel high in favour, perhaps a kinsman? He looked me over and spoke to a steward. I flinched as the servant came closer, and a sickle-bladed knife was held to my throat. I was certain my life was lost, but the knife, after threatening me to keep me docile, cut away my tattered clothes.

I fumed with a mixture of fear and righteous humiliation, both of which were absurd. To fear was pointless, since my life was in the lap of the gods, and as for humiliation, I was arrogant about my body. What nonsense it is to claim outrage when one's best features are displayed.

Mine surely were. Naked, I found myself held, turned this way and that, as a threesome of servants and two women, veiled in gorgeous peacock blue, came in to handle me. I kept my eyes down and was silent, though I wondered what was being said, laughed over, when the one I took for the Jackal spoke.

When I saw the whetted razor I recalled the pitiful gelded slaves I had seen in the market. I had always wondered where they came from, how they were made. I might have struggled then, but it was too late. Two brawny, grinning Nubians held me down on the deep, soft carpets and I was helpless.

Oil smeared slickly across my breast and belly, and one of the women, with a touch like a dove's wing, whisked the hair away, leaving me smooth as a child to the very groin. My legs were spread sinew-snapping wide and also shaved, before I was turned for my back to be done. I held my breath as the cheeks of my arse were parted, to be shaved there too.

Still seated on the cushions, vastly amused, The Jackal smiled and nodded. He had a deep, rich voice, not snake-like or unpleasant. His eyes glittered with unholy mischief, and I knew by their look, I was not to be killed. Perhaps I would be traded, exchanged for a Saracen prisoner? I could hope.

He clapped his hands, and a garment was fetched. The robe was the same peacock hue as the women wore, and so thin, so flimsy, I might still have been naked. A girdle tied it at my waist and I had the flimsiest slippers to wear, just enough to keep the sand from scorching the soles from my feet. How would I escape, clad this way? This state of near-undress was surer than iron manacles.

Already the camp was breaking. They had delayed only long enough to treat the wounded, and now they were eager to go. I had no work to do, but was never unobserved for an instant. To my astonishment I was not restrained in any way save one: I was clad just enough to keep my tender Saxon skin from burning in the heat, with only foolish shoes on my feet, no hope of a weapon, no flask of water.

All around the camp I saw only crags, barren hills and more parched hills, baking, stony and shimmering with mirage-lakes. If I made off in this state, I would collapse in five miles and be dead in five hours. Almost in tears with painful frustration, I bit back my fury and fear, and simply went where I was pushed.

I walked with the slaves and women behind the carts which carried the wounded. Women sang, muscular Nubians carried heavy loads and children were scolded, like children anywhere. I was ogled by men and women alike, to my indignation, though it was flattering. I bunched the flimsy robe at my belly for a morsel of privacy, too late realising how this stretched it over my behind.

Where were we walking? The sun set dead behind us, so we were marching eastward, away from the sea. We had put many a mile behind us by nightfall. At the head of the column were the warriors, then the wagons bearing the tents and wounded. Then, slaves, captives, women and children, and behind us, the freemen shepherds driving the sheep and goats, followed by a rearguard of a few soldiers to guard the lagging tail of the caravan.

Dust stung my throat and eyes, but it was no harder walking with these people, at the speed of the wagons and children, than trying to keep pace with Jean de Bicat. My grief was not physical that day, for I was no more hot and thirsty than any of the others. My skin, slick and hairless, felt peculiar, but even that was not unpleasant. I might have razored myself as a jest, to make Edward laugh or have him hot with unholy lust.

My grief was simply grief. I was apart from Edward for the first time in many months, and I knew he would believe me dead. Would he forget me, relegate the memory of me to the back of his mind, and soon it would be as if I had never been? I almost wished he could. I had no wish to be forgotten, but I did not wish him to suffer an agony of grief.

I wallowed in it and was morbid, but in the forefront of my mind was one thought. I would live, escape and find my way through the Saracen ranks. I would come upon King Richard's camp and announce myself as the prodigal. I would be feasted, and tell all I had seen of the enemy. The King would hang on every word, for I knew their secrets, where they camped, where they drew water, what trails they marched. Later, Edward would bed me with a wildness and fervour that told me vividly how he had mourned me.

All this soothed me as we marched, and I was astonished to realise it was twilight. We made camp only briefly, to eat, and then walked on in the cool of the evening. The stars and moon were very bright, the sky indigo, like writing ink, and the parched land grew cool and pleasant. It was far better walking by night than in the furnace heat of day.

In my flimsy shift I was soon chilled and my hairless skin prickled with gooseflesh. I rubbed my arms, hugged myself as the others cloaked themselves, and there was laughter. I was allowed a cape that covered me to the waist, but below it my haunches were cold. This was the means by which I was kept from any attempt at escape. It was this or bind me, and I will say that I never cared for being bound.

At last, when I had begun to think we would walk till dawn, a shout from the head of the column stopped us all. In a trice fires were lit, tents were hoisted and water brought up from the well we had just come upon. The horses were fed and watered before any of us while two of the men went into the darkness to butcher a goat. Soon the meat was hissing and spitting over a hearth. Women called their children to their skirts; bread began to bake and coffee brewed while the soldiers' slaves cleaned their master's armour and sharpened swords.

I sat warily by a fire with the Nubians and wondered for the thousandth time what was to become of me. No one approached me with work to perform. Perhaps they assumed I would be useless, and they were probably correct. I was not to be trusted with a knife or a nag, nor to safeguard the precious children, and when it came to cooking, I would have created havoc.

Not much before midnight, fatigue and tiredness captured me

and despite my belly's growls of hunger and my healthy fears for my safety, I curled up on the rug beside the huge Nubian, whose name was Nadim, and closed my eyes. I slept soundly until a vast, hard hand on my arm woke me, and I found a cup of strong coffee and a piece of meat thrust on me.

Goat meat has a peculiar flavour, even when it is spiced heavily with garlic, but I chewed and gulped, so hungry I barely tasted it. The coffee was strong, bitter and black, but it was hot and eased the knot of tensions in my middle. I woke fully, as if I had enjoyed a whole night's sleep, and looked across the camp toward the great tent where the chieftain of this clan bedded.

It was half an hour before a steward fetched me. He was a tall, rawboned man, but I could not see his face for the windings about his head. One hand half-drew the jewelled sword from his scabbard, and he pointed me toward the fine tent. I saw only pain before me if I refused. I peered into the dark face of the Nubian beside whom I had walked so many miles, and Nadim's amused look made me swallow.

Tapestries swung into place behind me as I entered the tent, and at first it seemed I was alone with the Jackal. But one 'wall' was not a wall at all, but a screen of some gauzy stuff, not quite transparent. We enjoyed the illusion of privacy, but beyond that diaphanous screen were two brawny guards, and I saw the glimmer of gold candlelight on the blades of their magnificent, curved Islamic swords.

Scented oils burned in polished brass lamps, filling the air with perfumes I could not name, and which swiftly dizzied me. Shadows flickered and writhed like live beasts on the sides of the tent, which were thick enough to keep out the chill, heavy with tapestries and rugs as thick as a man's finger. The carpets were rich and deep under my slippered feet. Before me, the Jackal himself reclined on a couch, in a state of comfortable semi-undress.

No man could have been less like Edward. Where Edward was as golden as sunlight, my host was raven dark. Where Edward was slender, this man was like a wrestler, and where Edward shaved his face like a boy, the Jackal wore a thick black beard. Yet he was hand-some in that swarthy, exotic way of the Saracen.

His robes were red and gold, hardly closed about his slim mid-dle, while his legs and feet were bare. He was sucking on a hookah, and I smelt a faint whiff of hashish. The guardsman who had brought me stood behind me while the Jackal looked me up and down, and at a nod from his master my cape and shift were taken.

Naked and as smooth as a child from head to toe, I stood with my eyes down and my head bent. My belly trembled, and I gritted my teeth. If I fought – much less if I injured him, or attempted to – I might die, and what would become of my grand plans for escape?

The soldier stepped out and took with him the only garments I had, insubstantial as they were. My captor set aside his hookah and held out his hand. At that moment it was an invitation. If I hesitated it would become a command. The luxury of request would become the bark of an order, and in a trice intimacy would become violence.

I went to him and summoned Edward to mind while I knelt at his feet. He bared himself for me to put my mouth on him and suck him up to lance-hardness. He was big and thick, his rod like iron against my lips. In a moment, he knew I was experienced, and likely thought me a man's catamite. I had no slightest chance of claiming innocence.

I sucked diligently, and he tasted clean. Like all Muslims he bathed often, it is part of their faith – a part I was grateful for. His skin had been delicately perfumed. He smelt of violets, which was strange on a male, but pleasant. I nuzzled his breast, which was as smooth as my own, and very gently I teethed his paps, which made him chuckle.

All this time my eyes stung, for I believed I was betraying Edward. I recalled the dream in which he imagined I had been with another man. There had never been truth in it, until now, but I was not foolish enough to struggle. If the Jackal believed me a catamite, I saw the security in the misconception.

When he turned me over his couch, spread and entered me sharply, I breathed deep, upturned my arse and let him have it. He used me with vigour but he was not brutal. He was no more energetic than many a man, excited with his wife. He was thick and long, but no more virile than Edward.

My conscience would have been easier if I could have taken refuge in pain, but I was oily after being shaved, I was accustomed to a well-endowed man, and the Jackal hardly hurt me at all. He pumped for long minutes and touched that nub inside that can make a man come alight in a bare half second. I ignited, and though my face twisted in shame, my cock got up and my balls churned.

He spent with a deep, hard thrust and a jerk against my tender innards. He pulled out then, reclined and sucked his hookah as he handed to me a scarlet kerchief. With this I was to mop his groin. This service performed, I was about to draw away, but he had seen my erection and caught me by the wrists. Both my hands were set on my belly, and he lay back to watch.

My cheeks heated. How fine a sight it is to watch a comely boy love himself! I closed my eyes and did as he wanted. I was tense and hot and, denied, I would have suffered. My seed damped his carpets, and while I was still gasping he handed me the kerchief. On hands and knees I cleaned up my mess, and heated again as I felt the strange caress of his bare foot on my behind. His toe probed the moist heart of me, and I writhed away.

He stood, touched my hair and took back the kerchief. I sat at his feet, quivering, wondering what else could befall me, but he had closed his robe and at a clap of his hands the guardsman reappeared. My shift and cape were set about me and I was shepherded out, back to the fire where I would sleep with the Nubians. Nadim snorted with laughter as he saw me, and I was grateful for the darkness that covered the heat of my face.

Yet it was comradely teasing. After the moon set, many slaves paired off. There was humping and sighing, and everywhere the scents of fucking under the trees that grew around the well. Nadim had a lover, a big, ugly man who, despite his grim face, had the kindest ways I have ever known.

When I ate bread and figs and drank milk at dawn, Nadim sat with his arm about me and sang a tribal song, perhaps from the land of his boyhood, when he was as free as I had been just a day before.

*　*　*

This was the pattern of my bondage. I counted fifteen sunrises and sunsets while we walked eastward, resting only from late morning to mid-afternoon, when we would shelter from the ravages of the sun. With evening camp was made, food eaten, and I waited for the soldier to fetch me. The Jackal would open his robe and I would suck him hard. If he came in my throat I would suck him hard again and kneel on his couch to be plundered. It was no more than that, and less strenuous than many a wife is said to endure. I could not beg for pity.

Six times on the road I was shaven, when he felt the prickle of hair returning to my breast or behind, and I was razored with as much care as the first time, while my captor watched, chuckled, and pointed out this and that area that had been overlooked. My skin was more supple than it had ever been, and below my belly I was like a little boy.

I worried at first that I must entertain other men too, but a bark from the solder who took me nightly to that fine tent was enough to warn off the others, and I was grateful. When he was done with me each night I was taken away, and in six days my fellows' teasing stopped when I had a small gift.

That gift was worse than a whipping, for it made me feel like a traitor, as if I had betrayed Edward in every way I could. It was an ivory bracelet, engraved in the strange, beautiful Arabesque design. It was slipped onto my right wrist by the soldier, and I wept as I took it. The soldier's name was Mansoor, and he was his master's trusted servant, not a slave but a freeman, high-born in his own right. He was much taller and heavier than I would ever be. He tipped up my face, saw my tears, and frowned in puzzlement. I flayed myself alive.

Worthless harlot! Vile serpent of a witch-arsed boy-whore! Wicked scorpion of an unprincipled sodomite! Cock-defiled trollop of corrupt honour! Strumpet of blackened heart and irredeemable grace! I railed at myself – I do not recall the worst of the names I heaped upon myself as I kicked along in the hot, stinging dust that day.

Come sunset, eyes red-rimmed with sky-glare, dust and bitter tears, I shuffled into the tent once more and stood naked before him, newly shaven, adorned in my bangle, the image of misery and ingratitude. Worthless youth, indeed. I could have been in shackles, emasculated and sold in Dimashq – Damascus. I had no cause to antagonise my new lord, who had spared my back the rod, spared my skin the sun, and had treated my arse with gentleness if not actual affection.

He opened his robe as always. I knelt and put my mouth on the cock which would soon be in me, but grief choked me and I could barely do my work. I expected the sting of the whip, and would have welcomed it. I could have wallowed in misery and told myself, *You have defied him, you have not betrayed Edward!*

Hands cupped my face and he slid out of my mouth. The man whose name has been likened to Satan lifted me onto the couch and called through the screen in his strange language. I curled on my side, expecting to be punished within an inch of my hide, but the screen lifted and an elderly man stepped into the bedchamber.

He was paunched, grey-bearded, he had the look of a scholar or pedagogue. His hands were folded into the sleeves of a grey and pink robe, and he looked into my face, saw my fright. To my astonishment he addressed me in a strange mix of English, Latin and French.

"Boy, what affrights thee? Thou hast been cosseted, stroked, never struck, and made a gift. Art thou ailing?"

My mind whirled. I was as much a prisoner as if I was bound hand and foot – is there any surer cage than a hundred leagues of the most hellish desert in the world, that not even the nomad travels easily? Wisely, I got down on my knees and kissed the hem of the old man's robe. I knew the customs of these people by now. I had taken pains to observe them.

"My lord, what is to become of me?" I whispered. I felt a hand on my flank as I kissed the hem of his robe once more, and since the elderly gentleman had not stooped, it was my master's possessive touch. I shivered. "Sire, I have been treated well, but where are we marching? The march must end soon! When it does, what is for me? I am afraid." Every word was true.

"Afeard of what, boy?" The old man asked, puzzled.

"That the Jackal will geld and market me," I whispered. I did not have to feign the wobble in my voice. Every terror I had kept hidden rushed at once to the surface like a stream breaking its banks. "Is this where I am bound?"

"I know not," the pedagogue said. "When we reach Dehjur I shall speak out against the abomination of castration, but I can give thee no guarantee. It may be that Masjed ibn-Zahran, 'the Jackal,' is needy of funds. The marketing of handsome, white-skinned Christian boys is a profitable enterprise."

I shivered and looked up at the man who had entered my body so many times already. "Sire, is this your will? Forgive me, but I am afraid."

He looked at me, puzzled, and spoke to the scholar, who answered, making my master's brows arch before he gave a gust of laughter. The pedagogue echoed the humour.

"This is not the Jackal! He fights beneath the black banner, but ibn-Zahran is safe in Dehjur, with Salah ad-Din himself, since a month past."

Again my mind reeled. I had sense enough to remain on my knees but looked up at the teacher. "Then, who is my lord? All this time, I have thought... "

"He is Jahrom Rafha ibn-Qasim, a young half-brother of The Jackal, and a Captain of the Knights of Islam." The old man smiled, greatly amused by my naivety. "He is a lover of boys, as is known to thee! It is in his heart that he will purchase thee for himself."

"And leave me whole?" I begged.

The teacher said a few words to Jahrom Rafha, and with that, withdrew. The screen moved back into place, granting us the illusion of privacy. The Captain stooped, lifted me by the arms and put me back on the couch. He spoke to me, and while his words meant nothing, through the screen came the voice of my interpreter as Jahrom Rafha traced the shape and felt the weight of my balls. "Castration is an abomination," he said. "No lover of boys does this. One loves boys for their own sake. If one desires a girl, there are girls without number."

"But you shaved me," I murmured as he sat beside me and opened his robe once more.

"Men of this tribe shave their bodies. We have no fondness for bears."

The only hair on his body was about his heavy genitals. The rest of him was smooth. Barbered. I closed my eyes and took him back in my mouth. Forgive me, Edward, I prayed, but if I am to live, I must look to survival! I prayed this over and over as I gave him every pleasure I knew. I was wild, desperate, as I tried to repair the damage I had already done. At last I straddled him on the couch and rode him until he burst in me.

Exhausted, I slid onto the carpets and with my eyes closed went on, using my hands. He enjoyed the dessert for his eyes almost as much as the meat of the main course. As I began to come his hand covered my own, and I spent within his fist. He was not smiling, but frowning at me.

"Thou wert a catamite when brought here. Thy body was long deflowered."

"I had a lover," I confessed.

"One true lover?" The Captain's large, leathery hand remained clasped about mine, and my dwindled cock.

"Aye, Sire, I loved him dearly." Tears stung my eyes.

"A knight?" He released me, gave me the kerchief to clean us both.

"A knight," I agreed. "But all that is past. I have left that life behind."

"So thou hast," he agreed almost sadly, and I forgot that it was the scholar, speaking through the screen. Jahrom Rafha touched my face. He said no more, but when I had cleaned him he kissed my lips for the first time and I shivered at the bristle of the full beard on my face. Then he clapped his hands for the soldier to return me to the Nubians with whom I felt a certain kinship. We were all slaves.

Where was Dehjur? I racked my memory but was sure I had not seen it on any map. Perhaps it was an oasis, merely a desert camp. Even if Edward searched for me, how could he find it? I was lost. My hopes and dreams ebbed like summer rain. I lay awake, watching the fire, and I was still awake in the small hours of the morning when the camp stirred and voices shouted urgently. I sat up, clutching the thin shift about me in the chill, and saw at once what the shouting was about. My heart skipped.

There, over the palms, crackling and licking, was a mass of blue-white lightning. The wind stirred, dust whirled into the air, wolves howled out of it, and my pulse hammered.

In the Christian ranks they swore it was a Saracen magic, but I saw now, it was no trick worked by these people. The storm was as strange and evil to Jahrom Rafha as to the Crusader knights.

Prayers were wailed while people hid their faces and men drew their swords. Several soldiers mounted frightened horses and rode out toward the whirling dust-storm, though ibn-Qasim tried to call them back.

Then, as suddenly as the furore began, it was over. I sat shivering by the fire, feeling very young, very naked and vulnerable. I was still a boy, despite the fact I had sprouted hair on my chest and was growing fast. A flick with the razor, and the hair was gone, and I would never be as tall or muscular as the men of this tribe.

Slaves and freemen alike clung to the hearths, spoke in whispers, prayed and studied the sky. We were all afraid, and these Knights of Islam were as impotent as I was.

* * *

We marched faster with the morning. I helped to load the wagons – I had begun working alongside them – and when we were ready to march I ran up along the serpentine caravan, looking for the teacher. He was the only man who spoke a language I could understand.

I knelt at his feet before he mounted his horse, and he bade me

130

rise. "My lord, what happened last night? What was that storm?"

"Christian devilry," he told me tartly. "Their priest-magicians make that poisoned magic to prove the power of Christ. Get up out of the dust. Thy robe will be in tatters."

I clambered to my feet. "Respectfully, teacher, in the Christian camp, where I spent considerable time, they are afraid. They say the storms are sent by Saracens, who have invited Satan into the world."

His brows arched and he pulled at his beard. "True?"

"This, they told me." I glanced at the head of the column and saw ibn-Qasim conferring with his officers in the shade of the great black battle flag. I ached for a glimpse of Edward.

The old man said no more to me, and as the column moved off I dropped back to walk with the women and slaves. But that night Jahrom Rafha was waiting with questions before he wanted my mouth or body.

He pressed a cup of fermented date wine into my hand, and I sat at his feet, resplendent in my bangle. He put his feet in my lap, and I massaged them as we spoke, which is a great pleasure among his people. Again, the voice of the teacher came through the screen but I was intent on my lord's feet and easily forgot the interpreter.

Edward was on my mind every moment, and when I was with ibn-Qasim, even more. The nearness of a man's body, the promise of pleasure, made me want Edward so keenly it hurt like a wound. Jahrom Rafha yanked my hair to arouse my attention, and I kissed his foot contritely.

"In the Christian camp, they say the windstorms are Saracen wizardry?"

"Satan, Sire, answering your call. They are very afraid."

"Wisely," he said. "Who shall not fear the devil risen at the behest of men! But the Saracen has no such power. If we had, dost thou imagine we would not have scoured the Infidel from Palestine?"

I nodded thoughtfully. The thought had occurred to me.

He touched my hair. "If thou shalt enter my house, thou must accept the true Faith."

"Become a Mussulman?" My eyes widened. I searched inside myself for a spark of rebellion, but was too numb to respond. All I cared for was surviving. "As you wish, Sire, so shall it be."

"Then shalt thou be accepted in the Mosque in Dimashq," he mused. "There will be no talk of market! Mind," he added as I rubbed his feet, "thou shalt be circumcised. Become like me." He opened his robe and I transferred my attention from his feet to his cock. "The deed affrights thee?"

"It does," I muffled against his musky skin. "It will hurt, I imagine. But it is beautiful afterwards. I know this now. I had never seen the cock of a Muslim before you sent for me."

He laughed, and so did the old man, who translated every word.

131

"Thou shalt see Dehjur tomorrow. I shall confer with my brother and mayhap with my lord Salah ad-Din. I shall see to thy education, rites and initiation as soon as may be, but first... " he sighed. "First, there is *Ibrahim.*"

He spoke the name with a shudder. I looked up, holding his long, thick lance between my fingers and stroking while I took away my mouth. "Who is Ibrahim? Should I fear him?"

"Hide upon hearing his name, run if he approaches," Jahrom Rafha advised. His mouth compressed, as if the mention of Ibrahim made him angry. Or frightened.

This also shivered me. I had never imagined ibn-Qasim afraid of anything. He gave me an unreadable look, and then caught my head and firmly pushed it back down. I was safest doing my few duties well, and I set about my task at once. But my mind was free to wander while my body was besieged, and where my thoughts wandered, Jahrom Rafha need never know.

The name of Ibrahim haunted me. My skin prickled with the shivers of healthy but unreasoning dread, and I turned more and more to Edward. It was two weeks since I had seen him, and I was pining like a lost lamb, though I had nothing to complain of and much to be grateful for. I was a catamite, but it was a small price to pay for comforts and survival.

In the Templars' camp, not a day went by without the crack of the whip, the abject cries of a man shown the cruel end of the birch. In this camp, in a week no one had been flogged, love was made nightly after prayers, and praises were sung to God with stirring devotion. These Saracens were devout.

I was silent and dutiful, quiet and polite. As we neared Dehjur, Jahrom Rafha spoke often of my covenant with 'the truth Faith,' but in my mind this was hazy as sea mist, on the distant fringes of my dreams, while my every thought was with Edward.

* * *

And so, begging forbearance, I shall tell part of Edward's story, as I have pieced it together from his own words and the testimony of friends.

Chapter XV

The fighting left more than a dozen knights and soldiers dead and several more grievously injured. Three members of the company were deemed 'missing,' and Paulo Delgado was one of those. Of the missing servants and squires nothing was known, and the Templars refused to send men to search. They feared, rightly, that the Saracens would double back and fall on them again.

It had been a rout. Edward's force was assaulted from the fore and flanks, and cut to bloody tatters. Late in the battle, Jean de Bicat was wounded in the arm and shoulder, and thereater he remained in a constant state of grace after a hasty confession. As the day's heat began his wounds were expected to fester, and he might die before the ragged, ailing party could return to the safety of the camp.

Edward was scratched and nicked, not badly hurt, yet I know he suffered more than his fellows as the Templars broke camp and swung their tired horses about for the flight back to Jerusalem. While the others rested he took a single squire who was game to accompany him, and walked into the hills where the *djinn* had sprung from no-where. Over and over, he called the name of Paul, but heard no an-swer, and at last Brother Francis sent a page to fetch him back.

The rag-tag column turned for home, and the sun punished them as much on the return as on the ride out. Since de Bicat was tied to his horse, his brains foolish with fevers and pain, Edward found himself in command. It was he who must face the Lionheart, give account of what had happened and accept King Richard's wrath.

They were seen by scouts, half a day's ride out, and by the time they arrived at the sprawling camp King Richard was well aware they had been assaulted, hurt, sent home like whipped curs. It was said his roars of fury cut across the camp like the blare of the lur, but his ministers counselled sense and patience, since fine knights, Normans, even Templars – and Jean de Bicat himself – had paid a high price for misfortune.

Sir Lionel de Quilberon was waiting as they toiled up the long, rocky incline toward the pavilions. His eyes searched for this and that face, and he noticed the absence of the lost squires at once.

He approached his old friend with a grim expression. "Edward, are you well? What became of Paul?"

Edward swallowed on his dust-dry throat and took a goblet of water as he watched the stewards carry de Bicat into the care of the surgeon monks. "He vanished into the sands, there was no sign of him. I cannot say he is dead, for I saw no body."

"That is bad," Lionel sighed. "If he lived... you know what be-comes of boys his age, lost in Saracen lands."

"Well do I know!" Edward snapped. "The thought haunted me every cursed mile of the way back! I would raise a band to search, but... "

"But it is too late already," Lionel finished, "and how would you explain these frantic passions to the King? If Paul were your son, the heir to Aethelstan, he might have listened."

"My son?" Edward's eyes were grey as a stormy sea. "He is my lover, Lionel. Or, was." They were alone, no one could hear.

Lionel's face was as swarthy as the Arab and the Jew. "There's nothing new under the sun, Edward. You're not the first and you'll not be the last to fall in love with a comely boy. It is a shame, I grant, a crying shame, but for the love of God, be silent. Pray for him, if you can recall how to pray, but say nothing in the hearing of others. 'Tis one thing to confess to me your lust for the lad – "

"My love," Edward whispered. "Lust, is it, base lust, like a dog on heat, no more than the hunger of flesh for flesh, a beast that rises up in me and makes me want his arse?" He shook his head slowly. "Once, I thought it was. I was wild with wanting him at first, so wild I hardly dared touch him, afraid I would injure, with my too-eager hands and the dreadful things I longed to do to him."

"Dreadful things?" Lionel cocked his head at Edward. The monks who had carried away de Bicat shouted for their confessor. "Listen. Brother Bicat may be dying."

"Devil take him," Edward spat viciously.

"You've no love of Templars." Lionel caught Edward's arm. "You must see the King, and soon. He is anxious for your report and any scrap of knowledge you gleaned about his enemies. Best come and wash. You're the colour of the road, and you smell like a nag! Come with me, I've fresh fresh linen and scents."

Edward's name was already being shouted as he followed Lionel to the pavilion where the banners of England, Normandy and de Quilberon fluttered. Henri scampered up, wide-eyed, and when he heard the news that Paul was lost his face crumpled. Lionel caught him, picked him up in one brawny arm and blotted the boy's eyes with his cuff.

"You were his good friend, I know," he said bluffly, in that rough-gentle way of his. "Aye, this is bad, Henri, but there's nothing to be done about it. Now, tell that bellowing steward that Sir Edward is washing half the dust of Palestine from him, and will be fit for an audience soon."

In fact Edward was standing like a statue, half bare and stupefied, looking at his drawn, haggard face in the mirror. He should wash, he should scrape the blond stubble from his cheeks. But he could no longer move, as if the mirror laid bare his soul. Lionel closed the tent, and deliberately laced it shut. It was he who stropped a razor, filled a basin, stripped Edward to the skin and pushed him into a chair. Edward was numb. On the road he had moved like a thing of cogs and chains and wheels, an engine, no part of him thinking properly, no space in his mind for any conscious thought save one. I was lost.

"Edward, collect yourself," Lionel begged urgently. "The King will not wait for ever!" He took his friend's face between his hands. "Edward!"

"I never told him, not once." Edward's voice was hoarse, as if he had shouted over a battlefield half the day and his throat was sore. "Not once could I find the words, the courage, to say it aloud."

"To say what?" Lionel soaked a cloth and began to swab the dust, grime and crusting of rank old sweat from him.

"To tell him I loved him," Edward murmured.

Lionel sighed. "It's often not seemly for a man to say that, even if he feels it. One thing to admit the truth to a woman, but when his desire is for a boy – "

"Where is the difference?" Edward snapped back to reality with a start. He took the cloth from Lionel and began to scrub himself hard with it, brutally, as if trying to take off his skin or scour away a weight of wrong he had done. "Love is love! The deed is almost the same, and in the dark who can tell the difference between a black cat and a grey?"

"Say that to a gentle priest, and be ready to flee for your life," Lionel warned. "No night is dark enough to blind the eyes of God."

"Where was God when the Saracens assaulted us? On whose side did He smile? Why does He tell us to wrest Jerusalem from the Saracen, then abandon us? Where was God when Paul wandered out to watch the fight, and the storm came up? It howled like a Fury, like a great beast in the sky. It was the end of the battle -- none of us could stand, let alone fight. By the time it cleared the Saracens had drawn back beyond the ridge. Brother Francis and I made the decision to let them go. *Let* them go? They had punished us badly. No matter how we snapped at them, they thrust steel into us. The windstorm blew up in the last nick of time, else we should all have been killed. I was for sense, and pulling the men out of the fray sooner, but de Bicat would have none of that."

"And he shall pay a dear price for the foolishness," Lionel added. "He looked nearer dead than alive when I saw him last, his skin all grey and his head lolling."

Edward only grunted as he washed his belly and plunged his arms to the elbows into the water. "And all for what? So the Saracen shall be driven out of Jerusalem again! This is the Third Crusade. We have driven them out of the Holy City before – it was said, Christian knights rode in blood, their horses were fetlock-deep in it, when Jerusalem was liberated ninety years ago. Not a Saracen was spared that time. How much more blood does God thirst for?"

He sank into the chair, the stropped razor in his hands, but made no move to shave. Lionel took the blade, perhaps fearful that he might cut his throat rather than his beard. Edward sat back, sweated, running with water, and closed his eyes as he was swiftly shaved.

Voices called and Lionel answered with a sharp bark: "Tell His Grace, Sir Edward will attend upon him momentarily!"

As yet Edward was naked, wearing just the gaunt face of unconcealed grief. Lionel's big hands moulded to his shoulders, and felt only bone. Edward had lost flesh on the road. "You must command yourself. Richard is waiting upon you impatiently, and that bellicose bumpkin of a steward is right. He'll not wait much longer before patience expires."

"I know." Edward dragged his hands through his hair. "It is a mindlessness that affects me, Lionel, often at night, when I miss him most."

"When you would do dreadful things to him?" Lionel threw clean hose and linen at Edward, and sprawled on his bed to watch him dress with clumsiness that betrayed fatigue, sleepless nights and grief.

"Dreadful things?" Edward produced a faint wraith of a smile. "He taught me otherwise. The touch of a man's hands can be gentle, a man's mouth is as warm and sweet as a girl's. His body as yielding in welcome. Buggery is the strangest of acts, Lionel. A man stretches out to the finest feelings he can aspire to, filled with love... yet he plunges the lance of himself into the organ of direst corruption."

"The same could be said of women," Lionel snorted. "They are vile, bloody creatures, on a regular basis, some female strangeness that has to do with the phases of the moon." Edward recoiled, and Lionel laughed. "You know little of women!"

"I shall accept your word, and castigate men less." Edward was dressed now, having borrowed a robe of royal blue, and was combing his hair. "Corruption, I said... yet, where can a speck of corruption be found in the body of sweet youth?" He sighed. "I understand none of it. I know only that I love him, and never found courage to say it. I came to crave him, and could not sleep without him. I would use him with what tenderness I could manage in my excitement, and afterwards I held him as if he were my own. Know you not, Lionel, what plagues me? He never knew! He never knew what I felt for him, only that I used him!"

"He *was* your own," Lionel said awkwardly. "I think he knew more than you give him credit for. Now, enough of this. Show the King a brave face, for an hour at least."

"A brave face?" Edward mocked himself. "My face is gaunt. The visage of a dead man looks out of the mirror with live eyes."

Lionel tilted his head at his old friend and sighed once more. "True, Richard will see the scars of pain about you. But good men died in that encounter, and their lives were lost for nothing, since you took no prisoners. He wanted prisoners more than anything, for their knowledge of the Saracen's routes through the desert, his devilry."

"He wants Saracens to torture?" Edward was grim. "I'll not fetch young bodies for the rack and the iron. Let some righteous bastard like de Bicat do filthy work like that."

"Aye, but don't let the King hear you say so," Lionel counselled. "Remind yourself, you are a Saxon, and low in favour because of that winsome yellow hair. Beg leave of the King, quote a sickness, if you like. You surely look sickened. There have been fevers here, a boiling of the guts and brains which afflicted many of us in your absence. If you tell the King you are laid low with the ague, they will leave you well alone for days, or weeks."

"And what of you?"

The burly Lionel shrugged his massive shoulders. "I must command the next company that goes to hunt. You know that."

"You ride by the same trails we took?"

"So I believe. We ride on Richard's order, and what he orders today is built on the confessions tortured out of prisoners captured in the weeks before we arrived."

"I go with you," Edward murmured.

Lionel puffed out his fleshy, stubbled cheeks. "This is madness! I know what is in your mind. You think to ride the same road and search for the boy."

"And what of it?" Edward demanded. "There is more honour, and more sleep, in that course than sitting here, pretending to be overcome by sickness!"

With that he strode out and left Lionel shaking his head in profound exasperation. Lionel knew Edward better than any man, and knew he would be immovable. Still, he followed his friend and was with Edward when he entered the King's pavilion.

The air was stifling. On the tables maps of Palestine and beyond were set out, and Richard was playing with chess pieces which simulated the armies and wandering tribes of Saracen and Turk. As Edward appeared and his name was called from the entrance, Richard paused and looked over his shoulder. Edward knelt, and when the King gave him leave to rise, he approached and accepted wine.

The Lionheart sat in his carved chair and studied Edward over the rim of a cup. He could see with half an eye the suffering in Edward's face. Masses were being said for the soul of Jean de Bicat, and the surgeons swore that the only saving of his life was the swift amputation of his arm. His wounds had rotted in the heat. Before Richard was a Saxon who, Brother Francis declared, had fought like a Norman and brought home his surviving men safely. There was no disgrace in Edward's efforts.

"You saw their banners and engaged them," Richard prompted. "On the map, show us where."

Edward leaned over the table and set an ebony chess knight on the site of the battle. "The sky darkened, the wind blew up a storm from this direction. It is said in the markets, Sire, the prevailing wind at this time of year is wont to raise the sand this way, it often happens."

"Word is, also in the market," Richard added, "the Sultan of Egypt, Saladin, is near Jerusalem. You have heard this?"

But Edward shook his head. "I have not, Sire. Be cautious that it is not a ruse to fool us."

"Wise," Richard agreed. "Still, the men who told us this were tortured one by one, and each gave a like testimony without prompting from another."

Did he see Edward's eyes close? Did he see him sway by the table? Lionel took a step forward as if he feared Edward might fall, and was ready to catch him.

"Aethelstan is unwell," Richard remarked.

"The ague, Sire," Lionel said quickly.

"No," Edward argued. "The heat, the road, and watching the suffering of others, knights who are my brothers in faith and loyalty, if not blood." The lie was sound.

The King sighed, leaned over and put a heavy, ringed hand on Edward's thin shoulder. "You have honoured Aethelstan. You fetched back the better part of your company, while Brother Francis told us he feared no one would return at all."

"Sire." Edward bowed his head. "Sir Lionel de Quilberon is to take the next company."

"So he is." Richard returned to his wine.

"I beg leave, Sire, to ride with him."

"For what purpose?" Richard looked down that long nose at him, and at Lionel.

It was left to Lionel to speak when Edward seemed overcome. "Your Grace, his squire was lost. Edward wishes to search for him."

A frown knitted Richard's brow. "What mean you – he was killed? Unhorsed?"

"Separated from us by the storm," Lionel corrected. "Edward fears that he may be a prisoner."

Richard gestured with his cup. "If that is true, Aethelstan, best get another squire, for the boy will be ball-less, buggered, and at market by now. You know the price a handsome Christian boy fetches."

"I know," Edward said quietly. "I would at least try to search, Sire. What harm can it do if I accompany Sir Lionel? I'll rest easier upon my return, knowing I did all I could. I promised his kin I would safeguard him."

"You are uncommon loyal," Richard observed, "which is commendable in a man. All right, Aethelstan, do so. You took no prisoners, this time. Why?"

So began the lengthy questioning. How many knights did he observe in the fight? How many Saracens were killed, how many escaped uninjured? How many horses? Did he see the camp? Where went the road, after the battleground? Many and tiresome were the questions. Edward answered as accurately as he could, for over an hour in the stifling heat.

At last, dismissed, he allowed Lionel to shepherd him back to the tent, send for ale and a meal, and stretched out on a soft bed for the first time in weeks. Lionel watched his laboured breaths, and for a time suspected that Edward was indeed becoming ill.

There is no cure for grief but weeping or action. In Edward's mind the time for tears had not yet come. Time to weep, he said, when he had searched and found nothing. Then he would rail at God and let loose his sorrow. But for the present he would *move!*

He called for a boy to squire him when Lionel's company rode out. They were to march two days later, and Edward spent most of that time asleep. He woke to eat and bathe, then slept again like a dead man. Sleep was the salve his wounds needed, for they were wounds of the soul. And sleep freed him to wander in dreams.

Such dreams they were – the kind Paul had once suffered. One returned over and over to Edward, at first shocking him, and later pleasuring him past sanity. He lay on his bed before a fire while snow whispered at the shutter and the wind howled about the walls of Aethelstan Manor. A click at the door, and he looked up at his visitor. Tall, robed in dark velvet, he came into the room, stood by the bed and kissed Edward's face. Not a word was said, though kisses became caresses, and soon they were bare. Lust overcame honour, pride and fear. The Saxon knight was on his belly in the soft cushions, the cheeks of his arse were spread, he was slicked with fragrant oils and pierced by a shaft as blunt and thick as a cudgel that fetched pains, and then inspired pleasure he could never have imagined.

He woke with a cry, startled and afraid. When his heart slowed and the rush of cold sweat had dried, his belly churned with a mixture of fear and longing. He had never anticipated that he could desire to be plundered like a maid, by a boy younger than himself, rankless and but half Saxon! Yet, where does rank have any place in love? And Edward was in love.

Time and again through the merciless nights while he waited for Lionel's company to leave, he threshed in remorse. Was Paul a fey, able to hear his thoughts? But Edward was silent even with Lionel, who could plainly see the nightmare his old friend was caught up in.

At last the company was at liberty to go. Dawn lay in the east and Richard Lionheart appeared, robed in red and gold, to farewell them. Lionel called his men to order. Reins were gathered, mastiffs bayed, harness jingled.

Edward did not look back into the hard, hawkish face of the King, but turned his eyes to the east, where the storm had swallowed his squire.

Chapter XVI

The scholar who translated for Jahrom Rafha and myself was a teacher named Haroun Bedi. I learned that he was a fair man, and he showed me many a small kindness, for which I was grateful. I was not craven, but when the Saracens prayed I was quiet, when they looked at me I lowered my eyes, and when I was called to duty I was respectful.

One curious thing did Haroun Bedi tell me. To espouse their Faith, I must embrace only one great Truth, and I wondered how many of the Christians who were at war with the Saracen and Turk knew this. It is the heart of the Islamic warrior. Their armies swept like a storm over the Orient, and when they captured a town, when its sovereign surrendered, only one thing was required of the conquered people before they would be embraced as brothers and sisters, and invited into the empire of Islam. This, Haroun told me, was the reason the Knights of Islam conquered with such ease. Not because they are better warriors, though often I think they may be, but because the peoples of conquered lands were easily wooed.

Did I have faith? Haroun asked, and ibn-Qasim waited for my reply. I kept my eyes down and said, "All my life, priests have done such evil before my eyes, and lovers of men like myself have been burnt as witches... I have never had much faith, Sire. How could I?" The two looked at each other over my head, and then I learned this great Truth.

I must stand up in a company of men and say, loudly and clearly, in a language they could all understand, "There is but one God, and Allah is His Name." With this said, I would be the brother of every Muslim. Would I renounce Christ with those words? This troubled me. I had read of saints who had been roasted alive before they would renounce. Would these Saracens roast me? Might I renounce with my lips, and keep my heart in abeyance? If Allah is but a *name* for God, might I speak this foreign name, and no blasphemy done? This was my puzzle as we approached the place called Dahjur.

It was an oasis with white-walled houses, a fortress wall, date palms nodding in a hot, dry southerly wind from Africa, and outside the wall clustered a host of tents, strings of camels and mules, and more gaudy banners than I could count.

I saw the crests of great houses and celebrated knights. Most were unknown to me, but to my astonishment I recognised one, and was so speechless, Haroun Bedi cuffed my head. I pointed out the banner I knew. "See there, my lord, that flag. I was once a guest of that chieftain."

"A guest of Imrahan?" Haroun demanded. "Lying is a sin. Thou shalt have three strokes of the switch for those words, after thou hast done thy duty this night. We shan't show thy lord a welted bottom for his pleasures, but after he is done thou shalt come to me, lift thy robe, and I shall welt thee properly!"

"But, it is true!" I insisted. "I was with my knight, chasing the mules, and – "

"Be silent!" Haroun Bedi's eyes had a way of glittering in warning, and I sealed my mouth while I burned with indignation. To insist would earn me three more strokes. Still, I hoped to woo him. If Imrahan was in the fortress, would he not recognise me?

We came into the long shadow of the great building as the sun began to set, and out of the fortress rushed the friends, kin and lovers of those who had ridden with ibn-Qasim. I stood back, hoping to see Imrahan, but I recognised no face among the throng. I watched my Captain stride into the vine-hung courtyard within the iron gate, and as the air filled with cries both of joy and woe, for the living and the dead, I and a few other slaves acquired on this campaign were escorted inside.

We were taken to a washing house and inspected. I was merely dusty and had no fleas. I had been shaved just the day before, and had only to wash away the grime of a day's march and bathe my feet. I was given a rich, gorgeous loincloth and new slippers. The greater part of me was bare, but I knew Jahrom Rafha prized my looks. If he was to buy me himself so as to keep me out of the market in Dimashq, I would please him. Life came first. Second, escape. Third, my return to Edward. This was my only ambition.

The others were washed and similarly dressed, and we waited for a soldier to fetch us into the dim, cool interior of the fortress. Once more I was speechless when I saw marble, onyx and alabaster for the first time. I had never seen the glories of this world, nor smelt its richness. The very air seemed made of rose petals and beneath my feet the floor was cold and smooth as milk.

The walls were everywhere decorated with the Arabesques and the windows were half-shuttered with delicately fretted marble in the same design. My mouth gaped as we were taken into a long white room with a high ceiling and I heard Jahrom Rafha's voice at last.

But I could barely believe what I saw. He was on his knees before a much older man whose body was gone to fat, big-bellied, and whose brown face was jowlish, sagged and old. So this was the Jackal, Masjed ibn-Zahran. Despite the absurd talk in the Crusaders' camps, he did not ride with his warriors, but remained behind, sodded and debauched, while the young men did his fighting. And it was on the orders of this *toad* that atrocities were committed?

My mouth dried as Jahrom Rafha summoned me forward. I knew what was expected of me and made obeisance before the Jackal. He reclined on a couch with a hookah at his side, and a little black eu-

141

nuch, naked, gelded, plump and almost distressingly beautiful, held a platter of figs and dates. I was as unlike that child as can be imagined, and the lad in me wondered what the boy's duties were, while the full-grown man in me rebelled.

I had been made a catamite, but I have always been a lover of men. I saw no shame in being cherished by a rich man, if one performs the duty well and is appreciated for it. The Jackal's liking was for different flesh, and while I rebelled on the child's account, I was guiltily grateful that I would be spared ibn-Zahran's attention. I was already too much a man for him.

He was robed in turquoise silk. His eyes were like the crow, flaying the flesh from my bones as they raked me over. Jahrom Rafha stepped closer, stroked my shoulder, and what he said caused a flicker in the eyes of his half-brother, before whom even he knelt. I looked up at the Captain, let him see my fright. It would do me no service to be brave. Better that he knew I feared for my very life.

A tally-sheet was read out, plunder – of which I was part – itemised and accounted before the slaves were taken to the bedchambers while the captured provisions were stored. A soldier with a white-swathed face took me to a room high on the west wall, closed a door on me, locked it and left me.

It was a bedchamber, and from the windows I watched the last flickers of bloody sunset. I listened to the unearthly wail of the Imam calling the Saracen to vespers, and watched the western edge of the world. Somewhere, that way, was Edward. But I saw guards patrolling below the window, felt the breath of the desert wind on my face, and it began to dawn on me, belatedly, that I would never see Edward again.

Bitter tears stung me. I dared not sit on the bed lest I rumple it, so I sat on the floor and waited for hours before a servant appeared with food and a jug of fermented goat's milk. I ate a little, but was hardly hungry. I was too alone, too frightened and much too miserable. I was sixteen years, and I reckoned up the rest of my life.

If I lived to be sixty, how long would I be desirable to men? Not past the age of thirty! So I had fourteen years' bed-service before me. How many times would I raise my arse? How many nights were there in fourteen years? I was never good at arithmetic. And what would become of me when I was no longer wanted by men who desired young flesh? I might be a labourer or a scribe, or I might be gelded and become a servant in the harem, where the wives and concubines were shut away from the world of whole men.

I tormented myself until the stars of midnight were overhead, and I heard footsteps at the door. A key turned and Jahrom Rafha's face appeared. He smiled and took my hand. I knelt and kissed his slipper, as I had been taught, and it began again.

My duty was easy. I would undress him, make much of his paps, which were tender, dark brown and like pebbles. I would take his long, hot sword into my throat, and when he was excited beyond bearing I would kneel up and, slick with my own spittle, he would lance me deeply until he came with a little cry of pleasure. The touch of him inside me always roused my traitorous body, and after he was done I must turn over and finish myself, before I was given a kerchief to clean him and, lastly, myself.

We could not converse without the aid of Haroun, but he did speak to me, and sounded affectionate as he stroked my face and dealt my nipples a teasing squeeze apiece. I arched my back to push my chest into his hands, since I could not tell him I was grateful for his kindness. He chuckled, pressed his lips to my forehead and I heard the one phrase in his language I could understand already. "There is but one God, and Allah is His name." I repeated it in my strange accent, and he smiled. He spoke again, and fingered my cockhead. I guessed that he was telling me, I would soon be accepted into his religion. I would hurt a little, then my fear would be over, for when a man has made the covenant, his honour is not abused. The Book is filled with warnings to evil-doers. They burn in hell forever if they defile their brothers. I forced a smile and kissed ibn-Qasim's hand.

Soon enough, as he began to yawn, a knock announced Haroun Bedi to fetch me away. I stole a glance back at Jahrom Rafha, and as I followed Haroun I wondered where Edward might be. Readying himself to retire, I thought, all long, gold limbs, drowsy eyes and yellow hair. The ache in my belly was like a sickness I never wanted to be cured of. If I had nothing else, I could dream. But would Edward forgive me for what I had done, and must do, with Jahrom Rafha? Would he ever understand that I would have been dead long since if I had snatched up a sword?

The pedagogue took me to his own chamber, and I found my own bed in the corner beneath the window, where the night wind was cool. His books were on the desk, four candles lit; a beautiful Quran was open and his writing materials lay in disarray. He had been teaching a class just minutes before. The birch switch lay across a stool, and I sighed once more as I saw it.

A servant had turned down his bed already. I turned back the sheets of my own while he unwound his turban and let loose his long white hair. Then I fetched the birch, took the girdle from my hips and bent before him to present my bare cheeks with clenched teeth and squeezed-shut eyes.

"What is it to lie, boy?" He asked curiously.

"It is a sin, my lord," I responded. I knew the words.

The first stroke was dealt with good conscience, and stung like a wasp bite across both buttocks. I would wear the welt all day, and if it did not fade before I went to Jahrom Rafha, I must explain it.

"And what is it to sin?" He prompted.

"To sin is to insult the Prophet," I said hoarsely, tense with anticipation.

The second stroke was heavier than the first, an inch or two below it, adding fire to fire. I bit my lip, groaned softly, and could not help wriggling as sweat sprang out on me.

"And what is it to insult the Prophet?" he asked cheerfully as he lifted the switch up high for the last stroke of my lesson.

"To insult the Prophet is to insult my own soul and break my heart, my lord," I said windedly, trembling.

The third stroke was hardest of all, and I jumped clean out of my skin. I smarted like the worst sinner, but I remained bent, in case he deemed my crime worth more.

The switch caressed me on both striped cheeks. "Mayhap, 'tis enough," he decided. "Art thou hot below?"

"Burning, my lord," I confessed, "like fire."

He swatted me smartly with the flat of his hand. "Put on thy night robe and sit, if the couch may be borne! Stand if not. One lesson only, since it is late."

A robe of peach-pink silk waited for me. I put it on and tried my rump on the couch. I could bear it, and I waited for the lesson from The Book. Each night, now, I would have one or several, depending on the time, until I knew my new catechism and was ready to face the elders, a surgeon's knife, a new Church. Haroun Bedi put his hand on my shoulder and read,

"'Have We not given Man two eyes, a tongue and two lips, and shown him the twain paths of Right and Wrong? Yet he would not scale the Height. Would that thou could know what the Height is! It is the freeing of a bondsman; the feeding of an orphaned relation or a needy man in distress; to have faith and enjoin fortitude and mercy. Those that do this shall stand on the right hand; and those that deny Our revelations shall stand on the left, with Hellfire close above them.'"

Every word I repeated after him in his curious blend of Norman French, Latin and Saxon English, which he had learned from sundry captives like myself. Then he asked me what I made of the lesson.

Wriggling on my sore behind, I said, "The Book says, grant mercy, show kindness, abhor the cruel and greedy, let no man suffer unduly, not even a slave."

He smiled at me and touched my head. "Go to bed, and meditate upon the lesson."

I slid into my bed under the window and laid on my belly, with the night wind cooling my rump. "My lord, they taught me, Jesus Christ said the same words."

He had snuffed the candles. "So he did. He was a True Prophet."

I watched his shadowy form slide into his bed robe, and between his sheets. "But, if we accept Christ as a Prophet, are we Christians too?" I was genuinely puzzled, but as soon as the words were out I

144

was worried for the skin of my behind.

But Haroun accepted it as merely the query of a curious boy. "Nay. To us Christ is a Prophet, not the offspring of God. Allah needs no son to do His labours. To claim that He does, and would send a mortal man into the world as his son, is blasphemy! Now, go to sleep."

"One question only," I begged as my rump began to ease in the cool breeze. He gave an acquiescent grunt. "My lord ibn-Qasim taught me to fear the name of someone called Ibrahim. Run, he said, when I see him coming, hide if I hear his name. What must I run from, and how shall I know him, so that I may hide?"

The pedagogue sat up and my belly flip-flopped. My backside gave a curious twinge and I prickled all over. Haroun was a fine teacher, but had a heavy hand with the switch. The birch is part of teaching and learning, and I never evaded that part of my lessons. But I was sore already, for nothing I had done, and a dozen fresh welts would punish me all the more atop those others.

To my relief the old man sighed. "Ibrahim is a magician, dark as night, black to the very soul. Thou shalt find him in the deeps under this fortress. Rarely does he emerge, save to make a pronouncement. Ibrahim is the Great Deceiver born in man, with witchfires in his eyes and the blood of demons in his veins. He is the Jackal's counsellor and most private adviser. Ibn-Qasim's advice is wise. Run from him, for his sorcery is vile. He has things in his warren that may not be imagined. Now, sleep! What has thee fidgeting? I did not break the skin of thy fair behind. Did ibn-Qasim bruise thee within? Needst thou a healer with a soother or a salve? Or did he not see to thy pleasure? Caress thyself, as boys do, lull thyself to sleep, but be quiet about it! I am old, and need my rest."

He turned over and punched his pillow. I fell silent, but his words hummed in my mind. The mention of dark magic thrilled me. The suggestion of a magician's lair beneath the fortress set my bones trembling.

Magic, to me, suggested a means of escape.

I was awake half the night, and yawning at dawn as I breakfasted and was set my lessons. I must learn to speak all over again, and Haroun Bedi had been given the task of teaching me. As I rose, with care he examined my behind and tut-tutted over the welts. So, while I ate, I had my first lesson, bent over the table with my bowl and spoon, repeating words and phrases, and a boy sat on a stool behind me and massaged my striped cheeks with olive oil.

It was the most maddening experience, and I was terrified that Haroun, on the other side of the table, would find my attention lacking, for it surely wandered. The wicked boy thrust his thumb into me, making me flinch and get up hard. I glared at him, but the table hid my belly and thighs and I parroted my words well enough to please.

I knew enough by bedtime to say to my lord, "Good evening to thee, Captain, art thou well?"

And I understood as he said, "Very well, sweet one. Come to me and show me thy pleasures."

I had spent some considerable time thinking of ways to amuse him. I imagined all the ways I would fetch Edward pleasure, and I practised every one of them on Jahrom Rafha. He spoke to me again, but I did not have the words, so I shrugged my apology and sucked his heavy balls, which seemed to suffice.

Then, back to Haroun Bedi's chamber to sleep, no welts that night, but a lesson from The Book. With morning, another lesson, more words. I learned the parts of the body, from 'nose' and 'lips' to 'cock' and 'balls', without prejudice or shame. I learned foods and drinks, how to say, 'Permit me to serve thee' and 'How may I help thee?' and, 'My lord does me great honour with his presence.'

"There," Haroun said drily, "thou hast the ability to compliment the Captain tonight! He is fond of thee, and if thou art not grateful, swiftly become so!"

"I am, my lord," I said quickly. "Tell me how to say this to him. Tell me how to say to him, 'I am grateful for thy kindness and patience, and shall earn both with good service for many years.'"

He cocked his head at me and frowned. "Thou art a strange boy. Others have tried to run away. But then, thou wert a catamite before, so those duties do not trouble thee, as they do trouble pious youths." And he taught me the phrases, which I repeated until I had them safe in my memory and pronounced them well enough to be understood.

"My lord," I said as I tidied his books, "I know I must be guarded, but might we walk out? I long to be in the open air."

He gave me a gauzy cloak. "Keep thy skin from the sun. Ibn-Qasim instructed me to keep thee inside till thou art white as almond blossoms." He arranged the pale blue cloak about me and pulled up the hood to shield my face.

That morning we walked about the rampart and down the stone steps into the great, wide courtyard, where banners fluttered and the camels were watered at deep stone troughs. And there, I saw the odd-smelling doorway which led into the cellars of the fortress. Ibrahim's lair. I shivered, felt the tug of wilful desire to defy orders and go down – seek the magic, try to capture a tiny speck of it for myself – but just then I did not have the courage or the foolishness for it.

In the courtyard I heard an expression of astonishment and looked up to see a face I knew. I threw back the hood and let him see me more clearly. "My lord! Dost thou not know me?" I was able to say this in his language, in my barbarous accent. "Dost thou not recall me, Imrahan?"

He recoiled and spoke in his thickly accented English. "I saw thee in the company of the Saxon knight, Aethelstan – the squire, with the hot eyes of a lover. Why art thou in this place?"

I knelt at his feet and slithered hopefully into English. My grasp of their language was as yet too weak. "I was captured. I know not if Edward lived or died. I was brought here after a great battle, and Captain ibn-Qasim bought me for himself, to keep, for I don't know what price."

"So Ibn-Qasim would," Imrahan said drily. He took my chin in his fingers and lifted my face. "You're a handsome boy, and even more so, razored girl-smooth. I see Ibn-Qasim's mark all over you! But you loved the Saxon. I saw it at once, when you were my guests. Did he teach you how to pleasure a man?"

"Rather, Sire, I taught him," I said as my face heated.

Imrahan chuckled. He was more handsome than Jahrom Rafha, and much younger. He was also a lover of boys and young men, and I hoped he liked my looks. The first and last ambition a catamite can have is for gentle, handsome lovers and a soft bed.

"You are safe in ibn-Qasim's company," Imrahan mused. "At least for the moment."

"Sire?" As he bade me rise, I clambered to my feet. "Things are to change?" Fear sharpened my voice. I shot a glance at Haroun, who wore an exasperated look. He now knew he had whipped my bare backside for nothing. Haroun was a fair man who would lay on with conscience when the stripes were warranted, and deal a caress or a kiss when good deeds were done.

"Things might change," Imrahan said carefully. "I am here with many of the chieftains, my half-brothers and cousins. Salah ad-Din himself was here until a few days before ibn-Qasim's party arrived. The Sultan has gone to Jerusalem. There was... disagreement."

The mention of politics piqued Haroun's interest, and worried him. He came from an excellent family, but the fortunes of his clan were as mutable as the moon. I was reminded of Aethelstan. "A disagreement?" he asked.

To my annoyance they spoke then in their own language, and I was hopping with frustrated curiosity before they parted and Haroun Bedi hurried me out of the sun before my skin could begin to brown by even a shade.

"Tell me, my lord," I begged. "Tell me what he said!"

"Thou art impertinent," he accused with a hard glance.

"Then welt my buttocks to blood, but tell me!" I flung myself down at his feet. "It is my life!"

"Hmm. Thy breast requires the razor," he observed, and sent for the boy who did that for me.

I sat on the couch, fuming and fidgeting as I was oiled and shaved, and begged again, "Please, my lord, it is my life if not my liberty. What did Imrahan tell thee?"

Haroun Bedi sighed. "Thou art a cursed importunate flea, but...

147

I welted thee for no good reason, and am in thy debt. Imrahan reported a great rift between my lord ibn-Qasim and his half-brother. They fought yesterday. They may fight again, and if they do, leadership of their armies is a matter to be decided. Who will fight with Salah ad-Din, and who will fight with he Jackal? Masjed ibn-Zahran and the Sultan are of two great houses, and have never been at peace. Salah ad-Din desires to strike a bargain with the Christian Crusaders, to fetch an end to war before every soul in this land perishes."

"Thank Heaven," I said, and closed my eyes with a groan. I set my forehead to the cool marble floor at Haroun's feet. "There is but one God, and Allah is His name."

The teacher studied me thoughtfully. "The Jackal is for war, but ibn-Qasim is with Salah ad-Din. Now, if Jahrom Rafha and his brother fight, it will be a battle for the banner of the house. And if Jahrom dies... " He looked me up and down as I was shaved by the boy, between my spread thighs, where a man grows cursed hairy. "As the Jackal's fair-won prize, surely thou shalt be marketed in the way that will fetch the best price." He frowned dolefully at my balls.

I swallowed hard and sat down fast, which might have achieved the surgery before its necessity, for there was a razor between my legs at that moment. The boy swore, cut his finger as he avoided my tender parts, and wailed as he saw his own blood. I was hardly thinking as I wrapped the cut in a kerchief. Haroun fetched the books and I forced my mind to lessons. My memory was poor, and for my teacher I will say that a dozen times that day he could have beaten me mercilessly, but he knew I was tormented and punished me but once, so lightly that I felt little and no stripes showed when I went to ibn-Qasim at midnight.

For the first time, in the saffron lamplight, the Captain took me into his bed, and I curled against him while I suckled his sensitive little paps. I said, in my barbarous accent, "I fear for my life, my lord. I learned, the Jackal is at thy throat. What becomes of me?"

He kicked back the sheets and I began to work. He stroked my hair as I sucked him. "I shall do what I can to assure thy safety. I spoke to Imrahan."

Bless him, he was choosing simple words and speaking slowly. I could follow him now. It is odd: learning Latin, which is never spoken from day to day, the memory refuses to hold the words. But learning a living tongue which is used every moment, fluency comes quickly.

"I know Imrahan," I said against his musk-hot cock.

"So he said. He told me of thy knight, the Saxon Aethelstan. Thy beloved."

Tears hurt. I sucked harder but he pulled me into his embrace, as if he had seen my grief for the first time. "Sire," I begged, not knowing what he wanted. "Have I displeased thee?"

"Nay. But I fear Athelstan died on a Saracen lance. If he was brave and kind, he may be judged mercifully. He never made the covenant in life, but upon the Day of Judgement, at the Cataclysm, he may be deemed a worthy servant and shown the gates of Paradise."

I had never considered this, and I made a wounded sound. If Edward were granted Paradise, I would be satisfied. Paradise was said to be more wondrous that the Heaven for which Christians hope. I imagined it as a Garden filled with fruiting trees and vines and flowers, where men enjoyed beautiful boys, never worked or ailed, drank wine and ate the finest food, for ever.

Grateful, I straddled his hips and rode him slowly, the way he liked. I pictured Edward in that Garden, wreathed by vines and shaded by fig trees; I saw dapples of shadow play across his face, and his eyes smiled at me. His arms opened, inviting. It was him that I straddled, then, him gently reaming the heart of me. Bliss burned like a slow fire and I was not aware of ibn-Qasim until I came.

It was the first time I had come with him, without handling myself, and I stilled, gasping. He stroked my back, which was toward his face, for he liked to be able to watch his spear move in and out of me. My hands gripped his shins as I got back my breath, and I feared a rebuke. This was *not* the way slaves behaved.

He chuckled. "Have I pleasured thee, in the taking of pleasure from thee?" He patted my flank. "Breathe deep, then ride me to the end."

Revived, I began again. Now, I was aware of my company, but Edward was still with me, gentle on my mind, even when the Captain filled me with his seed and I fell down to lie at his side.

We lay still for some long time, talking in whispers, before he rang a bell for a servant to take me away. At last, I knelt at the bedside and kissed his hand, a small show of gratitude which must have touched him, for he smiled, and next day I had gifts.

Chapter XVII

And so I passed my days, while my knowledge of their language and Book grew. I dreamed of Edward and lazed in the heat of the afternoon, drank coffee with Imrahan, played chess with his boys, some of whom were his bed companions, others his sons. And while ibn-Qasim argued and fought with his brother, and the old men of the hosted tribes listened and debated, I watched the iron-bound, strange-smelling doorway which led into the deep warren under the fortress, the lair where Ibrahim made strange magic.

News came one day that the Sultan had fought a great battle, and King Richard had been wounded. Salah ad-Din had cost the Crusader army dearly; many Templars lay dead, while the knights of

Islam returned home richer in gold, horses and slaves for the market and the harem. A vast feast was held, and I stuffed myself with mutton and apricots, and called down blessings on the name of Salah ad-Din, who had conceived of a treaty to end the blood-letting.

During these weeks, Ibn-Qasim grew restless and angry, even when I went to him at night. He was angry with his brother, not with me, but he was too quick in bed, coming not once but twice in just an hour. He liked to fuck me on my knees, deeply, without respite, for a long time. Then we would lie together and eat figs, and when he saw me wince he gave me the hookah. With two or three breaths of the hashish my pains were nothing. I felt drunk while he made apologies for my bruises.

As I learned the language, Haroun Bedi taught me much more. I was not circumcised, not yet properly one of his people, but when the Imam called the others, one morning I followed, and they allowed it. I washed my hands and face as I had often seen them do, and knelt in that curious way. I knew the whole litany by heart, and spoke it five times that day.

After this I saw a great change in the way I was approached. No door was ever locked on me. I was shown a measure of respect, as the bed companion of Ibn-Qasim. I had the freedom of the whole fortress, and even the market beyond the gate, as far as I could comfortably walk.

Once, I wandered out and voices called me back urgently. I thought I had presumed too much, and would be confined once more or even beaten, but it was just a boy with a cloak for me, to ward off the sun, so that my skin would continue to grow pale.

Free to wander between lessons, I rambled. I had a silver band for my ankle, with bells that tinkled as I walked, and a necklace and bangles for my arms. I was already much more slender. I had not worked in so long, my body was once again a young boy's, and I was so often shaved, I thought I was more akin to women; but my mind was more than ever that of a man.

In the heat of afternoon, when the others were resting in the shadows, I wandered the whole fort, from the high ramparts to that door which lured me with its strangeness, its smell, the sounds from within. I stood in the deep blue shade, listening intently for hours. What I heard, I never understood. The voice of Ibrahim wailed ungodly chants or incantations – I almost crossed myself, and stayed my hand at the last moment.

"Listen thou, unto the voice of Lord Hastur, and the lamentful moan of the Maelstrom, the insane clamour of the divine gale that whips among the mute stars. Hear ye the One who roars, dragon-fanged, in the womb of the world; that One whose endless roar imbues the immortal sky of deep-hid Leng, that One whose power sunders the mountain and smashes the fortress, yet no man may know the fist that strikes and the spirit that ravages, for unseen and odious is the Destroyer. Hear ye the voice of that One in the midnight hours, echo ye His name; supplicate when He does pass thee by, yet utter not His name upon thy lips."

This was dark magic from the distant past. What it meant, I never knew, but I learned much later, of the sorcerer whose Book of Shadows this was likely read from. It was called the Book of Dead Names. Al Azif. Abdul Alhazred was an enchanter of the blackest magic, in Dimashq, and Ibrahim was his acolyte.

My blood ran cold, yet the lure of the cellars was more terrible than I can describe. I smelt sulphur, blood, and I heard the cries of prisoners. A woman or a young boy screamed pitiably once and then was silent; a man screamed for a long time in pain or fear before his throat was stilled forever.

But one voice I heard often, and it spoke rather than screaming. It was the voice of a young man, and he also was foreign, probably a slave like myself, for his accent was as strange as my own. I knew he was young, for his voice was light. He spent many an hour talking with Ibrahim, whose voice I had come to know well, though I had not yet seen him. Ibrahim had a sound like rusty iron nails, full of corruption.

The young prisoner spoke in arcane terms I did not understand, couched in riddles, and I heard a sound of despair, or deep pain, deeper than the physical hurts of the body. Pain of the soul.

That young man haunted my dreams, and one day good conscience urged me to question Haroun Bedi. It was early in the morning, and I had just had my first lesson in the language. I had learned a poem, a lovesong from the Greek, by Meleager, who was besotted with a boy called Myiscus and wrote the most sumptuous poetry for him. I recited the whole verse twice in my best accent, and when Haroun was satisfied, and poured us lime juice, I asked,

"Who is the young man held captive in the cellars? The one who spends so much time conversing with the magician."

Haroun Bedi's eyes narrowed, and then spat flames, and I knew I had asked the wrong question. I received a tirade in his native tongue, too fast and vastly too varied for me to follow, then another in French and Latin, blurred to gibberish with fury. All I gathered was that I was never to go back to that door, not to look, not to listen.

"I promise! My word on it!" I swore as I hoisted my robe and bent over the table. "Teacher, I swear I meant no wrong!"

He punished me with the full weight of his arm. Not since Edward's groom had birched me had I been hurt so. I pressed my face into my arms and bit my lip as a trickle of blood ran down the back of my thigh. I counted twenty, but only five drew blood. Then Haroun was exhausted, flung down the switch and ran from the room. I laid on my bed, aching and biting back tears that were unseemly for a youth of my years. What had I asked that was so wrong? I would never ask again, nor mention that I had heard anything at that door. I had better respect for my skin.

I was stiff and burning, but after a time I knew I had stopped bleeding and I must attend to myself. No one came near me. At noon, when the day was at its hottest, I sat in a basin of water and washed away the crusting of brown-dried blood. I rubbed in a bit of salve and put on my robe, afraid to show my face outside, for fear word of my indiscretion had got about.

But Haroun had told no one, and not until late evening did my crimes become known, when I stripped for ibn-Qasim. I kept my back to him as long as I could. Then, he traced the twenty stripes while I knelt with my poor arse lifted for his pleasure, and he demanded,

"Explain! Haroun took off thy skin! How hast thou angered him?"

"In truth, Sire, I know not," I muffled against my arm, grateful when he tickled my balls, trying to tease me out of my unhappiness. "Unwittingly I listened at a door." That was a lie, but a wise one. "I heard a young man in the cellars, who seems to be held prisoner. I wondered if he is a slave like myself, and if he is needy. I was about to ask my teacher if I could do him some small service or a kindness. The Book says one must take care of bondsmen. I myself am thy bondsman, and would have been most needy, but for kindnesses shown me."

"While Haroun has taken no care at all of thy cheeks," Jahrom Rafha remarked. "Lie down. I'll not bugger thee tonight, thou art too tender. Suckle me instead, and I shall tell thee a little."

As I pleasured him, between lush sighs and deep groans he told me what I already knew. No one, no one at all, went near the cellars save ibn-Zahran, the Jackal, who went to confer with his adviser. Ibrahim was an astrologer and magician, whose work was midnight-dark. He possessed an ancient Book, filled with vileness, and he should at all costs be avoided.

"And the prisoner?" I asked as I dried him with a kerchief after swallowing the salt welling of his passion.

He put me astride his belly and I fisted my cock for the delight of his eyes. "Some weeks past, a storm ripped out of the desert, as they often do at this time of year. We watched from the east ramparts. Dry lightning and wind roared like a dragon, the sand whirled like a spinning top, and in the midst of it we saw banners, phantom riders. We sent out our own riders – cautiously. They found no prints of horses' hooves, the wind had erased them all. But they found the footprints of a single man. Mayhap he had been unhorsed by the wind. He ran into the desert and we hunted him by these tracks." He bit his lip in puzzlement. "Ibrahim is convinced he is sent by the Great Deceiver. He is a servant of Satan, conjured by the magic of the Book of Dead Names."

"Horned? Black winged?" I panted as I grew breathless.

"Green skinned," Jahrom Rafha said quietly.

My hands stopped. "Forgive me, Sire, I misunderstood. I heard thee say his skin was green!"

"Thou hast perfectly understood," Jahrom Rafha said in acerbic tones. "We found his skin green as emeralds when he was fetched here. He had been clad in the finest, most gleaming mail I have ever seen, and the finest silk. Ibrahim has him now. He speaks our language, after lessons like thine. And that is enough! Milk the seed from thy sweet boyish shaft, then lie back and recite me some verse before sleep."

So I pulled a helpless, muted coming from myself and sprawled on my belly. While he fondled my welted behind I spoke verses by Solon I had learned earlier that day, and he was happy. He kissed me, warned me not to return to the door where – unwittingly, he believed! – I had overheard the magician. Then he rang the bell for my escort.

My belly quivered. I had not seen Haroun Bedi since morning and I wondered if he would be still enraged.

He was, and he looked cruelly smug when I took my lessons standing. That night I had endless lessons, long past midnight. The Book, words, verses, tests without number which I passed as best I could.

I gave him my undivided attention, and no cause to strike me. At last he threw down the books, sighed hoarsely and grabbed the hem of my robe. I bent, wincing as the scabs pulled. Would he switch me again? I was afraid he might, for a whipping on top of yesterday's stripes is twice a hurtful as twice the stripes at one time. But he merely grunted over the welts and pinched me where the skin was whole.

"Mayhap, I beat thee too hard," he observed. I kept silent. "What said Ibn-Qasim, before thy mating?"

"He did not mate me, thinking me too sore."

"Hmm. So his pleasure was spoiled."

"Nay, for I sucked him, long and sweetly," I whispered. "I am his good servant."

"And wert thou too indisposed for the other?" He questioned.

"I've not sat on my arse all day, and can hardly bear the weight of thy hand." It was the truth. I smarted mightily where he palmed me.

He sighed and let go my robe. "Go to bed."

I undressed and lay on my belly. "I am forgiven?"

"Thou art not, knave, nor shalt thou be!" He snuffed the fat, smoking candles. "But the thief can be punished only once for the theft of the same camel." He slid into his bed, and in the moonlight shook a finger at me. "See that thou art not caught stealing any more camels, for next time, being well warned, it shall be the scourger for thee, and the nine-tailed lash. It shall not end simply with woe to thy comely young bottom!"

The warning was more than fair. Then, why did I feel the lure of that cellar more than ever?

* * *

All the next day, I could think of nothing else but the magician's lair, and every smart of my buttocks only reminded me of Ibrahim, the green man, and unholy magic which surely would – if I stole it like a camel! – free me of this place.

If I had been less preoccupied with foolishness, I would have heard the furore. Men were dangerously close to fighting, swords were drawn, and in the sprawling camps outside the walls, some of Imrahan's people, and many from other clans, were restless.

Some had packed their tents and left before sunrise. If I had been aware of what was happening in the long, marble halls where bondsmen like myself were not permitted to go, I would have known that ibn-Qasim and his brother had at last reached the end of their patience for one another. Now, they would fight.

The Jackal desired to spill every drop of Christian blood in Palestine, no matter the cost. Christendom, he said, was a plague that must be driven out. Jahrom Rafha counselled peace with honour, favouring Salah ad-Din's treaty, which would grant even Christian pilgrims a road, a safe way from the ports to Jerusalem, not to plunder, but simply to worship.

If I had only listened to the chatter of the guards who lounged in the shadows, I would have heard all this, albeit at second hand. But between lessons, dark magic consumed me with its promise of impossibilities. Escape. Freedom was like a bird just out of reach.

Jahrom Rafha retired with the old men, trying to thrash out their differences, taking Salah ad-Din's part and counselling peace and treaty. Haroun, being old and quickly tired, demanded his afternoon sleep. And I, young, impetuous, and oblivious of the fracas raging around me, deliberately disobeyed every command or word of advice given me.

I crept to the doorway, and I drew the bolts. The hinges squealed for want of oil and a waft of something foul-smelling came up from the near-total darkness within. I stepped through and at once was wreathed in shadows and coolness. The door closed, and I found myself at the top of a steep flight of stone steps.

My slippered feet were silent as I crept down into a pool of lamplight. It was an alchemist's workshop! On the left side was a library; before me, the floor was painted with a pentacle of enormous size. Black blood stained the ground within the magic circle, and I remembered the cries I had heard, the death throes of helpless people.

Heart in my mouth, I looked for the magician, but Ibrahim was absent. An enormous crow perched in the light of the lamps, preening oily feathers. A big, black cat looked drowsily at me from the magician's chair. The desk was littered with curled, yellow scrolls covered in arcane script I could not read.

And then the young man's voice made me whirl around. He was sitting on a rug in the corner of the workshop, naked, chained by the ankles to the floor... and his skin was as green as the hills of England. I gaped, deaf to him, though he had spoken in the tongue I knew well enough by now.

Little by little my brain ceased to spin and I forced myself to listen. He was very nearly as beautiful as Edward. Was he twenty years old? No sign of age or corruption showed about him. He was slender, almost thin, but wiry-strong, with cropped black hair and large golden eyes that seemed so sad.

He said, "Who art thou? Shouldst thou be here? The black one will surely bleed thee if thou art discovered."

My eyes devoured his nakedness. He was long-limbed, with a sweet cock, nicely thick though not very long, and smooth, near hairless balls, tucked up tight. He covered himself with his hand as he found my eyes lingering there.

"I heard thee from the door. Art thou a captive?" I whispered. He gestured with his chains. "Hast thou tried to escape?" I thought, he was older than me, he might have more courage or resources. Since my capture I had felt more boy than man. Fear has a way of making a boy feel very young, and an old man very old.

But he closed his beautiful eyes and leaned his head against the wall. "There is no escape. If I ran, where would I go?"

I knelt on the carpet beside him. "Run home!"

He looked at me, eyes luminous in the lamplight. "I have no way to go home. I have told the magician this a thousand times. He wants me to make magic, but I have none to make. See there, on the table. Maps of the sky he has made me draw. Aye, I can chart the sky for him — it is my trade! But he thinks I can speak strange words over the maps, read something from a book, and construct a chariot to ride through the sky on the wings of the windstorm! His own evil has driven him mad."

I was breathless. "A chariot in the sky? Is that possible, even for a sorcerer?"

"Nay, it is *not*," he said scornfully. "But when I tell him this he flies into a frenzy. He would beat me to death, save that he fears me." He touched his pale green skin. "Because of this."

"Thou art green as leeks," I said breathlessly.

"T'will fade," he said distractedly. "'Tis only a dye. It was thought to be *pretty*, and like a fool I agreed to wear it... I was very drunk that night. The colour will fade soon enough."

"Then, art thou not a demon?" I examined him, head to foot, but

155

the closer I got to him, the more a man he seemed. "Art thou like me?"

"A man, and a prisoner." He sighed and shrugged his slender shoulders. "Thy heart would beat in my breast, and mine in thine."

"Then..." I looked about at the alchemist's tools, most of which I could not even name. "He is wrong about thy magic." The young man nodded. "What is thy name?"

"Thou couldst not pronounce it," he told me softly. "Call me Qabir, as Ibrahim does. The name will suffice."

"Canst thou not get home, with a fast horse or a stolen camel?" I pressed, and my buttocks twinged at a mention of camels.

"Too far," he sighed. "Unless..." He bit his lip, closed his eyes, an expression of hopelessness. "I know where my people will be, a month hence. 'Tis a time of gathering, before the journey home. If I could be there, where they rendezvous... "

He fell silent, and as I heard a squawk from the crow I took fright. I was sure Ibrahim was returning, and jumped out of my skin. I leapt up and shuffled anxiously, and Qabir knew I must go before I was discovered. This time it would be a heavy flogging, a grown man's punishment, not the annoying sting of a boy's lesson.

"I shall return when I can," I promised breathlessly before I ran. At the door I stopped to listen, opened it the slightest crack and slipped out into the shadows. I threw the bolts and slipped away along the walls, as unseen as I had slid in.

Agitated, I spoiled my lessons that evening, and Haroun Bedi was exasperated. He spared me the rod, for I was still sore from his last heavy-handedness. Instead of getting welts, I wrote the whole strange, curled alphabet five hundred times on scraps of discarded paper. This kept me occupied and frustrated till well past midnight, long after I had been with ibn-Qasim, had my last lesson, and Haroun had gone to bed. Still tender from my lord's pleasure, I fidgeted, writing as fast as I dared. The letters must be finely drawn, or woe betide me!

But my mind and my heart went again and again to the cellars. I could see the door from my window, and when at last I crawled into bed, with my right hand cramped after so much writing, I could not sleep a wink.

* * *

I did not dare return to Qabir the following day, but I watched to see when Ibrahim came out. I had learned he emerged at dawn, midnight, and some days at noon. At dawn he communed with the gods of the Orient; at midnight he read the stars and at noon he often had an audience with the Jackal, and would foretell the future. I believe he predicted the fortunes of ibn-Zahran, so that the Jackal was no more than Ibrahim's puppet.

That night Jahrom Rafha was agitated. He fucked me so hard I almost wept, then apologised and gave me hashish and sweets. "Forgive me, boy," he begged. "My brother has me at the end of my patience. I must fight for the right to take the reins, and 'tis tomorrow I do battle."

"A great battle?" I wondered, sleepy with the drug. "On horses, with armour, lances?"

He stroked my breast, tweaked my paps, made me wriggle deliciously against him, and sighed. "I fight in single combat with my brother's champion, Suwayrah. Dost thou not know him?"

I shot bolt upright, my hands splayed over his own smooth chest, and my voice almost squeaked. "He is near seven feet from toe to crown, with arms like the trunks of trees and legs like a bear! If he is thy brother's champion – "

"I shall likely die tomorrow," he said. "I have asked Imrahan to snatch thee away before my brother can lay hands on thee. Look for Imrahan when the battle has gone against me. Do not tarry! The Jackal has seen thee, heard of thy slender body and knowledge of the bedchamber, and has reckoned thy worth in Dimashq. There will be no brotherhood of Islam, if he can lay hands on thee. He shall not stop at the small rite of circumcision, but shall geld thee utterly, balls *and* cock. A Christian gelding of smooth skin and tender years fetches a high price." I shook, and he pulled me against him. "Tears? For me, Paulo?"

He had never used my name before. "So much do I owe thee," I muffled. "So much hast thou done for me. I have not repaid a tenth part of my debt. Let me remain the whole night. Don't send me away. Let me show thee in a night all I may never show thee in the years we may be robbed of."

He stroked my hair, and though I longed for Edward, though I made abject apologies to my own lord, I showed Jahrom Rahfa Ibn-Qasim every skill I could imagine, and gave him the soft insides of me as often as I could make him rise.

It was the last time I would be with him, and I knew, as if I was fey, tomorrow my real battle for survival would begin.

Chapter XVIII

I left him at dawn, when his steward called discreetly from the door. He kissed me, touched me all over in farewell, and when I returned to Haroun Bedi, expecting the usual lessons and prayers, I found instead a knife, heavy robes, boots and a goatskin water canteen, bundled under my bed. I understood at once: these were my lord ibn-Qasim's orders, in the event that he was defeated. My heart jumped into my throat and I knelt at Haroun's feet.

"If I have treated thee harshly, boy," he said bluffly, "know that it was in the way of education, as I treat all boys whom I am charged to make into men. Thou art a better man for it."

"I know, my lord." I looked through a blur of tears. "I learned much, and the discipline was not harsh. Ibn-Qasim will die, won't he?"

He seemed very old of a sudden. "I believe he will. And that old fool, ibn-Zahran, will fight Salah ad-Din as well as the Lionheart." He sighed. "Thou shalt watch the combat with the household, but stay well back. When thy lord falls, as fall he must, do not tarry to grieve. Look for Imrahan. Put on these robes, take this knife for protection, and hide among Imrahan's bondsmen. Wisely, he leaves the fortress immediately, lest he and the Jackal begin a blood-squabble which would finish them both. Thou shalt have safe passage with him."

"I know Imrahan," I mused, "but, safe passage to where? Not to Dimashq! I have given good service, the best I could! Are gelding and market my reward?"

"Such is for Imrahan to decide," Haroun said in that mock-stern tone. "If he sells thee, then he sells thee. Knowing Imrahan, he will find thee a master who is a lover of whole boys, not the kind who desires a mutilate. A youth of fair looks and some skill at loving is of great value, if I have heard aright... even if he is whole."

I was dazed all morning as I watched for the sorcerer to emerge, and beautiful, green-skinned Qabir haunted me. When Jahrom Rafha was dead, the Jackal would be on the rampage and Ibrahim would be called upon to produce his unholy miracles. Qabir was upon the threshold of disaster, and his time was all run out. He had no magic and he would die, surely as night follows day, while I made clean my escape.

The Book heaps scorn upon the coward who leaves his brothers to their plight. Haroun had drilled this into me, and when I saw Ibrahim leave for his noon audience with the Jackal, I stole into the cellars again.

The blood-challenge was to take place at sunset. Jahrom Rafha had spent the whole morning in preparation – prayer, meditation and the care of his weapons, the tools of war. I had one chance, and with the audacity of youth I took it. I fled quickly down the stone stairs and called ahead of me, "Qabir? Qabir, 'tis only me! Tell me quick, where is the key to thy shackles?"

He was sleepy, and sat up, rubbing his eyes with the backs of his knuckles. "He hangs the key up on the wall there." He pointed across the workshop, to where a vast assortment of black iron keys hung over the benches full of strange devices. "'Tis the key on the big ring, with the scrap of green thread wound about it."

I had him unlocked and out in a trice. "Stay in thy corner," I begged. "Sit on the shackles when the magician returns, never let him know thou art loose."

"But the door is always bolted," he protested, though a light had kindled in his eyes. "How shall I get out?"

"I shall unbolt it when every eye in the fortress is turned elsewhere," I vowed. "We have the ungodliest of diversions. At sunset ibn-Qasim will fight for his life, and he will die. When he does I am to flee, and Imrahan is waiting for me. Hast thou seen the little gate in the south wall?"

"I know which way is south, at least," he said drily as he carefully concealed the leg irons beneath him. "I shall find the gate."

"I shall look for thee. Is there a robe in this stinking place, some rag to wear?"

"He has black robes, red, white robes, one for every kind of atrocity." Qabir looked ill. He caught my hand in steel-like fingers. "I do not even know thy name! Thou art not Saracen, but a different race, like me, this I can see."

"A captive, taken in battle. I am Saxon. My name is Paul," I told him. "If we escape we can share tales of our homes and people. Now, I must run!"

My heart hammered but I made it out of the cellars without incident, largely because the fortress was humming with furore. Ibrahim remained with the Jackal the entire afternoon and I watched the sun slide down with a chill feeling. Soon Jahrom Rafha would be dead.

Suwayrah was less a man than a monster. It was said that Ibrahim summoned him out of the pit one night, with a sacrifice to hideous devils. Oh, I believed! Suwayrah strutted before his many admirers, clad in a burnished casque, glittering chainmail and white leather and horsehair plumes, big and broad, twice my height, thrice my weight. Sickness churned in my belly as I thought of the contest.

I grieved for Jahrom Rafha, not because I loved him, though I had become accustomed to his hard body and gentle voice, but out of gratitude. I would love only one man in my life, but ibn-Qasim had kept me whole, and played the greatest part in sending me back to Edward.

As sunset bloodied the sky, it began. I swallowed my sickness, forced myself to watch, and looked for Imrahan. I saw him with a knot of his people at the main gate, in the east wall, and he caught my eye and gave me a nod. I clasped hands and bowed, then slipped back, unseen among the ranks of men who had long ago ceased to notice me. What was I? The Captain's catamite. Good for a brief joke, so long as it was not too coarse, lest ibn-Qasim object. I was good for a pinched bottom, and I would run an errand for anyone who asked. I was merely one of my lord's possessions, taken for granted, like furniture.

If it had not been for this single-combat he must fight, I could have lived my whole life as a bondsman in ibn-Qasim's house, first as a catamite, later as a teacher of youths newly acquired. I would have been safe, happy, if not entirely free. Now, I slipped away as I saw the Jackal and Ibrahim come out onto the balcony of ibn-Zahran's rooms, to watch the combat.

No one saw me unbolt the door into the cellars, but I called through the crack, "Qabir!"

He needed no encouragement. His face was at the door even then, and he was wrapped in a black robe with a hood about his head. "Now?" He begged. Even in the last fading daylight he was half blind, so long had he been kept in the dark. His skin was dusky green – exotic and surpassingly lovely.

"Wait here. Let the combat begin. Thou shalt hear the ring of swords. Then – the gate in the south wall."

He nodded, and I ran. I stood at the back of the throng and watched as Jahrom Rafha came out to fight. He walked proudly; he was tall and muscular, but Suwayrah was half bear and half demon, and it could end only one way. My lord fought fearlessly and he was on the road to Paradise, no doubt about it. He believed with his whole heart. His friends and kin called Allah's name for him, begged that he should be shown every comfort, every honour, in the Garden.

With a thundering heart I dragged myself away. I took the stairs up to Haroun's chamber, and with shaking hands dressed, took up the knife and skin of water and slipped out quickly, silently. I heard the ring of swords, still, as I left the building. My lord was giving good account of himself, and for a second I wondered if he might win after all.

But I glanced into the courtyard where it was taking place and saw him bloody about the chest and arm, lame in one leg, hardly able to lift his head. Suwayrah was merely humiliating him. My gorge rose in fury and I would have shot Suwayrah dead if I had possessed a bow.

Painfully, I turned my back on the scene and slipped into the shadows. The ring of swords grew quieter, less frequent, and tears burned my eyes as I saw the black-robed, hooded shape at the gate.

"Qabir?" I called. He showed me his beautiful green-skinned face for a scant second. "Come this way. I know where Imrahan is camped."

We scuttled about the outside of the wall, in the deep shadow, as the sun dipped beneath the horizon. Imrahan's banners fluttered in the evening wind, and we saw that the women and children had already loaded every possession and were ready to move out at a word.

Nor was Imrahan's the only clan making ready to go. All those who had favoured Jahrom Rafha and Salah ad-Din were leaving, bound in every direction, and even when the sorcerer discovered that his prisoner had gone, he could not guess which way to rush to find him.

I showed myself to the soldier who guarded the women, and he nod-ded at once. He had been told to expect me. I slipped my arm about the black-robed Qabir, who had kept his hood over his face.

"My brother bondsman, my lord," I said to the guard. "May he accompany me? The Jackal will maim and sell him, as he would me." Qabir knelt at his feet, head bowed, hands clasped. He knew the nice-ties as well as I did.

The burly soldier stood aside and we hurried into the last stand-ing tent. Qabir caught my wrist, and his eyes looked out of the cowl of his hood. "When Imrahan sees me, green as a cursed snake, like as not he will cast me out."

"Nay," I argued. "I shall speak for thee. Let me think – a ruse is as good as the truth, often as not! And in any case, 'tis better to be cast out into the desert where a man can run and hide, than be shut up in a cellar, waiting for Ibrahim to flay thee alive when he cannot make thee conjure magic!"

"True," he agreed. "If I were loose, perhaps I could still find my way to the place where my people gather for the journey home. There is time, I think... I only need to see the night sky."

A great roar rose from the fortress, and my heart gave a painful lurch. "That is the death cry of a good man," I said hoarsely. "Jahrom Rafha ibn-Qasim, is dead." For him, the war was over.

Now we waited only for Imrahan, and we did not have long to tarry. He strode out of the main fortress gate in a righteous fury, and clapped his hands to call his company to order. The last tent was dropped in minutes, and while it was being loaded onto the last camel, the first animals were already leaving.

Qabir and I hung back, fidgeting, waiting for his attention. When he had arranged his heavy travelling robes and turned toward me, while his steward brought up his horse, I knelt at his feet and touched my forehead to the sand.

"I owe you my life, Sire."

"Your balls, rather," he said drily. "Hurry, now. We have a bright full moon and must be far away by dawn."

I scrambled up and summoned Qabir. "One more has run with me, Sire. Don't send him back, I pray thee."

He grinned, teeth very white in the first moonlight. "After hav-ing stolen their precious Christian catamite, what else matters? I can lose my head but once, no matter if I steal a sheep or a lamb! But hurry, I said, or be left behind."

He was already in the saddle of a magnificent Turk with red leather harness, and I caught his stirrup. "Where do we ride? East?"

"West, to join Salah ad-Din. He is at this moment marching on Jerusalem, where we pray he will treaty with King Richard."

The breath was knocked from my lungs. West to Jerusalem, where I refused to believe Edward was not safe. My body caught fire as if a fever blistered me, and I hardly felt the ground beneath my feet as Qabir and I stumbled behind Imrahan's bondsmen.

We trudged until dawn, when the women and children were too tired to go on, then pitched camp and fell down to sleep. Qabir kept himself covered, but he was sweat-drenched. He could not hope to keep his secret for ever. We lay by the fire, heavy eyed with weariness, and I touched his skin.

"What manner of dye is this? What madness made thee use thyself as a bolt of linen?"

He groaned and made a face. "I am a Tartar. Hast thou heard of my people?"

"A little." I was too exhausted to be impressed.

He yawned deeply. "My people raid everyone, everywhere, and pickings are richest on a battlefield. We wait for the knights of Islam and Christendom to beat each other bloody, then we strike out of the windstorm, take what we like, and vanish back into the dust. My clan was poor as goatherds two years ago, but we have looted and pillaged across thy battlefields, and the more impoverished thy kings become, the richer we grow. Gold and silver chalice. Gem stones and the fairest slaves. The men of our clan are fierce, but few to make war brazenly. We sneak, we thieve and grow strong."

"Hiding behind the windstorms," I murmured. "But surely the wind never made thee green!"

He laughed tiredly. "Nay! 'Twas a vat of dye that greened every last inch of me, and I was so drunk I thought it amusing!" He waved a hand vaguely into the north-east. "Yonder, in a brothel in the mountains, I know not where, save I saw the Sword of Orion from the doorsill at midnight. We stopped for a night's debauchery. My kinsmen swore I was more comely than the harlots. The hussies became more daring, attempting to outdo each other. One danced naked with his skin green as a grass snake. I demanded to know how it had been done, and was shown the dye. Next I knew, I was bathing in it!" he sighed. "They held me under, even my face, and I laughed. I woke next morning with a head like a melon and tried to scrub it off, but it is fast and only time will fade it."

"Still," I said, amused, "thy kinsmen were right. It is comely. Even if it would have been the death of you, at Ibrahim's hands."

He made a quiet sound of derision, and was asleep. Darkness soon enveloped me too, and I knew nothing for hours. I knew Imrahan would call for us at first light, and when he did I caught Qabir by the wrist and made him go with me.

Imrahan was in his tent, barbering his handsome jaw, and it was already too warm. The day seemed set to be scorching. I was near naked and sweated heavily. Still robed, Qabir was sickening and Imrahan glared at him as we knelt at the Saracen's bare feet. He gestured toward the figure of my unlikely comrade.

"What ails him?" He asked in English. "Surely he is not a leper? Have you brought corruption among us? If he is a leper, he may travel with us, but at a safe distance. You should have told me he was sick!"

"He is not a leper, my lord," I said quickly. "Quite the reverse, in fact. He... " For an hour my brain had raced. If I told the truth, that Qabir was a Tartar raider separated from a pillaging party, he would lose his head in an instant. I swallowed and chose my words carefully. "He was a priceless courtesan, as was I. His masters played strange games, and their marks still show."

"Scars? Their brutality has disfigured him?" Imrahan's frown deepened. "The Jackal is a barbarian!"

I shook my head. "They sought to make his beauty more exotic. They prized him for his looks, yet were eager for games. Be warned! I'll show you his beauty, with that dire warning!"

"Show me, then," Imrahan said, with a sigh, as if I were being tiresome.

When I stripped the robe from Qabir and left him standing naked, slender, gorgeous and as green as emeralds, Imrahan was less bored. He gaped first at my friend, then at me. "And thy masters did this to thee?" he said to Qabir in the Saracen tongue which was the only one Qabir seemed to understand.

He bowed low, almost to his knees. "They did, Sire." I had told him of my plan, and though he groaned, claiming it would never work, he had no option but to agree to it. "They dyed me with some stuff, and it won't bathe off. I have tried to remove it! They said it must wear off, and it will, but slowly, my lord. Forgive me."

Imrahan laughed. "Forgive thee? Rather, with these looks, try to stay out of the beds of my men! They will have to have thee for the curiosity of knowing what it is like to cuddle a snake-lover... and what colour thou art 'tween the cheeks, and inside thy tender body."

"The same colour as thee," Qabir mumbled. "'Tis only a trick of dye which made the sorcerer believe I possessed a magic greater than his own."

A linen shift was fetched for him, and something similar for me, and we lounged away the heat with the women. I have never seen a man gaped at so often, and with such lasciviousness as Qabir was ogled that day. He was fondled, fucked half a dozen times before my bemused eyes, and no man even cast a glance at me! He tipped up his sweet little behind to show his colour within, and seeing his smoothness and moistness they had to have him. He was not hurt – lovers of boys were gentle in Imrahan's camp – and he bore their attentions without complaint, for which they gave him fruit, sweetmeats and bracelets.

At late afternoon we broke camp and the march began again. Now Imrahan was keeping a watch out behind, fully expecting riders to come after us. When they did, Qabir and I put on the same robes as

Imrahan's guards, and covered our faces. So clothed, and given swords to hold, we were unrecognisable. We stood back and listened as Imrahan verbally flayed the men who had pursued him.

Afterward we marched slower, at a pace better suited to the women and children, and I watched the west with a horrible fascination, waiting for landmarks I would recognise. When would I see the well where we had drawn water for a night? When would I see the red stone outcropping shaped like the head of a hawk, or the hill where I had watched the battle, when the windstorm rose and I was separated from the company of knights?

But Imrahan was bound not for Jerusalem directly, but for the camp of the Sultan Saladin, and soon I realised we were on a different route, parallel to the road I had ridden with Edward's knights, and not far from it. I counted the long, hot days, dredged my memory and tried to fathom where we were.

By night I lay watching the stars and talking to Qabir. By day we marched, hot, thirsty, dusty and tired, yet free and consequently cheerful. I told Qabir of England, and Edward. I spoke endlessly of him, his charm, courage and looks, his home, even the girl who would be his bride upon our return. If Edward had lived. This doubt I admitted only once and in a hushed voice. It was too painful to bear.

Qabir heard me out but refused to speak of his home, until I began to wonder if he had been disinherited, cast out by his father. Was he a prostitute in his own land? Many beautiful youths become courtesans in the east, as they did in the great days of Athens. Male whores are not respected, as freemen are respected, but they exist, and grow rich. They are held, just as in Athens, in the same regard as women, slaves and foreigners. But if a man can live with being of the same lowly status as any woman and all foreigners, he can be a whore, and rich.

My suspicions grew when I watched Qabir bedded by half the men of Imrahan's company. His skin was so fascinating, beautiful and seductive, he was never without an admirer, and his bottom was gently abused more often than mine had been, in Jahrom Rafha's bed.

I had my own duties in the travelling camp, and as a bondsmen I had no real right to refuse. If a man had desired me I would must comply. But Imrahan knew I was grieving for Edward, and bade his men let me grieve in peace for a week at least.

As Fate worked her wondrous way, a week's peace and celibacy was long enough.

* * *

Early in the morning of a day that would be as hot as hell and as dry as the deep desert, we saw the dust of an approaching column of cavalry, and my sharp young eyes saw the first hint of the colour of their banners. Red and gold, to anyone in that land, meant King Richard.

Hoarse with excitement, I tugged Imrahan's stirrup leather. He looked down at me and I shook the hair out of my eyes. "Sire, it is King Richard's banner. There is a company of knights coming. For pity's sake, don't fight them. Where is the need of a battle? King Saladin is already on his way to meet the Lionheart. Too many have died already, my lord. Let them go by. Or let me go ahead and say we are just a trading caravan from the east, with a load of spices. They'll not know, if you conceal our banner! They may let us go on our way if we don't show them our swords. Please!"

He chewed his lip and gazed at the distant, blood red, wind-fluttered banner. "That may be the best course. Very well, Paulo Delgado. Run on and speak with them. Say I have sent you because you have the gift of their tongue, while no one else in our number is half as fluent. That is true in any case! Hurry. I shall keep a watch out from that hill. Mind, if *they* choose to fight, they shall be answered!"

I kissed his hand, picked up the dusty skirt of my robe and ran. I had weakened while in the fortress. I was as soft as most catamites, but the days of endless marching in the heat had begun to tone my muscles once more. I was not quite gasping when I came to a curve in the trail where the knights must pass by, and there I waited, finger-combed my hair to something like neatness, and coughed to clear my throat.

These knights must be searching for Saracens to torture for their knowledge. Any man who was privy to Saladin's plans would do. The less they knew of Imrahan's business, the better, or a battle would be joined. The prospect of another battle sickened me. This, from the lad who had dreamed of the death and glory of holy war!

I waited by the gnarled old olive trees, hands folded in my sleeves, my head bare, my eyes respectfully lowered. My pale skin, brown hair and my blue eyes would mark me out as Saxon or Norman, and I placed my faith in this.

The horses pranced about the bend in the trail, and as I was seen the leaders reined back. I kept my eyes down and bowed low. I had my speech composed, every lie carefully constructed. As the harness jingled closer and the heavy clop of hooves was almost on top of me, I bowed even lower and cleared my throat. I had taken a breath, but in fact I never spoke.

A voice I had heard only in my most cherished dreams for so long whispered against the breeze, and for a moment I thought myself mad.

"I don't... " he said breathlessly. "I cannot see clearly. Lionel, tell me — it cannot be! After all this time, it cannot be!"

Sir Lionel de Quilberon was equally breathless with disbelief. He swore lividly. "By Christ, it is. I don't know how or why, but it is,

Edward!"

Edward? Weak about the knees, heart thudding, I looked up, one hand shielding my eyes against the glare of the sun, and I saw his Saxon blondness, the collar of bright chainmail about his neck, his honey-gold skin, Aethelstan blue livery and the white rose on his breast.

He swung out of the saddle and came toward me, and despite the trials I had endured, the anguish I had suffered, it was this last test I failed utterly.

Before he reached me, much less laid a hand on me, and before I had seen even his face clearly, the world spun like a dervish, my knees buckled and I fainted dead away.

PART FOUR: FRIENDS AND ENEMIES

Chapter XIX

Cool water bathed my face and breast and his hands on me, anywhere, so long unfelt, were the stuff of fantasy. Through my sealed eyelids the sun was red as blood. For a long time I lay in a confused muddle, floating in heat and dislocation, knowing there was something I must remember but without the stamina to grapple for the thought, while he bathed me from brow to belly.

And then a warhorse neighed, a sword clashed, and in the distance a gruff voice said, "Is he dead? Edward! I say, is the boy dead?"

Memory flooded back with a painful rush and I struggled up. Hands that had coaxed moments before restrained me before I could begin to thrash. I prised open my lids and saw the shifting dapple of trees above me. If I turned just a little I saw a blond head, stormy eyes.

Edward.

Tears glittered on his lashes, his cheeks were flushed, and he took a breath as I began to move. As I tried to sit I discovered myself near naked, with my head in his lap. Behind me, Sir Lionel de Quilberon's gruff voice said, "Ah, he lives after all."

"Overcome with heat and weariness," Edward whispered. "It has happened to him before. This is no land for a Saxon, a creature of the woods and forests. Hush, Paul, sit up carefully. I've already examined you, but you are whole. Tired and hot, but whole."

He helped me up and I knuckled my gritty eyes. In fact, it was shock that had cost me my wits. I was in fine fettle. I had eaten with Qabir and the others – Imrahan never short-changed us by so much as a crust. I had long ago learned to manage on less water than is the rule for a European, and the miles on the road had rebuilt my muscles. My skin was still hairless, my arse unwelted and, happily, tightened a good deal. I had been chaste for days.

"Edward," I whispered, but he held a flask to my mouth, and first I must drink. I slaked my throat of dust and began again. "My lord, what are you doing here?"

"What am I –.?" Edward recoiled. "What are *you* doing here, is the better question! Where have you been? You can not simply walk out of nowhere, fall down at my feet, and no questions asked!"

"I have a tale to tell," I said thickly while my eyes devoured him, and I tried to remember the proprieties. I might have grappled with him, thieved his breath with kisses, but a dozen knights and a handful of Templars were watching. At last Sir Lionel began to grow impatient and I roused myself. "Are you here to fight?"

Over my head, Edward and Lionel glanced at each other. Lionel came closer. "You know we are, boy. King Richard's plans for the liberation of the Holy City have not suddenly changed."

"Then you ride to disaster," I said in a soft, diffident tone which nonetheless stung like a wasp. "Beyond that hill is a Saracen army that will cut you to pieces. But there is no need for it. Not any longer." I looked at Edward, imploring him to believe. "Do you recall Imrahan? You could not have forgotten him!"

He nodded readily. "I remember him well. A gentleman, by all accounts, Saracen or no. What of him?"

I took a deep breath. "Imrahan and a great host are massed beyond the hill. For the love of God, don't throw yourself on their lances. They'll kill us all, and those who are not killed will be sent back to the fortress, as slaves."

"Sent back?" Edward was hanging on my every word. "Fortress?"

"Aye, my lord, I have just come from there with Imrahan. Good fortune has been my companion, but, fight now – " I glanced at Sir Lionel " – fight, and you consign yourselves to death and your squires to the slave market. You have not the numbers to match the host across the hill, and I tell you again, the battle is needless."

Lionel stood, fists on hips. "Explain, boy. I am listening!"

"My lord, Imrahan is against the Jackal, like many of the Saracen chieftains. They are for peace. Imrahan is journeying to host with Saladin. I know little more, Sir Lionel, save that it is not bloodshed Imrahan desires. If it were, he would have delivered me and Qabir to Damascus, and would be making war with Ibrahim's black sorcery, under the banner of Masjed ibn-Zahran, whom you know as the Jackal."

"And who," Edward asked softly as he studied my face, "is Qabir?"

"A captive like myself. A courtesan because of his beauty. He and I made it away together, and we have Imrahan to thank for our freedom and our manhood." I clutched his sleeve. "My lord, believe me! Send a messenger to Imrahan. Come with me yourself, you and Sir Lionel. I speak the language passing well, and Imrahan speaks both English and French to some extent. Learn the truth from his own lips." I closed my eyes, shook my head. "Fight, and the devil will be to pay."

With a noisy sigh Lionel de Quilberon stooped and patted my bare shoulder. "You are cursed sure of yourself."

"All this time I have been a slave in their camp. I accepted their ways, learned their language, and would soon have embraced their Faith," I whispered. "I was treated well, fed and watered, and beaten seldom."

"Beaten?" Edward's fingers bruised my arm.

"Only the birch," I said quickly. "A boy's punishment, during lessons. It was lightly dealt. My own master was a fine man." I looked into his troubled eyes. A storm of emotion lurked behind his calmness. I tried to smile. "This will keep till later," I murmured. "For now, let me tell Imrahan you wish to speak with him. Oh, believe me! To fight today is to die, and the nightmare begins again!"

"I believe you," Lionel said at once. "The question is, will the Templars have any part of this? You must convince Brother Edmond, not me."

I got to my knees. My head was steady now and I was aware of the buzz of the flies, the shimmering heat over the distance, the snuffles of tired horses and mules down the cavalry column. I saw the Templars' red banner and gold standard, saw the knight commanding them, still mounted on a magnificent grey steed at the head of his contingent. My clothes were folded at Edward's side, and I quickly pulled them on.

"I do not know Brother Edmond," I mused. "Is he a fair man? What became of Jean de Bicat?"

"The surgeons cut off his right arm," Edward told me with a look of distaste. "It was badly wounded and rotted on the ride back. He raved about seeing the devil summoned to the Saracen cause, and archangels. The Templars think they were religious revelations, some of them are petitioning to have him canonised. At any rate, his fighting days are over. He says he'll take a band of missionaries into the midst of the Saracens, and convey to them the message of Christendom."

Convey... to Saracens? I almost laughed! They, who pray five times every day and learn their scriptures by heart? Doubtlessly, Jean de Bicat would try to instil in them the belief that the flesh is wicked and lovemaking is sin. Only hellfires await such men as Edward and me. Well, I thought, we shall see!

"Speak to Brother Edmond," I said as I girdled my robe. "He may fling his Templars onto Imrahan's lances. If he does, let him, but keep back your own men. I tell you, Imrahan marches to host with Saladin himself, and it is a treaty of peace in his mind, and in the Sultan's, not a holy war that has become a torment to us all." I frowned at the Templars.

Stubbled cheeks puffed out, Lionel looked from Edward to the armoured monk, and back. "I am in command of this rag-tag, tired and hungry column, so the odious duty of confronting the friar falls to me." He pulled straight his cloak. "A fair man, I'd say – for a Templar. But he'll be hard to convince. How many fighting men march with this Imrahan? Many more than we?"

"Five times the number of your company," I told him. "And that is a wary estimate, since even slaves will pick up a bow or an axe and fight when their backs are to the wall. Consider their fate, if they were taken alive. Even a maggot fights at the last."

The Norman nodded soberly and set a hand on Edward's shoulder. "Let me talk sense to the friar. Fetch up a horse for the boy and stand aside, Edward. You know you're in no fit condition to do battle. If it comes to a fight, God's teeth, you'll take no part in it – and those are the King's orders since I speak with his voice. You understand?"

Edward began to protest. It was a matter of honour, which can be a delicate question.

"No argument!" Lionel said sharply. "You commanded the last column. By all accounts, you've no right even being with this one. Your presence is a favour, my own and the King's. You are unwell, and you shall keep out of the fracas, if battle cannot be avoided. If we fall, take the boy, and run! Someone must get back with the news of what befell us."

The blond head bowed for a moment, and Lionel was satisfied with Edward's expression of agreement. I was faint with anxiety. No sooner had Lionel gone to confront the Templars' commander than I spun toward Edward and caught his arms.

"You are sick? Unwell? Injured? Edward!" Fifty nightmares I had endured during my captivity returned full force like a punch to the body. "Edward, what ails you? Where are you hurt? Are you whole?" My eyes raced over him.

He stepped back against the coarse trunk of the palm beneath which he had put me, for shade. His eyes closed to slits but I saw the tears on his lashes. For a moment I feared the worst.

"I am sick at heart," he said so quietly, only I could have heard. "Or, I was. I am mended now... almost mended. To be sick at heart is worst of all. A canker that not even the finest surgeon can cut out."

My pulse raced. "Edward? Something ails your heart?" I almost set my hand on his breast, and stopped myself at the last second.

He nodded slowly, but a faint smile touched his mouth. "I am sore there, as lovers are. I missed you more than I would have believed I could."

Warmth suffused me and I leaned heavily against the tree. "I thought you meant you were ill." He had mourned me? I was dizzy with joy.

"I was sick, tired and old without you," he said even more softly, as if I were a priest and this his month's confession. "I punished myself a thousand times."

This puzzled me. "For what? I can think of no wrong you have done."

"You have no imagination," he chided. "I punished myself for reticence." Now, I was confused, and simply waited. "How many times did I bed you, Paul? Twenty, thirty? I lost count. It all became a wonderful muddle of happiness, exhaustion and tangled limbs."

"I also lost count," I admitted, and my cheeks heated not with embarrassment but with desire. "But why do you punish yourself now for what you did to me then? Have you second thoughts about us?" Fear nibbled my belly like a tapeworm.

He sighed, exasperated with himself or with me. "You don't know what I mean?" I shook my head in genuine confusion. He took a deep breath, held it, exhaled slowly. "I shall lay bare my heart, if I must. It is past time." His eyes were tranquil as those of a painted saint. I was reminded of the likeness of St. Bede in the Saxon church near Sleaford. "I love you," he whispered, and could not look at me as he said it. "I never had the courage to tell you, as if I thought it belittled me, and that was an insult to us both. Is it God who puts love in men's hearts? Then if I deny what I feel, I deny heaven! I punished myself a thousand times, for I thought I would never have the chance to tell you. The things I did to you, lover's things, wonderful and terrible... if I abused you – "

"Edward." My tongue was so thick I could barely speak. "Never once did you abuse me. Even if you had hurt me I would have understood, it was in urgency." My eyes blurred with tears; I wanted his mouth, his tongue, his hard, hot arms. "I love you," I whispered. "Every hour we were apart, I thought that. I thought of you every time – "

Every time I was held down on cool sheets and lifted my arse. I stopped myself before I could say it, and icewater ran through my bone- marrow. I had two choices.

I could keep the truth from him. He need never know what kind of slave I had been. Yet he had already seen my shaved body. They had all seen it when he cooled me after I fell at his feet. Edward must be filled with suspicion. What folly it would be to hide the truth. One day, however long in the future, the tale could get back to him and he would know I had lied. He might never trust me again.

My second choice was fraught with risk, but I had no option. I must tell him, and make my peace with him if I could. Would he still want me, knowing what I had been? I recalled my fantasy from the feverish days before we were lovers. If it would take a thrashing and a basin of hot water to make me clean again, I would accept his anger, weather it all and buy my way back into his affections.

"Paul, what is it?" He plucked a strand of grass from my hair, which had grown long and was getting into my eyes. I was of a mind to cut it, but I knew Edward would like it this way. "You are haunted," he added.

"I am," I murmured. "I have my own ghosts, my own tales to tell."

After a long silence he said, "Aye, but they must wait till we have privacy, an evening to ourselves. This is not the place for heart-felt confessions! Though, Christ knows what this next hour may bring. We may all be dead by tonight."

All this time, Lionel and Edmond had been disputing noisily.

Now, a dozen other knights and Templars joined in, and the decision was a matter of numbers. Lionel had a few more on his side than the Templar, otherwise Edward and I should have been standing on the hill, watching with the squires and grooms and keeping our horses to hand, ready to run when the Saracens cut down the last of the fools.

Lionel turned his back on the Templars and strode toward us with a furious glare on his face. "Settled!" he shouted. "Paulo Delgado, go to the Saracen and tell him Sir Lionel de Quilberon is ready to talk!" He was in a righteous temper, and behind him he left a company of men neatly divided.

I gathered the skirts of my robe. "I shall say that Imrahan will talk with a man he knows already – with your permission. He recalls Edward and spoke highly of him to me."

"Very well," Lionel said tersely. "But you'll not go alone, Edward. A guard of knights go with you, and myself, though I'll stand aside and let you do the talking if this is what the Saracen prefers."

"Wise," Edward agreed. "Is it far, Paul?"

"Not so far that I cannot run it in minutes," I said, and was already on my way. Leaving Edward again was more cruel than a whipping, but Imrahan must be wondering what had become of me.

I gave Edward a smile as I hurried off. He was smudged and gaunt after the weeks he had grieved. He was right, the sickness of the heart is the hardest to bear, and no quack can cure it.

I took the shortest route over the shoulder of the sun-bleached hill, and spotted Imrahan's lookouts before I had gone a hundred yards. I saw the gleam of a casque and waved, so they knew who it was. The man waved back, and I recognised his face. He let me pass and I hurried on. My robe snagged on the coarse grasses and I was in tatters when I ran into the camp.

Of a sudden it was a camp of war. Men were in their armour, swords were being honed and the women and children had been sent away in my absence. I looked for Qabir, then realised he would be with the courtesans. Qabir was every man's darling.

Imrahan was magnificent in mail, white robes, a gleaming steel helmet with a high white plume of horsehair. He wore two swords over his shoulders and his eyes creased against the glare as he watched me come down the hill. I flung myself at his feet and fought for my breath.

"I spoke to the captains, my lord," I panted. "It is good fortune past believing! I know them well. One is Sir Lionel de Quilberon, a Norman, but a better, kinder man never lived. With him is my own lord, Edward of Aethelstan. He rode this way, looking for me – it was on these trails that he lost me! With them is a company of Templars headed by a man I do not know, but more knights are for Sir Lionel than for Friar Edmond, so de Quilberon has command." I looked up into Imrahan's face. "If it pleases you, he and Edward wish to talk.

They have no call and no wish to fight. I cannot speak for the Templars."

He waved me to my feet and considered me with pursed lips. "No trickery? If there is trickery, this will end in blood. I cannot keep my men on the leash if I bring vipers into their midst."

"No trickery, I swear," I said urgently, switching into his language. "I make thee a pledge, before witnesses. If there is trickery, spill my blood first. A drop or all I have, at thy pleasure." I spoke loudly, in full hearing of them, and they understood. It might have been a rash thing to say, but I had nothing else to offer.

Imrahan accepted my bond. "Go back, fetch them by the road. We will meet them here. Give them my word, there shall be no ambush."

Once more I took the hill as fast as my legs could carry me. I waved, showed my face to Sir Lionel's lookouts, and they sent me through. Lionel and Edward were already mounted, along with their escort. A horse was waiting for me, and a squire handed me the reins.

Breathless, I settled myself in the broad leather saddle. "Imrahan is waiting," I panted. "I gave him the word of a Christian captain," I warned Sir Lionel, "no trickery, I beg you." I glanced at Edward, almost in apology. He knew there was more. "The bond I placed upon this was my blood. I had nothing else to give."

"Good enough," Lionel decided, and lifted his hand.

A pace before us, the standard bearer kicked his horse and we moved off. For the first time I found myself at the head of a column of knights rather than with the squires and servants, in the dust at the rear, but I was too anxious to revel in it. I remember a buzzard, hunting on widespread wings over the parched hills, the movement of the horse under me, and the strong smell of animals and men who had been in the field for weeks. Edward was beside me, tight-lipped.

We moved slowly about the long bend in the trail. It was important to make no threatening move. Every man with us was armed, and the difference between a mission of peace and a pitched battle was a matter of a single word, even a gesture from Imrahan, whose men attended on his every expression. I begged any and all gods to hold them leashed.

Imrahan was in the forefront of his men. He was on foot, hands clasped before him, plumed helmet on his head, and his handsome face was bare. To left and right of him stood his most trusted warriors, his brothers and cousins, who would die for him if needs be. I counted twenty helmets clustered behind him, and behind them, a force of archers, though every man had set his bow and quiver at his feet. We were in no immediate danger, and would be safe unless Sir Lionel's men made the first move. I trusted Imraham implicitly.

Fifty yards from their position, we drew rein and dismounted. Imrahan came forward as I hurried toward him. I wondered what my fellows would make of it when I knelt at his feet and touched my forehead to the dust. The gesture was for Imrahan's warriors, all of whom I knew, and almost all of whom had so gently used Qabir, fed him sweets till he grew sick, and given him jewellery till his arms were heavy with silver.

"My lord," I said to Imrahan in his own tongue, "the knight with whiskers and shoulders like a bear is the Norman, Sir Lionel de Quilberon. The Saxon thou knowest."

"To thy feet, boy," Imrahan invited, and as I stood he raised his voice and called in his heavily accented English, "I bid you welcome. If you come to make peace and keep men's blood in their veins, you are welcome indeed."

Twenty knights swung out of the saddle, and Edward and Lionel strode at the head of them. Edward smiled at me and then at Imrahan, and offered the Saracen a deep bow. "We meet again. I hoped we would, and in peace. Paul told me he is indebted to you."

"Perhaps." Imrahan nodded toward the great, open-fronted pavilion. "I can accommodate your men inside, but I wager you would rather leave ten or fifteen without, so as to be at ease. You cannot sit and speak of peace when every second you fret for your safety." He smiled. "My word of honour upon this, Aethelstan. In my camp, you are safe until you lift your sword against me."

"I have no intention of lifting my sword." Edward took a step closer, held up his arms and turned aside. "Take it from me. I am an envoy of peace today. What need have I of a sword?"

Very slowly, with his left hand, Imrahan drew the broadsword from Edward's scabbard. We all felt the tension of Christians and Saracens alike: a naked sword in the midst of us was like a taper held close to a candle. But Imrahan turned the point down and drove it deeply into the sand at our feet. Beside it, flanking it to left and right, he drove in his own two swords.

"Trust, Sir Edward?" Imrahan offered his right hand.

"Trust, my lord." Edward gripped his strong brown wrist for a moment and then stepped aside to allow Sir Lionel also to take it. "Paul spoke of King Saladin. You march to join him?"

"We do." Imrahan gestured us toward his tent, where servants had set out the cushions, coffee and sweetmeats. "Has the boy told you, Salah ad-Din proposes a treaty by which your people and mine may know peace at last?"

So began talks which to me seemed endless. Fifteen knights stood outside, but though they were flanked by a like number of Saracens, swords remained sheathed and drinks were carried out by Imrahan's bondsmen. In the tent Lionel, Edward and Imrahan talked on and on. Often, I was asked to interpret, when language became a barrier. My knowledge of the language was invaluable.

Two hours after they began, the Imam called the Saracens to

prayer and Imrahan excused himself. As he passed me he put his hand on my shoulder and looked questioningly into my eyes. I nodded, and followed him. I saw Edward's astonishment as I washed face and hands and knelt with the others. I knew every word by heart and would never forget them as long as I lived.

The prayers were brief, passionate, before we returned to the tent and Imrahan took up his discussions where he had left them – the matter of prisoners of war. Edward's eyes were on me still, and I flushed. He was frowning, troubled. What things we must address when we had privacy!

Food was fetched, slices of lamb, apricots and onions, limes and lemons in crystallised sugar, figs and dates. I was too agitated to eat, and so was Edward, but Lionel and Imrahan ate a great deal. They were locked in discussion and I could tell they liked one another. They were worlds apart, yet, at the root of them, both were honest men, and warriors. That was their brotherhood. Surely truth matters most. More than love? Or is love itself a kind of truth, and not to be denied?

I became drowsy in the heat while the men smoked, drank coffee and tried vainly to conceive of some way to place the Lionheart in direct communication with Saladin. Without this communion, a treaty would never be wrought. If peace were to come about, we may well be the instruments of it ourselves. Fate wheeled about us like stars about the pole, and we felt a little grand.

Perhaps we felt too grand. Complacent. In the heat of mid-afternoon we were careless, and for that sin we were almost snuffed like candles before we knew what was upon us, and could blame no one but ourselves.

The Templars raged over the hill in a full charge – a magnificent sight, lances and shields, gleaming helmets, feathery hooves, flying cloaks – all the splendour of the tournament. Save, at the joust, killing is not the object. That day, sport was the last thing on the minds of the Templars, damn them. They would *taste* blood.

The Saracens made ranks and Lionel's men milled about, not knowing what to do. Before they could pick up their arms they found themselves thrust to the ground, weapons confiscated. Steel chimed like bells as the Templars joined the battle, obviously hoping that the engagement would be a rout, since they were mounted and the Saracens were on foot.

Foolishness. Truth? The foot soldier has the advantage in these engagements, though noblemen who revel in the tournament and the charge detest to hear it. A horse at full tilt cannot easily move left or right, there is a force that prevents it, just as the spin of a fast-whirling top keeps it upright.

A Saracen would stand still, offer himself as a target, and at the last moment simply step aside, grasp the downthrust lance and unseat the charging knight. When he crashed down, like as not unconscious from the fearful impact, he would be skewered, like a fish spitted for the fire. The screams were pitiful, blood crimsoned the sand and my heart was in my mouth.

At the entrance to Imrahan's tent Edward and I stood close together. We could only watch impotently. Before us, at our feet, Lionel's men were flat in the dust, knives, swords, arrows keeping them honest. Behind us in the tent, two guards held Edward at sword-point, but it was unnecessary. Imrahan swore bitterly as he watched the sudden carnage, and I wrung my hands.

It was but a brief battle yet twenty Templars lay dead and five horses were crumpled, hamstrung and crying piteously for help. I cannot bear the sounds of animals in pain. I fell to my knees, hands over my ears. As suddenly as it had begun, it was over. The brawny Saracen blacksmith put the horses cleanly and mercifully out of their misery, and the bondsmen dragged out the dead knights. Three of Imrahan's men had been killed, five more were injured.

White-faced, Edward and Lionel could only wait. Lionel had told Imrahan of the Templars, of Edmond, and how he hated their orders. Imrahan knew enough of Templars to accept what he said as the truth. But we fretted now, for the deceit looked plain as day. First, Edward entered the Saracen camp and lulled them into false security, then the Templars struck, knifed the enemy in the back. How could we make Imrahan believe we were not vipers?

Anger tightened his wide mouth. He returned to us with a grimness that spoke plainly: Who will answer for this? Lionel sighed, swore and clenched his fists till the knuckles were white as bone. Edward opened his mouth to speak, and I, impudent youth that I was, got between them and threw off my robe.

I stood before Imrahan in my linen and showed him my breast. "My lord, spill my blood first. It was the pledge I made thee," I said hoarsely. "My word on it, this was none of our doing. 'Tis the Templars that were not to be trusted. My pledge was good, I did not break faith with thee!"

He stood, hands on hips, head cocked at me. "Thou art the most reckless youth," he accused. "I shall deal with thee momentarily, but for now let me have it out with the captains!"

Chastened, I stood aside and bowed as Imrahan moved smoothly into English. "The boy says *that* was the Templars' doing. They wish to destroy my kind, to the last man. This I know! But I ask myself, am I duped?"

"No." Edward looked at me. "I half suspected Edmond would never allow us to make peace today. As we told you not an hour ago, part of our mission is to take Saracen prisoners who can be questioned – "

"Tortured," Imrahan corrected icily.

"I fear so," Edward admitted. "The Templars are known to slaughter whole Saracen villages in search of treasure or secrets, or because your people would not be converted. I am... " He took a breath and began again. "Forgive me, Lionel, but the time has come for truth, no matter the cost. Imrahan, I am godless. I take no part in what Templars do, or are, or say. I cannot speak for Lionel, and I saw Paul pray with your men. But I have no faith, none at all, so you may believe me where you doubt the word of a Christian, who might lie to protect that rabble of Templars."

A frown knitted Imrahan's brows. "You are a most uncommon Englishman."

"I am a Saxon," Edward said acidly. "A Saxon in a Norman land. Imrahan, you know little of my land and people, but I tell you this. The Normans come to England as invaders, just as they came here. They beat, rape, kill and enslave my people as they do yours. Saxons are tortured, sold into bondage, used as pack animals, starved, flogged and hanged. The Normans do nothing in your land that they have not done in mine. Some of us survive, but none of us prosper." Edward put his hand on my shoulder. "The boy and I came here to try to make a place for ourselves among the Normans. We hoped to serve our foreign masters well enough to earn favour. We came for selfish reasons, and it was a mistake. Now, we desire only to survive, and go home."

Silence echoed him for some time, before Imrahan sighed. "A most uncommon Englishman," he said once more. "And you, de Quilberon? You, the Norman, devout in your faith, loyal to your King!"

"I was born Norman by an accident of birth," Lionel said drily. "I could as easily have been born a blackamoor! A King is a King. Born a blackamoor, I would have been loyal to a chief dressed in feathers, and there is the end of it. I love God, where Edward doubts His very existence. But what's to say I'll not learn to doubt the Almighty tomorrow while Edward stumbles over faith? As for the Templars?" He shook his head emphatically. "They are outside my comprehension." He paused and looked Imrahan in the eye. "Are we your prisoners?"

"Should you not be?" Imrahan asked shrewdly. "I have twenty knights of your company. Both commanders. My men will gather your squires and servants. What shall I do with you?"

Lionel looked sidelong at Edward. "Let us go on our way. We are too few to harm you."

"True," Imrahan agreed. "But you take with you knowledge that could destroy us. That not very far from Jerusalem is a hosting of the knights of Islam, among whom Salah ad-Din is to be found. No, de Quilberon, I would be a fool, the Sultan himself would slit me, ear to ear, if I let you leave with the secret that could be the end of us all."

"Then – " Edward stepped closer to me, a gesture I appreciated

" – we are prisoners?"

"Consider yourselves my guests," Imrahan mused. "However, you shall be guests who leave at my pleasure, not your own. I yearn to trust you, Aethelstan. I believe I can. But until I am sure I must hold you. What would you do in my position?"

"The same." Edward considered the men with whom he had ridden. "We are twenty knights, fifteen boys, ten stewards. Forty-five in all, and some of our number are little more than children. Treat us fairly, allow us dignity."

"And in return, what shall I receive?" Imrahan was ready to bargain.

For a second Edward and Lionel looked at each other, and Lionel answered, being the commander of the ill fated party. "Obedience, my lord. You have my pledge, my men will cause you no harm, nor try to, until we are reconciled and free to go. It is my desire that we may be of service to King Saladin in the matter of the treaty, in which I perceive the hand of destiny. What better allies to deliver to Saladin, at this of all times, than ourselves?"

Imrahan saw the sense of this. "I grant you fair treatment," he agreed. "For now, you will surrender your arms and armour, and your horses. You will be on foot, like most of my people. You will travel with us, eat when we eat, drink when we drink, and receive what comforts my people enjoy. Paul, I give into your personal charge this man, Aethelstan. Who knows him better than yourself? Attend to his obedience, and you keep him safe."

Heaven help me, Imrahan was teasing mercilessly. I was still half naked, sweating in the sun. I knelt, bowed my head before him. "You trust me, my lord?"

"I have learned to trust you," he said offhandly.

"What of my pledge?" I took a quick breath. "I owe you blood. My promises were broken before your eyes."

"So they were." Imrahan came to me, and I almost physically felt Edward rebel as he drew his dagger. "What was the pledge? That if deceit came out of this, I could take a drop, or all the blood you possessed?"

"It was, my lord." I clenched my fists to stop their damnable trembling.

"Then... " The tip of Imrahan's dagger touched my left breast, piercing the skin with the tiniest wound. A faint drop of scarlet showed over my heart.

Edward burst forward, Lionel could not hold him back. "For pity's sake, it was not the boy's fault! Is it blood you want? Then take a man's, if blood enough has not already been spilled today! Fight me for my blood. If you can spill it, you can have it! But leave the boy, he wronged no one!"

"A most uncommon Englishman." Imrahan smiled. I felt the tip of the dagger, leaving only a tiniest smart behind. He showed the knife to Edward. "He promised me a drop of blood to atone for the deceit of your fellows. What do you see?"

"A... drop of blood," Edward said between gritted teeth as his hands clenched into my shoulders.

"Then, it will do. One drop was the price decided, and it is paid." Imrahan cleaned the dagger on my bare shoulder and resheathed it. "What think you, Aethelstan? I am a barbarian?" He laughed quietly. "Put on your robe before you burn, boy, and attend to this man of yours." He moved smoothly into the language Edward, Lionel and the others could not understand and said to me alone, "I believe he loves thee right well. With faint hope of winning, he was ready to fight and he knew he would die for thee. For thy love."

"I know, my lord," I replied in his language. "We have been lovers for some time. Trust him to my care. His word binds him, he shall cause thee no fretting."

"Thy pledge?" Imrahan teased.

But I was not jesting. "Aye, my lord, my pledge."

I dressed as the men began to dig a long, deep trench into which went the dead bodies of Templars and horses, and those of Imrahan's men who had died. Edward followed me into the tent but said nothing to me, nor to Lionel. He and Lionel drank water while the graves were filled and covered, by which time the squires and servants had been brought around the hill, and the tents were swiftly dropped.

We travelled only a short distance that evening, to join the women and children of Imrahan's clan, who were encamped not far away, where they had been safe from the battle. And it was there, despite Lionel's protests, that the necessary was done.

Though Lionel and Edward were left free the other knights, servants and youths were shackled about the ankles. The leg-irons were light, and a yard of chain between them permitted a full stride, but shackles are shackles, and pride was bruised. This was the price of their entry into the caravan, and after cursory protests Lionel and Edward kept silent. Save for the irons, Imrahan's people would not trust the Normans, and the mistrust was not unfounded.

Three Saracen dead were being mourned, five injured were being nursed. Lionel's people were alive, and knew they were fortunate. Trust must be earned, and they would not earn it overnight.

Meanwhile, Edward was entrusted to me, and as the sun set in a lake of gold and crimson I took him to the small tent I shared with Qabir. As usual by night, Qabir had gone with a paramour who would making free with the tender welcome of a lover's body. The tent was empty, leaving Edward and me to face each other at last, and I trembled more at the thought of this than at the spectacle of battle.

Chapter XX

The tent smelt of jasmine, which Qabir liked to burn because it calmed him and settled his belly. But as I led Edward into the scant privacy, my Tartar friend was the furthest thought from my mind.

The evening was already chill. No Englishman can imagine this without having experience. No sooner is the sun down than it is dark, there is almost no twilight, and when the sun is gone the sand fast cools and the air is like a draught off an icy lake.

Servants had visited our tent with coffee and food, and we would not be disturbed. I closed and tied down the flap. If Qabir returned he would call through, but this was unlikely. He had so many admirers, as soon as one man was finished dandling him he would be swept up by the next. It was not unusual for him to share the beds of four or five men between dusk and dawn, and every one would cherish him, make him feel a prince among consorts. His comfort was their concern, and though he was fucked a great deal, he came to no harm that I knew of.

I fumbled with the tent flap, my fingers clumsy with anxiety. Behind me, Edward threw down his heavy mail coat and stood like a statue. A single lamp burned, the brazier was lit and the jasmine smouldered in the brass burner. At last I got the tent secured and turned toward him.

He had dropped his mail coat in the corner, out of the way, for the tent was not large. He seemed thin, and in the semi-darkness I saw hollows beneath his cheekbones. So greatly had he grieved? My heart twisted and I knelt at his feet, as I had knelt before my Saracen master. But ibn-Qasim had never gone to his own knees beside me and crushed me against him. He had accepted my obeisance as his due, but Edward seemed to crumple, and the next I knew I was in his arms. I buried my face in the Saxon gold of his hair.

I wept and he soothed me, when by all accounts it should have been me soothing him. His hands stroked me through my robe, and slowly I calmed. In that moment I felt more boy than man, and Edward knew, and let me take my time. He lifted my chin in his fingers, and put his mouth on mine. I opened for his tongue and he plumbed my depths with a kiss so hard, it raised the iron tang of blood. Tasting it, he gentled, and we toppled onto the cushions and lay entwined, kissing more softly for a long time, while his hands explored me.

When we parted he brought the lamp closer and studied my face as if he had never seen it before. My mouth was swollen. My jaw was as smooth as the rest of me, but he had discovered this already, and now was waiting for explanations. One fair brow rose, and I swallowed hard.

"I stumbled into the storm, Edward. When I found my feet I saw a horseman. One of the Saracens... "

So began the tale of woe and survival. I was in his arms again, fed, safe, my hopeful cock throbbing against his thigh. I had no need to grieve for wrongs done me, but I knew I must tell the whole truth – he would demand no more and accept no less – and this frightened me more than any act ibn-Qasim might have desired.

First, I told the story in broad terms: the march to the fortress, my teacher, my lessons in language, the Book, what I had seen of military forces, the sorcerer and his prisoner, Qabir. Edward absorbed all of this, but the frown creasing his brow told me that he knew I was skirting the truth. After I had described Imrahan's arrival, and the battle between the half-brothers at the head of the clan of the Jackal, and our escape, I fell silent. Sweat beaded my face. Anxiety wilted my erection, and Edward saw that, too.

"There is more," he guessed. "What is so dreadful that you cannot speak of it? You were birched, you said, but not so cruelly that it left scars." He turned me, lifted the hem of the robe I still wore, though it was loose and gaped to display the better part of me. He stroked my buttocks affectionately. "These cheeks are perfect and there is not one welt on your back. If you were flogged, it was done carefully to save your skin. Did this happen? What was your crime?"

"No, Edward," I said hoarsely, "I was not punished, save by the teacher, mostly for being a wilful student with an awful memory! It was the same in England for us both."

He let me turn again, and knotted his hands in my hair. "You are as smooth as a little boy. Who shaved you, and why? Answer me, for I am fretting. Were you not raped?"

I bit my lip hard. What could I say? He groaned, taking my silence for an admission. I caught his hands and found them shaking. "Edward, I was not raped. I was merely used."

He took a breath. "What mean you?" And he took his hands from me, as if I had grown hot as a coal.

With a belly full of butterflies, I told him. I did not dare look him in the eye for fear I would see pain, or worse, distaste. One would have been as bad as the other. If I hurt him, I hurt myself.

"I was a slave," I said quietly. "I told you, for me it was bondage in the fortress or the market at Dimashq, where I would have fetched a high price. A fair skinned eunuch, pretty with paint, skilled in the bedchamber. I was fortunate, Edward. I had no rights or options. When the Captain desired me, I could not refuse. I gave him what he wanted without a struggle. Had I fought, I would have been bound, or beaten for audacity. Every moment, I had one dream: to keep whole and make my break for freedom! I let the Captain have me, and he was fair to me. He was the only man who had me, I swear – I was made love to, not defiled. He was fond of me, and bought me. He offered to let me accept his Faith, and become free in a way, and I agreed."

Still, I could not look at Edward, but he was listening intently. "I was fed and clean, taught their language and writing. At night I went to my lord's bed. There was always oil, I was never unduly hurt. I would use my mouth, then straddle him, or kneel. He liked to watch me attend to my own pleasure, and sometimes recited poems. Then a soldier took me to the room I shared with my teacher, for a lesson before bed. I slept alone. Edward, I was not brutalised. Am I dishonoured? Should I have fought? If I had, he would not have wanted to keep me, he would have let them sell me. If I lifted a hand against him, I would never have seen you again. I could have hidden a knife and cut his throat, but I would have been dead before I could get out. What choice had I? Edward, absolve me. For God's sake absolve me!"

I said all this in a hoarse whisper and he was silent. He did not bring me closer or thrust me away, and as I ran down like a waterwheel in summer he sat against the pillows and rested his chin on his fist. He seemed to be looking into the distance, with hazy eyes. I could say no more. To go on protesting my innocence would make the truth begin to sound like a lie, so I waited, and Edward neither moved nor spoke until I was about to leave the tent, sleep outside with the slaves, which I fancied was where I belonged. What place had a harlot in the bed of a Saxon knight? Ice had frozen in my belly and I was exhausted.

In the instant before I would have left he found his voice. "I knew it must be something like that," he said with an odd, far-away sound, as if I was hearing him on the wind. "I thought, a beautiful boy would be owned, traded, used. I imagined, passed from hand to hand, the way your strange friend Qabir is being shared. If there was only one who bedded you, I must be grateful. How defiled could one Saracen make you?"

Defiled? I choked on the word and squeezed shut my eyes. He was hurt. He could picture every scene I had described, and he would bear them painfully. His was a gentle birth and upbringing, and until he met me he had never laid hands on a man or boy. All his life he was chaste, and I went to him as a virgin. He could touch me without qualm, I was as pure as a novice nun.

Now, he imagined me despoiled. Pain racked me and I could not defend myself. All I had were empty excuses. I rocked on my heels and hugged my chest, punishing myself. I *felt* defiled. I was sullied!

My old fantasy returned to haunt me, and my heart beat harder. Despoiled, was I, like poison to his hands and body? Trembling, I got up. In the corner was the enamel bowl and ewer of water, left for me to wash before evening prayers. Beside it, a phial of sweet oil, cloths and towels, the little niceties the Saracen and Turk enjoy.

Without looking at Edward, I filled the bowl, dropped a washing rag into it and draped a towel over my arm. From the cushions opposite I picked up a thick leather strap, one of the bindings with which the bundle of rugs and cushions, and the tent itself, would be thonged for tomorrow's march. He seemed to realise what I was doing when I put dish, towel and strap down beside him, and stripped. I closed my eyes and said hoarsely,

"I am disgraced in your sight, and in the sight of heaven. But here is the mending of that." And I turned, knelt with the bowl between my knees and leaned my weight on my elbows for the leathering that went before the washing.

He remembered as well as I did. The strap slithered through the cushions like a live snake. I heard the rustle of his sleeves as he doubled it and wrapped it about his hand. I choked off a cry, half of dread, half of disbelief. He was going to strike me! Never had Edward raised his hand to me, it was beyond my imagination.

I clenched my teeth, prepared to be welted to blood if need be. Rather a day's soreness and an arse full of stripes than the loss of Edward's affections. I would have taken any punishment.

The tough leather caressed me, around my buttocks and through my cleft, slithering over the heart of me. He sighed. "What is this? You are shaking. Do you think I'll thrash you?"

"I have done the worst by you, my lord," I said breathlessly, cheeks blazing. "I cannot turn back time, but I can make amends. Hit me. Hit me!" The strap swung like a feather against my uptipped rump. "Harder," I hissed through clenched teeth. "Hit me!" By then I needed it. I felt like dirt, and needed the purging.

Just once, he did strike me, the way one urges a horse to speed, a good blow, heavy and unstinting. The breath rushed from my lungs at the sudden white-hot burn, then the strap fell into the cushions. He caught my hips and pulled me back and down, over the dish. Panting as if I had run miles, I shut my eyes as I heard the splash of water.

His hand, wrapped in the cloth, slid between my legs. He washed my cock, my balls and, over and over, my anus. Each time he wrung out the cloth I felt a little more cleansed, a little more virgin. He pushed my shoulders forward and down. I doubled over the dish, held my breath as he pressed a thick wad of cloth inside, withdrew it and began again. As he did this, though it stung, I relaxed one muscle at a time. In some way the strange rite washed memories from my mind. Recollections that had been sharp as a knife when he began dulled, misted, until scenes and sounds I had engraved into my memory during the weeks at the fortress were somehow cleansed from my brain.

A fifth time he pressed a thick wad into me. I grunted at the sting, but I was so lax by then, I was dreamy. When the cloth pulled out I felt a towel. The bowl was taken away and I heard a stopper being removed from a bottle... smelt the scent of cedar. Fingers entered me, thick, slick, gentle as he readied me.

He was making me his own again. Tears burned my eyes and I

spread wide, waiting and eager. I would have given him everything I had ever given the Saracen, had he granted me the opportunity, but his robes were simply hoisted about his waist, and before I could speak or move he was in me. The sudden fullness knocked the breath out of me. I forced back, impaling myself. His hands cradled my hips and his rhythm, which I had expected to be hard, even merciless, was slow. Had he purged the pain from himself, at the same time as unburdening me? He was a different man now. He was Edward again.

We went down among the cushions and I sprawled on my belly, head pillowed on my arm. I longed for his skin on mine, his bare chest on my back, but I felt only the rub of his clothes. Still, his breath was moist in my ear, his cock thick inside me. I was content. Harsh breathing warned me of his coming, when my own cock was rampant and I needed more. I snaked both hands under, grasped it tight and pulled urgently as he began to spend. He panted into my hair, bruised my shoulders, thudded against my insides before he was leaden, vulnerable in the aftermath of the storm.

I had been so tense, swift pain stabbed me as I followed him. Edward did not move, but continued to press me down until I was squashed and suffocated. I would not speak, even to beg for air. I could think of no better way to die than crushed beneath him, thoroughly fucked, whole in body and spirit. I *was* whole, purged, I felt almost virgin. At last he returned to his senses and took his weight on his hands, either side of my shoulders. He kissed the crown of my head.

"I hurt you."

"No." I smiled against the cushion. "The bathing smarted. The strap stung. But you were my salvation. I am your own, Edward. It was all I could do, to live and come back to you. All else was folly, and you know my alternatives." I prised open my eyes and dared look at him. His face was peaceful, his eyes calm. "Tell me I am your own."

"Oh, you are," he said ruefully. "If ever I doubted, I know better now. I have never known a boy beg to be leathered! I am so sorry. I must have made you feel... understand, it was the shadows in my own mind, none of your doing."

With that he withdrew and I yelped at the sharp little pang this brought. I was so sore, I could hardly bear his examining fingers, and was grateful to be bathed again, and re-salved. Then he turned, took me in his lap, and I slid my own arms about him.

"Tell me," he whispered, "everything you did in the Saracen camp."

"The details?" I muffled against his warm, hard breast. "My lessons, the bedchamber?"

"Everything." He stroked my head and let me kiss his tongue. "Are you hungry? You seem well fed. A lad your age needs his food."

We ate as I told him all I remembered, from the beauty of the marble and the softness of the silks that are brought west down the Silk Road, to the dark magic of Ibrahim, the dreams of glory of the Jackal's followers. The elegance of Arabian horses, the sweet singing from the harem, the call of the Imam, the wisdom of the Book.

He wanted to know the secrets of the bedchamber, and I spoke of perfumed oil, the freedom of men to love boys in that Saracen clan. Other clans, I know, read into the Book lessons which may or may not be there, and many Saracens and Turks count love between men as the same kind of sin as adultery. Again, I had been fortunate.

It was very late when at last, tired and hoarse, I fell silent. He held me still, scarcely believing he had me back. The guards were changing their watch, which meant it was midnight. Edward was bare under a heavy rug that shut out the growing chill. I poured cold coffee, which is as refreshing as the hot. We had eaten all but the last of the dates, and I had brought these to our nest among the cushions when feet pattered on the sand outside.

The flap twitched as someone tried to open it – it could only be Qabir, no one else would intrude. I looked down at Edward, who lay with his head pillowed on one hand, and swung on a robe. I moved to the flap and in the Saracen tongue called, "Who is it?" Though of course I knew.

"It is I," Qabir answered. "Why am I shut out?"

"I have my lord to bed," I told him. "What doest thou out of some other man's warm bed?"

"I want my cloak, my kerchiefs and jewel box." Qabir sounded annoyed with me. "Let me in!"

I looked back at Edward. Qabir, who had been loved by most of the men in this camp, would never understand why I would shut him out. "A moment," I whispered, and then to Edward, in English, "It is my friend, Qabir. He wants his things."

Edward sat up and finger-combed his hair. "Let him in. I would see this green-skinned beauty!" He was bare to the waist as the rug fell about his hips, and the word 'beauty' best described himself.

I opened, and Qabir hurried out of the sharp wind. I had spoken at length of this one, whom Ibrahim believed had the power to conjure magic to crush the Crusader army. Here was the man himself, and I watched Edward's face as he appeared. Qabir wore only a thin linen shift, and he was cold. Who had tossed him out without a cloak? Or had he run from someone? Imrahan would admonish the man who hurt or upset him! I wrapped a cape of my own about him and fetched him closer.

He had heard so much of Edward, he must have felt as if he knew him. His manners were perfect. He knelt, touched his forehead to the carpets and did not rise until he was told to. I took him by the shoulders and found his skin like ice.

"Qabir, thou'rt frozen! Where hast thou been?"

"On the hill," he said tersely, in the Saracen tongue we shared. "I needed to see the stars. As a lad I was apprenticed to an astrologer, and you know I made charts of the sky for Ibrahim. The position of the stars tells me the day and the time, and the way we are marching. We are marching in the right direction!"

I was puzzled, and barely noticed Edward's dumbfounded expression as he gaped at Qabir's skin. I was still trying to warm Qabir's hands when Edward plucked at my friend's shift.

"Ah, God!" Qabir groaned, "I am too cold!" But he had learned, a slave did not refuse. He shrugged out of the shift, knelt and presented himself. "Tell him to be quick, for I'm frozen. The wind is sharp as a knife, and I had nothing to wear. I was to have gone straight from Sarab's bed to Rashid's, but I had the chance to walk, and I took it!" His teeth were chattering.

Edward was speechless as he saw the whole of the green body. Qabir was beautiful, but that dyed skin made him irresistible. For a second I wondered if Edward desired him. I swiftly took Qabir by the arm and wrapped him in a rug.

"He does not want thy arse, importunate harlot, merely to see thy skin, for its colour! Edward is mine, he'll fuck no other, and has had me once already tonight. I doubt he can rise for a while, and when he is hard again – out with thee, grass snake! The ripening of that lovely pizzle is not for thee!"

Qabir looked up and smiled. "Thou knowest what I thought. Not a pole in this camp has not lanced me."

"Impudent flea," I accused. "I have not skewered thee, and I have a well-sized pole." I looked at Edward then, who was captivated, and moved into English. "His skin was dyed for a prank. It will wear off, but not soon enough for his liking. He is the warmer of many beds, and all he yearns for is to return home."

"By sorcery, as Ibrahim thought?" Edward asked bemusedly.

"On a horse, with a tail-wind! He says he is a Tartar, far from home, as I told you. His people are pillagers, but be sure, Satan has no part in this. Qabir was as much a prisoner in the fortress as I was, and his master was not so kind as mine. While I was fondled on a soft bed, Qabir was chained in a cellar." I shuddered. "He would have died, had I not brought him out."

"He is frozen," Edward observed. "Stir the brazier and put another rug on him. Then come to bed, Paul. It has been too long since we lay together. Can he understand me?"

But I shook my head as I poked the brazier with an iron rod. "He was taught only the Saracen tongue, and speaks it with as barbarous an accent as I do!"

"What was he doing out there, in the cold?"

"Reading stars, to tell the time and day, and where we are going.

He is an astrologer of sorts." The fire brightened quickly and Qabir shuffled closer. "He said we are marching in the right direction, but what he means, I cannot guess."

"Ask him!" Edward began to comb his hair.

I itched to comb it for him, but turned back to Qabir and put his question. Qabir's lips pursed. "Thou knowest what I meant," he accused. "Time and again I tell thee, if I am to return home, I must meet my clan on a certain day, in a certain place."

"Tartars, a hundred leagues from home," I observed. He nodded, sighed, and I fear I believed him addled in the brains. What chance had he of meeting them? It was wishful thinking. He was lost, as we all were.

"Well?" Edward yanked a strand of my hair.

I repeated Qabir's nonsense and Edward's eyes widened. "He is mad," I said drily. "He is more likely a slave, hurt so badly in his capturing or breaking-in, he cannot even recall his name or where he is from. Pay him no mind. He is harmless and beautiful. Mark my words, he'll end his days some man's beloved, in a bed in Dimashq or Bagdad." I kissed Edward's stubbled cheek, and shifted into the Saracen tongue. "Art thou warm now? Take my cape, and thy things, and give us privacy! I shall rouse my lord and I desire greatly to be fucked, but not with thee watching. Is Rashid waiting for thee?"

"I imagine so," Qabir said tartly. "And he desires as greatly to plough the field of my behind!"

"Then enjoy it," I scoffed. "Sounds of enchantment have I heard from thee when thou art reamed with gentle but firm determination! Rashid is an honourable man who will first warm and feed thee, then oil and bed thee on cushions."

"True," Qabir admitted. His eyes glittered as he rummaged for his things and clutched my cape about him. "I shall tell him I was taken ill. A quickening of the gut." He caught my arm. "I know the time, the day and the place! If fortune is with me, I will go home!"

Then he fled, and I shook my head over the follies of a mind too tormented to remain sane. I let him out, and he vanished into the shadows. Edward was waiting. He opened his arms and I went into them, hungry for his mouth. He gave me what I wanted as he blindly stripped the robe off me, and I returned to my senses to find myself swaddled in the rugs, half under him, but before I could turn him to sensual pursuits he shushed me.

"I cannot rest. Advise me – who else will I ask? Shall I trust Imrahan? He has already shackled a company of knights!"

"And would *you* trust a company of glory hunters and barons' men not to make mischief when your back was turned?" I asked shrewdly. "In England, every man in that infamous little army of Sir Lionel's trod Saxons underfoot. Why would they be any kinder toward Saracens? Knowing that, should Imrahan trust them, without at least imposing a little on them in the way of shackles! It is less than he could have done. There is a fiendish way of collaring a column of men for a march, where every man has his neck in a running-loop, a noose, and if one flees or falls he strangles all the others. Imrahan has done the least he might have!"

"He is probably wise to chasten them with a yard or two of chain," Edward mused. "But what of us? You have known Imrahan much longer than I have."

I rolled onto my back, pillowed my head on my arm and studied his attentive face. In the firelight he was very beautiful. His hair cloaked his shoulders, and I rubbed a strand of it between my fingers. "He is for peace, but not all the tribes are. Imrahan and many others march to meet Saladin, but that is the beginning, not the end. Not even Saladin can order men's hearts. Before he can offer any kind of treaty to King Richard, he must woo his own people. That will not be easily done."

Edward frowned deeply. "You foresee a war, pitting Turk against Saracen?"

"Maybe," I admitted. "I have already seen it happen, brother against brother. Ibn-Qasim, my master, was killed by his brother's champion, fighting for the right to captain that clan for Saladin, rather than send his men back to war. The Sultan may have to fight them all before he can speak to Richard Lionheart."

"And in the midst of this, what of us?" Edward caught my wrists and made me stop stroking him. I was beginning to rouse him, and he knew I could make him lose his mind.

"I do not know," I admitted. "But we are better and far safer in Imrahan's charge than in the company of Templars. We may not be entirely free, we may be headed for some kind of bondage, but we shall be free as eagles when the truce takes shape."

"If it takes shape," he corrected. "Suppose Saladin fights the Jackal and is defeated. We are captives. Anything might be done with us."

But I shook my head and gripped his hands. "Imrahan respects us. Do you know, the Mussulman calls Christ another Prophet? There is less distance between us than you imagine, Edward. It is not impossible that we could call each other brothers... merely unlikely. In the teeth of disaster, Imrahan will turn us loose and put the sword back into your hand. You may have to fight again." I touched his face. "I have heard, a magical Garden awaits the righteous. If a man lives well and dies bravely, he is deemed fit to enter, and there lives forever, without sickness or want, enjoying wine and food, and the lovers he desires."

"They taught you this?" He leaned down over me, his chest pressed heavily on mine, warm and hard as only a man can be.

"It was in the Book," I whispered.

"You believe?" He kissed my brow.

"I do not know," I sighed. "I have seen so much, good and bad, that it is jumbled in my mind. I may be years sorting out the confusion. What does it matter? They told me, God sees into the hearts of men and cannot be duped! He is watching even now, and knows I am struggling to live well and decide what is right. He will appreciate my struggles, knowing they are the rites of passage of a boy into manhood."

"You speak like a Saracen," he accused, but he was not mocking.

"Do I?" I wrapped my arms about him, wanting to feel his heart. "I could have been one of them. They taught much I shall never forget. Forgive me."

He nuzzled my neck. "You have changed. You are more a man than when I lost you."

"Hardship changes anyone," I murmured. His hand was sliding over my belly, and I kicked down the rug. My eyes slitted as I watched him palm my eager shaft, which had wilted and required coaxing. "I am not changed where it matters most," I added ruefully. "Let me turn over, and prove it."

I was trying to offer my arse when he held me back, and his hand tightened on my cock. "I dreamed, when you were lost. Over and over. I was shocked at first, then less troubled, and at last when the dreams came I welcomed them."

I rubbed his arms, revelling in his lean, hard muscles. "What bedevilled you?"

"You plundered me," he whispered.

For a moment I thought I had misheard, but he dragged in a breath for courage and shivered, and knew I had heard correctly. I rubbed his arm once more, but I was trembling too. He had touched something in me that had never been touched before.

"Have no fear," I soothed. "I would do no such thing, Edward." But oh, how I wanted to!

His eyes were dark, like luminous obsidian. "Not even if I begged and seduced you?"

"You want... ?" My mouth flapped like a stranded fish. I struggled desperately to sit. "I could not!"

He cocked his head at me, one hand on my hip. "I have a repulsive arse?"

"You have a bottom fit for princes, a rump like a peach! But you are an earl, I could never do it to you!"

"I am a sodomite," he said without scorn either for himself or me. "I am unrepentant and content. I often dreamed I was plundered by this young cock."

I groaned as if he had wounded me. Some sinew was alive inside and every word tickled it. "And enjoyed – ?" I asked breathlessly.

"Greatly." His voice was soft as ripped silk. "I'll have that from you now. I know how it is done – I am virgin, but not ignorant!" He

189

had the phial of oil, and I watched him coat his fingers. I gaped as he knelt, spread his lean thighs and slid those fingers upward. He sighed, and though I saw nothing I knew what he was doing. At last he turned to show me. "Enough?"

Wanton, he knelt with his shoulders on the cushions. I had never seen him behave so, nor dreamed he could. His rump was white as flax and the heart of him was pink, tight, quivering. I laid the pad of my finger on him and, heaven help us both, it slipped in. He made a tiny sound. Inside he was like butter, hot, soft and smooth, clean and wholesome, smelling just of the oil. I kissed his back, and he smiled. I waggled my finger, trying to find the deep-buried nub, and thrill him.

He yelped when I found it, and writhed helplessly, which gave me a dizzying sense of power. "What are you doing to me?"

"Showing you the pleasure you give me," I muffled against the skin of his backside. "This is what men love of men. This is what monks do, in the closed cells of every monastery, though they deny it. What witches do in the shadows on Beltane eve, and how shepherds make love, out of the sight of their masters." I slid in a second finger.

He had been enjoying it, but now he frowned. "You're hurting me."

"I know. I must make this clench soften... remember my first time? This is but a little pain. Endure, and you will feel only pleasure later."

Sweat beaded his brow, and he gripped the pillows. "Then push in three fingers, since you are well hung for a youth your age. Go on! I am a knight, and can bear it."

It would hurt, and I was cautious. He stretched, hissed through his teeth and squeezed shut his eyes. I kept my hand still until he relaxed, and all the while I was tormented. My heart thumped, my head spun and my breath rasped. I was a poker, hard as iron, hot as a brand, weeping tears of frustration. The minutes of my torture were the mirror of Edward's, we paid the price in equal measure. I gritted my teeth and courted patience, trying to help him to this new knowledge with great gentleness. For a time he was taut as a bow, then he fell onto the cushions and his breathing was as easy as mine was harsh, his heart at ease while I was feverish.

"Fuck me properly," he growled. If that is three fingers, I am ready."

I gulped and did as I was told. My balls were white-hot as a new-forged sword as I moved between his thighs. How fine is the body of a man, lean, hard and glowing with heat. I nudged into place, touched him there and almost came at once. Without encouragement, he lifted his hips as he had seen me do, which spread him wider. His muscle had softened and he was ready. Trembling, I positioned myself and pushed. In I slipped, with no resistance, no obstruction. The knight was open, virgin as a maid, and he was mine – a half-realised dream come true. I was in by a hand's span when he sobbed and I realised I was hurting him. I stopped, withdrew a little to ease him, and he gripped me like a fist. His muscles rippled, which to him was swift pain and to me, swift pleasure.

I kissed his shoulder. "Suffer a moment more, and you will feel the enchantment."

It came soon enough. I nudged in, touched that nub, and he jumped like a wayward horse. Now I had him! I tried a thrust, and he groaned. A deeper thrust buried me and he arched to meet me. His head tossed, his face twisted. Power filled me – not a realisation that I had the ability to hurt, though I surely did, but that I could give him pleasure that made him mine. Now that he had felt this, how would he ever be free?

I soothed him and we began to rock together. It was difficult to find a rhythm, but when we did it was deeply satisfying. He moved with me, with the same perfection as I had always moved with him, even the first time, but he was tense, aching to be released. I was tight-leashed and could have gone on, but I must let him finish, and get out, before he paid a high price for my pleasure, so I drove him on, put my hand under his belly, and found the lance of his cock, the fleshy eggs of his balls. He came with a shout, and that cry, the rush of seed in my hand, were all I needed to follow him.

I went down on his back, breathing the scent of his musk and seed. He whimpered into the cushions, a sound I had never heard before. Slowly I regained my breath, and parted from him. I saw just one drop of blood, and wrung out the cloth that had bathed the defilement from me, to wash us both. Then I stooped between his legs and kissed the sore heart of him with my tongue. He struggled awake as he realised the homage I was paying him, and I helped him turn, took him in my arms and held his face against my chest.

"It was pleasurable," I guessed hopefully.

"It was... " he cleared his throat, as if he could not command his voice. "Strange, and wonderful. Painful and unpardonable... beyond my imagination. I love you." He looked into my face and a blush stained his cheeks. "Am I the same man who sailed from England?"

"Yes." I kissed his forehead. "You are Edward of Aethelstan."

Tears glistened on his lashes but he smiled, and I pulled up the rug before we could begin to chill. In the midst of passion, heat, cold and even pain diminish. Nothing else is noticed till the uproar is spent.

"Sleep," I whispered. "It is past midnight and the camp will break at the hour before dawn. We have a long way to go."

But he pulled me into his arms, teethed my nipples and was not content until he had explored me with his tongue. At my belly, he arched back to study the instrument that had stolen his virginity, measured it with his fingers, held it up and pressed my balls in fascination. "You will fuck me often," he said as he lay beside me again. "In this

191

camp, I am no more a knight than you are. We are prisoners, it hardly matters that I was noble born and you were not. Indeed, it is you who knows these Saracens best, not I."

"I know a little," I admitted, "but I had only begun my lessons when Qabir and I had to flee."

"Qabir," he mused, "is a strange one. Little wonder he beguiled the sorcerer."

"He is insane, pay him no mind. He is probably from no further away than Cochin. All else is the ravings of a mind which could not endure captivity without cocooning itself in fantasies."

Yet Qabir had never seemed insane, and my arguments did not much impress even me. Every word Qabir said convinced me he was sane, and intelligent. He had been Ibrahim's prisoner too long, perhaps, and was on the brink of madness. Now that he was free, cherished by lovers who sang of his beauty, he might become sane again, a little at a time.

But Edward was fascinated. "I have heard of the Tartars," he mused as we settled to sleep.

"So have I, but I doubt he is one! He is dreaming to make his captivity easier."

"Perhaps," Edward agreed. "But tomorrow, ask him where they come from, what they want, where they are at this time. Has it occurred to you that he may well be from Cochin, but his first masters may have been Tartars, who sold him to the Saracens! They might accept mercenary work, in our pay."

"Fight for us? We might raise an army of our own?" That thought had escaped me. I was never one for puzzles, and I hate a mystery. Edward, by contrast, seemed to thrive on mystery. I wriggled closer. "I shall ask."

"In the morning, first thing. Even if he is raving, there may be a seed of truth in what he says."

His voice grew thicker, his hands heavier, and he was asleep. He was limp as a rag after what I had done to him, and I might have been drunk, but the only wine was him. All the same, his reasoning impressed me and my mind wove in circles as I drifted to sleep.

Chapter XXI

The Imam roused us in the hour before the sun rose, and Edward shook my shoulder. "Keep in their good graces, love, even if the words are like warm oil on your tongue. The day may come when it makes the difference between life and death for us all."

We kissed ravenously before I snatched up robe and cloak and hurried out. The Christian knights were yawning and scratching in their tent. Qabir and Rashid, his last man, stood by a smoking fire. Rashid had enfolded him as if Qabir was his long lost beloved, and as I watched he knelt at Qabir's feet and kissed the elegant green hands before he also hurried to answer the Imam.

We washed faces and hands and knelt. Every word tripped from my tongue, and they were not quite like oil, despite Edward's suspicions. I mused upon what I was saying. Salutations to a God who promised to care for the weak and sick, vengefully chastised wrong-doers, and promised the just a magical Garden as the reward for a good life. If only I owned the faith, rather than just the yearning to believe.

At my right was Imrahan, and in that moment we were of the same rank. Before heaven all men are equal. Then the Imam fell silent and we stood. I bowed before Imrahan and he smiled. He was again the chieftain, and I the captive who was somehow not quite a captive. My position was odd, which seemed to amuse him endlessly.

"Thou enjoyed a good night?" he asked with a shrewd glance at the tent I shared with Edward.

"A fine night, Sire, filled with love," I told him.

"Then feed him, and help break camp. We have far to go."

I caught his sleeve. "A moment of thy time, my lord. I am fretted. What shall become of us if King Salah ad-Din must battle the other warlords, and is defeated?"

He sighed. "A grave question. I know not, but I shall look to thy welfare. I can make no fairer promise."

I bowed again as Imrahan rejoined his cousins. The little boys were serving our swift breakfast of simmered dates and honeycomb. I took a basket of food, and as I turned toward the tent I saw Qabir, and remembered what I must ask.

He was still with Rashid. The warrior's arm was about his shoulders, and Qabir looked exhausted. He had been coupled often, kept awake and busy until all hours of the night. He would doze whenever we stopped to rest the animals, and when we made camp he would sleep sound until his admirers summoned him.

As Rashid answered the call of his lieutenant I joined the yawning, smudged-eyed and half-awake courtesan. "Slept thee well?"

He gave me a glare. "I slept hardly at all. Every time I closed my poor eyes that damned Rashid would wake me in the most ticklish way! Now, a finger thrust up me, now, his shaft in my lips, and my own shaft slid into a cup of cool water so that I leapt out of my skin and came up hard again!"

"And dost thou not love such pleasures?" I snorted. "But tell me, what saw thou in the stars? I know nothing of stars, save that they are brightest at midnight."

He helped himself from my basket. "I can tell thee the names of scores, I know where they are on any day of the year, and by the

193

setting of the sun and the rising of the planets I can tell where we are."

"And where are we?" I asked shrewdly.

He gave me a shrewd look. "Jerusalem lies yonder. The fortress is back there, and my home, north-east."

I bit my lip. Qabir seemed so sane – sad, hunted, wild with grief, but not mad. He would watch the distance as if he yearned to catch sight of something, someone. "Tell me," I prompted, "so I may tell my lord – "

"Thy lover," he said, cheering of a sudden and grinning at me, all white teeth.

"My lover," I agreed blithely, and glanced after Rashid. "That man is crazed over thee."

"He loves me." Qabir was agitated. "I have tried time and again to fend him off and make him know they are but games I play. I cannot go with him, as he wants, and be his beloved for all his days and mine. I am going home! Rashid will not believe me. See, he gave me this." He showed me his right hand.

On the first finger was a concubine ring, immeasurably old and precious. I whistled to show my appreciation. "So, tell me. When wilt thou meet thy tribe?"

"It is not for thee to know," he snapped. "I'll not have thee tattling to Imrahan and keeping me here."

I smiled, humouring him. "I would not tattle! Edward wishes to know if the Tartars would take mercenary wages, fight for us."

His face darkened as if a chill wind had blown on him, but he took my wrist in friendly fashion. "Best that thou never meet them. If thine eyes behold them, be silent as a hare hiding from the hawk until they are gone, or it may be the end of thee. I should not like to see thee come to harm. Much hast thou done for me. They would kill thee or take thee slave, and my people are... not kind."

I recoiled. What brutalities had he seen? I took his hand before he could go. "But what do they come here for? Tell me, so I have some tale for Edward."

He turned his face to the morning sky. "I have already told thee. Wealth. Plunder, jewels and slaves. Secret books, Books of Shadows, sorcerers' tricks. The magic of immortality."

"Immortality is the magician's trade," I mused. "I have often heard of it. I knew a witch, in England. I would go with her, gather herbs and hear tales of the Craft. She spoke of sorcerers who had the secret. One was called Merlyn, servant of the great King Pendragon."

He cocked his head at me. "Men would murder for that secret. The magic is worth more than all the wealth in the world."

I blinked out of a half-trace. "It seems nonsense to me," I admitted.

Qabir laughed and slapped my back. "To me also! But men kill

194

for the sweet sorcery of it, and for treasure or slaves. Mark me well. Set eye on the Tartars and *run*. Hide until they are gone, or thou shalt be with them, and wishing thou wert dead."

With that he ambled away, leaving me chilled. Knights sometimes returned to Jerusalem with stories of terrible slaughter. Saracen sorcery was being blamed – some swore that Saladin himself was the wizard who made some men vanish while others were brutally slain. I had always thought it was the work of Saracens crazed with grief, and part of the time it must have been. But Qabir was right. A battlefield is the perfect place to thieve, and no one would ever know where the raiders came from. They could have come from Normandy itself, where many barons had been impoverished, and were vengeful.

I returned to Edward, and at a glance he knew something was amiss. Before we ate or dropped our tent I told him what Qabir had said.

He had been busy with oil and a borrowed razor, his face half smooth, half greasy stubble. He stood listening with the razor in his hand, and seemed to forget what he was doing as I warned him of Qabir's countrymen.

Absently, he rubbed his jaw, smearing the oil about. "If Qabir is sane and correct, we are marching into the midst of these raiders. I shall be the first to hide!" He threw off the drear mood with an effort. "There is a saying among Imrahan's people. Better a live dog than a dead lion."

I sat with the basket on my knee, and when he had patted dry his face I gave him his pick of the food. All about us men were rolling the tents in preparation for the day's march. Wains were loaded, captives fed. The morning was already growing hot, and I begged a cloak for Edward, with a hood to keep the sun off his face, for he would surely burn. Then I set to and took down our tent with the ease of long practise, rolled and thonged canvas, rugs and cushions, and just as I finished Sarab and Rashid arrived to dump everything in the wain.

Imrahan was on that magnificent dappled grey, his casque shining in the sun, and at his heels were his cousins, brothers and trustees. Behind them, his household and servants, among whom we would walk. Behind us, the wagons, and then in the rear, the captive knights, grooms and rear guard. Sir Lionel de Quilberon frowned over his men, who were shackled behind the wagons, but he held his tongue and actually bowed when Imrahan rode by. The men had believed themselves doomed to dishonour and execution, and would take bondage over death. Also, they had heard the tale of a treaty, and prayed they might one day go free.

So began the day's march, as many had begun before it, and many would begin after. By my side Edward walked at an even pace, and we talked endlessly to pass the time, of home, England, Aethelstan

– the family and estate to which he longed to return. We spoke of love, and of fucking too, and blushed like a pair of roses. He confessed to the rapture of being coupled, and I made him promise to do it to me as soon as the tent was up, evening prayers said, food eaten and Qabir swept away by the first of his admirers.

"I shall, on one condition," Edward promised me, eyes sparkling with teasing humour which was at odds with Sir Lionel's surly temper. I waited. He leaned closer. "After I have had your sweet boyish arse, you will fuck mine."

I shivered, giggled, which was unseemly for a lad of my years. "I shall be glad to perform any serve you desire." I looked up at him, and my heart beat harder. "I do love you, Edward."

"As I love you," he whispered. It was still difficult for him to say it, especially in the full of the sunlight.

The column marched at a slow, steady pace that did not tire us. Among Imrahan's clan were babes in arms, old stewards, many women. We had several camels, a string of donkeys and a herd of black goats which were driven along beside the road. They were milked twice a day and some evenings one was slaughtered to provide meat. But for most of the march we ate dates, honeycomb, bread and a sweet porridge made of grain simmered in goat's milk and sweetened with honey. The fare was odd, a little rough, but there was plenty. It must have been nourishing, as we were in good health, and the men who had been injured in the skirmish with the Templars began to heal.

I longed to ask Imrahan when we would reach our destination, but dared not be so importunate. Though I was very nearly one of them, I knew I could press my luck. I never feared that Imrahan would punish me, but I did fear his displeasure. He might cease to smile at me, trust me, and might refuse me the small courtesies that made me welcome.

Still, I longed to know when we would reach Saladin's encampment, and won my answers by devious means. Not only Imrahan would know where the King camped. His cousins would know, and one of the more distant cousins was the same Rashid who was so besotted with Qabir that he ran errands for his courtesan, and fetched him his food at midday. I overheard him begging Qabir to take the Faith, be his beloved, run his house. He swore he would sell his women, empty the harem and give Qabir his whole heart. Qabir kissed him and said nothing. Rashid had heard every argument he could make, he had no more to say.

Qabir's eyes were shrewd, and every dusk he waited for the stars, noted which rose where on the horizon, and when. He knew our location, the time and day. I realised he was navigating by the heavens the way mariners find their way at sea. I was impressed, and wondered if he had been snatched off a vessel, sold to Tartars. I was still not sure if I could believe his incredible stories.

That afternoon I joined him in the shade of the fronded date palms nodding over the shadoof, which is a counter-weighted device for bringing water out of the deepest well, without a man toiling much at all. I put a drink into his hand and he tilted his head at me, eyes half shut against the sun, and pouted.

"Dost thou want something of me?"

"How canst thou tell?" I batted my eyelashes at him.

"My sore behind is not for thy delight," he said testily, and turned his shoulder on me.

"I do not desire it," I scoffed. "I have had my lord's, he has had mine, and we are content! But I want a favour." He turned back, sipped and waited. I stroked his silky hair. "Thou art well into Rashid's affections, and could take liberties. Do me a service tonight, when he is rapt with pleasure. Ask him a question, tell me the answer tomorrow."

He finished his water and threw out the dregs. "What question? Rashid will tell me, unless it is to Imrahan's damage."

"It does not concern Imrahan," I said affably. "Merely ask thy beloved – "

"He is not my beloved!" Qabir protested. "He is in love with me and I am fond of him, but I am going home! I know where I am, and what day this is, and *I am going home!* "

He was so emphatic, I recoiled. "I shall rejoice that day," I assured him, though I still feared he was deluding himself. "In the meantime ask Rashid this: how far shall we march before we reach Saladin's camp?"

He chuckled. "Thy feet are tired?"

"I am eager to see the King," I said drily. "Wilt thou ask?"

"Aye." He stood and stretched both slender arms over his head. "It has bearing on my own arithmetic – to make my rendezvous I must part from this company at a given point."

"They will send riders to hunt thee," I protested. "Qabir." I took him by the arms. "Thou art the darling of many men, but thou art a slave, a bonded courtesan to whom Rashid offered a home and safety."

He wrenched out of my grasp. "Then I shall do as many a slave has done! I shall run away. They shall not catch me. By every calculation I have made – and I was always gifted at the arithmetic of astrology – I have not far to go and my brothers await me. Let Imrahan send riders. They shall fly into the teeth of such woe as songs are sung of!"

The glare on his face warned me to say no more. I drifted back to Edward, who sat with Lionel in the shade on the other side of the shadoof. The two men, Norman and Saxon and close as kin, looked up at me. I gave Sir Lionel a bow and said to Edward, "I asked Qabir to learn how far we have still to go."

At that, Lionel grunted. "My own men have begun to ask the

same question. They have their bearings, you see, and if they were able to make a break for freedom – "

"Stupid," Edward hissed. "Counsel them that if they run into the desert, if the sun and the scorpions do not kill them, marauding Saracens will! They are too far from home. Where is the nearest Christian stronghold? A week's march at least, and every day we move further from it."

"I have told them all that!" Lionel got to his feet and planted his fists on his hips. "But they are noblemen to whom the chains and captivity and depravity they see about them every day and night is more than can be borne!"

"Depravity?" Edward and I chorused.

Lionel squirmed. "Men and men. Doing that. Even you. You think it has escaped the notice of Etienne, and Sir Jacques Pournelle?" He shook his shaggy head. "They revile sodomites. Mark me well. If they are alive when you two return to Richard's camp, they'll make trouble you may not survive. Often, sodomites are burned as witches, you know this. They burn the devil out of such men." He sighed and placed one large, brown hand on Edward's shoulder. "I am not your judge. I only beg you to beware. God knows where the road takes us."

With that he left us and Edward put his face into his hands. "My lord," I whispered, "trust Imrahan. He has promised to look to our welfare. Qabir will tell me how far we have to go."

"And then?" Edward roused himself and leaned back against the sun-hot wood. "What's to become of us?"

I could not answer, and my heart ached for what I had brought him to. By loving him, I had made him the enemy of his brother knights, and where that would end, who could know.

Chapter XXII

What I knew of the desert seasons was scant, and I lost track of time. Was it autumn as we toiled toward the camp of war over which flew the banner of King Saladin himself? For the first time since our ship tied up at Joppa I saw the sky cloud over and grow dim, and I waited for rain. None came, but like a gift from heaven the punishing heat diminished, the sky and sands did not blister the eyes and the day's march was less an ordeal.

Qabir was wild with fretting as the sky dulled. Rashid coddled him, fed and even cuddled him in an effort to quiet him, but even a gentle fucking could not much calm him. Rashid wrung his hands and bade Imrahan send the physician. Though Qabir protested mightily he was held down and examined from crown to toe.

Nothing physical ailed the grass-snake – whose skin had gradually begun to return to normal and was now only a faint, dusky green. But it seemed to me, a malady of the mind grew worse in him every day. Bruised and sore after the physician's ministrations early in the evening, he sat by the fire, put his head into his hands and wept while Rashid hovered, at a loss to know how to comfort him. There was no way, but I sat beside him, offered him strong coffee and set my arm across his shoulders.

"The sky will clear soon," I promised

"It must," he muttered. "Without the stars, how shall I know when it is the night, and when I must run like a thief?"

"Thy mind is made up," I concluded soberly. He nodded and sipped the coffee, shivering. "Qabir," I whispered for his ears alone, "thou shalt never make good thy escape. Imrahan will send men to recapture thee. If not Imrahan, then Rashid will fight to keep what is his."

"I am not his! I am a freeman!" Qabir wrenched away and for the first time in my seeing, when a man solicited his favours he spurned him and stalked into the shadows between the tents.

Edward had seen all this, and I shrugged at his unasked question. "The boy is mad, as I've always said." We spoke English, which was as well, since Rashid was close by.

"Mad or not, he is miserable," Edward remarked, and then paused as Rashid approached. He spoke not to my lord but to me – I, who prayed with him and spoke his language after a fashion. Edward stepped aside and cocked his head at us as Rashid petitioned me.

"The physicians found nothing wrong with his body," he began. "Thou hast known him longer than I. What is his madness? What vileness was done to him to addle his mind? How may I mend him?"

"I know not." I sighed. "Save, keep him safe and do not abuse him. And should he run into the desert at night... " I looked at Edward and bit my lip. "I beg thee, Rashid, let Qabir have a whole night alone before he is brought back. He cannot run far enough to escape, and one night may be the mending of him." I shrugged helplessly. "It is his obsession."

"I have seen." Rashid knuckled his eyes as if he was tired or close to weeping.

"King Salah ad-Din commands the finest physicians," I added. "Perhaps they can discover his illness. How long before we arrive?"

"Four, five days." Rashid looked after Qabir and wrung his hands. "He mutters about the clouds and riders and the wind. What thinkst thou he means?"

"He thinks a clan of Tartar land-pirates will take him home," I murmured. "Be gentle. He may have been captive for a long time, and the dream of liberty is all he has left. Deprive him of it and he may die. Rashid." I looked into Edward's stormy eyes. "Is Qabir thy property?"

The Saracen sighed. "I bought him from Imrahan soon after we left the Jackal's fortress. He was a courtesan, not a freeman."

"And we?" I nodded at my lord. "Edward and myself, and the other knights. Who will buy us?"

Rashid fidgeted and swallowed, unwilling or unable to speak, and at last edged away. I returned to Edward. He slid his arm about my waist, and I told him everything Rashid had said. "Who shall buy us, indeed?" he asked grimly when I was done. "I think I must speak with Imrahan."

"It would be wise," I mused. "Four days or five, before we are in Saladin's company, then... " I caught his sleeve. "While we are in open country, our chance of escape is slender, but we have that chance. If we seized arms in the night and fought we might get horses under us and simply flee. But once we are in the King's encampment – "

"We will be surrounded by ten thousand armed Saracens, at the mercy of a King who must nurse so great a grievance against Christians that he may not hesitate to make sport of us." Edward touched my cheek. "Let me speak to Imrahan, then to Lionel. We have waited and been obedient, but our time may be running short."

My mouth was dry as he kissed me and turned toward the Saracen's tent. I was not to follow, it would have been ill mannered, so I wheeled about, skirted the fire, approached the tent from the opposite side in the cover of smoky shadows, and knelt, unobserved, to listen like a spy.

Edward was as polite and courteous as ever. I heard the rustle of cloth and guessed he had been invited to sit. A brass cup rang quietly against the side of a jug of coffee; the scent of hashish wafted like head-buzzing incense. Edward was treated as a guest, but I had begun to wonder if it were a ruse to lull him, get him to market whole and sound. In that condition he would fetch the best price, no matter what manner of market – an auction of pleasure slaves or ransomed knights.

"Forgive my intrusion," he was saying as I knelt to listen. "Only put my mind at rest and I will be gone!"

"On what matter, Edward?" Imrahan asked pleasantly, as if he were Edward's firm friend. Ruse?

"The matter," Edward said slowly and deliberately, "of liberty. What becomes of us, when you have delivered us to King Saladin?"

A pause, and then Imrahan said, "That is for the King to decide. Does a mere Norman baron, or a Saxon earl such as yourself, make the Lionheart's decisions?"

"No," Edward admitted. "Then, advise me. All I know of Saladin is legend. Shall we be executed cleanly, or sold like sheep?"

"I cannot say," Imrahan admitted regretfully, "but I can tell you what I believe." His voice dropped and assumed a confidential tone. "Salah ad-Din is wearied of the war and filled with horror at the atrocities which have been committed by both our armies. Once he was consumed by a thirst for revenge, but now he speaks of peace. One day the old law of eye for eye, tooth for tooth, must be set aside, or every eye in the world shall be blind, every tooth drawn. Salah ad-Din would sooner speak of peace than vengeance, and it is my belief that he will not wantonly execute knights in his charge, for that would incite King Richard to more bitter fury than ever."

For some time they were silent, before Edward said quietly, "Then we shall live. But how, Imrahan? As slaves?"

"That also is for Salah ad-Din to say," Imrahan warned guardedly, "though I can pledge you my own good faith. If the day comes when you and the boy are sold, I will pay your price, just as Rashid has already paid Qabir's. You can make fair remuneration, upon your return home."

"You trust me," Edward murmured.

Imrahan sighed audibly. "You are a Saxon, outcast in your own land, no less than the Saracen is outcast here. How shall I not trust you? Be at peace! If I had wanted to sell you I could have done it already!"

"You could have – ?" Edward echoed, and my own belly gave a lurch at Imrahan's words, and his wry laughter.

"You think you are unnoticed?" he asked, much amused. "Shoab and Malik lust fiercely for you. They have never kissed or humped a white-skinned, yellow-haired Saxon of either gender! I was offered the market price for an ungelded Christian male still in youth, and when I refused I was offered a fine price for your casual favours for a night here, a night there. At a word, I could have grown wealthy from your favours. My men understand that at this time you and the boy are my property."

"I ... " Edward floundered, and silenced himself. "I believe I am in your debt."

At that, Imrahan chuckled. "I believe you are! So be at peace. You will go before Salah ad-Din bare-headed and humble, you will kneel before him and place your faith in him as I believe you never placed it in Richard Lionheart! Then, trust that boy to pray for mercy, and if all else fails, trust Imrahan to take your part." Fabric rustled and hands slapped as they clasped. "I like you, Saxon. I see honesty in your eyes."

With that, I crept back to our tent. Our meal was waiting. The smell of mutton and figs had once seemed strange and unappetising, but now my mouth watered. I held open the tent and saw the burly shape of Lionel de Quilberon sitting on our cushions by the brazier.

"What brings you here, my lord?" I asked as I warmed my hands. The night was already chill. "Is there ill news from among the knights?"

Lionel was growing browner with every day in the sun. He turned up his broad, blunt nose. "They sent me to spy! They saw

Edward go to Imrahan."

I rested carefully on the cushions where Edward would soon lie with me. I was weary after the day's march, stiff with fatigue, ready for ease. "What shall I tell you, my lord? We shall be delivered in a few days, and Imrahan assures us we shall not be executed."

"Set free?" Lionel pressed.

"That is for Saladin to decide. But Imrahan believes the Sultan is for peace, not revenge."

The shaggy head nodded, but Lionel's expression was sour. "Then we are objects of barter. I thought as much."

"Objects, my lord?" I helped myself to a palmful of food.

"We may be traded for Saladin's captains who were captured in a raid just before Edward and I left." Lionel sighed. "We may be ransomed or held hostage, our comfort wagered against the comfort and liberty of Saracens in Richard's hands."

"Imrahan said he would pay the market price for my lord and myself," I whispered.

His brows arched as he got to his feet. "And what of the rest of us? He is well acquainted with the two of you, but most of my men are wearing his chains!"

Something in his voice made my belly curdle and I caught his sleeve. "You are not telling me the whole truth!"

He was silent, debating if he should speak at all, then he leaned closer, and I strained to hear. "We have a few days before we lose all chance of a fight for freedom?" I nodded, and wondered if I should have kept that news from him. Lionel's mouth compressed. "Then there will be a battle. These men have marched in chains for many a bitter mile, they'll not walk into Saladin's camp, meek and docile as a flock of breeding ewes!" He nodded grimly as I recoiled. "If you and Edward wish to keep safe, take no part in it. I have warned over and over, it will be bloody, and there is little chance of winning, but they will fight anyway."

My throat was dry as dust. "They will all die."

"As they believe they will be executed by the King." Lionel squared his massive shoulders and stood up straight. "Imrahan may see to your liberty, but that pledge weighs little against the burden of dread my men have borne for too long." He stepped to the open flap, and turned back for a moment. "Warn Edward. For his sake, and for your own."

He was gone then. I sat looking into the fire, numb and yet churning with foreboding. I had known all along, it must be. Lionel and Edward had commanded the finest knights who would never meekly bow their heads and accept captivity.

The food was good and plentiful but I could not eat. I left the bowl on the brazier, keeping it warm for Edward, but it was almost an hour before he returned. A glance at his face, and I knew at once that he had heard the news already. He laced shut the tent and knelt in the warmth with me.

His expression was grave. I studied him against the firelight and tears stung my eyes. "Edward?"

"I spoke to Lionel on the way back here. Imrahan made me certain assurances – "

"I was spying outside," I confessed, ducking my head as if I was ashamed when in fact I was not. "Lionel was here, waiting for you. He told me to warn you."

His eyes were storm-silver. "I have an ill feeling about my bones. As if thunder is at hand, lightning is on the horizon, and we wait only for the tumult to break."

I nodded miserably. "Something terrible is going to happen. Please God, my lord, have no part in it."

I flung myself at him and he caught me as if I was a child, not a youth well turned sixteen, almost as tall as him. I pressed my face to his chest and begged him to promise he would take no part in it. He shushed me, gently at first and then with a slight tone of impatience at which I fell silent.

"What do you want of me?" he said against my hair. "That I watch my brothers fight, and turn my back on them?"

"That you watch fools fling themselves onto Saracen lances," I corrected bitterly, "without any chance of victory or liberty. That you should have better sense than to waste your life and mine."

"You would not be called upon to fight," he remonstrated.

I drew back, showed him a face that must have been haunted and hollow. His eyes widened. I must have appeared older and bitter. "If you were dead, what makes you believe I would struggle to live? Where is the reason for living when every day is cold as ice, empty." I swallowed and lifted my chin with unseemly defiance. "Throw away your life, and you waste mine. I'll likely be dead the same day."

His eyes closed. "I told Lionel, this is a fool's errand. I begged him to speak sense to his men, but the likes of Pournelle and Ferrand never listen. They neither read nor write, and understand nothing but the sword and the reek of blood." He sank down onto the cushions, his face very pale.

I bent over him, breathless with fear. "Edward, are you sickened?"

"Tired," he murmured. "Weary to the very marrow of my bones. I could lie here in peace and die in your arms tonight. Would we go to that Garden, stand before the Great Judge, swear ourselves pure, without the sins of hate and negligence and cruelty that damn men to the flames... Would we live forever?"

"I read their Book... I do not know. Imrahan believes."

"Imrahan was born to the faith." He looked at me out of haunted eyes. "Make love to me. I have a feeling about my bones. We may have few nights left together."

Fear trembled my limbs. Sweat sprung out on me and I was use-less, unable to rise or govern my mind. He was strangely calm, as if he had accepted that terrible things were about to happen, and no power under heaven would prevent them. He whispered to me till I calmed, and did as he had asked. Bare in the firelight, he was golden, passive beneath my hands and mouth. He wished to be mine tonight. I think he had had his fill of command and yearned to be free of duty.

What intuition guided him? If I had known, I would have been impotent with terror. I suckled his paps until he moaned. With the nails of my fingers I drew patterns in his flanks; I took the long, hot lance of him into my throat and fumbled for the oil. My fingers en-tered him and he made them welcome though they hurt for a mo-ment. He twisted on my hand but my mouth kept him poker-hard and diverted him from his pains until he was ready for plunder. Then I fucked a knight of Christendom, on his back like a maid with his long, fair legs over my shoulders. I sheathed myself in him like a living broadsword into a living scabbard, and he mewled like the kitten I had cherished when I was a boy.

Musk, heat and despair clouded us. This was the only escape we had, and we pushed each other harder than we should. My shoulders were scratched and bruised when we were done, and he was tight-lipped in discomfort. When I had my breath back I made him kneel for a bath of tepid rosewater, and ointment that would ease him for sleep.

"I have hurt you," I murmured as I worked, and he made some noncommittal grunt which left my guilt raw. When he was clean and salved, I covered him and tried to crawl away, to let him rest in peace. He caught my wrist and tugged me into the bed.

"You were vigorous, and it was what I wanted! It was still an act of love, and even at our wildest I was pleasured. It was afterward before I realised what I'd invited." He kissed my mouth tenderly. "How often did I ride you like that in our early days, when I'd waited too long?"

"Often enough." I admitted. "It was mad and exciting. I never complained." I tucked my head beneath his chin.

"Nor am I complaining." His fingernails scratched through the beard on my jaw. "You feel less like a boy every day."

"I do not feel like a boy at all," I admitted. "The things I have seen, heard and done... " I sighed heavily.

"What? Tell me." His lips pressed my forehead.

"Shall we ever see England again?" I tugged the blankets over our heads. "Lately, I have begun to pine for home. I yearn for the woods, the Aethelstan hills, the friends and kin I left behind. And a girl-child awaits you, do not forget Edwina Montand."

"I never forget her," he confessed. "If we do not see home again, it will be worse for her than for us. She may enter holy orders, if she is quick, and lucky. Otherwise, her marriage to Yves Guilbert will be a wedding made in hell."

She would suffer greatly and die young, and Guilbert would inherit the estates that should have buttressed Aethelstan. The man who had wed a child and been the death of her would own the whole shire.

"She will be thirteen now," Edward whispered. "Guilbert will leave her virgin until she is fourteen, and then if she does not swiftly get behind the wall of a nunnery, she will be in his bed."

"And soon in her grave, while her lands go to Guilbert as the bride-price," I added. "And Aethelstan?"

He heaved a deep sigh which gusted across my cheek. "Guilbert has the ear of the Sheriff and the Bishop of Durham. It may take a few months to prove that I am in debt, or a witch, a heretic or a traitor. Before long I would be called to answer for my crimes, and if I were not executed, I would be fined of my lands. What of Aethelstan?" He kissed my mouth lingeringly. "Aethelstan will be a *man* who hires his sword for pay. It is the only trade I know." He spoke calmly, as if he had long ago resolved these scenes.

I propped myself on my elbow to look down into his fire-dappled face. "And Edwina?"

"Will be mourned," he murmured.

"And Paulo Delgado?" I set one hand on his breast to feel the thud of his heart.

His eyes glittered. "I would hope," he said quietly, "my squire would accompany me as a man just as he attended me as a boy. If I'm to be a mercenary soldier, you are my equal. I'll have no serfs, nothing to my name save the spurs I won, and what honour I have left."

"I would not be left behind," I swore. "I love you."

He gave a wriggle. "I am certain of that if nothing else! You rode me hard, as if I were a horse you rode to battle!"

"You put the spurs to my sides and made me," I reminded him.

For the first time in so long he smiled, but it was a sad expression. "I did. You are an obedient lad."

"Duties like that," I said, flushing brightly, "are easy to fulfil."

He bruised my ribs with his embrace, and we settled to rest, but we were awake most of the night, and with morning were sorely the worse for wear.

* * *

Discontent ran rampant through Lionel's party. Black looks were given Edward and myself, as if Pournelle, de Malestroit, Ferrand and others could scarcely bear to see the two sodomites who had turned traitor.

Was I right or foolish to feel stabs of guilt? A merciless hand thrust the blade between my ribs countless times. I had brought Edward to this – fetched him to a time and place when men who were not fit to polish his boots openly curled their lips in scorn and shouldered him aside.

Tight-mouthed with anger, or perhaps with shame, Edward answered with silence and a turned back. In a moment's privacy I knelt at his feet, pressed my face to his belly and made abject apologies. He said nothing, until I thought he believed me guilty of all I said. Then I felt his hand on my head in absolution.

Imrahan was aware of the restlessness among Lionel's ranks, and I noticed that when we broke camp the captives were chained more tightly and double-guarded. The looks they gave Edward and myself grew even blacker when we were free and they were imprisoned more surely than before. I heard the word 'traitor' as we passed; later, the word 'sodomites'. I saw Edward's taut features, and whispered for his attention.

"My lord, if those men make it to freedom and rejoin the Lionheart, we do not dare go back, not to Jerusalem, not to England. If we did, we would be tried."

"And burned," he finished. He raised his eyes to the sky, which was still thickly overcast, though it did not rain. "All is in the lap of the gods, and us with it. Fretting will avail us nothing." He studied me strangely. "Pray for us."

I called upon anyone's God, anyone's Prophet – Wotan, Tor, Cernunnos, Mithras, any saint I could remember, anyone I thought may look down and see a terrified mortal. When the Imam called I went with Rashid and Imrahan and prayed fervently, not least for faith. When all else is exhausted, and a man is at his limits, what remains but faith? Alas, I had none.

Qabir wept, cursed, swore and shook his fists at the sky all that day, and his grasp of the language broke down with pain. His own native speech was incomprehensible as he accused and impeached the sky.

"That tongue," Lionel said, frowning, as we stopped to drink in the afternoon. "Not Latin, Greek or French. You recognise it, Paul, the tongue of your father?"

"Not Spanish," I assured him as we watched Qabir stalk between the horses and the shadoof, all the while muttering like a madman. "Not Italian either, since Italian and Spanish are similar. Nor is it the Hebrew tongue, which is more guttural, and not the Saracen language, in which I have some fluency."

"Then, what?" Edward wondered. "Ask him."

I had no fear of Qabir even now. When I approached him he looked at me wildly. His eyes were pink with weeping yet he was still beautiful. "Green grass snake," I began, trying to tease.

He shook off my hand. "I could call thee white plucked chicken!"

"I am sorry," I sighed. "Tell me how to help."

"Thou canst not," he groaned, falling to his knees and beating the pebbles until I caught his hands and held them. "Clear the sky for me! Call a wind from the sea that sweeps away the clouds! Time is short, and if I cannot see the sky, how shall I know the hours of night apart?"

"Time is short?" I echoed.

"Rendezvous," he whispered. "A time of meeting, going home, joy past bearing." He squeezed shut his eyes and began to mutter again in that incomprehensible language.

I knelt beside him, watching over his bowed head as Imrahan called his men together. At the rear of our column, with the slaves, asses and camels, were the chained knights. I felt their hate and rage, and looked at Edward, who was drinking while Lionel filled the water skins.

"That language, Qabir," I said when my friend paused for breath.

"The tongue of my home," he rasped. "How often must I tell thee? Over and over till I am without breath! I am no more part of this cursed land than art thou!"

Behind us, Rashid made a strangled cry. He was as distressed as Qabir. I joined him as Imrahan mounted that magnificent dappled grey and moved up the length of the column, with a jingling of harness and the heavy clop of iron-shod hooves.

"Then, he is mad," Rashid said brokenly. His eyes never left Qabir. "How long has he been without his right mind?"

"A long time." I took Rashid's arm. "What knowest thou of the treatment of slaves?"

His eyes darkened. "I can imagine what horrors he endured. It is little wonder that he is mad."

I nodded sadly. "Knowest thou, his master at the Fortress was a sorcerer?"

He gave me a bitter glance. "A sorcerer from whom wise men fled, and upon whom none dared look. If my beloved belonged to Ibrahim, I do not wonder that he lost his mind." He dragged in a painful breath. "He shall come with me, nonetheless. Make him understand, for he listens to thee. I shall cherish him all his days, and Salah ad-Din's physician shall see him when we are encamped."

"I shall tell him," I promised, but it was a lie.

To say this to Qabir, no matter how kindly Rashid had meant it, would have driven him further out of his reason. Qabir lived for only to see the stars, know the day, the place, the hour, and we all believed him mad.

What astonishment awaited us all when the courtesan was proved sane – for the sky did clear, one night later, and calamity thundered about our heads.

Chapter XXIII

The day's march had been wearying. We had bathed and eaten, and Edward lay with his head in my lap as we watched the flames lick about the charcoal sticks in the brazier. I had rubbed him with oil to loosen his muscles, combed his hair and laid out his night robes, but he was still bare as we ate, enjoying the coolness. Outside, the breeze would soon be very cold; inside, it was pleasant after the heat of day.

The sky had cleared, and as I stroked Edward's shoulder and wondered if I could seduce him, though he was tired, I thought of Qabir. His stars were bright; the night was like twilight with the illumination of a full moon, and the strange madness would surely possess him.

I suppose I was listening for the shouts of alarm as someone caught sight of the runaway and gave chase. Even in his madness, Qabir was as valuable as Edward or myself. Still, I knew he was safe – he was Rashid's, it was for him to decide how his bondsman would be disciplined. Rashid would 'punish' him with kisses and the sweets and scents Qabir liked best. Every bondsman should have so gentle a master.

But the shouts were not those of a guard, calling hunters to return a stray lamb to the fold. My heart skipped I sat, dislodging Edward from my lap. Imrahan's men were bawling in the tongue he could not follow, and he looked warily at me.

"What is it?" He set aside our platters.

"The storm, wind and dry lightning,"I whispered. "The sorcery." Wide-eyed, I swallowed. "Edward, Qabir said the rendezvous would come soon, the time of gathering before the journey home." All at once I was wide awake and in my clothes before he could stop me.

"Where are you going?" His hand on my arm held me back.

"I must see," I hissed.

He was rushing into his own clothes as I stepped out. The whole camp was a frenzy as men pointed into the north-east, drew swords and swept up their women and boys. The camels tore on their halters; a child screamed in fright. I looked about in the wind-tossed firelight and cupped my hands to my mouth.

"Qabir! Qabir!"

What use to shout his name? Rashid appeared out of the shadows, sword in hand, a heavy, dark cloak wrapped about him, his lips compressed as he strode toward me. "He has gone," he said grimly. "Give him a night to himself beneath the stars, didst thou advise. But – what of that?" He flung his arm at the sky. "Satan's own wind is rising, and Qabir has run into it! He shall perish if the demons come upon him. Has thou not heard their hooves and swords?"

I swallowed on a tight, dry throat. I had heard those sounds with my own ears, or I would never have believed them. Was this the time of rendezvous for which Qabir had longed? Coincidence! It must be no more than sheer chance that the sky cleared, the storm appeared, and we were in this place. I watched Rashid gather his cloak over his arm and stride away into the indigo gloom.

Even then lightning had begun to flicker and the wind whipped sand into my face. It had begun, and my heart raced. A moment later Edward was with me, and torchlight gleamed on the blade of a knife he had hidden in his sleeve. Properly, neither of us was allowed a weapon, but he had kept that knife hidden about him since he had learned how many of Imrahan's men lusted for him, and that at a single word it could be himself on his knees, arse upturned.

"Qabir has run," I said breathlessly. "He cannot have gone far. I think I can find him."

"Why?" He demanded in that steely tone of command to which men jump in obedience. "You told me he instructed you to hide when his people came!"

"But he is mad!" I protested. "This is but a storm out of the desert." I covered my eyes as the flickers of dry lightning came closer.

"Aye, a windstorm," Edward shouted over the growing gale. "And suppose a company of Tartar raiders uses the wind and storm as a shield, knowing that fools call it Saracen sorcery and flee, leaving them to pillage where and as they will!"

Horrible fascination gripped me, just as it had when I had been warned to stay away from Ibrahim's lair. As I defied Haroun Bedi, at the cost of welted buttocks, so did I defy Edward. My devil got into me. I had to know, or die.

I ran, leaving him in the fiery ring of the torchlight, likely bewildered and angry. In seconds the shadows swallowed me and the wind sang in my ears. With the camp behind me I felt horribly alone, and shivered with healthy fear. I called Qabir's name, prayed to see his figure in the patches of moonlight, but what I saw was a flickering vision from hell.

Ibrahim believed in the power of devils, and that Qabir could speak some arcane verse and create a chariot that would ride the wind. I stood, frozen, like a rabbit mesmerised by a snake, and watched the storm gather when any man with sense would have taken to his heels.

It flickered and whirled over the rocks and the stunted trees that somehow survive in that merciless land. Lightning spat and crackled, the wind was like a spinning top, and I heard the drum of hooves, the clatter and chime of swords.

The moon was high, riding well clear of the last sporadic clouds, but the air thickened with sand and it was hardly possible to see. Grit and dust half blinded me. Was Ibrahim right? I saw no wind-borne chariot, but the swirling air and lightning maddened me until I could believe I glimpsed all kinds of devils.

Movement at my shoulder made me jump out of my skin. I leapt, cried out, but Edward's hand clamped over my mouth to silence me, and the next I knew he had dragged me bodily into the shadow beneath a tree. From there, huddled against him, I watched.

Qabir was clad in a robe and cloak. He held a lantern in his right hand and the polished lid of a kettle in the other – an unlikely combination of chattels to steal, I thought, until I saw that he was using them to signal, sending flashes and pulses of light into the heart of the windstorm, the way a lamp can be used to signal from a window.

The air sucked itself up, so thick and fogged with dust, a knife would have cut it. Every hair on my scalp stood on end as the lightning flickered closer. I had heard of lightning being attracted to trees, and almost fought to my feet to flee, but Edward held me down in concealment.

And then I saw the shape, like a shadow inside the storm. A man-shape on foot, glittering and gleaming, with flames where his head and hands should be. Fear choked me but I could not look away. Ibrahim was right, the darkest sorcery was rampant before me. My fingers clawed Edward's arms like talons.

A dozen paces before us, Qabir threw down the lamp, cast off his cloak, tore the robe from his shoulders, no matter the chill, to bare his skin to the sporadic cascades of white light from within the storm. He was still dusky green though the dye had worn off with sweat and rubbing, and he spread his arms to show himself to the fire demon, as if he longed for the creature to demolish or devour him.

I knelt up, the better to see, oblivious of Edward's hands as he tried to hold me down. The shape loomed closer, stepping through the dust, and I blinked my eyes clear as Qabir waved and shouted.

All at once, I saw. It *was* a man, clad all over in the finest chainmail that gleamed like silver. On his head was a casque of a kind I had never seen before, so brightly polished that it flashed back the light of the twin torches the man brandished in both his hands.

My heart thudded. Weak in the knees, I watched the man toss down one of the torches and his helmet, and hold out his hand. Qabir went to him and they embraced, sealed lips and kissed ravenously. I heard my friend give a cry as he was gathered up, held tight, but before he would allow himself to be dragged away he turned back in our direction and called into the darkness.

"Paul, I know thou art there!" He smiled, and one hand on his lover's arm stilled the man. "I swear, thou shalt come to no harm. I have told him thou wert the saving of my life!"

I stepped away from Edward and showed myself. Qabir did not come to me, but he smiled and nodded. "See, thou unbeliever! Is Qabir mad? He is bound for home this night! And I owe my liberty, my life, to thee. I have nothing to give but gratitude, which shall last life-long, and a word of wisdom. Hide when the storms appear, for thou knowest the reason my people come, and I shall grieve at thy death." He stepped into the veil of dust. "Fare thee well, thou and thy mate. Keep safe and think affectionately of Qabir, for he shall surely remember thee."

Then the storm of wind and parched lightning swallowed him. An arm in silver-polished, gleaming chainmail wrapped about him to hold and guide him as he vanished. I fell back into the lee of the tree where Edward had kelt, watching cautiously, his knife gripped in his hand.

We clung together like village loons, shivered by the wind, prickled by the strange lightning, wreathed in shadows and in disbelief. Even then the storm was ebbing. It withdrew into the north-east like a great beast and soon would be spent.

Dust-throated, Edward murmured, "They call the whirling storm *djinn*. Sorcery?"

"If it is," I whispered, "the Saracens fear it as much as anyone. Did you see the man?"

"I saw." His arm slipped about me. "Tartar?"

"So Qabir swore... and I called him mad." I took a breath and coughed sand from my lungs. "I was wrong. Qabir is as sane as you or I. The sorcery Ibrahim lusted for, and King Richard fears, does not exist. He is going home, and I rejoice for him."

Edward collected his wits with an effort. He held my face between his hands to make me look at him. "We also will go home. Believe, boy."

"I do," I said hoarsely, and pressed tight to him. "I am glad for Qabir. Once, we both thought he would die in Ibrahim's lair."

But the wind had dwindled and Edward was no longer listening to me. "Christ Jesus," he breathed, "what is *that* ?"

I heard it then, too, and for a second time that night my mouth dried. The bell-like chimes of swords called though the darkness and my fingers bruised his shoulders.

"Fighting," I gasped. "Lionel's fools are fighting – they have seized weapons in the confusion!"

"Imbeciles," he said bitterly as he pulled me close to him. "They will die, every last man!"

I think he would have joined the battle had there been a chance. Honour and chivalry were his second language, and Edward was no less a knight than any Norman whose spurs are given to him un-earned. We scuttled back to the camp, stopped on the fringe of the firelight, and he had his knife in his hand, a pitiable weapon against the swords and lances of Imrahan's warriors. The captives had seized their opportunity. In our absence, as men milled about, shouting about the devil in the sky, they had set upon the guards, taken up arms and slaughtered seven Saracens and Nubians before Mansoor, Malik and

Shoab called back their cousins and rallied a force to control them.

Already as Edward and I began to watch, the fight was half spent. A dozen men lay dead or dying. One of them was Rashid. He would know never know that Qabir was gone... never mourn for his loss.

Another of the fallen was easily recognised, and my heart burned like a brand as I saw the body of Lionel de Quilberon, the lance still buried in his belly, his limbs twitching slightly.

The sight of Sir Lionel lying dead made Edward a little mad. I held him back when he would have set upon anyone in the fracas, Mussulman or Christian alike, for he held them all responsible for Lionel's death. My hands, like steel shackles on his arms, kept him out of the battle but our movement on the edge of the fireglow did not go unnoticed. And our crimes and sins were not to go unpunished.

Sir Jacques Ferrand saw us. The big Norman, who had always hated Saxons in general and sodomites in particular, cast the lance and there was no stopping it. I would have thrown myself before it like a martyr but, God help me, I had no chance.

It was I who screamed as the lance speared into Edward's right side, and I caught him before he fell.

I was sure he was dead. His body was cold, his hands lax, and now I was so oblivious of the battle, I would not have known if Richard and Saladin had both appeared like avenging angels. I had time only for the weight in my arms as I took Edward across my knees and held him as if my life depended on it.

PART FIVE: SALADIN

Chapter XXIV

His eyes were glassy, his skin grey. I swabbed his face with my sleeve, deaf to the sounds and sights about me until I heard a voice which spoke so softly, close to my ear, that somehow made itself heard while shouts and roars went unnoticed. Imrahan himself knelt beside me, casque beneath his arm, sword naked and bloody, his face grimed with ash, sweat and the blood of others. His eyes were filled with pain. His friends and cousins were dead, and in that instant grief made us kindred.

"Is he dead, boy?" He peered into Edward's face.

"Hanging onto life," I murmured hoarsely. "It was the Norman, Ferrand. Curse all Normans, may they rot, may they burn on spits over the fires at the Cataclysm, may their bellies crawl with maggots, may they spend Eternity upon their knees, scrubbing the paths in the Garden at the feet of the Faithful!"

His hand fell on my shoulder. "As thou hast spoken, so shall it be."

I blinked on scalding tears. "Sire, Edward took no part in the combat."

"I know. I saw it all. He had a knife," Imrahan mused, "but I thought it was for thy defence. Thou art his bedmate and it would be the amusement of such as Ferrand to slay thee wantonly." He got to his feet. "Yusef, help the boy. Take Aethelstan to his tent, clean him and prepare a place for him in the wain tomorrow."

I kissed Imrahan's hand. "Bless thee, Sire."

But first Edward must survive the night, and if he did, the journey to Saladin's encampment would be a trial. Imrahan watched with a look of regret as his cousin and I took him to the tent. I was given water, cloths, oils of mandrake and olibanum. An old woman and a little boy worked with me, long into that night, sponging him as he grew fevered, and pressing his wound to staunch the blood.

Many looked into the tent, and prayed. Malik, Salim and Yusef, who had desired Edward, sat with me after they had disposed of their own dead. Sometimes he wandered deliriously, feeling no pain. Often, he was so deeply asleep that he was beyond even dreams. But just before dawn, he came to his senses and knew me, and fear gripped me more vengefully than ever.

It is said that a dying man will regain his right mind for a few seconds before death. I pressed Edward to me, careful of his wound, kissed his mouth and tasted his tongue for what might be the last time. Then I put my ear to his breast to hear his heart. It beat faintly, wild and fast.

At dawn, when the wailing voice of the Imam summoned us, the old woman bade me go. She would not leave him, she swore. She would press the wound, listen for his voice and send swiftly for me if he spoke. Reluctantly, I tore myself away.

I knelt between Imrahan and his cousins, and I made a pledge to the One in whom their faith was unshakeable. If Edward lived, it would be by a miracle. I would see in this miracle the hand of the Redeemer. If Edward lived, I swore on my knees, I would embrace the faith of those who had protected us, and repay the debt I owed them all.

As we rose Imrahan regarded me speculatively. "What was thy pledge?" he asked me in a moment's privacy. "Come! I saw thee, it was graven on thy face."

I confessed to him, while weariness overtook me. I was almost too drained of strength to stand. "Edward will live now only by the most wondrous of miracles," I slurred. "And I shall not forsake the Worker of wonders."

He touched my face. "Still, prepare thyself for his death, boy. All petitions are heard, but sometimes the answer is no. If the time has come for Aethelstan to go to Judgement, then it shall be. What of thyself? Wilt thou return to England?"

The strength went from my legs and I slumped to my knees. What was there for me in England? What was there at all for me, without Edward? Yet, if he lived forever in a Garden of peace and plenty, what more could I ask?

"There is nothing in England for me," I whispered. "The woods, the soft rain, the very smell of England would taunt me with memories. I could not return without him, Sire." I took a deep breath as the sky brightened from powdery pink to brilliant blue. "When I belonged to Jahrom Rafha, he said I would be as family if I made the covenant of thy faith. Thou art my owner now. If Edward dies, keep me." I took his hand and kissed it.

He hoisted me to my feet. "It is the least I can do, boy. I shall attend to thy rites. You shall be a bondsman in my house, and in my bed, when Aethelstan is a warm place in thy heart, and thy young body has begun to yearn for the relief of a man's loving. Thou shalt know when grief is spent, and when to turn to me. Yusef!" He clapped his hands to summon his cousin, and gratefully I hurried back to the tent.

Edward was unmoving, lily-pale, waxen-skinned and sweated. Still he cried out as he was lifted and carried, and threshed as he was set into the bed of the wagon with the bags and a lamb that was being hand-reared. I would walk beside him, and as the wain began to roll I took his hand. Did his fingers tighten about mine? I swallowed my heart as Imrahan called out from the head of our caravan.

Behind us we left a grave, for there was too little wood to burn our dead. The grave was marked and servants and slaves would return for the fallen. But also we left behind Sir Lionel de Quilberon, and I sorrowed, even in the midst of my pain over Edward, that such a man should lie unmourned in a foreign land.

I looked back at the site where he lay and wondered if I would ever see Henri, or Lionel's wife and children, so that I might tell them he died in battle. Then I looked west, where our long morning shadows stretched before us. Far away lay the camp of the man whose name was legend: Saladin.

I recall little of that day, save the glare of the afternoon sun, and Edward's mutterings as he wandered in the grip of fevers, and Imrahan's frowning face as he came to offer his compassion. I could not bear to watch Edward's struggles, and but for Imrahan's kindness I might have broken like a twig. A touch, a look, a sigh close by my ear. I kissed his hand in thanks and recalled his promise... If Edward died and I remained as a bondsman in his house, as I had decided, I would one day warm his bed, for his pleasure and my own. I would never love him, but I liked him and was grateful, as I had liked and felt gratitude toward Jahrom Rafha.

Every mile on the road I expected to be Edward's last. I set a cloth on his skin so the sun did not burn him; I gave him water when he woke and could swallow; at night I washed and massaged his body, and bathed the wound. And I beat the ears of every god I knew, demanding to be heard.

Somehow, Edward still lived when we came upon a finer sight than I had ever seen. Our caravan toiled up the eastern slope of a hill which rose and rose as if it would clamber into the very sky, and I thought, from the summit we must see Jerusalem! Then we crested the shoulder of the mount and on the west slopes I saw a thousand banners, ten thousand horses, and five times that number of soldiers and their boys.

This was the Saracen host, a company to strike dread into the heart of Christendom, from one tip of doomed, beleaguered *Outremer* to the other. Salah ad-Din had recaptured the Empire, and when I beheld this host I did not wonder that he had done it. As far as my eye could see were the tents and fires, paddocks and enclosures of the army that was ruining England by paupering her, without ever laying foot on English soil!

In the midst of it all was a building, part palace, part fortress, of granite, sandstone and marble, with high battlements from which flew the banners of the greatest clans.

At the sight of these walls Imrahan sighed and touched his breast. "I am come home at last."

I took note of everything I saw as the wain wheeled Edward into the shade of a courtyard. Fountains played and a dry, dusty breeze rustled the branches of the olive trees. Women and boys hurried out, knelt before their lord, who had been absent for so long, and at a word from him they lifted Edward out. Imrahan bade me go with him.

The room where he was put overlooked the east hillside. From the fretted marble window I could look across the whole camp, and it was a glorious sight. Out of the sun, inside walls so thick that the air was cool and smelt of roses, Edward was set on clean sheets while a bath was prepared. An old eunuch helped me carry him and lower him into the tepid water, and he soaked for an hour while I bathed him and worried over the wound.

The eunuch's name was Tauseef. He was tall and spindly but surprisingly strong for one so slender. Though he was old, his skin was soft and smooth. He slipped off his trousers to save them from the water as we bathed Edward in preparation for the physicians, and I saw that not only were his balls quite absent, but his short, thick little cock was circumcised too. I gave a deep shiver. If Edward lived, that contract awaited me.

Edward stirred to half-awareness as we dried him, and I held a cup to his lips. His eyes cracked open and he looked at me, his tongue formed words but he did not have the breath to speak. His head lolled on my shoulder once more as Tauseef let out the bathwater, which ran down a conduit to the olive groves.

The wound was poisoned. Even I saw this. Time and again I had washed it, but the roots of the poison were deep and no matter how I bathed it, the corruption grew worse. Tauseef puffed out his swarthy cheeks as he looked at me over Edward's prone body.

"Hast thou seen worse?" I asked desperately.

"Aye," The eunuch answered in his light, womanish voice. "But only upon men who died. Never have I seen worse wounding upon one who lived."

I slumped at the bedside and Tauseef took my shoulders in his hands. He assured me that Imrahan would fetch the finest physicians, they would soon be here, but I did not have the heart to answer.

The doctors arrived at noon. I had prayed in the passageway outside, with the door open so I would hear Edward's voice if he so much as whispered. The men of the household had mats on which to kneel, and when I joined them I was given one, to save my knees the punishment of the marble floor.

A beautiful silver mirror stood by the fretted marble window. I caught sight of myself and was shocked. How I was changed. My Spanish blood and the Palestine sun had conspired to make me as swarthy as any Saracen. I was taller than some of them, heavier than others. My jaw was beard-shadowed, and I was hollow-cheeked. It was not a boy in the mirror, but a man, no matter how I felt at heart.

I asked for a razor and was given a fine blade, whetstones and oils. I shaved face, breast and my private parts, as the others did. It was local custom, though I am certain it sprang from sheer vanity. Then I bathed and dressed in a fresh robe. Scores were folded in the camphorwood chests that lined the walls of our room. I was ready when the physicians arrived, and bowed before the three tall old men.

Head to my knees, I stepped back with a whisper of thanks in their language. I wondered fleetingly if they took me for a Saracen, for I surely looked like one. They stripped Edward, listened to his pulses and lit a brazier. A stone was set to heat, a poultice made of reeking garlic and herbs, a kettle set to boil. I shook with dread as they worked. I always hated quacks.

The wound was poulticed and the hot stone placed on a wet cloth, over the mess of smelly herbs. Then, I was grateful Edward was not conscious, for he threshed in a frenzy of pain. The bed was soon soaked with his sweat as the heat and herbal stuff drew out the poison. The doctors bound the tormenting thing to him, strapped him to the sodden mattress and left him to me, only to return an hour later when he had just begun to ease, and repeat the horrible process.

Again, he screamed his lungs hoarse. That time, being much weaker, he seemed to faint. For a terrible instant I thought they had killed him, but his chest continued to heave and I bit my tongue to keep silent. Once more they left him for an hour, while I bathed his furnace-hot skin and kept his gasping mouth wet.

I was trembling with fatigue when they returned, and about to beg that they not repeat the treatment. But this time when the stone was removed the wound was bathed with salt water, dried with a boiled-clean cloth, and touched with the red-hot iron.

The smell of the cauterised skin sickened me, but it was for the best. Edward plunged into deep unconsciousness, and Tauseef sat with him while I stumbled away to drink and force down a little food. I saw Imrahan on the great balcony that ran about the whole palace, and he spared me a moment.

"The physicians spoke to me," he told me. "They have rooted out the poison which was killing Aethelstan. If he lives out the night he will grow well, so they said."

"He is sleeping now, Sire," I mumbled.

"And thou art close to thy limit," he added. "Go, sleep beside him. Little wilt thou achieve by punishing thyself... and thou hast a little ordeal to undertake soon. Hast thou forgotten?"

I shivered and shook my head. "When, Sire?"

He smiled at me – mischievously, since he knew my apprehension. "Tomorrow or the next day, when we have time to spare for the small matter of thee," he promised. "First, I share news with the Sultan. News," he added, "of the Lionheart."

"Send for me when it is time," I said breathlessly.

Imrahan chuckled. "Faintheart!"

With a few figs and a little milk inside me, I returned to Edward and lay on the rugs by the bed. He was deeply unconscious, feverish but without pain, and the wound in his side, a brand the size of the palm of my hand, had been dressed with ointment. If he slept till morning the edge would have gone off the pain, and I would beg hashish for him, to keep him doped until it eased further.

He was thin now. It was a sharp-boned, thin-ribbed, frail-looking man in the bed beside me. I would hardly have known him, save for the colour of his hair. His face had grown elfin, he had a delicate look which both frightened and attracted me. Beside him, I felt bigger and stronger, and I felt the first stirrings of the protective, possessive, nurturing feeling that is native to a man. Still, I would not be content until I saw his eyes open, sane and alive.

This came at dawn, when trumpets began to blare over the vast camp of war. I always stirred early, since I must soon go to answer the Imam. I must shave and bathe Edward, and I must ask Tauseef what duties were required of a bondsman here.

I was on my feet before I was fully awake, stumbling after a fresh robe, when I heard a moan and the rustle of sheets. My belly turned to water and I fell to my knees among the rugs where I had slept. I took his hand, touched his stubbled cheek. He had gone a week without a razor. His beard was the colour of ripe wheat and silky. I stroked it and smiled into his eyes, which were wide, weary but awake. He licked his lips and searched for his voice.

"Where are we?" he asked. "How long?"

"Imrahan's fortress," I told him. "It is almost a week since... you have been doctored."

"My side feels... branded," Edward croaked.

"The wound festered. Imrahan fetched the finest physicians."

"Water," he begged, and drank with difficulty as I held a cup to his mouth. When he set his head back he was sweated with effort, and I mopped his face. He caught my wrist in a hand that seemed too delicate to belong to a warrior. I sat on the bed, careful not to jar him, which might open his side.

"Where are the others?" he murmured exhaustedly. "Lionel?"

I bit my lip. "They are dead." I kissed his forehead. "All of them. They had no chance."

"Ah, Christ." His eyes closed. "Lionel too?"

"He died fighting," I said softly, "as befits a knight."

"Lionel," he moaned, and his hands clung to mine with surprising strength. Tears leaked from his closed lids as he grieved, and slowly he drifted back to sleep.

This time it was a peaceful sleep, natural and healing. I bathed, shaved and crept out when the Imam called. Upon my return I fetched some food, just soft fruit, but he did not stir for hours, and I spent most of that time sitting by the window and watching the camp.

I was guilty. I should be working, and I half expected Tauseef with a catalogue of duties to occupy me, but when Edward stirred once more at noon we were still alone. I was with him at once, and lent him my hands as he tried to move.

He wished to empty his bladder, he ached to shift his spine but his side was painful and in moments he was grey with distress. I unwrapped his wound, found it bleeding a little and dressed it with ointments once more. The scar would be awful. He had been almost without a mark before this campaign, and I cursed King Richard for fetching him to this.

As he slumbered through the afternoon I wondered what news Imrahan had of the war. Tauseef knocked with food and small personal gifts at sunset. Among these was a Book, for my own use. One long forefinger tapped the engraved leather cover and he whispered, so as not to wake Edward,

"Meditate tonight. Tomorrow, thou art called!" He winked and cast a glance at my belly which made my skin prickle. He thrust the Book into my hands and popped a date between my teeth before quietly stepping from the room.

I read by candlelight while Edward slept. Now and then I would bathe him, and when he woke at midnight I helped him to the close-stool, fetched him a drink and changed the bedlinen. Then he was asleep again, and I returned to my reading.

The Book promised and threatened by turns. Retribution and reward, life everlasting... hellfire and torment. I had learned so much from Haroun Bedi, but I still had much to learn, and of only one thing I was sure. I had seen a miracle. I closed the Book and stood by the bed. Thin to the point of emaciation, his side bandaged with aromatic herbs, his face bearded... Yet he was alive and grew a fraction stronger every hour. In a week he would stand on his feet; in a month he would sit a horse, when by all accounts he should be dead. All life is a thing of wonder. Edward's life was a miracle.

Tauseef knocked before dawn, and I was ready. He took my place with Edward, while a boy with gazelle eyes guided me to a part of the fortress I had not yet visited, and showed me into a chamber of cool alabaster and rich red velvet drapes. Imrahan was there, and three other men before whom I bowed politely.

"Well met," Imrahan greeted me, and made fleeting introductions.

One man was a priest, one a surgeon, one a witness. A censer burned pungent frankincense; a Quran in red, blue and green inks lay open beside a phial of spirits and a surgeon's tools. My head reeled, my belly churned, and when I was invited to sit, I was grateful to. The Book was placed in my hands, my head was anointed with oil, prayers were spoken over me and I had only to say that one phrase to please them all, as Haroun Bedi had taught me long before. Then I kissed the enamelled cover of the Book, and it was taken from me.

I looked nervously at Imrahan. He was smiling, not teasing but encouraging. When the surgeon came I trembled badly, and fumbled with my clothes. A thick gauze pad was placed in my right palm. I sat my cock on it and closed my eyes. A cold wash of spirits... a strange caress. Of the cutting I felt nothing at all, so sharp was the knife, but like any cut it began to sting. Soon the smarting became fire. Another wash with spirits made me hiss through my teeth, but it was already over. The gauze was wrapped tight and tied.

I bled much less than I had feared, and when another bandage was wrapped about the first to protect what was tender and hurting, I was done, as simply as that. Imrahan gave me a tiny cup of fermented date wine and kissed my forehead.

"My brother," he said warmly, and he put into my hands a sickle-bladed knife, a weapon of my own, which was the measure of my freedom, and a tiny, beautiful Quran, small enough to slip into a pocket.

I stood, wincing, and closed my robe. Surgeon, priest and witness left, and Imrahan sat on the chest under the window. "Thou shalt be sore, but it heals swiftly, without trace," he promised. "It bleeds less than you think and is seldom dangerous."

"And afterwards is beautiful." I walked stiffly, spraddle-legged, to the window, and gritted my teeth as the smarting settled into a steady pain which would accompany me through the whole day. "Thy brother, Sire?" I rested one shoulder to the wall by the window and looked over the camp.

"Truly." Imrahan slapped my buttock playfully. "How is thy beloved Infidel?"

"Better," I said cautiously. "He is sleeping, and sleep heals. The physicians wrought their own miracle."

"They should," Imrahan said drily, "They are Salah ad-Din's own."

For the moment I was diverted from my anguish. "The Sultan's?"

Imrahan nodded. "I spoke to the King as soon as I had washed the dirt of the road from me, told him a great deal of Aethelstan. Salah ad-Din has uses for such a man, and offered the services of his doctors. Aethelstan shall grow strong, have no fear for him, nor for yourself. Thou art my bondsman. My family."

"I am grateful," I said, wincing as I knelt, knees widespread, on the rug at his feet – not an attitude of deference, but of comfort, given my predicament. "By law thou art bound by honour to cherish bondsmen." I flourished my Book. He nodded. "But what of Edward?"

"Would he... ?" Imrahan considered my groin thoughtfully.

"I know not," I admitted, "It is not so simple, Sire." I took a breath, settled myself as comfortably as I could on my haunches, and told him the story of Edwina Montand. He frowned as he digested this and pulled at his chin. "So, Edward may serve Salah ad-Din well and faithfully for some time, but he must return home," I finished. "His house and the life of a woman are at stake."

"I see," Imrahan agreed. "This also, I shall tell the Sultan. In any event, Richard seems disposed to treaty. We may be at peace before long."

"News?" I moved too fast, the small wound punished me and I palmed it firmly with a wince. Imrahan pretended not to notice, which was polite. "News, Sire?" I began again, in a hoarse voice.

He seated himself comfortably with a cup of coffee and lifted his bare foot into my lap as Jahrom Rafha had done countless times. I spread my knees to ease myself, moulded my hands about his foot to massage it and waited expectantly.

"The Lionheart is angry," Imrahan said slowly. "In his absence, his brother, Count John, seems to have granted the French many of his Norman holdings. King Richard desires them returned."

"He must fight for them," I said cautiously, concentrating on my work for diversion.

"And soon," Imrahan agreed. "Philip of France has been warring for some time. The Land Pirates have ravaged the country, and there is grief not merely in thy homeland. Richard weighs the cost of this holy war against his losses in Normandy... He desires to be elsewhere, fighting for gain. Our peace shall likely be wrought out of gold, not steel."

He switched feet in my lap; I wiped my sweated brow and began again. "If my lord Saladin were to offer an honourable settlement ...?"

Imrahan sipped and nodded. "Peace, honour, and more important, the freedom to make war in Normandy!" His lip curled. "What of *Outremer*? What of the 'holiness' of this war, for which so many Saracens have died?"

I shifted uncomfortably. Pain is insidious. I wanted to sink into a tepid bath. Sweat trickled about my sides and the gauze, soft as a dove's wing, felt like a mailglove. I wondered how long it would be before getting up hard was quite safe. If I rose in that way, I would open the half healed cut, and I was grateful that Edward was so ill, fucking was the last thought in his mind. He would not attempt to rouse me until he was recovered, and so long as I did not rouse myself, I could manage.

"The Sultan requires Edward?" I asked through clenched teeth as I massaged Imrahan's foot.

He touched my face. "Art thou fretted for him? Or is it pangs of another kind?"

"Both, Sire," I admitted. "I do hurt."

"I imagine so!" He kissed my cheek. "Bathe there, and rebind it. And to answer thy question, it was the King-General's suggestion that Aethelstan would undertake the duties of an envoy. He will carry messages between our camps."

I made it to my feet with a curse. With my back turned tactfully, I opened my robe. To my annoyance the bleeding had stopped and the cutting was no more than a scarlet line about the crown of me. I was furious! Given my discomfort, I would have liked to see real blood to pardon my commotion. I washed and salved as I spoke, and used a new gauze pad, which I realised had been left for me.

"I believe Edward would welcome the duty, Sire," I said. "But if I may, let me caution thee. He is so weak and ill, and his side is a great brand, the size of my palm. It will be a month before he can sit a saddle without tearing open what the physicians worked so hard to heal.

"By which time," Imrahan mused, "all will be in hand. Inform him that he may be called to this duty."

"I shall." Eased, I returned with a slow gait and spraddled legs which would betray me wherever I went for a day or three. Men by the legion experience this, it is most common. "If Edward is healed too late for the duty, what work will he do? I mean no impertinence, but he is proud. Menial tasks will insult him. If demeaning work is to be done, let me do it and make no mention of it to him."

Imrahan smiled faintly. "Loyal puppy! Thy cautions are well taken. Saxon honour will not be overlooked."

I should have knelt or bowed in response, and dithered, loath to move. At last, flushed scarlet, I ducked my head and said, "Forgive me. I am indisposed."

Now he laughed aloud. "No need to explain! Many are circumcised in adulthood. I think it pains the babe no less, but he cannot speak! Sit in a warm bath. Show thy beloved. A few days hence it will be beautiful."

I managed a creditable bow and walked carefully to our room, where Edward lay resting, more or less at peace. Tauseef was with him until the moment I returned. At my peculiar gait he giggled and fled, and I latched the door behind him.

Bare to the hips in the warm air, wide awake, thin and tired but clearly mending, Edward watched me with a curious look as I tottered to the bath and opened a spigot. Water was precious. I was permitted a hand's span in the alabaster tub, no more than that. Once used, the water went to irrigate the trees, nothing was wasted.

"That eunuch speaks a barbarian kind of French," Edward said slowly as he watched me fiddle with my robe. "He made odd remarks, about pruning and cultivating." His voice was a whisper but his heavy eyes followed me. "What did he mean?"

How could I lie? I shrugged out of the robe with my back toward him, slipped off the bandage and inspected myself to make sure it was not too unsightly. Soon it would bruise, but for now it was merely swollen, and since I had been 'pruned' the swelling was unnoticeable.

I had the grace of the Saracen male, whose cock is gorgeous, with a seductive look of nudity.

I turned back to Edward, held myself in my palm and stepped to the bed. "Please don't touch. It hurts."

He was speechless. One fingertip almost touched, drew back, and his hand fell to the bed. He gaped. "Was this to make yourself beautiful before me? You always were, when you were whole!"

"I'm not gelded," I remonstrated. "All is intact, I assure you."

"So I see." He tilted his head at me and looked me in the face. "You are like them."

I leaned down and kissed his bearded mouth. "When you were on the edge of death... I knew, if you lived it would be a miracle. I promised, if you were given back to me I would make a blood sacrifice. My blood, spilt with great gentleness from the instrument of love."

Wearily, he watched as I lowered myself into the water. The fire cooled and I leaned against the curved alabaster. "That," Edward observed, "had a heathen sound about it."

"Did it?" I felt a thousand years old and as tired as him. I shook my head slowly. "I always had faith of a kind, but in what? Ranulf is devout, but the Church would burn him for it." Edward's brows rose and I nodded. "His gods are older than Saladin's or Richard's. As old as time." I splashed my smooth chest. "I always believed in *something*. It never seemed important to call it by name."

"You are wise past your years," he whispered as he rested back and closed his eyes. He was asleep in moments, exhausted by the effort of speech.

I lounged until I was comfortable, then left my ration of water in the bath – I would need it again – dried, and salved myself with the ointment that had healed his branded side. A blood sacrifice? There was more truth in the remark than I had realised.

Tauseef had sent for food, and I sat at the window, watched the camp and ate fruit and bread while Edward slept. Cavalrymen rode under the walls with a jingling of harness, a thunder of hooves; a forge roared as swords and armour were repaired; a chandler rumbled along with a wain laden with grain. I could watch the whole world pass me by, and I began to drowse as the day grew warmer.

The Imam wailed, and I put on a robe to join the others. I knelt at the back, awkward and prickled with sweat, but the teasing I expected was absent. I had made the covenant, and it may have been unseemly for them to tease.

When I returned Edward had woken, so I changed his bandage, fed and bathed him. At his beard I paused, kissed his lips and said against his ear, "Would you trust me with a razor?"

"Upon which part of me?" He jested, and touched my belly, though not my cock, which he knew would have stung.

"Your face!" I suppressed a helpless flinch and stepped back.

"Your beard is most becoming, but I love you best smooth as a boy. I want kisses, and all this masculinity is a hindrance!"

"Very well." He sighed. "You've done all else for me since that night." He settled as I fetched my shaving knife. "Tell me of it."

"The battle?" I oiled his face. The razor made a soft scritch-scratch as it whisked off his beard and left him as smooth as me, and paler. My hands and arms were dark against his pallor, and soon, if we remained in this land, I would pass on the streets of Dimashq as a Saracen... even if I were stripped naked.

As I worked I spoke of that terrible night. The storm, Qabir, the battle, and Sir Lionel de Quilberon. Grief welled, and Edward's eyes glittered with tears.

Finished, I sat cautiously on the mattress and took his face between my hands. By heaven, I would put flesh on his bones! We both must heal before we would be ready for love, but I could kiss him, and when his arms circled me weakly I was gratified.

His hands delved under my robe, lifted it away and loosened the linen. He wanted to look, and I obliged him. Reclined on his pillows, I held my breath as he carefully took me in his hand.

"It will be beautiful," he said almost reluctantly.

"I have always thought so," I agreed smugly. All my life, I would have this beauty. What was a temporary smart?

He looked up at me, and for the first time I saw his eyes dance with weary but genuine humour. "It was for vanity that you did it!"

I squirmed as his fingertips came too close. "It was for Imrahan, in whose hearing, in a depth of despair, I made a pledge. Have you forgotten, Imrahan owns the both of us. It behoves us to remain in his good graces, for if we fall... " I looked away. "An auction block is not impossible."

"Then, you did this to keep us safe."

"In part. And in part because... " I took a breath. "I believe I saw a miracle, and I owed a debt of blood."

He laid his hand over his wound. "A miracle of knives and branding irons!"

I took his hand away from his side and kissed the palm. "You should have died on the road. The trail was hard and the sun vicious. You lived long enough for Saladin's own surgeons to treat you." His eyes widened. I nodded.

"Saladin's own?" Edward swallowed. "But, why does the King even know I am alive?"

"Imrahan," I told him, and gave him the news I had heard that morning. He listened intently, but he was exhausted once more, longing for sleep, as I yearned for another bath. I told him of the duty Imrahan proposed, the work of the envoy. I also would have a part to play, since I spoke the language.

Then I kissed his mouth and bade him rest, for sleep heals as no medicine ever did. At first he watched as I lounged in the water, but when next I glanced at him his eyes were closed.

Chapter XXV

He slept the sun and moon across the sky each day for almost a week, while I bathed him, massaged his limbs and fed him every bite he would eat. He did not stir to love, and I was grateful, for in those first days a swift, boyish passion would cause me woe! In fact, I was soon mended, and twice Edward caught me admiring myself. I had thought him asleep, and the sound of his ripe laugh made me scarlet to the ears.

But he thought it beautiful – the first act of love he was capable of showed me this. One morning, seven days after the surgeons tortured him and gave him back his life, he stretched without pain, kicked away the linen and showed to me a body that was not quite so gaunt.

I stood at the foot of the bed, surveyed him from toe to crown, and with a thrill saw his shaft arched over his belly. My own cock rose for the first time in more than a week, and I dropped my robe, knelt beside him, and when he pulled me down I tucked carefully into his good side to kiss.

Three nights, I had dared sleep with him. Now he was ready for more. He wanted to see me, hard like this, and I moved about to oblige him. It was graceful and elegant, and he admired it, first with hushed words and then with his mouth. His tongue found the tiny scar that had all but vanished, shivering me. When he was better I would ride him, but at that moment it was more than enough for me to press my hot face between his slender thighs, and take him in my throat.

That was the real beginning of his healing. As we finished he whispered that he needed to make water, and I must help him. His side pained him, his face was waxen and he leaned heavily on me; he could not stand straight, but hunched over with his arm pulled in. Anxious, I stood back and watched. His spine thrust sharply through tight-drawn skin, his hips were bony, his muscles wasted, and I knew he needed meat and milk, fruit and bread, fresh air and the sun.

He leaned on the wall by the close-stool and could not move when he was done. I half carried him to the nearby chair and he sat while I knelt between his feet and bathed his fine, heavy genitals. The Saracen custom is to be cleanly, a habit I had learned.

"I'll remake the bed," I offered as I dried him and washed my hands.

"No." He touched my face with fingers that shook. "Get me a robe. I'll walk."

I bit my lip and frowned at him. "You are not well enough. Please, go back and lie down."

He arched a brow at me. "I'll stagger as far as the garden you told me about, and sit in the sun for an hour before I totter back!"

I had described the garden several times. It was a short walk for a well man, but a long journey for one whose every step cost him dearly. Tight-lipped with disapproval, I fetched a robe of deep blue silk, as near to Aethelstan blue as I could manage, girdled it about his hips rather than about his waist, and lent him my arm.

"Carefully. One step at a time," I cautioned as I helped him through the door.

"You are my keeper, nurse and mother?" he demanded testily, but leaned heavily upon me and shuffled doggedly into the passage.

"I am your squire, nurse and lover," I corrected with a swift, surreptitious kiss for his neck. "And I fear for you. Carefully, now."

The garden was really a courtyard filled with enormous stone pots in which grew palms, ferns, little trees and enormous flowers, fruiting bushes and thorny roses. Sunlight was filtered and dappled by boughs overhead, and deep shadows crept across the cracked, mossy flagstones.

A fountain played in the centre, casting rainbows into the air when sunlight struck through the spray, at late morning and early afternoon. Above was the harem, where Imrahan's thirty wives and concubines, two-score boys and eunuchs, and his hundred-odd children lived. Singing, music, incense and laughter filtered down from the screened windows, where I saw shadowy forms beyond the drapes. The women had heard about the Saxon knight, and despite his frailty they would see the beauty that had seduced me long ago.

Edward settled on the corner of a bench and gave a sigh of relief. The walk had exhausted him. It would be an hour before he was ready to return, and I wondered if I should summon a litter. But he would never have that. I hovered like a wren with a cuckoo chick in the nest till he caught my hand and bade me come closer.

I cast a glance at the windows and murmured, "My lord, we are observed."

"By bedboys and eunuchs! And what is this 'my lord' gibberish?"

"You *are* my lord," I said as I let him tug me onto the bench at his side.

"I am your fellow bondsman," he said drily. "Imrahan owns both of us, body and soul. You, he would not sell. One day he may grant you the gift of freedom. But me?"

"He would not sell you away from me," I argued. "He knows I would die without you."

He closed his eyes. "Will King Richard accept the services of a Saxon in the pay of Saracens?"

I stroked his thin forearms. "Richard is eager to get out of Palestine and make war in Normandy. He will clutch at straws, no matter who bears them. Carry Saladin's messages. It is an honour granted by the enemy whom Richard has learned to respect."

His eyes opened, blue-grey in the brighter light. "The honour we need, think you, to return to England and rebuild my house?"

"Aye," I said cautiously. "But first, grow well. You are weaker than you know."

"I know it well enough," he argued.

"Your side?" I was up then, on my knees at his feet, hand in his robe, searching for wetness about the wound. But it was dry, hot, scaled like a lizard.

"It itches!" He swore. "I could scratch till it bled, and it is the effort of a saint to let it be." He smiled crookedly. "I am mending. Come here and kiss me."

I embraced him carefully and was astonished. My arms were round with muscle, for I make muscle quickly. My shoulders were broader, my breast and legs bigger than his own. So I had grown again. He pressed against me, and after his wounding I realised with a start, I was stronger than Edward. The old, foolish fantasy had come about, but I wished it had not been like this. I held his head against mine, kissed his ear, and his arms shook as they embraced me. I thought it was with frailty, and murmured nonsense to him, until he began to laugh.

"For the love of heaven," he chuckled, and ouched as the laughter hurt. "I am healing! I am weak as a boy – but in a month I shall be your match once more, and then shall outstrip you and be stronger. I am a soldier and you are not. Do you enjoy the ability to master me?"

"No," I said, and it was half a lie. I had dreamed of holding him, protective and possessive. But not like this.

He gave me a curious expression, part amused, part abashed. "You have grown. Have you not noticed?"

"I have," I admitted. "I may be taller than you in a year or two. Does that discomfit you?"

"No." He yawned against my cheek. "I knew your father, and he also was tall. I knew when I took you into my house, you would be like him." He sat back and looked at me, fingered my hair, which was long on my shoulders. "You have grown more handsome too. You are almost a man, Paul. If I treat you as a boy, I am wrong. Your boyhood days are over."

I was taken aback. "You'll still love me?" I asked, faltering. "Even when I am a man? I can razor my body and face, if you prefer. I do it now, living in this house."

He took my hand with a companionable squeeze. "I shall love you when we have grown old together. It is not a matter of the flesh, but of the heart. Now, enough. All this is for the bedchamber! Tell me

227

what you know of Imrahan, Saladin, the army and all. I've lost a week and must somehow catch up! Our lives could depend on it."

News arrived almost hourly. Dispatch riders lamed their horses to fetch every story from Jerusalem and the desert strongholds. To the west were Richard and the Crusader army, and to the east, the Jackal and his sorcerer, so intent on the annihilation of the Infidel that they would not rest until this whole land was drowned in blood.

Just that morning Tauseef had given me the latest snippet of news. The eunuch and I stood in the shade by the olive trees, eating oranges and watching the waterwheel, and he told me that a contingent of Saracen cavalry had fought a terrible battle. Against Richard or Templars? I asked. His eyes were filled with dread, for it was brother pitted against brother. They had fought the Jackal.

"Ibrahim was on that battlefield," I murmured, and Edward hung on every word. "Ibn-Zahran is riding at the head of a band of Saracen knights that even now draws closer to this fortress."

"But surely, if Saladin knows where he is," Edward began, "he can root out his poison?"

"That battle was just fought," I said, hushed, recalling Tauseef's face as he told this tale, "and the Jackal's company won. Saladin's cavalry were massacred to a man. A few squires escaped to fetch out the news. Even now, Imrahan and Saladin are conferring with the chieftains. If they fight, they may not win."

His hands were like talons on my arm. "How far away is the Jackal?"

"Tauseef said he is camped five days' slow march from here. Not very far." I knew what was on his mind.

"This place is a fortress," he said tersely. "Could it be held under siege?"

"I know little of military matters," I sighed.

"Oh, Paul!" He stirred, pressed his side and turned toward me. "You know as much as is necessary! How many approaches are there to this hill?"

"Three," I told him readily. "From the east, where we came; the west, where Saladin is camped, and north, along the ridge of the hill."

"And up here we command water, orchards, grazing for animals." He rubbed his face. "That is not the makings of a dangerous siege. We may be safe."

"Safe?" Now he had lost me.

He pinned me with a hard look which demanded that the boy become a man at a snap of the fingers. It is often how a boy must mature, or perish. "Safe," he repeated, "while the Jackal and Ibrahim challenge Saladin."

All at once I knew what he meant. We would have seats at a tournament, we would watch the contest fought out beneath these walls, as if we overlooked a pageant and joust. My mouth dropped open and he nodded.

"At least we cannot easily be besieged," he said tersely as he clambered to his feet, "but if the battle is lost we must have a means of escape. Horses."

"If you rode it would break open your side," I protested as I shouldered his weight and helped him stand.

He grunted with effort. "Then, when next you bruise the ears of the Almighty, beg for ibn-Zahran to be held at bay for a week, two weeks, until I can straddle a horse without a price to be paid in agony."

I had seen one miracle, could I hope for another? Ibrahim terrified me more than ibn-Zahran. I had seen the Jackal only twice in all the time I spent as a courtesan. I saw, *felt*, about him something sweet-rotten, as of flesh that has gone over-ripe and begun to decay, but I had little terror of him. A single knife thrust would be the end of him, and a boy or woman could manage that. But what I had seen, heard and smelt when I crept into Ibrahim's lair was branded into my memory.

I made Edward comfortable when he had toiled back to the room, and left him asleep as the Imam called. On the cool balcony I knelt with the servants and guards. I was free, accepted as one of them, and my grasp of their language was good enough for me to laugh at their jests and sit enraptured by the storytellers.

The jingle of camel bells announced the arrival of another party on its way in, and when we had rolled the prayer mats and helped ourselves to fruit and water I looked into the blistering sun to see their banners. I did not recognise the green standard, but I knew the face of one of the men who rode in the shadow of it, and as he tied up his dusty, tired horse, I met him in the courtyard and knelt at his feet with a smile of delight.

Haroun Bedi was astonished, delighted, and grasped my hands to lift me to my feet. "Thou hast grown," he observed approvingly. "I wondered what became of thee!"

"And I of thee, my lord! I thought the Jackal would murder thee after ibn-Qasim was put to the sword." I spat into the dust. "A curse upon the Jackal, and his sons after him."

"I ran," my old teacher said acidly. "I rode alone for much of the way, on dangerous roads, and was twice set upon by bandits before I had the good fortune to join a spice caravan from Hind. And thee?"

"Imrahan kept me safe. Along the road we came upon a band of knights, a battle was fought... Edward of Aethelstan is with us. We are Imrahan's bondsmen, last survivors of that doomed party. And I... " I blushed. "I had my rites."

This astonished him. "'Twas not merely lip-service? I taught thee, but not a word did I think was believed!"

"I was a diligent student!" I protested "Dost thou require to see the very cock of me, to be convinced? Nay, my lord. I belong first to

Imrahan, second to Aethelstan. Shouldst thou wish to give me further lessons, I shall happily accept, but as to welting me, first procure Imrahan's, then Edward's approbation. And it will not be given."

For a moment he gaped, and then laughed at me. "A welted arse is a swift spur to learning, but not without permission."

"Never didst thou ask my permission before welting me." I bristled.

He swatted my behind. "Not thy permission, impudent flea. Jahrom Rafha was thy master, his permission to teach boys as they have always been taught was granted without the asking. Once only did thou and I show him welted buttocks, and amply were they earned."

"On a slave's behalf," I objected. "I went into the sorcerer's lair and fetched out the prisoner. I saw him loved, and watched him vanish into the storm!"

Haroun was gaping once more. "Deliberately didst thou defy me?"

"I did." I lifted my chin. "And an innocent lived because of it."

"Rascal!" He shook his fist at me. "Flea upon the rump of a manged camel! Worm in the gut of a poxed ewe sheep! I promised thee flogging if thou defied me, and the whip shalt thou have!"

"But he would have died," I remonstrated, and wondered if he meant it or was jesting. For the life of me, I could not tell. What else could I do but call his bluff? I drew myself up to my full height, and by this time I was taller than he, and broader. I made quite a fine figure. "I am Imrahan's now," I said curtly. "Take up the matter with him, and if he deems my crime so dire, I shall be flogged. It was the price of the life of one who was well loved among Imrahan's men, and if I must pay with a back full of stripes – I shall pay!"

I bowed deeply and left him as his companions called him. I saw Imrahan from afar an hour later: he was eager for news, and who better to assail for it than Haroun Bedi, who was a scholar? Would Haroun tell him my transgressions? Of course he would, and Imrahan reckoned me still among the boys of his household. If I was wicked, I knew I would be disciplined like any of the others.

The maggot of doubt gnawed at me all afternoon. In the early evening Edward and I ate together, and if I was to be sent for to give account of myself it would be soon. I gave Edward careful forewarning.

He stopped eating to hear me out, and averted his eyes. "What right have I to keep you from discipline?" he asked bitterly. "You are a fool! If you had said nothing your teacher would never have been able make woe for you."

"I know," I agreed dolefully. "I've begun to forget myself. You said yourself, I am almost a man. I've begun to think and behave like one, and often it is unwise!" I nibbled a date. "Let me go and see if

Imrahan wishes to chastise me. I cannot bear the waiting."

"The waiting?" Edward snorted. "When is the last time you were shown the end of a whip?"

"Never," I said breathlessly.

He punched the pillow at his shoulder as he arranged himself to sleep. "Take it as best you can. See if Tauseef will doctor you, and if not I'll do what I can." His tone was disapproving and anxious.

"You... " I faltered. "You have been scourged?"

He glared at me. "By a monk, for the sin of watching boys bathe. It is no tickle, Paul. You'll learn the folly of your loose tongue to-night!"

I closed the door quietly and crept away. Sweat prickled my sides and my knees shook. Could I offer Haroun some other penance? Could I woo Imrahan, beg a less painful restitution? How could I go back to Edward with a ruined body, when I realised he had been hoping for love that night! I kicked myself black and blue as I shuffled along and showed my face to the burly Nubians. They were bondsmen and did not require a bow. They knew me, passed me inside and I stepped into the very chamber where I had had my rites.

Imrahan, Haroun and several men I did not know sat smoking and drinking coffee. From the polished casques on the cushions beside two of them, I knew they were the Sultan's men. A scribe accompanied them. You would always recognise a scribe by the blue stains on his fingers and the writing box at his feet.

Eyes turned to me and I bowed back-creaking low before Imrahan. My old teacher looked sternly at me, all whiskers and glittering eyes.

"The boy reads minds!" Imrahan exclaimed. "Come. The Captain is Neyriz Azurah, a cavalry commander." He indicated the hook-nosed, pock-cheeked man at his left, who sucked indolently on a hookah. "Tell us all that is know to thee," Imrahan invited.

I knelt at Imrahan's feet. "Of what shall I speak?"

The captain leaned forward. "Tell us what numbers the Lionheart commands. Archers, horsemen, soldiers. How many ships? How many warhorses does he stable?"

"I know but little," I warned. "I was a squire, privy to scant details. Still, I was curious and squires talk amongst themselves!" I looked at Haroun. His face gave nothing away.

They questioned me while the sky dimmed from peacock blue to starlit black. Through the windows I watched those stars and wondered where Qabir was. In the arms of the handsome man who had caught him up into the storm, I hoped. If I was to pay for his liberty with my skin, let that liberty be sweet! I told all I knew, careful to warn when I was speculating; I drew charts from memory, even wrote a list of the knights I knew who fought with Richard, their names and estates.

My knees ached and I was hoarse with talking, but Azurah was pleased, and before he and his fellows left he asked my name, my house, so that he might summon me when he needed me. "I am Delgado," I told him with a thread of pride, "of the house of Imrahan. I belong to the Earl of Aethelstan, who is also my lord's bondsman."

The Captain swept up his companions and bade Imrahan a good night. The door closed and Imrahan stood, stretched and cast off the windings that had bound his head. His dark hair spilled loosely and he tossed a silver comb to me.

I got up stiffly, stood behind him at the window while he took the night air, and combed his hair as I combed Edward's. It was silky and lovely, but blond was my preference. Haroun poured cold coffee and collected the litter of maps with which they had worked.

"Thy teacher tells me," Imrahan said offhandly, "thou art at fault."

I swallowed. "Sire, I am no longer a student, but it is true, I did disobey when I was under the hand of Haroun Bedi... once only, to save of a man's life. The man was Qabir, Rashid's beloved."

He swept the comb out of my hand. His eyes were shadowed, I could not read them. "Still, Haroun claims thou wert a disobedient puppy and have been promised the services of the scourger."

I ducked my head. "My lord." I hesitated. What could I say?

"Against the wall," Imrahan said, low and velvet with menace. "Learn thy place and thy duty. The lesson is taught but once, if it is well learned."

I shuddered as I dropped my robe to bare my back, pressed against the cool marble and shut my eyes. Footsteps behind me; the rustle of a garment. I steeled myself and felt –

A lash that tickled, made me jump with surprise. A second that itched me, a third like a breath of air. I opened my eyes, looked over my shoulder to see Imrahan with a peacock feather in his hand, about to lash me again. Laughter creased his face as he brought it down across my shoulders.

"My lord!" I protested. "What is the meaning of this?"

Another tickling lash. "A lesson," he told me, "for thee, *and* thy teacher. Nay, boy, stay there! Thou art to have twenty strokes! And thou, what hast thou learned, Haroun?"

As the feather counted out the foolish punishment, Haroun pulled at his chin. "That the boy has become more man than a boy, and is obedient to the last," he said wryly. "Fully did he expect whipping, but he went to the wall without argument. He is thy true servant."

Imrahan nodded. "And thee, boy?" He lashed the feather across my bare back for the fifteenth and sixteenth times.

"That I can trust my lord to judge me fairly," I said, weak with relief, counting seventeen. "That I was wrong to disobey my teacher, but Qabir's life was worth a flogging." Eighteen. "I would have paid the price. I was ready to accept Imrahan's wrath and keep faith... " Nineteen. "I am grateful to be judged guilty yet forgiven, since my

232

crime was committed on another's behalf." I took a final, twentieth lash of the feather, and kissed his hand.

"The boy," Imrahan said aside to Haroun, "is nearer man than boy. Dress, Paulo. Is Aethelstan waiting?"

"Aye. He is stronger." I sashed my robe. "My lord, he is fretted, also. If this stronghold falls, we must not allow ourselves to be captured. In ibn-Zahran's hands, we are dead meat."

They shared a bleak glance and Imrahan's hand fell on my shoulder. "It was I who spirited thee out of his clutches before! Shall I now let thee blunder back into them? Tell Aethelstan, if this stronghold falls, Salah ad-Din and all of us will fall with it. Ibn-Zahran is massed for battle, but we will stand – a last stand, if need be. *Here* is where the Lionheart's holy war is won or lost, though King Richard may never know it. His fortune lies in the hands of ibn-Zahran and Ibrahim."

I withdrew to the door. "My lord," I said softly to Haroun Bedi, "where is the Jackal now?"

He waved his hand vaguely into the east and his lip curled in scorn. "We are safe for twenty days. Ibrahim will not sanction battle till the stars are in the right conjunctions."

Almost three weeks? I bowed and hurried back to Edward. In twenty days he would be mended. If worst came to worst, Imrahan would see that we had horses, a means of escape. I racked my brains to recall maps, and thought I knew the route to the coast. I could spirit Edward through, since I spoke the language, was swarthy and dark haired, and even stripped I would pass for a Saracen. In twenty days, Edward could make that run for freedom.

Behind us we would leave an army in disarray, thousands dead, a land in the grasp of a madman whose name even Imrahan shivered to speak. Ibrahim weighed heavily on my mind, like a great black bat. If he defeated the forces of Saladin, his victory in this Third Crusade was almost assured.

Our lamps still burned and Edward was awake. He sat against the pillows, and in his lap was my Book, which he could not read though it fascinated him, since every leaf was illuminated. He set it aside as I bolted the door. "Well?" His voice was steely. "You were disciplined?"

"I had twenty lashes." I dropped my robe and showed him my back. "With a feather from a peacock's fan. It was a lesson in discipline, the acceptance of place and duty. Trust. I went willingly, believing I was to be flogged, and accepted judgement. Imrahan was satisfied."

He held out his hand. "You were lucky! A lesser man would have flayed you. Come here. And in future, learn when to keep your mouth shut!"

"Shut?" I set my lips upon his own.

"Shut," he whispered against my tongue. "But... now is not such a time."

I gathered him up, unable to credit that this bag of bones was my Edward. I was so afraid I might hurt him, I scarcely knew how to make love to him. At last I put him on his back, oiled myself and mounted him. His blood-hot lance stole my breath, but I kept my eyes open and watched him. If he showed signs of pain I would be off him in a trice.

But ecstasy lit his face, bliss shone in him as he teased my paps, dealt my own cock and balls the clever touches and strokes I liked best. Lust and love scintillated in his eyes and I felt more cherished than ever. He exhausted quickly and came in me long before I was done. Smiling, I bade him lie back and watch me. I had often done this for Jahrom Rafha, and every night I had sworn I would pleasure Edward so, ten times for every one I had shown Jahrom Rafha. Here was the first time. I rode him delicately and gently, showed him the dessert for his eyes, then with leaden hands went for bowl and cloth, water and scent, to render us sweet for sleep.

To my intense gratification he curled in my arms, set his head on the pillow by my own and closed his eyes. He was mending. I was sore, soft and open between the legs, and there was no surer sign that he was mending. I would feed him, I told myself. I would put muscle on these bones, so that he would be ready when the time came.

Twenty days. Was it enough? It must be. Edward's wound had not wept or bled since it was cauterised. His fevers had not recurred, and the pains had diminished. Now he needed strength in his legs, suppleness in his joints. I could urge him to his feet, help him walk carefully, coax him to eat and rest when he must. The same stars that had shown Qabir the way home would show Ibrahim the road to battle. I buried my face in his hair and squeezed shut my eyes. It was so little time to be at peace, for once the Jackal's armies moved, Palestine might never know peace again.

Chapter XXVI

Of all the time Edward and I spent at Imrahan's stronghold I have but one regret. I was never privileged to see Saladin closely. Edward met him twice and described him to me in detail, but I saw the legend only from a distance, mounted on a magnificent black Turk, clad in a scarlet cloak and burnished armour. Later, I glimpsed him again, wonderful and terrible in the firelight as he exhorted his men on the night before battle. He stirred even me, and I had seen enough of blood and battle to be disillusioned by dreams of glory. But twice Edward was summoned to the Sultan of Egypt, and when he returned I hung on his every word.

I spent an hour on him before I let him out of my sight. Before I was done his face was smooth as a boy, his hair was like silk and his robes were fit for princes. I begged the loan of rings for his fingers from Haroun and Tauseef, and offered work in exchange for a new pair of rich, embroidered slippers. Till then, Edward had been as as barefoot as I, since he had not ventured from the cool halls and gardened courtyards, but I would not have him barefoot before Saladin Rex.

I wondered if I might be called to act as his interpreter, but Saladin, so Haroun told me after cuffing my ear for my audacity, spoke English and French as well as Latin, Greek and several Oriental languages. He was a scholar as well as a warrior. I ducked my head and admitted my admiration, which was both what Haroun wished to hear, and the truth.

The first audience fell a week after Edward regained his feet. He was still thin, and would take months to regain full strength, but I did not fear for him any longer. A kind of glow surrounds a man in good health, and Edward had that look again, though he was not yet strong. I thought it was a miracle then, and have thought so ever since. My small sacrifice was gladly made.

The day had been hot and Edward was sore after sweating on the wound. The brand was livid, the size of my hand, glistening like a carbuncle now the scabs had peeled. He had not scratched, and the healing had been the faster for his patience. I bathed it in rose water and rubbed it with ointment, and he was at the least comfortable when he went to the King.

The company had gathered in the feasting halls, an entourage of knights, captains, scholars, scribes and astrologers. I yearned to be there, but Haroun had already cuffed my head. Not even he was to attend, though Edward had been summoned by name. My lord was slender, fine and splendid, he would hold up his head among them, and though he was a bondsman he would display the stubborn Aethelstan pride. His skin was boyish, pale, and they would be fascinated by his fairness. Many would look lustfully upon him, but none might have him. I was complacent of that. Edward was mine.

Afternoons, he had taken to walking about the balconies and gardens. I would lend him my arm when he needed it, but he became more reliant on his own legs as days passed and he strengthened in body and spirit. He would sit watching the honey-skinned, gazelle-eyed boys, and I remembered that he had once been punished for watching boys this way. Yet he watched these boys only with passing interest, and at night, or in private moments, turned to me.

We shared every pleasure we would conceive of, without shame or restraint. Imrahan's clan were of a tribe to whom the love of male for male is considered near divine. I learned that this is an article of faith in a cult that predates the time of the Prophet and springs from the age of the Pharaohs. Those people say, in a man who loves men is born the soul of both male and female, and when both spirits dwell in a single body there is a kind of divinity. Nightly, Edward and I rejoiced in this belief, and our freedom to love purged the guilt from him – he, who had been led astray by an impudent flea!

The Nubian who escorted him to Saladin was the same man who had gathered our belongings when we had chased the mules after the storm, a lifetime ago. He had not forgotten that day, and neither had we. We shared a smile and a word of hope, that Saladin could conjure some magic. What is peace, if not magic?

Then he took Edward and I paced in a turmoil of fretting until the stars of midnight shone over the vast encampment. I was alert, listening for sounds that might signal trouble, but the first I heard was the soft slippered footfalls of Edward's return. He was tired to the marrow of his bones, for they had taxed him past his present limits. I bade his escort thanks, and as I latched our door my lord slumped onto the bed and had not the strength to disrobe.

I undressed him, from the slippers I had begged to the rings I had borrowed. "Tell me!" I begged, when he seemed disinclined to talk. He lifted a brow at me as I opened his robe. "Tell me of the King," I cajoled. "Is he tall? Is he grand? Is he handsome?"

"Not as tall as I expected, nor as handsome. Not as young, nor as powerfully built," Edward admitted. "Perhaps kings are called handsome and heroic by people trying to earn favours! But Saladin is what they say of him. He has the eyes of a great man."

"A great man?" I had him bare, and oiled my hands to rub him, as I did each morning and night, to tone his muscles. "He is a scholar, a warrior, poet and philosopher, Haroun told me." I was rubbing his breast, and paused to kiss his nipples. "Edward, tell me!"

"Curiosity is a curse," he warned.

I pouted, which made him smile. "Did he ask you to act as his envoy?" I demanded. "Imrahan said he would."

"He did," Edward mused. "If there is any message left for an envoy to carry." My hands stopped on his breast. His eyes were shadowed. "Dispatches arrived earlier. Ibrahim commands more than respect in the distant tribes. He has called men from as far as Kush and Hind, where he commands with fear. Those tribes are held in thrall by sheer terror, and will surely fight for him."

"Then Saladin may be vanquished before he can meet Richard," I whispered.

He caught my wrists. "I spoke to Imrahan. He promised me horses, weapons, and safe passage if the tide of battle runs against us." Edward's teeth worried his lip. "You can pass for one of them but I shall be hard to disguise. Can you smuggle me to Joppa?"

I studied my Saxon beauty and puffed out my cheeks. "I think not. Safer to join a band of knights, even Templars, and run for Jerusalem. We should take news to King Richard, and then no more can be asked of you. You are skin and bone, and wounded. You'll fight no more this campaign. Richard's quacks will tell him so at once."

"Jerusalem." Edward let go my wrists and rubbed his eyes. "The King's astrologers read the same stars as Ibrahim. They know when the battle will begin, to the very hour."

"Fourteen days." I kissed the scar. "By then you will be strong."

"Not strong," he corrected, "but I shall survive. Oh, come to bed. It is not rubbing I need, but a sound *fucking!*" He said it crossly, as if he was annoyed with himself.

"What irks you, love?" I pressed to his side. I yearned to call him 'beloved,' and 'sweetest rose of night,' names the Saracen part of me could lay tongue to easily, but the Saxon would not countenance. I slid into the language Haroun had taught me to say all those things.

He looked suspiciously at me, as if he knew what I was saying. I would not translate, and he turned onto his good side with care and a sigh. I cuddled into his back and reached for the olive oil.

"I asked what irks you," I repeated as I slipped my fingers in, too gentle to make him even flinch. He must not move quickly, but step cautiously and move slowly even in bed.

"I irk myself," he admitted, sighing as I worked. "It is unseemly for a knight to have such yearnings!"

"Yearnings?" My fingers slipped out and the smooth, trimmed crown of me nudged him. What sensations I felt now! I have a notion that men of these tribes are cut for sensuality. I believe the cock of a Saracen is more beautiful and more sensitive. I shuddered with delight as I entered him.

"Cravings," he groaned as I joined us. "I need to feel you in me. I itch and ache until you are there, which may be unseemly for a knight."

I nuzzled his neck. "Think you, Imrahan does not have such longings?"

But he was beyond speaking and merely lay still and let me give him what he had wanted for hours, perhaps the whole day. Afterward I washed us and we slept sound – too sound, for I was late for morning prayers, and swore I would pray twice in the afternoon to make amends, which appeased Haroun Bedi.

* * *

Horsemen rode from north and south to join the great army, and I was told that these were the remnants of the forces King Richard had battled with in recent months. The wives and daughters of these men had been butchered by the Templars in atrocities that will not be forgotten for a thousand years. I saw their wild eyes, and I thought they were a match of Ibrahim. What can sorcery conjure that a fury for

237

vengeance cannot?

The stars wheeled, Mars rose toward Scorpio and the moon thinned away to nothing. Soon it would be new moon again, with the sun in the House of the Lion, Mars in Scorpio, and Saturn ascendant. This was the celestial alignment Ibrahim desired, and Saladin's own astrologer had pinpointed the exact hour of battle.

Edward walked further every day, and when I found him alone in our room, bare to the waist, repeatedly lifting a heavy stone, I did not caution him. He was ready to tax his body. He also knew that time was running short.

Two days before the heavens decreed the moment of battle, Imrahan sent for me, and I met him in the courtyard at the postern gate. From there, one looked down the hill, west into the setting sun, toward Jerusalem. Two horses and a mule stood in the palm-shaded stable; harness and light travelling gear waited for us, rugs, goatskin canteens, and a selection of knives and swords.

"Here is thy way out," he told me soberly as I stroked the bony face of the lovely, patient mule. "Let Ibrahim find thee here and thou shalt not live to be sold in Dimashq. He surely knows who stole Qabir."

"Does Ibrahim scry?" I whispered, as if by whispering I could hide.

"Who can say?" Imrahan stirred restlessly. "Be ready to flee. Leave thy flight to the last second, and thou shalt sign Aethelstan's death warrant. He would fetch a fine price."

"I shall spirit him out before the Jackal knows we were ever here," I assured him. "But surely, Sire, the host camped beneath these walls cannot be defeated!"

"What of dark magic?" he asked. "The storm winds of Satan – "

"Are only storms, Ibrahim does not command them," I insisted. "I saw the truth, the night Qabir left us." He looked closely at me. "I disobeyed everyone and went after him. I was on the very brink of the storm, and saw it for what it was. Just a wind, a swirl of dust and sand, strange dry lightning, which Qabir's people use as a mask to hide behind. Ibrahim cannot conjure that trick, and if Qabir's brothers ride out of a storm, they will fall on Jackal or Lionheart with equal hunger."

"I thought the boy was mad," Imrahan admitted. "Rashid loved him."

"He was mad with despair," I admitted. "And he was fond of Rashid. Qabir gave much pleasure, Rashid was not short changed in the last weeks of his life."

Imrahan sighed heavily and touched my shoulder. "Prepare Edward. The time is near, I feel it, I need no astrologer to tell me when a battle is coming. I can smell it, like rain in the air."

He left to attend to his cavalry, and I stood in the stable, let the horses get the scent of me, learn the sound of my voice. Animals are afraid of strangers, and these must soon be ready to serve us with the loyalty of old comrades.

That afternoon, in the shimmering heat when the rest of the house was sleeping, Saladin once more sent for Edward. The Captain, Azurah, waited for him in the courtyard, and when I saw him I knew the hunt was up, with a vengeance. Edward shot me a glance but said nothing, and the last I saw of him before late evening was the swirl of his robe.

I fretted the hours through, and when I could bear the torment of ignorance no more, I searched out Haroun Bedi. He was teaching a class, and I waited at the back, hands folded, lips sealed. He looked up over the heads of the boys and frowned, but my manners were faultless. When the youths left I knelt and kissed the teacher's slipper, which pleases one of his generation.

"Dost thou want a lesson?" he asked, and tugged my hair to raise me to my feet. "In what art?"

"May I know a small truth?" I begged. "They have taken Edward to the camp. He has been with the Sultan for hours. Knowest thou what it means? Must I ready our nags for flight this very eve?"

He stroked his beard and his brow creased. "I know not, but stay here a while, I shall find out."

Grateful, I loitered by the fountain where the lessons had been conducted. I gathered the chalks and slates, cleaned and stacked them, tidied Haroun's scrolls and his Book. I was so accustomed to making my hands useful, I no longer knew how to be idle.

Minutes later he returned and I picked up the slates and scrolls to carry them back into his chambers. "The Sultan is giving into Aethelstan's care a letter," he told me. "A letter bearing the signature of Salah ad-Din, and directed to Richard Coeur de Lion."

I took a shaken breath. "Then, we leave before battle begins." In his cool, dim chamber I put down the slates. A chalk fell; I retrieved it without thinking and remained kneeling at Haroun's feet.

He placed his hands on my shoulders. "Thou shalt leave at the last safe moment, and recall, upon thy honour, thou art Imrahan's bondsmen. Thou shalt have a Saracen escort part way to Jerusalem. Then, deliver to the English King the document of treaty."

"And return?" I looked up at him.

His forefinger rested on my nose. "I spoke to Imrahan but a fivesome of minutes ago. Tell me, boy, what dost thou desire most in the world?"

Flustered, I struggled for words. "Edward's love and Imrahan's respect."

"And to return home to the wet, wild land of thy birth," he added shrewdly. "To be a freeman."

"That too," I admitted. "I never brood over what is impossible."

"Not impossible," Haroun Bedi scoffed. "Many ways can a slave earn freedom. Twenty years of good service, or a single act of surpassing bravery. Imrahan offers a pledge, to thee and Aethelstan both. Deliver the treaty to the Lionheart, and thou art free." He eased his old frame into a chair. "It shall be perilous, and not taken lightly by those left behind."

"Perilous?" I echoed as I got to my feet.

"Thou art the last survivors of thy company, and might be seen as traitors... especially thou, whose body shows the mark of a covenant with God." He glanced pointedly at my groin. "Take care. Woo thy King with honeyed words. Beware priests, who would torment and burn thee. To them, now, thou art a defiler."

I was dizzied, but he was right, and it was an aspect of our task I had not considered. I bobbed a bow and left him to his contemplations, and hurried back to our own room. It was dim and smelt of jasmine; songbirds carolled on the balconies and the hot wind stirred over the parched hills. I leaned both elbows on the window ledge and looked out over the sprawled, massive and still growing camp. My belly churned with anxiousness, disquiet, fear and pride. We would be free, if we could only run the gauntlet of Crown and Church.

Weary, I stretched out across the bed as the sky darkened. I did not see the sunset; I slept through evening prayers and was still asleep when Tauseef knocked with a basket of food in the evening. He wondered if I was ailing, but I only thanked him for his concern, took the food, bathed, and paced as I waited for Edward.

When he returned he was grey about the lips with fatigue, long past any appetite for food or love. I bathed and rubbed him while he told me, in a hoarse whisper, all he could remember of what he had seen and heard. He brought with him, wrapped in a yellow calfskin, a rolled letter closed with scarlet wax into which was stamped the signet seal of Salah ad-Din Rex.

The time was *now*. The stars foretold battle and my spine shivered with foreboding. The letter lay with my Book on the chest by the window, under the fluttering candles. My eyes were drawn to it, over and over, as I lay in his arms.

"What does it say?" I whispered. "Did you read it?"

He spoke against my neck, warm and gusty. His hand was between my legs, cupped about me, warm and possessive, though he was past rising. Who knew when we would have the opportunity to make love again. Hell was about to be let loose and we must run like the wind.

"It is an invitation," he told me. "That letter bids Richard send an embassy to an oasis in what is now no-man's-land. There, the two shall meet."

"And make a treaty of peace," I breathed.

"Armistice. Peace with honour." He tugged me closer. The strength had begun to return to his arms and in the last week his side

240

had healed considerably. It was still pink but now he could move and turn. In a year he would forget it had ever happened. "The treaty," he went on, "promises that the Saracen shall be allowed to live in his own land without fear of persecution, yet also grants Christian pilgrims the right to enter the Holy City."

"King Richard will grasp at that," I guessed. "He longs to fight in Normandy, to recapture what Count John has lost."

"I pray so," Edward sighed.

I lifted my head. "Pray? You are godless!"

"A figure of speech," he retorted. "Tomorrow our escorts meet us, and we ride west."

"But battle is set for the day following," I protested.

"Saladin does not wish harm to befall me," Edward said acidly. "Or is it the letter upon which he places the value of a hundred sapphires?" He snorted. "Either way, it matters little. We are to leave after the heat of day is past. By dawn we shall watch the battle from a safe distance, and when Saladin has overcome ibn-Zahran we ride fast and straight for Jerusalem."

"When... ?" I echoed, stroking his thin-fleshed back. "That victory is not certain, Edward."

"So Imrahan told me. If we see the battle lost, we *run*, and take the news of what we saw. At least the Crusader army might get out alive if only they know to flee!" Edward sighed heavily and kissed my face. "Do you know, we are to be free?"

"My teacher told me. An act of valour is the price of our freedom. Haroun said... " I bit my lip. "Beware of Richard, priests and Templars. We'll have explanations to make, and if they dislike one word they hear – "

"Shh." He kissed my mouth deeply. "I am still a knight, and I fetch Richard the letter that frees him to make war in Normandy. That will conjure the trick for us."

I placed my faith in his judgement, for Edward knew the ways of barons and princes better than I could ever hope to. But, if he was wrong? I pressed my face to his shoulder and tried to sleep.

Chapter XXVII

The day following was filled with restless work, hot and dry as dust. I saw little of Edward. Imrahan and other officers commanded him every moment, while I packed the belongings we had been given, checked harness, sharpened swords, groomed and saddled the horses. At last I spared myself an hour to bathe and gobble a meal.

The encampment was in full cry. Riders rushed in, late in the blistering afternoon, with news that the Jackal was but five miles from our stronghold. With many others I climbed the archers' fire-steps atop the walls and, sure enough, I saw their banners in the distance.

The time had come for us to leave. As the sun began to smoulder on the western horizon Imrahan sent for me, and for the final time I knelt at his feet; for the final time he fetched me up, kissed my cheeks and mouth, and whispered into my ear, in his language, words I shall cherish for ever.

"Thou art my brother. No matter whither thou goest, the covenant remains immutable as the stars. I have a gift of parting for thee." He drew back and smiled. "Thou art a freeman."

I would have knelt again but he held me up. I kissed his palm instead, tongue-tied as a loon, and he passed me into the care of the waiting escort. Two men, each twice my size and clad in burnished chainmail and plumed casques, flanked me as I returned to the room to pick up my own small bag. I swung on my cloak, and bade farewell to Tauseef. He gave me a moonstone ring, kissed my face, and I embraced him. "Where is Edward?"

"Looking at the horses." Tauseef released me. "Ride like the wind. 'Tis the life and death of us all."

We made no mention of the fear that Saladin could be defeated by ibn-Zahran.

The horses were already saddled, and Edward was more than satisfied with the animals we had been given. One was a dappled grey Barbary stallion, the other a sleek brown Turk, both bred for speed, to race us to safety if we were challenged.

For the first time in so long, Edward was properly armed. At his left side, a broadsword, at his right, a short sword; leaned against the stable wall was a shield upon which a Saracen artist had painted a curious white rose on midnight blue. Not the Aethelstan rose as we knew it, but it would do.

I went to him as the stable plunged into dimness. The Saracen knights were already waiting for us, the sun was low and the wind moaned out of the south, where Africa broods like a great beast asleep in the earth. I looked up into Edward's stormy eyes and nodded mutely.

He could mount without my help, though he was not well. He was strong enough to make this journey, so long as it was a single ride and at the end of it he was given a soft bed and a week's rest. His lips compressed as he settled on the wide leather saddle, which squeaked beneath his weight. He gathered the reins in his right hand and urged the dappled Barb into the shadows of late afternoon.

The whole camp watched us go. Every man knew who we were, where we were from, where we were bound. A few shouted well wishes to Edward, blessings to me, for I was like them. I looked back and waved. Many of them I knew from a trail that led as far back as the Jackal's fortress. I saw Haroun Bedi on the wall, and bent my head. He raised his hand, acknowledging the valediction. I had been sent to him as a slave; I left him as a freedman.

Pride ached in my chest as I turned back to Edward. He was in a light mail shirt and surcoat of deep blue, a black cloak with a hood which was at that moment down about his shoulders, so that his hair was wind-tossed and like finely wrought gold. He wore his Saxon beauty as he wore his youth, purely, and without arrogance. I loved him all the more, and placed my trust in him as our escort swept us down the long decline below the fortress.

At the bottom was a river, fetlock-deep to the horses. We splashed through and toiled slowly up the rise opposite. How many hours had I spent at our window, looking across at this dry-burned hillside. How strange it was to crest the rise, turn back and look upon Imrahan's stronghold. I felt a tug of longing to return and mocked myself.

It would have been easy to pine for the loveliness of that world, but I remained a Saxon... or half-Saxon, whose heart and mind were scorched by the memories of home.

We camped on the highest point of the hill, and as the sky grew full dark I saw the first sliver of the new moon. She lay on her back like an empty cradle, filled with portents and omens. When the Saracens prayed, out of force of habit so did I. We heard the Imam from the camp of Salah ad-Din, wafted on the night wind, and that night the prayers were endless. They were saying rites for the dead, so that every man would face dawn having made his peace with his God. Many would not see sunset; many would be judged tomorrow, when the Gates of Paradise opened for the worthy and slammed in the faces of the worthless.

Let Ibrahim be struck down! I begged of any god who would listen. Ranulf would have called upon Wotan. Lionel de Quilberon would have spoken the name of Christ. I blindly begged one and all to cast the Jackal into everlasting darkness where the soldiers of peace would trample his broken bones.

At last the wind was silent as the camp settled. Five miles beyond, Ibrahim would watch the same stars and work his sorcery. I wished Sir Lionel was with us. I wished Rashid had lived to know Qabir was safe. And I lay in Edward's arms, wrapped in a cloak, knowing I would not sleep and watching the sky for the first glimmer of dawn.

It grew very cold. Edward and I pressed together as the fire burned out, and he was stiff with the chill and the discomfort of rough sleeping. He was not well enough to bed on the ground, and he wore a grim face as we stirred. The sky was brighter, the stars beginning to pale as rose and gold flooded out of the east.

Dawn. Banners fluttered, warhorses wheeled together, so far off that they might have been toys. From our vantage point we looked down on the scene, across the wides of the river that was like a natural moat between us and the spectacle. Masjed ibn-Zahran would never know we had been there. To be safe while those we left behind were at risk gave me a guilty pang.

"There," Edward said suddenly, pointing. "You see?"

We stood in the lingering chill, cloaked, while an iron kettle sang over the fire. The Saracens were silent and watchful beside us; they also had seen. Like a shadow on the grey-brown landscape, the army came on, a mass of cloaks and banners, black, dark greens and blues, the standards of many clans and tribes from as far afield as the lands of the Pathan and the Pushtu. They marched out of fear of Ibrahim, or to win vengeance for atrocities committed by Crusader armies.

Most of these men who rallied to the call to arms were from far beyond the Holy Land; they could not yet have fought, or they too would have been eager to treaty. Saladin's cavalry fell on them and battle raged like a live beast. We heard the roar, the chime of steel, and I fancied I smelt the reek of it. Battle has a smell, ripe and rotten, like something decayed.

Edward's hands clenched, white-knuckled. He knew better than I how the tides of battle run. He had been schooled in strategies and campaigns while I worked in Ranulf's fields, and beneath his breath he muttered curses that blistered my ears.

"What is it?" I hissed as the morning wore on toward noon.

"Use your eyes," he said tersely. "They are containing the outland cavalry, but at what cost? Saladin will likely win today, but after this he will be too weak to challenge the Lionheart. Richard will never know that his Crusade was won for him here, by a general called ibn-Zahran!"

Imrahan was probably on the castellated roof, flanked by his archers, where he could watch the scene of havoc. I smelt blood on the air, heard the screams of injured horses and wanted to run, to get away. I fell to my knees with the Saracens. Edward stood beneath a gnarled tree, hands clenched into the knotty wood, all of us praying the same prayer: *send down the Cataclysm upon them!* How many hearts sent out that exhortation? Was it Wotan, Camelus, Bellona, who stirred awake on some height above the earth? Or did some wicked *djinn* cast an ear to the cries of men, and make mischief?

The sky shadowed and I wondered if a storm was coming. I had never seen rain fall here and could not imagine it, yet the wind was in my face, stronger every second, and the sky was dull where before it had been burnished, like polished copper shields. And then I knew.

It came out of the south like a funeral shroud in the air, and fell upon the battle all at once. Edward caught me as it raged toward us, and flung his cloak over us both, as he had done once before. The whirling wind stormed across the scorched hills and tore apart the battle like the hand of the Angel of Death.

Not a mile to the east, the Jackal's camp must be devastated,

244

ripped up and thrown away as sticks and shards of wreckage. Knights were unseated, horses bolted. Above the chaos Imrahan's archers, with their elevation on the battlements, had only to take cover and wait it out before they emerged.

In the dark, stifling space beneath the cloak, Edward and I huddled and fought for breath. Fear drove us together. He pressed against me, his lips hunted for my mouth and I was glad to give it to him. How long the windstorm raged I do not know. Our senses were bludgeoned when it diminished, and such a weight of sand piled upon us that Edward, in his weakened condition, was unable to lift the cloak.

Sweating and cursing, I threw my own strength into the task, and we found the sky bright once more. Blinking on stinging eyes, we clambered to our feet. The horses and mule had been tethered to the tree and our guards had sheltered with them, holding cloaks over the poor animals' heads to save their eyes from the scouring dust.

Coughing painfully, hand clapped to his side, Edward peered at the battlefield and groaned. "Paul!"

I echoed his groan of relief. In the confusion of the storm ibn-Zahran's ranks had broken. Horsemen fell, animals bolted in fright, and now the archers perched on Imrahan's ramparts had only to mark their targets and bring them down like fish in a barrel. Foot soldiers burst out of the courtyards where they had taken shelter and fell on the shambles of the disordered army.

Our guards called blessings upon the Great Redeemer, clasped each other and wept with relief. The same tears prickled my own eyes, and when Edward offered me his arms I went to him. Then he gently thrust me away, and I looked into his face with some breathless awareness.

"Now," Edward said softly, "we must ride. The tide of battle has turned, they have conquest in the palms of their hands. Saladin will count this day a great victory, but it is only the beginning."

I swallowed on my dry throat and helped him into the saddle before mounting my own skittish, frightened horse. Our guards were already up, and waiting only for Edward.

With a last backward glance at the scene of carnage and glory, he turned the dappled grey Barb about and set our feet on the road to Jerusalem.

Chapter XXVIII

Smoke curled on the wind, dark and forbidding. There had been fighting. We saw the black and white banners of the Knights of Saint John at a town called Hamah, and there our Saracen escort left us. Edward let down his hood so that his Saxon colouring might be seen, and I took charge of the mule carrying our waterbags and bed rugs. I watched Edward hawkishly, as I had since the day before. The Crusaders' camp still lay a day ahead, and he was pained, fatigued, taxed by the heat.

The Knights of Saint John are hospitallers, whose mission is to care for sick and injured pilgrims. Their banner bears a white cross that to any Christian means succour and care. Edward sorely needed rest, as they must have seen as we approached.

Hamah had been razed to the ground, vultures circled, hoping to feed, and the bodies of two knights were being swiftly embalmed in brine. They must be returned to Antioch, Constantinople or Rome to be interred. They could not lie in the ground in this heathen place.

Tired and dusty, our horses toiled toward the hospitallers and Edward raised his hand to the commander. He was young, a fair Norman with pale blue eyes and an arrogant but not unkind face. He was on foot, flanked by four of his fellows who kept their hands near their weapons as if they feared we might assault them. It was absurd. Edward was close to the end of his endurance and I had only a knife, as befitted a squire.

"Greetings," he said in a dry, faint voice. "I am Edward of Aethelstan. I beg your protection on the road. I carry a message for the King and must deliver it with all speed."

He was plainly weak. The young commander clapped his hands, and Edward was lifted down, fetched water and helped into the shade of a tree. Sir Michel d'Oleron heard out a brief version of our story and seemed dubious until, at a word from Edward, I brought out the letter.

They knew the signet seal of the Sultan at a glance. Saladin's own hand had touched this creamy vellum and scarlet wax. With all due reverence I put the letter away and knelt beside Edward, who had begun to revive with the rest, water and shade.

D'Oleron conferred with his companions and reached a decision in moments. "We are bound for Jerusalem. You may ride with us. Indeed, you shall be in jeopardy if you do not. These roads are menaced by Saracens."

"My thanks," Edward said, as if it were an effort to speak. He held out his hand to me, in the belief I would help him up.

"Rest a while," I begged. "These knights have work to do. You can rest an hour at least."

"How far?" Edward drew a deep breath and his eyes narrowed on d'Oleron's face.

"We dine in the Lionheart's camp tomorrow eve," d'Oleron told him. "Are you injured, Aethelstan?"

"An old wound." Edward put his back against the tree and closed his eyes. "It was well doctored but will pain me for months yet."

"Then rest, as the squire advises," d'Oleron said indifferently.

"We shall ride on in an hour."

I fetched Edward food and drink but he was too tired to eat. It was strange to watch noon go by, and the hour of afternoon prayer unobserved. No Imam called, no Saracen in my sight knelt, and I must attend the hospitallers' Benediction when we camped that evening, or be thought an impious rascal. A heathen? Little they knew. And now I must safeguard my modesty. I would carry to the grave a secret only Edward shared

It was nearer two hours before we rode on, and we travelled at the speed of the wain bearing the dead. We left behind a Saracen town that no longer existed. I looked over my shoulder, where the smoke pointed into the south like a weathervane. Who would ever know what souls had perished there? The same thought troubled Edward.

He questioned d'Oleron, asking of the King and the war, and we learned that much had changed in our absence. Funds were as short as tempers; Normandy was almost forfeit, Richard was furious and in England many barons had begun to switch their allegiance to Count John. Richard was restless, impatient to be elsewhere. Edward glanced silently at me, and I nodded.

We slept that night in a corner of the hospitallers' pavilion, and though I bathed Edward and salved the scar, I could not otherwise touch him. D'Oleron glanced briefly at the wound but did not ask where he had won it. Benediction was sung in that lilting, strangely beautiful singsong chant, but Edward was excused, too exhausted to stand, and after my duty was done I hurried back to him.

I dozed at his feet, always half awake, listening for a sound of distress, but he slept like a dead man and in the morning his youth did him better service than any medicine. He was stiff and sore but able to mount his horse with my help. I caught his sleeve while we had a moment's privacy, and he looked into my upturned face in the cool dawn light.

"The last day's ride, and then I can do as you say, and rest. I shall survive. Have you forgotten, I won my spurs the hard way, in battle!"

I never forgot. It was the pride of Aethelstan, that in the teeth of Norman rapaciousness a Saxon could still command dignity, if he had courage. Or was it audacity? That day, as I watched Edward struggle, I wondered.

Four times we broke our journey to water the horses. Four times I almost lifted Edward off, and then back onto his horse. Only I knew how near the end he was, and by mid-afternoon I had begun to watch for any sign of that camp within sight of the Holy City.

The sun was down when at last we clattered into the midst of the gaudy throng of pavilions, wagons, horses, camels and dogs. Twilight had begun to thicken into night proper. D'Oleron summoned his brother knights as I slid from the saddle and stood ready to catch Edward, for I feared he would topple to the ground. As I took his hands and guided him he fought to keep his feet. I cast about for some face I knew, some man who would assist him, and I saw two.

The Templar, Jean de Bicat was maimed, gaunt, and looked ten years older than the day I had last seen him. The day I was lost. Edward had told me about him, but I had been unable to imagine de Bicat like this. His right arm was gone at the shoulder, he wore a plain brown habit, his head was tonsured, his feet were bare in the dust and his limbs were wasted. I was appalled at his grizzled face and ravaged body. He had come as close to death as Edward, but he had enjoyed less care and tenderness.

Help for Edward came from another quarter, one I hardly recognised. At that age, boys grow rapidly. Henri had shot up by a hand's span, filled out, and his voice had almost fully broken. He was a youth, he must be thirteen, and manhood was settling in. He rushed forward and took Edward's arm as he swayed with fatigue.

He babbled his disbelief as we took Edward into de Quilberon's pavilion, which was the closest and the best appointed. And his little monkey face crumpled as I told him of Sir Lionel's death.

"They all died," I whispered as I disrobed Edward and swabbed his feverish skin to cool him. "The squires and serving boys are alive, but only one knight survived that adventure. You are looking at him." I wrung out a cloth over Edward's shoulders, sending rivulets down his back.

"The squires," Henri demanded in his odd, deeper voice. "Where are they?"

"Bondsmen." I sighed. "They belong to Saracen masters, as we did until days ago. Now, that is enough, Henri. Fetch me food, wine and a quack, in that order! Then keep a watch out for the King's courier. Sir Michel D'Oleron will have told His Grace that Aethelstan has returned as a royal embassy. It'll not be long before the summons comes!"

"A royal what?" Henri's voice rose sharply.

"Enough, I said." I looked into Edward's drawn face. "Food, wine and a physician. Go!"

He scampered off, but at the entrance to the pavilion paused for a moment. "You have changed," he said thoughtfully before he rushed away.

I blinked at the observation, and was astonished when Edward said quietly, "He is right. I brought a boy to this terrible land. I take back to England a man. Ranulf will not know you." He looked at me with dark eyes, and his mouth softened, making me long for kisses. "School your face," he murmured. "All that is danger here, or have you forgotten?"

"I never forget," I said, hushed. "I'll keep my eyes down and say nothing, my lord, not a word to betray you."

"My lord?" he echoed, teasing and sad at once.

"Aye." I knelt before him. "Here, I am a squire, bonded to the house of Aethelstan. All else belongs in the bedchamber." I won myself a smile, and began to bathe him once more.

He revived under my hands and when Henri returned with fruit, wine, cheese and bread he was able to eat. I combed his hair, put aside his mail coat, fetched fresh linen and looked around for the quack Henri had begged. The man was an ancient, but he knew his job. A tincture of herbs made Edward blanch as he swallowed, but by the time the King's man arrived he was on his feet, in command of his wits.

I gave him the calfskin containing the letter and stood at the entry of the pavilion to watch him escorted away. He was a freeman once more, prideful, Saxon, and fair as no other man in this camp. Weary, and for the first time able to spare a moment for myself, I ate, drank the last of the watered wine and bathed, clumsy with fatigue.

Tiredness has a way of making the mind slow, and I did not notice Henri until it was too late. He had seen me as I washed, and he swore, the kind of language for which Sir Lionel would have boxed his ears.

"They cut you!" he exclaimed, horrified and fascinated, and crept closer to see.

It was too late to keep the secret, so I let him look, but I was vigilant for strangers. He stooped, peered at me and whistled. "I was a captive," I said quietly. "Much befell me that I will never tell, so do not ask. It is enough that I am free once more, and whole."

"Whole?" He touched me with his fingertips. "You call this whole?"

"I could have been bound for a church choir," I snorted. "You know well enough what I mean!"

His narrow little shoulders scrunched. "It hurt?"

"Of course it did. But not any longer."

He gave me a shrewd expression. "In bed, it is more sensitive," he guessed.

I pulled on my linen. "Much," I said drily, "and that is more than enough curiosity! Whom do you serve, since Sir Lionel wisely left you behind when he embarked on that hell ride?"

"No one. I look to my lord's chattels. Now, what is there for me?" Henri looked up at me with wide, worried eyes.

"You'll return with us," I guessed. "Perhaps Edward will give you a situation in his house. But if he does, fair warning, Henri! Find a bedmate of your own. I belong to Edward, and I'll not betray his trust and affections in your bed. Those days are past."

His jaw sagged. "You and he – ?"

"Are reconciled and have been intimate for a long time," I said with rich satisfaction. I yearned to sleep, as no doubt Edward yearned, but the King would occupy him until my lord fell face-down on a table.

I stretched out on the bed where Lionel would have slept, closed my eyes and never expected to sleep. If I had napped like a cat I would have been grateful, but exhaustion was insidious and I slept so sound, I knew nothing till midnight.

A rustling sound woke me with guilty start. Edward stood in the cool blue darkness, and murmured my name. I did not light a candle, but secured the canvas and caught his hands to press him onto the bed.

"Will you have a physician?" I whispered as he lay down with a breathy sigh.

"No. Rub me," he murmured. "I have drunk, eaten and sat, the whole evening. I am merely tired. A quack examined my wound before the King – I believe he wished to assure himself that the story of my wounding was true!"

"Had it been a ruse," I said bleakly, "we would have been in irons by now." I gave the scar a slather of oil. "The letter?"

"Was seized, read a dozen times, and even now they are composing a reply that will be taken out tomorrow." Edward caught my hands and pulled me down on top of him. "We are high in favour."

I was weak with relief, and so was he. I set my lips on his and found his mouth trembling. I tasted his wine and kissed him deeply. "Then our duty here is done," I said hoarsely a long time later. "We are released?"

"We are for home." He urged me to lie beside him and pressed me tight to him. "I have been given the duty of seeing to the return of Lionel's servants. His ship is still in Joppa, we leave in a few days."

"A week, even two," I argued. "You should take that time to rest. You are hurting."

He merely sighed. "I have a grant of land from the King. Distant from Aethelstan and likely worthless, but it will fetch a price or we shall have its income to buttress my flagging fortunes." He kissed my neck. "And we'll have Montand's estate, if Edwina will stand by the betrothal."

"If?" I snorted. "She loves you. Trust me, Edward, as one who also loves you. The way she looked at you is the way I look at you myself." I kissed his tongue. "What season is it at home?"

"Spring, I think," he said vaguely. "We have been gone a long time, yet not the years I feared."

"It is not the time, but the road we travelled," I said softly. "A month of hell is more wearing than a decade of heaven. I aged five years in the last three months."

His hands blindly stripped me, fondled my arse and fetched me up, half hard, the best I could manage just then. He fingered the crown of me, stroked the tiny, invisible scars which for all my life would be sensitive and ticklish. "The sooner I get you away from here, the better I'll like it."

"I'll look to my modesty," I assured him. "Henri saw."

"Saw you naked?" He lifted his head from the pillow. "You trust the scamp?"

"I told him I was gruesomely tortured," I said, to amuse him. "A barefaced lie, but he was keen to believe."

He set his head on the pillow. "Tell him to pack Lionel's wain. We go as soon as I can stand without feeling near to death's left hand."

"You need a surgeon?" I asked urgently.

Edward pulled me back down. "I need rest, food, sleep... and your tender ministrations," he corrected. I put my hand between his legs and heard a sound of humour from his lips. "Not even you could rouse me tonight, but soon I shall be capable."

"And then shall fuck me," I said happily.

He tousled my hair. "In what position?"

I cuddled closer. "I shall kneel with my arse up high and beg you to plough and seed me." He hugged me, and we settled gladly to rest. "Edward?" He grunted, half asleep already. "I love you," I murmured.

"As I love you," he assured me, against my ear.

PART SIX: HOMECOMING

Chapter XXIX

It was ten days before we left, and we rode slowly to the coast. Edward was tired, and the de Quilberon servants were mourning. The measure of a man is the affection his bondsmen have for him. There is a saying that deeds speak louder than words; so do the tears of genuine grief.

On the road I was Edward's shadow, and since he was clearly ailing no one questioned it. We saw few churchmen other than Father Robert, who was so ancient, he could not even remember his own scriptures. After the day's journey I bustled about, taking charge of the dozing Earl of Aethelstan, and I was praised for my troubles, Father Robert actually commended my loyalty. Had he known what amusements took place behind closed doors, he would have excommunicated me! Edward was not the complete invalid they believed. A little flesh covered his ribs by the time we neared Joppa, and by night he was ready to ride me as he rode Icarus.

It was good fortune that he had left Icarus behind, when he rode out to search for me. The poor horse was lame after the first hell-ride into the Saracen hinterland, and Edward left him to rest, and took another. But our real luck was that we took home with us not only Icarus, but the animals Imrahan gave us when we undertook Saladin's business. Both were whole males who would breed with English mares to produce the finest horses ever seen in the shires. The horse is the soul and spirit of the Arab. The word 'Arabian' will one day surely come to mean this breed of horse.

Nightly, we slept entangled; every dawn I slipped away before Edward woke and was busy when the rest of the company stirred. Father Robert praised me and offered me a 'better situation', in the service of his brother in Lincoln. Edward lifted a brow at me as I told him of this the following night. We were in bed, spent, and I was sore, aching and doubtless so was he, since we had had the pleasure of one another without stint.

"I have been thinking," he mused. "You should have an allowance."

"Money?" I rubbed my back on the sheet. "I've no need of money."

"For your future," he added.

"I have no future, unless it is with your house," I added blandly. He gave me a look, as if he took that for guile, but I meant every word. "You cannot afford to pay me," I argued. "I know the state of your purse! Give me your livery to wear, food in my belly and a warm bed. That will suffice. So long," I added, "as the bed is warmed by yourself."

He was silent while his teeth gnawed his lip, and I knew what was rushing through his mind. I took his hand, pressed it to my chest, where the hair was growing back and prickled me mightily in the heat. "I know you must wed the girl. I know we must be discreet. If I am granted one night a week in your arms, I'll be content all my life. I've had you to myself these months, and it has been Paradise. I own a thousand memories to keep me company when you are with her, or when we must bed apart for the sake of propriety."

He turned over, pillowed his head on his arm and studied me in the light of two cheap, smoking tallow candles. "You'd be content with that service from me?" He sounded dubious.

"Measurelessly," I assured him, and was due a surprise.

"I would not!" He sat and glared at me. "You know I am sleepless without you. I cannot sleep in a loveless bed, and I want no other but you." He swooped and kissed my mouth bitingly. "I am at the problem like a dog with a bone. Be patient. I shall resolve it by and by."

Dizzy with pleasure, I snaked my arms about him and pulled him down. We were already spent, and kisses were more than enough.

* * *

We stabled the horses in Joppa late one blustery afternoon, and I was astonished at the coolness of the sea wind. We were accustomed to the intense heat of the interior, where the days are blistering as an open hearth and the nights as frigid was a winter's gale. A cool, soft breeze wafted off the sea, and we basked in it as we strode through the waterfront markets.

The same merchants and hawkers were there, selling carpets, silks and spices, silver and copper... slaves. I regarded the little gelded boys and doe-eyed girls with a mixture of pity and resignation. The bondage waiting for them would be life-long and demanding, but if fortune smiled and they went to an owner such as Imrahan, it would be as gentle and fulfilling as many a marriage is not. I remembered both my masters with the greatest affection.

The horses were loaded aboard and the sail unfurled while dawn was still a glimmer in the east. The wind was poor and we would make slow time on the voyage home. Edward and I stood in the stern, watching the parched, grey-brown coast fall away. We would never return. We had stretched our luck past all good sense and were blessed to be homeward bound with whole skins. Many were not so fortunate.

The winds remained light, and the skies fair. By day we lounged in the shade and Edward gained flesh as I watched; by night we bedded carefully in a tiny, stifling cabin while the ship hugged the coast of Africa and butted into the westerly wind.

They were bittersweet days for me. I was eighteen years old at sea and Edward cherished me teasingly. Henri matured swiftly and was a young man when we saw the rocky isle of Gibraltar. He would soon find a lover of his own, and I wished him well.

Many weeks passed, and Edward strengthened. As we hugged the coasts of Spain and France, and at last saw the cliffs of home, the only sign of his injury was a pink scar I alone knew. He was supple and agile again, and once more stronger than his squire.

Eventually, when I had lost track of weeks and months, the ship nosed up the river to York in company with a trading vessel and a squadron of fishing boats. Crowds gathered as always, hungry for news from the Holy Land, as soon as we stepped ashore. But the news is always months out of date.

We told them that the two great Kings were about to make a treaty and end the Crusade, but by that day it was already sealed, and King Richard was bound for another war entirely.

Green, cold and damp, was England. Cool and misty, lush with forests the Saracen could not imagine, rich with a kind of magic even Ibrahim could not match. The stone circles that stand like sentinels on the windy hills speak to me of ancient magic greater than sorcery, more profound than enchantment. I devoured the sights and sounds and smells of England, and admitted I had pined more for home than I had realised.

Once more I had that strange and disconcerting feeling when I came ashore. I was so accustomed to the roll of the deck that now it seemed the solid earth bucked and heaved. It was an inconvenience, but it diminished after a day's patience. I barely noticed the discomfort of swimming senses, I was so intent upon the longed-for beauty of my homeland.

Yet England was in turmoil. In the absence of King Richard, his brother was high in favour with many of the barons. They and the sheriffs bled the Saxons and Normans alike of every shilling that could be stripped from them, to keep the army in the field. Young men were levied for the soldiery; the cream had already died in the Holy Land.

All around us as we rode out of York, we saw the scars of the war. The struggle to liberate the cities on the Pilgrims' Way had cost England dearly. I wondered if the Saracens would be consoled to know, they was not alone in suffering. In England also, women and children were hungry, boys were literally kidnapped for the army, hands were lopped, backs flogged, when taxes could not be paid. For the sake of holy war.

We bedded at a tavern outside York on the night of our landfall, and made our way homeward next morning. Riders rushed ahead to the Aethelstan estate, but first a painful duty fell to Edward's hands. Sir Lionel's widow and children were waiting for his return, and instead were about to receive the worst tidings of all.

The sun was warm on my back, but it did not have the punishing power of the Saracen sun. Larks sang on the wing and the orchards were ripe with fruit. Haymakers were busy by the river; cockleshell boats wove through the midwater currents as nets were cast over. This was the England I had longed for.

Edward wore a wistful face. The joy of homecoming was marred by sorrow. We were accustomed to the loss of Sir Lionel, but Lady Enid and her three children, the survivors from a brood of five, must face the grief anew.

Soldiers were on the road, marching beneath the banner of the Sheriff of Durham, but they bowed as Edward rode by. They recognised a knight returned from Palestine by his tanned face, his leanness, the bitterness of his expression. A pace behind, I rode the Barb and led the Turk, while Henri rode the pony that had been purchased from me on our departure, a lifetime before.

The woods were busy with children gathering herbs; corn was ripening, pigs rooted for last season's acorns and squirrels scampered through the branches that arched over the road. I would have been supremely happy, but I recalled Lady de Quilberon affectionately and could not bear the blow we were about to deal her.

She was older than Edward by some years and had borne Lionel a large family. Her eldest was my age, and we expected to see him on the property, since it was his responsibility to head the house in his father's absence. But we saw no sign of Christopher, nor of the other younger son, James.

Servants ran to tell the lady we had arrived as we loosed the horses in the yard. Edward and I stepped into the house while Henri hurried to remake the acquaintance of boys he had not seen in so long.

She was still a lovely woman, broad hipped and comfortable as a mother, with the face of a madonna and hair the colour of hay. Even I would call her beautiful – I, who never desired a woman for bed. Edward had the greatest respect for her. She joined us in the parlour where I had once served ale to Edward and Lionel.

There was the table where we had examined maps; there, the shelf where Lionel's few books were kept. The sunlight was golden and dusty through the open window. It gleamed on Edward's hair, and on the unbound hair of Lionel's daughter, a comely child of six years.

A glance at Edward's face, and Lady Enid did not need the truth put into words. She sagged into a chair and buried her face in her hands. He took her shoulders, stood behind her while the child, Martha, tugged her mother's skirt, wondering what was wrong.

"Enid," Edward whispered. "I am so sorry. If there had been anything I could have done – "

She lifted her eyes to him, pink from weeping, one Saxon to another. "How did it happen?"

"We were in the field, he died fighting, as befits a soldier." Edward spared her the details. "He fought well, as he always fought, and he was buried decently."

"A Christian burial?" Enid murmured. "He would have wanted it."

"He had rites and prayers," Edward said evasively, looking at me. I nodded, for I knew better than any of them the great similarities as well as the differences between those two faiths. Strip away the words, and the foundations are of the same stone, the spars and beams holding up each temple, the same wood. Edward sighed and touched her hair. "Where are your sons? They should be with you."

"Christopher was taken for the army," she murmured. "I've not seen him in six months. The last I heard, he was in Wales, where the tribes are rising. I have heard no more of him. James is dead."

"Dead?" Shocked, Edward sat on the edge of the table at her side. "Enid, what happened?"

"An accident," she sighed. "He fell from a horse and injured his head, he never woke. When the physicians could do nothing, I fetched in Mother Mary, but all she could do was usher him gently away."

Edward looked over her head at me. "That was dangerous. Mother Mary is whispered about. They say – "

"She is a witch." Enid rubbed her eyes as fresh tears began. "And not even her Craft could wake James. Oh, Edward, do you think I care? Mary is a witch, what of it? She has the power of healing, and Lionel turned to her too. She delivered both James and Martha into this world. It was fitting that she should ease James out of it."

I was surprised and pleased. Enid was like Ranulf. Beneath their pious, obedient surface lay a deep faith in the ancient traditions of our own land. Enid took Edward's forearms in hands that had grown rough with hard work. "What is left for me, Edward?" she asked, hushed. "I've no husband, they took my son, I've lost James." She swept the little girl into her arms. "I have only Martha. What are we to do?" And she was wild with fear.

A woman alone is prey. Enid did not even own the land, but was merely managing it for Christopher, until he returned. She had been left unmolested since she had been awaiting her husband, a Norman knight, but the news that she was widowed would soon reach the Sheriff, the Bishop, and Yves Guilbert. How long would it take them to gulp down a Saxon widow's home, her land and small fortune?

Edward touched her cheek with his fingertips. "Trust me. I'll not leave you to the wolves. First, let me see if I can find Christopher and fetch him home. On whose authority was he levied?"

"I don't know. Sheriff's men came one day, they had a paper, I did not see the signature. Christopher did not even have time to take a bag before they marched him away."

"To fight in Wales," Edward mused. "When was this?"

"February." Enid scrubbed her eyes and pressed against him. "Help me, for pity's sake."

"For your sake," he corrected tenderly. "Come home with us, Enid. You'll be more comfortable there than alone and grieving here."

She made a wounded sound. "You have not been home, then, before coming here?"

Something inside me coiled up tight as a drawn bow. Edward and I looked sharply at one another. "We came directly here with the news of Lionel," Edward said quietly. "What is it, Enid?"

"Tax collection," she told him bitterly. "Sir Laurent of Aiselby led the progress across the whole shire. Crown tax, Church tax, scutage, tax for the crusade. Your estate had little left after the fires last autumn."

"Fires?" Edward echoed. "The house – ?"

"Was safe, but your crops burned." Enid withdrew from Edward's tense body and blotted her eyes with her cuff. "The land has wintered and is green again after a great deal of work. You have a crop to reap soon, but last season's taxes were unpaid – unpayable, with you in the Holy Land, and the fire. The Sheriff took everything. The estate would be ruined utterly, had not Ranulf of Sleaford looked to the place, and Mother Mary herself moved in there."

"Dear God." Edward closed his eyes. "Still, pack. You won't stay here alone. Fetch the child. Let me see if we can pick up the pieces."

She looked gratefully at him, and my heart went out to her. When she had gone I went to Edward and lowered my voice to speak under her hearing, for she was only in the adjoining room.

"Her property has spoiled since we left and they took the young men for the army. Yours will be run-down also, but it is a matter for strong backs and willing hands. Give Ranulf a word's thanks for his efforts. And the witch."

"A word's thanks? He has my deepest gratitude. He brought you to me, and when we were gone he tended my estate." Edward touched my mouth with feather-light fingers and sighed. "I hoped to bring you home to a comfortable life. It seems I am to offer you only more hard labour."

I smiled faintly, sadly. "So long as I am in your company nothing else matters."

I meant that to the last syllable. I left Edward putting Lionel's books into a sack, and went out to call Henri's name. He was in the stable, filled with anger and bitterness. We shared a look, and in a second I saw that Henri had taken another step closer to manhood. Young men mature swiftly when times are hard.

"I had the whole story from the cowherd," he told me tersely. "The Sheriff was within his rights, but it was a cruel blow to the lady. And Aethelstan's crops burned to cinders last autumn."

"We know." I walked out of the stableyard, and with a mercenary eye I tallied everything I saw. When one must pick up the bits of a broken vase and remake it, every piece is to be hunted down and cherished.

It did not take Enid long to pack. Three bags were loaded onto a wain, two old plough horses was backed between the shafts and pair of milk cows hitched behind. Enid tried to apologise. "We have little left, Edward. It's been hard since... " She gestured toward the road, where the soldiers had marched Christopher away.

"After our service in the Holy Land I am high in favour with the King," Edward told her. "I have a grant of land and a little money. All is not lost." He took her hand and squeezed it tight before we mounted up for the short ride.

We could see where the fire had caught alight the ripe, dry wheat. If the eye was keen, it could still pick out blackened bark and scorched ground, but fresh earth and dung had been fetched in, tilled and ploughed, until the soil was good enough to bear again. New wheat was waist high, the corn stalks bent under the weight of the ears. But if the Sheriff's bailiff had not looted enough out of the estate in order to pay last year's taxes, we must pay those this season too. Little would remain to live on.

Yet the house was sound, the fire had not reached the kitchen garden. Cabbage, cauliflower, turnips and marrows grew in weeded, orderly ranks. Someone had been busy, and the finger of smoke curling from the chimney told us, they were at home. I wondered if it was Ranulf, but Enid caught Edward's attention as we neared the house.

"It is Mother Mary and her daughter. Pay them no mind. Had they not moved in, you would have returned to a ruin. The bailiff took even your hoes and spades. I gave Ranulf what we had to spare."

Grim-faced, Edward surveyed his estate without a word. The thatch was sound, the fences were firm, but the paddocks were empty of all but a score of squabbling chickens and a pair of geese. We dismounted, and rather than entering by the front door Edward looked into the kitchen.

Past his shoulder, in the dimness, I saw the old woman and her big, strong, half-wit daughter. Mother Mary stood and bobbed Edward a curtsy. Her grey hair was plaited over her shoulders, her body was whipcord thin and still strong, though heaven knew how old she was. Perhaps she knew herbs that maintain strength long into old age.

"I ain't trespassing, my lord," she began, as if she thought she must defend herself. "Ranulf of Sleaford gave us permission – "

"Peace, Mother," Edward said quietly. "Lady de Quilberon told me everything. I bring bad news. Sir Lionel has perished."

"Dear gods." Mary made a sign before her face which was not a cross. That banishing sign was enough to have her burned, had a churchman seen her, but she knew she was safe among us.

I entered the kitchen with Henri and took stock of the results of industry. I smelt cooking vegetables, saw a hare over the fire, a dozen brown eggs in an earthenware basin, herbs trimmed and drying in the warmth, a basket of kindling and wood by the fire, pickles and preserves in stone jars, mushrooms waiting to be cleaned and sliced, a marrow stuffed with rosemary, thyme and bread, waiting to be thrust into the ashes to bake.

"It seems," Edward said slowly, "I owe debts of gratitude to the most unlikely friends." He gave the old woman a brief bow. "You can call this your home, and be safe here, you and your daughter."

The daughter was wool-brained but quiet, child-like though she must have been as old as Enid. Mother Mary coddled her, kept her clean and dressed her like a maid. The child in the woman's body did not seem to suffer. Oddly, she was clever with her hands. As I watched, she was sewing rabbit skins, and the great iron needle was sure in her fingers. But her tongue could not make words and her head could not understand them.

The house was almost empty. Edward's books were gone, the linen had been taken, even the furniture. We found nothing much save the odd mouse and a toppled stool that had somehow been missed in the rampage of plunder. Edward picked it up, turned it over and set it down again. He would not look at me.

"What have I brought you to? That old priest who rode to Joppa with us offered you a situation in Lincoln. You'll soon wish you had taken it. When that day comes, you are free to go."

I snorted scornfully, and while we had privacy slipped my arms about him. "I do wish a better *situation*. I should like to be situated on my knees... and you on yours behind me, soon to be within me."

"Not what I had in mind," he remonstrated.

"I know." I palmed his lean backside. "Yet, that is what I want most. May I have it?" I was trying desperately to tease him into better spirits, but he resisted fiercely. "Edward!" I caught him by the hands, tugged him out through the front door, where the pivots screamed for want of oil. "It is a matter of hard work for strong backs!"

"There is nothing to work with," he argued, resisting even my tugging hands as I took him out into the sun, as if he would have liked to sit in the dimness and dust inside, and moulder.

I pointed out the horses, Icarus, Turk and Barb. "We have three of the finest stud sires this shire has ever seen," I said with the native shrewdness of the Saxon, who has always had to fight to survive. "Lady Enid has two young cows in milk. Did you see the chickens as we rode in, and the kitchen garden? Twenty-six hens and two cockerels. I can count!" I nodded at the woods. "The crab-apples and hazelnuts are ripening. Yonder is the river, and this is the best season for fish. I saw eight beehives when we rode off de Quilberon's estate. We have corn and wheat, and those woods are full of rabbits, and the odd wild pig if we're lucky. Mother Mary has been busy. Pickles, preserves, herbs. We shan't starve!"

He scented a hunt – the hunt first for survival, then for prosperity. Like any warrior his nostrils flared, and he cocked his head at me. "You want to begin again, and not throw the whole sorry muddle to perdition?"

I hoisted myself up to sit on the fence, caught him between my knees and held him. I would never have dared do this when I was a hopeful squire, he the lord whom I barely knew, and the stables filled with grooms! Now, Mary, her sweet half-wit daughter, and Enid – who cared not a fig for anyone's bedmates – little Martha and Henri, were our only company. I pulled Edward closer and kissed him.

"If you threw the muddle to perdition, where would we go? What of Lady Enid? And you've not considered the Montand girl."

"I can fight for pay." His eyes narrowed against the sky. "Barons without number would hire a champion just back from the Holy Land with honours. Tournaments and local skirmishing. The war in Wales."

"You could," I admitted, and bit my lip. "I would urge you not to. You have been direly injured already. Once is bad enough. Twice... and you shall die, and I'd swiftly follow. I've no wish to live without you."

"Rubbish," he scoffed. "You are young and strong, you would live."

"I might," I sighed. "If I did, I would take the first ship back and find Imrahan. I am his freedman, I can beg employment in his house and he would not send me away. Besides, the war is over, Palestine should be at peace."

Edward knotted his hands into my hair. "You hold him in high regard."

"I owe him my life, and yours," I said levelly. "Please, Edward, no more fighting." I looked across the woods toward the hills where Lionel's house stood. "I see the makings of a fine estate. In a year or two we'll have mares and foals, calves and more cows. Your fortunes will repair themselves."

"Taxes," he added pointedly.

"A colt from Icarus would pay them," I retorted.

At last he smiled with a peculiar mixture of mischief and sadness. "You are determined."

"I love you," I said simply. "I want you for my own, for all my life. I don't want to follow you to battle or some tournament, and see you put into a hole before the altar of the church, where your banner will stand until it rots to dust. I would be dead or with Imrahan within a year, and *he* would be my lord for all the years you threw away."

I had not meant to speak vehemently, but the words escaped as an angry rush, and Edward physically recoiled. "Then, I shall tie up my sleeves and put my back to work," he said with mock docility.

I kissed him soundly and jumped down off the fence. "No one here will chastise us for being two men with a single love between us. We are free to lie together, at least until you get the Montand girl into the marriage bed."

"Edwina," he said darkly, "is a child."

"Of fourteen years," I added. "Which is the age of greatest desirability, so they tell me. If you don't wed her, someone else will."

He knew whom I meant, and kissed me swiftly. "I had best visit her tomorrow, and the Sheriff. You stay here. This place needs a man, and you are the closest we can provide in my absence!" He was teasing, for when he stood beside me I was a hair's breadth taller, my shoulders were broader. He slipped an arm around my waist and drew me back to the house. "This evening we take stock of our situation, and tomorrow... " He looked over the Aethelstan lands from woods to river to hills. "Tomorrow, we begin."

"With what?" I would have been content to do whatever he bade me.

"That paddock will yield hay," he said shrewdly. "We must have a scarecrow, or lose the grain. We need extra stalls and an extra fence, or three studs will fight, given a mare to battle over. I'll ride to Montand's, and if Edwina will honour the contract, she can send down her mares. Her father had a stable of three or four good ones."

As I closed the door on its noisy pivots I embraced him, ravished his mouth and buried my face in his hair. The embrace was practised now, not a clash of knees and chins. When I released him his lips were red as cherries and his eyes were smiling again. "Ask Enid and Mary if there is anywhere to sleep," he suggested. "Otherwise, I'll go to Sleaford and fetch back what I can."

A few blankets had been salvaged, but not enough to warm our number. As I groomed the horses, Henri carried in fresh hay to serve instead of mattresses and Edward mounted Icarus. He was gone until late twilight, and I had guessed he would have met Ranulf and stayed to talk. Sure enough, Ranulf accompanied him when he returned. I was with the women and Henri, we had made ourselves comfortable in the kitchen. A cheerful fire, a good meal, and the world looked a better place.

We had eaten hare stuffed with hazelnuts and dressed with apricot preserves. Edward's meal was set aside, but Ranulf would have fed him. Henri was asleep by the fire; Mary and her daughter were sewing while Enid and her own daughter tried to comfort one another.

Iron-shod hooves rang in the yard and I picked up a knife before I went out. Twilight was mauve over the woods and midges danced in air that smelt of woodsmoke and the river. As I saw Edward I put down the knife. Behind him was Ranulf – older, stiffer, greyer, but still the same Ranulf. It was I who had changed so much, he blinked when he first saw me.

"I would have passed you in the street," he declared, "and not known you!" He embraced me swiftly. "Sir Edward tells me you gave sterling service."

"The best I could," I swore. "Have you eaten? There is plenty of food. I saved your meal, Edward."

"I ate with Ranulf at the inn," he told me. "Rolled behind my saddle there, rugs and blankets. Take them inside, and get some rest. You're half asleep!"

The day had been a century long and I was glad to do as he said. As I left him to talk with Ranulf I leaned down to whisper in his ear, "Our bed is by the warm chimney in your own chamber. Come to me soon."

He only nodded, for Ranulf was near, and I felt his eyes on me as I left. The bed was a mound of fresh hay overlaid with the blankets, and a quilt over the lot. The night was not cold, we had no need of the hearth, but I lit a candle and by habit I read my Book while the moon rose into the open window.

It was late before he came to bed and I had snuffed the candle to save it. The moonlight was still bright and my eyes were so accustomed to the dark that I could see his scar as he disrobed. I held the bed open and in a moment he was against me, hard and warm.

"What news from Ranulf?" I asked between yawns.

"Disturbing news," he said thoughtfully. "No one has seen Edwina Montand in months. Yves Guilbert wrote several times to her, begging letters that swore I had been killed. I imagine that message was sent home when we vanished."

His tongue silenced me for a long minute. I arched against him, felt him rub and roll my nipples, and got up hard. My cock tucked between his thighs while his own lay hot on my belly, and he began to hump so slowly that urgency was far off.

"Then, Edwina is unwed?" I asked as he kissed my neck.

"Ranulf says so. But no one has seen her in a long time. Her father is alive, but he cannot be well. More than likely, Edwina is at his bedside like a dutiful daughter." He kissed me once more. "Enough of that! I did not come to bed to talk about her, but to give you that *situation* you desired."

For a moment I grappled with his meaning, then remembered and laughed. "Any position will do," I told him, and put into his hand a phial of oil I had bought in the market in Joppa. Olive oil is the finest I know, when it is that part of a man to be eased, and for that purpose.

A scant minute later he was inside and not for a Sheriff's ransom would I have deserted Aethelstan for another employer.

We slept at last, and my mind was a jumble of chaotic thoughts, trepidation and misgivings. But Edward had scented a challenge, and a man of his dauntless nature could not resist. I was proud of him, and of my place at his side.

Had I known what was to come, I would not have slept so easily.

Chapter XXX

We rose to the sound of starlings scratching in the thatch. Chilled, since we had not lit the hearth, we had pressed together in the night and I woke with Edward wrapped about me, his thigh between my legs. I humped comfortably on it, which woke him too, but before we could settle into sleepy lovemaking, which is the best beginning to the day, we heard footsteps outside our door and I slid reluctantly out of the bed.

It was Henri, fetching tea and petitioning for a few pennies for market. The kitchen needed spices and dishes. The bailiff had emptied even the pantry. Edward gave him three pennies.

I saddled the Turk and let Icarus into his own paddock. Even he seemed glad to be home. Despite the shabby condition of the property, the empty, dusty house, I was filled with optimism that morning.

"I'll ride to Montand's," Edward said at mid-morning as he pulled on red leather gauntlets and buckled on his sword. "Look for me by mid-afternoon, I'll not stay long." We were alone in the stable and he leaned over for a quick kiss. "The lady will be pleased to see me, but I'll not presume on her without warning."

Could Edward 'presume', with or without warning? I imagined myself without him, longing for him, then suddenly given his company. More likely the girl would squeal with joy and not let him out of her sight. I held his reins while he mounted, and laid a hand on his thigh. He gave me a smile and turned west out of the gateway.

So sure was I that little Edwina would detain him that I did not wonder when he was still absent at late afternoon. I did not question his absence until twilight faded into night. Midnight came, still he was gone, and by then I realised something was wrong.

His words haunted me – he could not sleep without me, he would not sleep in a loveless bed. Had he bedded with the girl? I could not believe it, after he had told me he wanted no one but me. He would not deceive me. And he was not the kind of man to importune the virgin before the wedding.

I spent a bad night and at dawn I was on the fence, watching for him to ride down from Sleaford. I should have been working, and

Henri shouted my name. He was sneezing on the dust as he laboured with the women, sweeping out the house to make it habitable.

"Cloth-lugs! What are you doing?" He plunged his head into the horse trough to wash away the sneezes. "There's firewood to fetch in and rabbits to skin for dinner. What's the matter with you?"

"Edward is not returned." I hopped down off the fence.

"So he stayed to bed a comely wench," Henri said with complete indifference. "Know you not by now, every man is not like you and me. Some actually prefer women, and almost every man can bear them occasionally."

I might have taken umbrage but I was too restive, and I had already made up my mind. Henri was on my heels as I caught my horse and saddled him swiftly.

"Where are you going?" He trotted after me as I left the yard.

"To Montand's," I shouted back. "I am worried for Edward."

"Knock before you walk into the bedchamber!" Henri yelled. He was cynical for a boy his age.

The ride was the most pleasant is the shire. Durham is a beautiful nook of the world. I saw the River Tees, where salmon leap and seals play on the estuary sands. The Meeting of the Waters marks the marriage of two rivers, and all about the forests are the richest in England. Sleaford stands upon a hill, and Montand's fortified manor is at the highest point. His banners could be seen from a mile away, and I urged the Turk on up the rise, past the village.

A servant stopped me at the gate but it was just an old retainer, grey-haired and half blind. I could have bowled him over with a breath if I had wanted to force entry. Instead I somewhat imperiously gave him the reins of my horse and said, "I am Delgado. Where is Sir Edward?"

He bowed and stepped aside. "In the garden, my lord."

My lord? The old man's eyesight was poor; my stature, my speech and the quality of my horse had convinced him I was a gentleman. I was not about to correct him! I strode about the curved wall to the garden gate. Roses, lilacs, honeysuckle and sweet basil made the air light and fragrant, and the view over Sleaford as far as Aethelstan was breathtaking. A man would cherish an hour spent there.

Yet Edward was so preoccupied with gloom, he had not even seen me ride up the hill, nor did he hear my approach. I was almost in front of him before he gave a start of surprise and got to his feet. His face was smudged with sleeplessness, and haunted. My grievances as to my own night alone died unspoken.

"Edward, what is it?" My voice sounded odd in my own ears.

He caught me and we embraced tightly. "Baron Montand is dead," he murmured against my ear.

"Strange, that Ranulf did not tell you last night," I began breathlessly.

"He does not know. Nobody knows." Edward drew away. His face was drawn with fatigue. "Montand died two months ago and is buried in the back, there. His rites were said in secret by a friar from Yarm."

I was shocked. "But, why? He should have been honoured with a statue in the church, and his colours and weapons hung there, as befits a knight!"

Edward turned haunted eyes on me. "Come inside. I am so glad you are here. I could not leave her last night."

My heart leapt into my mouth. Was Henri right, had he bedded her? Hot tears stung, but I let him tug me into the dim, chill interior of the house. The stone walls never admitted the warmth of day. His hand bruised my arm, and I bit my tongue rather than questioning him. A moment later I was glad I had kept silent, for I saw the girl.

She sat by the hearth, dozing in a chair, attended by a crone who also was asleep as if she had nursed her through the night and was exhausted. This was likely the case. I stalled in the doorway, speechless and flushed. I remembered little Edwina as a flower, a bud still to open, just twelve years old. She was just past her fourteen birthday, yet she was huge with child, so swollen, her childish body was bloated and distorted. She was scant weeks from deliverance.

"Yves Guilbert came here and bargained with her father," Edward whispered. "The old man accepted gifts of money, wine and cattle. Then Guilbert required the lady's hand in marriage without delay."

"But she was betrothed to you," I hissed in outrage.

"And dispatches had already come from Palestine," Edward said sadly, "saying I was missing. Still, Baron Montand allowed the child to choose, and she said she would sooner enter the abbey. Guilbert was furious. He returned that night, killed a seneschal to gain entry to her rooms and spent the night with her."

I gaped. "She took him willingly?"

He shook his head slowly. "Over and over, he rutted on her. She was unconscious sometimes, half-aware at others. Her child was conceived that night, and she's not left this house since. Guilbert has not returned, as if he scorns her now he has fucked and buggered her, filled her with his bastard. She is for the abbey, but cannot go there until she is delivered."

"It cannot be long," I guessed. "She is so large."

"Two, three weeks." He pulled his hands across his face. "She was distracted last night, I could not leave her. She has only the old family servants to stand by her now. Montand passed away in his sleep, four months ago. They have kept the secret safe."

"But why?" I was so intent upon the poor girl, I had not thought it through.

"So long as it is believed that Montand lives, she is safe," Edward whispered as he ushered me out and closed the door. "If it is known he died without leaving a male heir, his lands are forfeit. Edwina would have nowhere to go, and no man will have her after this."

"So she keeps secret her father's death until she is delivered, gives the child to a wetnurse," I said softly, "and goes to the abbey."

He urged me back to the garden, and in the privacy of high walls and trees he crushed us together. "I must call Guilbert to answer for this. It is a matter of Aethelstan honour. Edwina was *my* betrothed."

He was right, no matter the consequences, and I did not argue. I held him tightly. "Where will you call him out?"

He had already considered even this. "Ranulf told me of a tournament in a week's time, over the river in Rotherby. Guilbert will be defending the trophy he won last year and the year before. The purse is a hundred shillings. We can put the sum to good use, but I care little for that. It is Yves Guilbert's death I desire. Nothing less will do."

I chilled but bit my tongue to keep silent. He must fight, and if he must kill a Norman – as he surely must – then the legal tournament was the place to do it, where no man could even breathe the word 'murder'. Yet my belly congealed and the thought haunted me, it could be Edward of Aethelstan who lay dead on the jousting field.

When we were home, for the first time since I had left Imrahan's fortress, I took the Book in my hands and called the name of the Great Judge. I pleaded the case as Imrahan would have, and petitioned for Edward's life, Edwina Montand's honour, and justice.

We had left behind a girl in tears, who hid when she saw me and would not show her bloated body to me. Shame is a terrible weapon we use against ourselves, and she was past comforting. But the servants would nurse her, we would keep the secret of Montand's death, and Edward's mind was made up. He would kill Guilbert in the full sight of the Sheriff of Durham, who was to judge the contest.

I gave him my silent support, tended his swords, mended his mail coat. And I rode with him to Durham when he went to bid the Sheriff greetings and announce his participation in the tournament.

* * *

Durham is the seat of a Prince Bishop, a County Palatine, and heavily taxed. Still, it is a town without compare and above its many houses rears a castle that will withstand the Apocalypse. The walls are eight feet thick, and I hear that if one desires a new room, it is cut out of the solid stone. It was built to defend bishops and barons in the days when every baron seemed to be at war with every other.

The Sheriff, Sir Marc de Chabot, was a tall, lanky man with red-gold hair, thin but handsome features, and good legs which he liked to show off in tight hose and short tunics, displaying his buttocks and the swell of his manhood. I wondered for whose benefit these courtship displays were made, as I stood back among the commoners, ankle-deep in stale rushes, and watched Edward.

A Saxon he may have been, but he had the King's favour, and it was all over the shire that Saladin had chosen him to carry the dispatch that offered the armistice and sent King Richard to Normandy. De Chabot reluctantly respected Aethelstan, gave him wine and sweetmeats and invited him to dine that evening.

I ate with the squires but we were close enough for me to plainly hear Edward's conversation. Normandy was the talk of this town and every other, but Edward and I could hardly have cared less. It was Lionel's eldest son on Edward's mind, and he broached the subject when the stinking-high pheasant had been picked clean and wine served with raisins for dessert.

"You levied Christopher de Quilberon for the army," Edward said quietly but insistently.

"Did I?" The Sheriff seemed unaware of the deed.

Edward was immovable. "He has been fighting in Wales for months, which is fair and good, since it is his duty." He lifted his goblet in toast. "However," Edward continued, "I must convey to him the news of his father's death, and since Christopher is de Quilberon's heir it is necessary for him to return at once to take his place."

De Chabot looked down his long, aquiline nose at Edward but he could hardly argue. Christopher was half Saxon, but he was half Norman, too. A drop of wine spilled on the table. De Chabot dipped his finger in it, traced patterns on the polished wood.

"Leave the matter in my hands, Aethelstan. I shall write at once, I assure you. Give my condolences to Lady de Quilberon. Sir Lionel was a great knight and shall be sorely missed."

The perfidiousness was nauseating. De Chabot cared nothing for people, great or poor, Saxon or Norman. Neither Edward nor I could remain in his company for long, and rather than stay in Durham overnight we left at early twilight and roomed at an inn on the road.

Travellers were ignored, save by the tavern thieves. As my lord's squire I shared his room, but the little cot at the foot of his bed went unused and I was pleased to slide into his arms.

"Guilbert will hear that you are to ride against him in the tournament," I muffled against Edward's shoulder. "He'll know why."

"So he shall." Edward's hands were like manacles on my arms, and I winced. He relaxed and kissed me to apologise. "Let him know Aethelstan is returned, and I am not ignorant of his evil."

"And his bastard?" I wondered as we settled to sleep, too distraught for lovemaking, too weary to rest.

"One thing at a time," he sighed. "Let me meet Guilbert in legal combat, then we turn to the matter of that poor girl."

"But, if you... " How could I say it? *If you are defeated?*

"If I am killed?" he asked gently. My teeth closed on a fold of his skin and branded him, a swift pain which he answered with a kiss. "If I am killed, look to the girl. Get her to the abbey, leave the child with the Church, which will likely inherit Montand's estate. But why do you imagine I'll be killed? Guilbert is a knight, but he is not the only man who can claim a pair of spurs."

I propped myself on my elbow and studied him in the light of the single candle. "I beg every soldier's gods for victory."

"If your supplications are unanswered, Imrahan would say it is time for me to go before his Great Judge."

"I do not believe that," I said fiercely. "Guilbert is the one who must be judged. You are the hand of vengeance!"

He stroked my arm. "I wish I had your faith."

"The only faith I have is in you," I retorted. "You are younger than Guilbert by many years, and stronger." I stooped and kissed his paps. "And you have lately fought on campaign, so you have the experience. Guilbert will not have faced a genuine foe in a decade."

Edward had fought like a young lion in Palestine. Guilbert was forty years old and had not fought outside of a tournament in so long, he must have forgotten what a real fight was about. He was only good for menacing children. My scorn was boundless, though I had heard the tales of him only at second hand, and never yet seen his face. I would see it soon enough.

We were home by noon, and haymaking took us into the fields. Edward had money, but not much, and he must safeguard it against accident rather than pay labourers to do what we could do ourselves. If there is one thing a Saxon knows how to do, it is work.

Clad simply in shirt and leggings like myself and Henri, he worked alongside us. I thought he had never looked so beautiful, and would have told him, save that the women were so near and I had no wish to embarrass him. Enough to say all this in the privacy of the bedchamber, intent on the serious business of love.

The clop of hooves caught my ears and Henri's at the same time and I straightened. I shaded my eyes and looked toward the gate, where a big bay horse had just turned in and was trotting toward the house. I called Edward very quietly.

He was bare to the waist, deliciously tousled, with a water cup in one hand and a scythe in the other. He could have been a peasant labourer, save that no peasant ever had his poise and dignity. I drew to his side and stood straight, a long knife in my right hand.

Was I protective, possessive? I had seen him naked that morning, seen the scar in daylight, and could not yet rid my head of the memories of his wounding.

Instinctively, I had known it must be Yves Guilbert, and the news of Edward's participation in the tournament had rushed to him so fast, it could only have been conveyed by the Sheriff. Toadspawn cares for its own. He was bull-like with male strength, dark but silvered about the temples, clean-shaven, his hair cut in a neat cap. His colours were red and black, and both he and his horse were clad in them. He wore a mail shirt, and his broadsword was at his left hip as if he expected to be set upon.

As he saw Edward his lip curled. Fury sent a waft of heat to my face but I had no need to caution Edward. He knew every quirk of the law which the Sheriff could use to send him to the rack or the block, or confiscate his title, spurs and estate.

"Good day," Guilbert greeted him in a voice thick with Norman overtones. "A fine day for honest labour."

"It will do." Edward twisted the scythe in the sun before him. "My property is in tatters, as you see. Hardly worth the effort of salvaging it."

"Would you sell?" Guilbert's eyes raked over the woods, the orchard, house and river.

So that was what he wanted. He could come by Montand's estate, since he, the Sheriff and Bishop were hand in glove. Almost the only land in the shire which he did not own belonged to Aethelstan, and he thought he could have it now for a song. I saw all this like a flash of pure white lightning.

Edward must have known for some time, for he said calmly, "I think not. It does a young man good now and then to get his hands dirty with honest labour, as you call it. This place will mend." He smiled, thin-lipped, a sham expression that did not reach his eyes. "And perhaps I shall bring home a purse after the tournament."

The Norman's pale hazel eyes narrowed. "I heard you were to ride." Edward bowed mockingly. Guilbert frowned at him. "You are not long returned from the Holy Land. You fought there?"

"Several times." Edward sounded smug.

"Then, you fight next against me," Guilbert added, soft and silky, like a snake.

Edward smiled again, no more warmly. "I know."

For a moment that stretched on and on, they said nothing, nor did they move, but were like statues, eyes locked. Then Guilbert nodded minutely and gathered his reins as his magnificent warhorse began to sidestep.

"Luck, Aethelstan." His gaze swept contemptuously over the estate. "You will need it."

"Oh, this poor estate will prosper by next year," Edward said with an ease and grace I envied. "I shall have Montand's bride-price to work with, and his mares to put to my studs."

I could almost hear Guilbert's spine crackling as he stiffened. "You'll wed the girl?"

"She is my betrothed," Edward said grimly. "I saw her. The foolish child allowed herself to be seduced in my absence. Her sin will be punished by Nature, with more agony than is meted out by the flogger. Childbirth is the keenest punishment. I shall not have a virgin to bed, and shall call another man's bastard my child! Well, it has been said, every man is the father of every child." Edward nodded soberly. "So be it."

Guilbert's face was puce with rage or dread. What passions thundered behind that mask! Had he seen the girl since the night he raped her – did he not even know until that very second that he had made her pregnant? Was he puce because he believed the silken lies Edward had just told – that Edward accepted a story of seduction, and did not suspect Guilbert? Then, Aethelstan would call Guilbert's child his own, and would never know who the father was! Worse, Guilbert stood to lose what could be a full-blood Norman son to a Saxon house! The web was tangled as the Gordian knot.

I was stunned by the lie also, for I had never expected it. Guilbert collected his reins and turned his horse without a word. A few paces away he stopped and looked back over his shoulder. "I shall see you at the tournament, Aethelstan."

I shivered and leaned closer to Edward. "May I leave you for a moment?" I whispered. "In Imrahan's home it is the hour when the Imam would be calling. I shall be back soon and am not shirking."

He was not surprised, and I took to my heels and was soon lost in the privacy of the woods. I knelt and my fists battered the grass as I demanded that some god high on some mountainside listen. Guilbert would be out to kill Edward, while a poor girl was to be punished by the agonies of the childbed. I bludgeoned the ears of every deity I could remember, and suspected they were all deaf.

At last, exhausted, I sprawled in the grass, and only then became aware of Edward. He had followed me and heard every word. I flushed but did not rise, and was grateful when he came to me, lay down beside me and took me in his arms.

"If I am defeated," he said wryly, "prayer is a waste of breath!" He kissed my mouth, tongued within, and deftly opened my clothes. Cool grass stalks caressed my cock, which began to burn in seconds. "Paul," he whispered. I opened my eyes. "I shall marry Montand's daughter," he murmured.

My erection wilted in the palm of his hand.

"Marry her," he repeated as he twisted around and kissed the smooth crown of me, which fascinated him. "Her child will be a bastard otherwise."

"Her child is Guilbert's, conceived in rape!" I groaned as he made me hard again with the determined tip of his tongue.

"It will be a helpless, woebegone infant," he argued, "destined for holy orders and likely castration by seven years of age, if it is a male!" He gave my balls a firm squeeze of admonition. "Edwina wishes only for the abbey, never fear. She cannot suffer the touch of a man's hand, and could not bear to have me in her bed. Trust me. I know a way to beat Guilbert, even if I cannot kill him."

I humped against his hand, fumbled with his leggings and bared him also. He was hard, a musky golden lance which I loved. I pulled him against me so that we crossed like swords, and we made love with the desperate urgency of boys so afraid they will be caught that speed is crucial.

Decent again, still flustered but in command of my breath, I said, "How can you beat Guilbert, without killing him?"

He twisted a hank of grass between his hands. "Wed the girl, and I become master of Montand's estate as well as Aethelstan. Edwina's child may be a boy, and if it is, I shall have my Aethelstan heir without ever needing to bed a woman."

"Guilbert's child!" I protested hoarsely.

He gave me a reproving look. "An orphan, deserted by a mother who took holy orders, while his father never knew him. A child who shall be nurtured in kindness, calling Aethelstan his home."

"And Edward his father." My face heated. "Forgive me."

He kissed me. "Forgiven. After the marriage I will release the girl and give the babe to Enid to raise for me, since she is alone now with Lionel gone." He stroked my hair. "So, I am the heir to Montand's estate, with luck I shall have a son, and soon that girl can renounce men and life, and go to the abbey where she belongs."

I gave him a rueful look. "You are cursed logical for a beauty."

Edward laughed. "You told me that once before. A beauty?"

I kissed his ear, nipped the lobe between my teeth. "Fairer than sunlight, sweeter than wine – "

"Hush." He slapped a work-roughened palm over my mouth. "It cannot be seemly to say such things to a man. And I think... " He looked me up and down. "You are too big to be my squire. I shall call you my valet."

"After the tournament," I insisted. "You need a squire for the tournament."

"Henri could squire me."

I was on my feet, fists on my hips. "I went to war with you – give me the pride of wearing your colours when you knock Guilbert on his nasty Norman arse!"

He laughed, took my hands, and I pulled him to his feet. "All right, you are my squire till then, but thereafter I shall call you my valet, and Henri shall squire me, if need be." He looked me in the eye, and had to look up a fraction to do it. "You've grown, in all ways. You are strong. And handsome." I preened. As he palmed my lower cheeks he lifted a brow at me in question.

"Later," I promised fervently.

He slapped me there, sharp enough to smart. "Then let us get to

271

work before the others suspect of us rushing into the woods to hump one another!"

"Which would only be the truth," I added drily.

* * *

The wedding was a strange affair. The friar from Yarm who had given Montand last rites performed it, but it took place in a dimmed chamber in a solemn house, and the bride wore a nun's habit which to some extent disguised her grossly swollen belly.

I went with Edward. The servants were present, but no one else saw Lady Edwina Montand wed the Earl of Aethelstan. Bride and groom held hands, a gold ring was slipped onto the girl's tiny finger, but Edward kissed her hair, not her mouth. She could not even bear his kiss, and I grieved for her.

The babe was a fortnight away, the tournament two days hence. She knew Edward was riding but seemed unmoved, as if she had never seen a tournament to know how dangerous they can be. She had lived a very sheltered life. I recalled the day she bade Edward farewell before we went to war. She had been nowhere, seen and done nothing. She was an innocent, and I have never understood why innocents are made to suffer most.

We rode away from Montand's estate with a document to prove that the marriage had taken place, and Edward wore a gold ring on his hand. My eyes were drawn to it, he let me caress it, feel its warmth, but he merely shrugged when I looked searchingly at him that night. He was bare, the ring was all he wore, that and his scar and the soft candlelight. I was oiling myself, ready for him, and could not help looking at the ring.

"Your wedding night," I said cautiously.

"Is it?" He pillowed his head on his hand. He lay on his back, on the rugs that overset the hay. We had not yet commissioned the Sleaford carpenter to make us a bed, which cost money. His eyes dwelt on me as I made myself ready. "My wife is big with another man's bastard and the marriage shall never be consummated."

"You will have the marriage annulled?" I set aside the oil and lay beside him. "How will I... ?"

"Lie down," he whispered, and a second later he was between my spread thighs, lifting my legs over his shoulders. "Aye, the marriage shall be annulled."

So with luck he would have his heir, the Montand estate, and freedom. I caught my breath as he speared me, and my thoughts whirled. Guilbert would fret with rage, but it was all quite legal.

If Edward survived the tournament.

Guilbert would be trying to kill him, and Robert de Chabot, who presided over the field, would encourage him to do it. I put these drear thoughts from me so as to enjoy the gentle fucking, but long after he was asleep I lay awake, watching the fire while my imagination flayed me without mercy.

My final duty as his squire was to fetch out his livery, check and clean his mail, hone his weapons and see that his horses were in the finest fettle. I thought he would ride Icarus, but he surprised me.

Not long after dawn, I was grooming the big stud. We would ride to Rotherby after breakfast, which was even then cooking. Mushrooms simmered in butter and wild garlic, corn bread toasted in the skillet. My belly rumbled with hunger and fretting, and I was so intent on the horse that I jumped when Edward's hands fell on my shoulders. He had come up behind me with cat-like silence.

"Prepare the Barb," he said softly.

"You won't ride Icarus?" I was astonished.

"Icarus is too valuable." He patted the horse's sleek neck. "His value as a stud is proven already. The Barb is as big, as strong, as quick and brave, but he has not yet serviced a field of English mares. Even now, Icarus is my best fortune, so we leave him at home and risk the Barbary horse."

He was right, as always. I switched my attentions to the beautiful animal Imrahan had given him. The Barb had the spirit, stamina and courage to carry a man through a battle. He would not find a summer tournament daunting, and in the Aethelstan blue livery he looked magnificent. I searched the woods after breakfast, while Edward bathed, and found a dozen white, wild roses. I carefully trimmed every thorn and threaded the blooms into the Barb's bridle. I would ride the Turk, a lighter and even quicker animal, though not as strong – and also a whole male capable of siring fine offspring.

Edward was ready when I rushed back to the house, and I scrambled through the task of dressing, shaving, polishing, so fast that I nicked my chin and tore my shirt. Swearing, I searched out a new one and ran down to find a compress for my face.

From the gate as we turned south, I looked back at the house and paddocks, which I thought of as my home now. I might have been born there, and worry stitched through me. Guilbert would be trying to kill Edward with every fibre of strength he possessed. If he did murder him, this estate could be lost, as Edward was still technically without an heir. The Bishop, the Sheriff and Guilbert would seize everything.

I would see Edward interred in the church, see his banner raised there, and the bastard child who inherited the name of a Saxon earl safely in the hands of the Church, for better or worse. Then I would find a ship, I would even make the voyage with Templars, if theirs was the only vessel leaving before winter. Imrahan would have me. He would leave me to thrash out my grief, and then would fetch me to him as a freeman in the bed of a freeman. I shuddered, chilled, though the afternoon was warm enough to raise a sweat.

Four miles away, through the trees, we saw the walls and rooves of Rotherby. Pennants and banners marked out the field where battle would be done for the entertainment of people who had never seen the real thing, and been sickened of it.

The images, sounds and smells of that day branded themselves into my memory, as lurid-bright as stained-glass windows. The river smelt of duckweed; onions were frying over a fire there, chestnuts in a skillet here. Jugglers and mummers competed for the attention of the rag-tag crowds that gathered to watch the spectacle; the Norman ladies and gentlemen kept apart from the rabble. Above it all were the rooves of many pavilions and the stand where our Normans lords would sit.

De Chabot was splendid in red robes and gold chains. The Bishop was not far away, in purple robes and ruby rings. I saw Lady Elspeth of Anjou, old as an oak tree, mother of three knights of Christendom who won fame when Richard Lionheart was a little boy. She was fawned upon even in her dotage.

A long field had been scythed flat for the contest. To one end were the pavilions for the travelling knights, pilgrims, soldiers of fortune; to the other, the stand where the judge sat and the pavilions where the local knights and barons' champions camped.

At that moment Edward was a soldier of fortune, which made us both rueful. I left him conversing more or less politely with a group of Templars and hurried to elbow my way into the pavilions, where I demanded the service of the bumptious lads in charge.

Several Templars were competing in the name of their monastery, and I learned later, they were of the same order as Jean de Bicat. Two brawny youths brought a dozen lances for Edward – lances are supplied, since they are shattered with almost every joust – and I had polished his shield until it could have done service as a mirror. Outside the tent, the Barb pricked his ears. He could scent a battle coming and relished it.

Swords, mace and chain, daggers, all were ready. Pages came to take the names of knights who would compete, and the rounds were made up. The finest and most experienced were not pitted against each other in the opening rounds, or else the champion of the day might well be an unknown. Edward must meet three much lesser men to win his way into the final round, as must Yves Guilbert.

The Norman wore black armour and a scarlet cloak, and his horse was in the same livery, with a black plume on his head. Guilbert rode with a favour in de Chabot's colours on his arm, and I caught Edward's sleeve as he mounted for the first round, in the shade by the pavilion.

"Beware," I murmured. "Nothing he does will earn him a caution. He'll be trying to maim you, and de Chabot will let him."

"I know," he said mildly, and I helped him into the saddle. The weight of a mailcoat, harness and swords makes a man heavy and the climb is hard. With the extra height he saw across the heads of the crowds, and waved. "I see Enid and Martha, and Henri. They have come to watch." He looked down at me and we shared a moment of closeness unsurpassed by any scene of passion. He almost touched my face, but not quite. "I wish I could wear your favour."

My eyes prickled with emotion. "Just ride well," I said bluffly. "You will spear through the others, but Guilbert will have his eye on you. When you meet at last he will know your value and will show no quarter."

"I ask no quarter," Edward said in the steely tone I knew of old. He took his first lance from me as his name was called and the awful helmet encased his head.

The Barb pranced away as the pennants ran up to mark the houses now competing. Up ran the Aethelstan blue and another, wasp-like black and yellow, which I did not know. That round lasted less than a minute. Edward knocked the boy off his nag, leapt down and held the tip of his sword gently against his throat, below his helmet. The young knight put up his hands and Edward helped him to his feet. They laughed and clasped wrists like comrades.

Others rode while we drank ale and ate a pork pastry. Edward was unconcerned as yet, but I noticed that his eyes never left Guilbert. We watched the Norman ride twice before Edward competed again, and Guilbert won both times with aplomb and arrogance that won applause from the enormous crowd. My belly was hot as a brazier.

Again Edward rode, and this contest lasted a little longer. His opponent was a better man, but Edward was younger and stronger, with a better horse under him. The older knight's mail was so heavy, when he was unseated by the terrible impact he could not rise unaided. Edward tucked his helmet under his arm and stood back as squires and pages helped him up.

Only one round remained, for Edward and Guilbert alike, before they had defeated their rivals and must face each other. Wagers were being taken, and I was so outraged to hear that Guilbert was the favourite while Edward was given long odds, I wagered two whole pennies. The man who took them was suspicious and leaned closer to me, wanting to know what I knew to make me risk so much.

"I was his squire in Palestine, you old goat," I said drily. "How long is it since Guilbert fought a real fight, not a sham fight like this? Aethelstan was fighting for his life just months ago!"

Even then Edward was unhorsing his last opponent before Guilbert. It was another Norman, a decent knight, but his skill was not extraordinary. He gave Edward a small battle. They jousted three passes, and when the man was unhorsed he sprang to his feet and drew his sword. That was his mistake. Edward was lean and swift – strong again, and more than a match for him. In moments it was over

275

with a clean surrender before injury could be done, but the crowd was pleased and the odds on Edward shortened while those on Guilbert lengthened.

Enid de Quilberon and her daughter were sitting with the Normans. The fact she had lost her lord on the Crusade won her a little favour. She was intent on Edward, hands clenched on the railing before her as the pennants were run up for the final round.

My throat was dry as dust. I watched Guilbert mount, and saw that he carried a mace and chain, the most brutal of weapons, an iron ball with sharp spikes the length of a man's finger. Edward chose swords, and an ancient Saxon tradition passed down to him through the line of his warrior fathers. Today, he carried a battleaxe.

They took their places and the crowd hushed. Horses pranced, plumes fluttered, helmets were donned at the last moment before shields were settled and lances lowered for the charge. The impact and splintering of wood was sickening, but both of them were still seated. My heart skipped wildly as stewards collected the smashed lances and brought fresh ones.

The horses took their places once more, excited now and fighting the bit. Guilbert was off first in a headlong dive, while Edward was a second slow in answering, but at the end of the charge it made no difference. Again, that splintering sound of breaking lances, so like the sound of breaking bone – the impact was shocking even to those merely looking on.

And Guilbert was off. He toppled backward out of the saddle and landed hard, with the weight of his chainmail. A rush of astonishment passed like a summer gale through the crowd. They had never seen the Norman champion unhorsed, but as I had told the old goat taking the wagers, Aethelstan was younger, stronger, with an incomparable horse beneath him and genuine combat raw in his mind. Edward was also hunting for vengeance, but only Guilbert knew it. Before my lord's eyes as he dismounted and drew the axe from the sheath beside the saddle would be the face of the young girl whom he had left, virgin and innocent.

Steel chimed like bells, over and over. Guilbert swung the mace on its long chain as if it were a whip, and Edward bore the blows on his shield. Dents I could have put my hand in were punched into the metal, and the shield could not last long. It must soon break away and leave him exposed to the punishment. My breath froze and I took a step forward, as if I could somehow stop it.

The only man who could stop it was Marc de Chabot, and he had not budged a muscle. He watched the whole event with slitted eyes, shrewd as a hoodie crow. He had known before it began, Guilbert was riding to kill Edward.

In minutes everyone in the crowd knew it too. Saxons cried out to the Sheriff, begging for the contest to be stopped. This was to have been a simple joust for entertainment, not a scene of ritual, legal murder. I knew better.

Edward staggered under the blows of the mace. He was down on one knee with the axe in his right hand, and Guilbert could not see the weapon. The shield blocked his view. But I could see it, and I knew what Edward was doing. My heart jumped like a frightened rabbit as the axe swung just one decent blow. I had spent a whole hour, grinding the blade to such sharpness, I could have barbered my face on it – I knew what it was capable of in the hands of one who knew how to use it. It would have felled a tree.

It hewed through the mail cladding Guilbert's right leg, and through the bone, above the knee. Blood gushed from the wound and the man toppled even as he swung the mace over his head like a horsewhip. He went down, and the mace he had swung so hard fetched him a vicious blow in the belly at the end of its in-curved swing.

The crowd leapt up, some screaming, some speechless. In the furore I rushed out and helped Edward off with his helmet. He was grey to the lips with distress as I cast it aside, and under the rising din I hissed,

"Are you hurt? He did not strike you, where are you hurt?"

"My arm," he said through gritted teeth. "My shield arm. Take the thing from me."

The blows he had sustained, though taken on the shield, had almost broken his left arm. This is common on the battlefield. Not all injuries are suffered by the vanquished, nor from blows that draw blood. I lifted off the shield, shocked to see its pocked, cratered surface, and threw it aside. With both arms I lifted Edward to his feet. He was heavy with the mail, sweated, waxen with pain, and his eyes were stormy as he looked down at Guilbert.

The physicians were fighting to save his life, but he was horribly injured. They could have saved him if they had cut off his leg and sealed the stump with a pitch brand before his blood gushed away, but his own mace had stabbed into his belly. When they tried to get his mail off they saw it was deeply embedded. He was dying, and would not last an hour.

The Templars' own priest said last rites over him as Edward limped off the field. It was a battlefield, no one who had watched was in any doubt. I went with him to the Sheriff's high seat and then held back, as befitted my rank. Edward held his left arm to his chest and could hardly move, but he bowed before de Chabot and squared his shoulders.

"Well ridden, Aethelstan." De Chabot's pale eyes bored Edward to the bone, and his face was a mask carved in wood. He held out a heavy purse, which Edward took. The value of next year's taxes, and the year after. "A most unfortunate end to the contest."

"Sir Yves," Edward said hoarsely, "was trying to kill me."

I swallowed hard and prayed the Sheriff would let the matter rest. For a long half minute it seemed he would not, and then he merely nodded and let it go. Hundreds of spectators, Norman and Saxon, had seen everything. Any one of Guilbert's blows could have smashed Edward's shield and his body. Edward struck Guilbert but once, in self-defence. Jahrom Rafha ibn-Qasim told me once, a great warrior needs to strike but one blow.

Edward set the purse into my hand and walked toward the pavilion. I knew he was hurt and I fretted as I gathered his horse and weapons and hurried after him. Henri appeared at my side out of the crowd and I gave the responsibility for the animals and gear to him while I ducked into the tent and closed it up behind me.

He was still in the mailcoat, sitting on the side of the slatted wooden cot, head hanging. Silent, I helped him out of the mail, and he winced as I moved his arm and shoulder. "You need a physician," I said as I saw the inflamed limb.

"I need hot compresses of rosemary and willow, and a soft bed," he argued. "I shall get both of those at home."

"Best stay in Rotherby tonight," I mused as I gingerly touched his swollen elbow and shoulder.

"We'll ride home," he said stubbornly.

"You know best, I suppose!" He glared at me; I kissed the glare off his face and helped him dress. "It is over, Edward, and the worst of it is a stiff, sore arm. Be grateful."

"I am." He took my hand. "Tell the Soldier's Judge I am grateful."

"Tell Him yourself," I grumbled. "He hears Infidels too, so Haroun Bedi told me."

He cocked his head at me, groggy now, and smiled wearily. "Help me dress. Get me out of this company of Normans."

I bathed him, got fresh clothes onto him, and he held his arm tight against him as we stepped into the afternoon sun, where Enid, her young daughter and Henri waited with the horses.

"There is a Saxon inn on the road," I suggested as I helped the lady mount that curious, awkward saddle women ride. "You can rest there."

"Aye," he said tiredly. "I think... " He paused, and I looked about to see what had made him stop. The Sheriff and several stewards were sauntering toward us, and Edward's breath hissed through his teeth. "Stay back," he murmured. "This could be trouble. If they say I have murdered Guilbert – "

But the Sheriff merely nodded to Edward and turned to the woman. "Lady de Quilberon," he said courteously. "I fear I have bad news."

She flushed, one hand clenched into the lace at her throat as she clung to the saddle. "My lord?"

"About your son, Christopher," he said in what I swear was mock-regret. "I am informed that he fell two weeks ago in a battle in the mountains. Many men were killed, and his captain reports that he fought with great valour before he was shot. An arrow in the breast, I believe."

Her eyes squeezed shut. I hovered at her knee in case she fell, but though she stooped over she did not topple. De Chabot lingered as long as he thought he must for the sake of propriety, then ambled on and left us to our anguish. Edward caught her hands.

"Enid, I'll not leave you to struggle," he said, husky with feeling for the woman. "I promise you. Come home with me today." She did not answer, and he looked for me. "Paul?" I was with him in an instant. "Ride behind her, hold her tight," he whispered. "She is faint, and could fall."

"To the inn?" I hoisted myself up and gathered the reins about her trembling body.

"Home," he corrected as he lifted little Martha in his good arm, up onto her pony.

I saw the twist of his face as he lifted the child, saw him pale and then flush as he hauled his own weight onto the Barb with one hand and took the reins. Henri was already mounted and fidgeting.

"I know a shorter way to Aethelstan Manor," the boy offered. He seemed years older than his age of a sudden. Enid was the nearest he had ever had to a mother. Martha was all she had left, and how would she hold onto her lands? Next season, when taxes were due, she would sell to the Church and take holy orders. Thus, the Church grows wealthier every year.

We had all reckoned without Edward's planning.

He was ill with fatigue by the time we reached home. Henri and I carried pails to fill the hooped wooden possing-tub with near boiling water, and then I chased them all out of the scullery and got in with him, and rubbed him with liniment which stung the eyes but eased him at last. Mother Mary produced a strong tincture in a cup of wine, and he drank it gladly.

By then his bruises were showing and I was appalled. He was purple and blue, as if he had suffered a merciless beating. His arm and shoulder were like a black pudding, and in the morning the limb would be stiff as a piece of wood. He accepted it with the stoicism of the soldier.

I dried him down, dressed him and combed his hair. "Am I your valet now?"

His good arm slid about me as I finished with his hair. I kissed him and he flicked my tongue with his own. "Later, love. I must look to Enid. I have been considering her plight since we had the news of Christopher."

I stepped away, thinking to allow them all the privacy they

needed, but he caught my hand and made me go with him to the kitchen where Mary was trying to comfort the distraught woman. I frowned but kept silent, trusting Edward as I always had. He sat on a three legged stool, turned his arm and shoulder to the heat of the fire, and though he held Enid's hand he looked up at me.

"I am wedded to the child," he said softly. "But it is a marriage in name only, to make her babe legitimate, and to give the poor scrap a name. Its father is dead, its mother will take vows as soon as she can travel." We had shared the secret of Edwina's condition, but outside these walls no one else knew. Guilbert took the secret with him to the grave. Edward looked at Enid and back at me. "With luck, it will be a son, and his name will be Aethelstan ... the heir I must have."

She was listening closely; her eyes were pink with weeping but she had the strength you often see about Saxons. We have suffered so much. Edward took a breath. "I'll give the babe to you, Enid," he said quietly. "And when the marriage has been annulled, which is simple – it was never consummated – " he looked at me again, though he spoke to her. "Marry me, Enid."

I gasped, and so did she. She was older than Edward, past her best, broad-hipped, her beauty was motherly even when she was calm and not ripped by grief like this. And she knew Edward and I were lovers.

"I don't... " she began raggedly.

"Hush, let me explain." He kissed her hand. "It is a marriage of convenience, to keep you safe and to further the fortunes of us all. You are a Saxon, as am I. Wed me and nurture Edwina's child as a Saxon. I hold the lands of Aethelstan and Montand; if you wed me, I shall hold safe the lands of de Quilberon also. In this shire, Aethelstan will be the strongest, a Saxon refuge in a Norman land." He paused and smiled at us both. "I'll not trouble you as a husband, Enid. You know by now, I have found my heart, he stands behind you. Wed me, take my fostered child as your own, and let me be your friend as long as Aethelstan prospers."

She pressed tight to him. He held her and looked over her bowed head at me. I touched his face gently and my eyes misted. Edward had thought of everything. I would trust him till the end, I thought as we three lingered and considered the twists of fortune that had brought us together.

* * *

Rievaulx Abbey
1230 A.D.

So ends the part of my story which I will tell. I could write of the good years that followed, but these are matters private to myself and Edward, and all that remains now is to set a few scattered details to rights.

Lady Edwina Aethelstan bore twins, two strong sons whom Edward called Lionel and Christopher. Mother Mary made their birth as easy as could be, and in a month the lady was well enough to travel. I rode with her, and left her at the gate. The nuns took her in, and we never saw her again, though at Yule and Candlemas we sent messages and gifts. She seemed happy. She lived many years and died peacefully, knowing that her sons were not bastards, and that both grew into men of honour and wealth, knights who were Norman by full blood, yet who called themselves Saxon.

They grew to manhood in the house which had been Sir Lionel's home, and which remained Enid's. Edward and I visited so often, we seemed to spend half our time with her. The wedding was fine, in a tiny church, a year and a day after the first marriage was annulled and the girl took her vows. By then Enid was resigned to the loss of Lionel, and I believe she was honoured and flattered to take the name of Aethelstan.

And well she should have been. On the day of his second wedding, Edward was fair and beautiful, clad in his colours, sword at his side, golden in the light of many candles. I was transfixed as always. Henri and I stood to one side and celebrated the wonderful event in our own way.

By then Henri had found himself a lover, a boy who was clever with horses, and who came to live with us. He had a squashed, pug-nosed face, not at all handsome, but he was unfailingly good humoured, kind, and Henri swore he was so gentle with his hands and body that lovemaking was a pleasure he had never imagined.

I knew what he meant. In that year, when Edward married for the second time, we had gentled and grown very easy at love. We could still be rough and playful, but we seldom indulged in wildness. I was taller and broader than he, and he never made me feel like a boy, nor behave like one. I was a man, turned nineteen years, and strong. For that, he respected me.

Edward commanded all the lands between Sleaford and the sea – Montand's, his own and Sir Lionel's were all one. The Aethelstan colours flew above them all, and we were secure. He sent Ranulf to oversee the Montand property, and we did not visit there often. Bad memories haunted us both.

In the Norman church by the river, Sir Yves Guilbert was interred with great pomp and ceremony. A statue was put up and his banner still hangs there, tattered with age. Strange, that he should be so honoured and beloved, when he was the very personification of evil.

My lord lived long and healthy, happy till the last, when he passed peacefully through a certain gate into a Garden where the privileges and pleasures of the blessed surely awaited him. One summer evening, long after we had both grown old, slow, grey and stiff, he said he was sleepy, and that he would doze by the fire for an hour before supper. When I went to wake him he was beyond recall, and I grieved as much as I had always known I would, on that day that awaits us all.

He lies buried on the hill above the house we loved. Christopher and his wife and three children live there now. I was welcome to stay after Edward left me, but I had no wish to. Being there without him was painful. I entered this monastery five years ago, and for the last two of those years have invested my efforts in this strange document.

The time has come to finish, and I am glad to. There is not much life left in me. I feel the tug of sleep and often Edward's voice calls to me in dreams and in the wind. I yearn to go to him, and I shall, very soon. I never liked to be apart from him, and this parting has been too long. I was taught, a place of peace and delight is the reward for a life of good service ... and this has been the measure of my life.

I leave behind me little save this document, but I swear that all that I have told is true.

May God or gods, by whatever name or names, send me soon to him I have loved all my life.

also by Mel Keegan from The Gay Men's Press:

Mel Keegan
FORTUNES OF WAR

It was in the spring of 1588 that two young men fell in love: Dermot Channon, an Irish mercenary serving the Spanish ambassador in London, and Robin Armagh, the son of an English earl. Separated by seven years of war, the two meet up again in the Caribbean, where Dermot now commands a privateer. The couple's adventures together on the Spanish Main make a swashbuckling romance in the best gay pirate tradition.

Mel Keegan's action-packed adventures already span the 20th century to the 23rd. Following the 'rip-roaring and colourful' *Ice, Wind and Fire*, and his 'unputdownable' science-fictions *Death's Head* and *Equinox*, Keegan now conjures up in the historical past a world where men both fight and love.

"A fine example of the genre" — *Gay Times*

ISBN 0 85449 211 9
UK £7.95 US $10.95 AUS $17.95

Mel Keegan
STORM TIDE

Sean Brodie, an American engineer on contract in Adelaide, and his partner of eight months, local boy Rob Markham, are struggling to save their relationship by hiring a boat for a week's fishing off the wild South Australian coast. As a storm approaches, they go to the aid of a luxury cabin-cruiser apparently in trouble, only to find that they've stumbled into a drug smuggling gang's offshore headquarters. A lucky escape is only the start of their troubles, as they find their pursuers have unexpected friends on land as well as sea.

Popular novelist Mel Keegan needs little introduction to GMP readers; this is his fifth novel for The Gay Men's Press. Following the two science-fiction titles *Death's Head* and *Equinox*, and his debut in historical fiction, *Fortunes of War*, Keegan returns to the present with an action-packed and gripping adventure set for the first time in his native Australia.

ISBN 0 85449 227 5
UK £7.95 US $12.95 AUS $14.95

Mel Keegan
DEATH'S HEAD

On the high-tech worlds of the 23rd century, the lethal designer drug Angel has become an epidemic disease. Kevin Jarrat and Jerry Stone are joint captains in the paramilitary NARC force sent in to combat the Death's Head drug syndicate that controls the vast spaceport of Chell. Under the NARC code of non-involvement, each of the two friends hides his deeper desire for the other. When Stone is kidnapped and forced onto Angel, Jarrat's love for him is his only chance of survival, but the price is that their minds remain permanently linked.

"A powerful futuristic thriller" — *Capital Gay*
"Unputdownable" — *Him magazine*

ISBN 0 85449 162 7
UK £8.95 US $12.95 AUS $19.95

Mel Keegan
EQUINOX

Equinox Industries is a commercial monopoly mining the gas giant Zeus, challenged by a growing faction for its environmental record, and suspected of manufacturing Angel. Enter Kevin Jarratt and Jerry Stone, lovers whose minds have been bonded together. In their second action-packed advetnrue, the heroes of *Death's Head* need their empathic powers as well as the 23rd century's technological wizardry to outwit their corporate enemies.

ISBN 0 85449 200 3
UK £6.95 US $10.95 AUS $17.95

Send for our free catalogue to GMP Publishers Ltd,
P O Box 247, Swaffham, Norfolk PE37 8PA, England

Gay Men's Press books can be ordered from any bookshop in the
UK, North America and Australia, and from
specialised bookshops elsewhere.

Our distributors whose addresses are given in the front pages of
this book can also supply individual customers by mail order.
Send retail price as given plus 10% for postage and packing.

*For payment by Mastercard/American Express/Visa, please give
number, expiry date and signature.*

_____

_____

Name and address in block letters please:

Name
_____

Address
_____

_____

_____